To Love
and
to Dream

To Love and to Dream

Elizabeth Nell Dubus

G. P. Putnam's Sons/New York

G. P. Putnam's Sons
Publishers Since 1838
200 Madison Avenue
New York, NY 10016

Published simultaneously in Canada by
General Publishing Co. Limited, Toronto

Library of Congress Cataloging-in-Publication Data

Dubus, Elizabeth Nell.
To love and to dream.

I. Title.
PS3554.U266T6 1986 813'.54 86-8138
ISBN 0-399-13172-8

Printed in the United States of America
1 2 3 4 5 6 7 8 9 10

This novel is dedicated to Roger Scholl, whose editorial skills are matched only by his compassionate humanity; to Sallie Gouverneur, who is a rare combination of business acumen and gentle wisdom; and to Claudette Price, who entered my life as book-buyer par excellence and stayed to become a friend.

If one advances confidently in the direction of his dreams, and endeavors to live the life which he has imagined, he will meet with a success unexpected in common hours.

—HENRY DAVID THOREAU, *Walden*

Part I

I

DECEMBER 1941

The hand pressing against her back grew heavier, its force shoving Caro forward into Larry Jordan's chest. She drew her head back and looked up at him. "I can't dance if you immobilize my spine," she said. Her mouth formed a polite smile, but the chill film in her blue eyes kept the air between her and her partner cold.

"Say, darlin', I'm just trying to get you to keep up with me." His hand tightened, and Caro felt as though someone had tied a five-pound sack of sugar around her waist; Larry's hand, his arm, his huge body, were appendages she dragged around the dance floor, silently counting the measures until the song ended.

She broke from him before the last note faded and headed for the ladies' room without a backward glance. For a moment, she stood on the threshold. Behind her, the band began another set, a medley of Jerome Kern songs. An image of the room formed in her mind and held, framed by the soft edges of the music. Shaded candles on white-clothed tables. Russets and golds and crimsons and hunter greens of the women's silk and crepes, bright flags signaling winter. Muted grays and blues of the men's suits. A sudden flash of light gleaming on white shoulders, as dancers moved under the mirrored ball that revolved slowly over the floor.

The ladies' room door closed behind her, and she walked quickly to the pay telephone set into the wall. She fumbled in her evening bag for a nickel, dropped it in, and waited for the operator to answer.

"I want to make a collect call to Skye Langlinais," she said. "In St. Martinville. The number's 3907." She could hear the Lafayette operator ringing the St. Martinville telephone exchange, and then the St. Martinville operator was on the wire.

"Who's calling Skye at this time of night?" the operator said.

Caro cut in before the Lafayette operator could answer. "It's Caro Hamilton," she said. "Is that Miss Ellen?"

"It's Miss Georgette, Caro. Is anything the matter?"

"I'm fine, Miss Georgette. Really. Just ring through, will you?"

"All right, Caro. But I told Beau when he put all those separate phones in, you children would be using 'em day and night."

"Yes'm," Caro said. She rolled her eyes at the girl who had just come in, someone she'd gone to school with at the Mt. Carmel Convent in New Iberia, shifted the receiver to her shoulder, and searched in her bag for her cigarettes. She could hear the phone ringing; she imagined Skye struggling up from layers of sleep to answer it, and she gave a quick prayer of thanks for the hunt tomorrow that had kept him home and sent him to bed early.

Skye picked up on the third ring, sounding awake and alert, as though he had been sitting waiting for her to call. "Caro wants to talk to you, Skye," Miss Georgette said. "She's calling from a pay phone over in Lafayette, but she's reversing the charges. I guess you'll take the call?"

"Put her on, Miss Georgette," Skye said. "Caro? Caro, are you all right?"

"I'm fine," Caro said. She waited until she heard Miss Georgette get off the line. "But my date's not. He's getting drunker by the minute, Skye. Can you come get me?"

"Where are you?"

"At Toby's. You don't mind, do you?"

"I'm on my way. Who are you with, anyway, that he would get drunk?"

"An oil scout I met at Becky Laraguier's. He seemed fine—"

"Caro, you know what those guys are like."

"Let's talk later, okay?"

"Right. Sit tight, I'll be there as fast as I can."

"You're a prince, Skye."

She hung up the phone and stood for a moment, smoke pluming around her. Then she crushed out the cigarette and sat on a low velvet stool in front of the mirrored dressing table that ran along one wall of the room.

"The band's great tonight, isn't it?" the other girl asked as Caro opened her compact and began to powder her face.

"I can hardly hear it over my date's heavy breathing," Caro said. "He's half-drunk."

"I thought he looked a little the worse for wear. Do you need a ride home?"

"Thanks, but Skye's coming."

"Oh, is Skye home too?"

Caro heard the quickened interest in the girl's voice and smiled. "Everyone is. The men are hunting in the morning and we're trimming the tree in the afternoon."

The girl got up and shook out her skirts. "How's Newcomb? I've thought about transferring there—but you know me. I don't want to have to study too hard."

"I can't speak for the other departments, but the art department is tough."

"Well, you're awfully good. Your work always took first place in high school."

"Newcomb's a little harder nut to crack," Caro said.

The girl laughed. "Maybe I'll just leave well enough alone and go to New Orleans for weekends." She picked up her evening bag and headed for the door. "Now, remember, if you need help—my date and I will be here for a while."

"Thanks. But you know Skye—if he says he's on his way, I can count on it."

She heard the sudden invasion of sound as the girl opened the door, and then silence as it closed behind her. Caro sighed. The band *was* good tonight. What a waste of an evening to have come with Larry Jordan. She put on fresh lipstick, touched her wrists and throat with perfume, then lit another cigarette. The first deep drag tasted like her perfume; she put the cigarette down and surveyed herself in the mirror. You don't look like a girl who attracts jerks, she thought. She lifted her hair off her neck, holding the mass of blond curls away from her and then letting it fall back into place. Her blue-red lipstick highlighted the pink in her cheeks, and the teal-blue crepe dress reflected the color in her eyes. She settled the portrait collar on her shoulders, shifting her eyes away from the expanse of skin its curving line revealed; she remembered the way Larry Jordan's eyes had fastened themselves on her throat, and shivered. Good old Skye. Thank God he'd been there. If she'd had to ask Henri or Raoul to come for her, she'd never have heard the end of it. She looked at her watch. He should be here in about twenty minutes. One more battle on the dance floor—and then rescue.

She put out her cigarette and rose, watching her reflection in the mirror. Someday, she told herself, you'll learn not to wear sexy tight skirts with slits up the front with a guy you barely know. She thought of her first conversation with Larry Jordan, at a brunch during the Thanksgiving holidays. "Becky tells me you're an artist," he had said. "I told her she must be mistaken. Pretty as you are, you should be a model."

"I'm not tall enough," she had said, and had turned away, already put off by the easy label he seemed to assign her. "Sweet and pretty. Can draw a little."

"Wait a minute," Larry had said. "Pretty girls can be artists too. Can't they?"

"I should think they could," Caro had said.

"So tell me about yourself. What do you paint?" He had seemed interested. So when he called and made a date for her next weekend home, she had said yes. Which was *her* mistake. But Larry had made a series of mistakes that were much more serious. He had arrived with a couple of drinks already under his belt, something she hadn't realized until they were halfway to Toby's. Then, though he had ordered dinner for both of them, he had not touched his, preferring to drink his way steadily through it.

She reluctantly made her way back to their table, walking with the same fluid grace that infused her dancing. Larry had worked through another drink and was signaling the waiter for more. Caro shook her head when he looked at her. She fixed her eyes on the dance floor, and on the main entrance beyond it, waiting for Skye.

"Say, Caro, your nose doesn't look that long."

"I beg your pardon?"

"You were in there so long I thought you'd fallen in."

"Don't be crude," she said.

"Don't you be such a cold fish. Dammit, Caro, don't you laugh at anything?"

"I haven't heard anything funny."

"Don't rile me, Caro," Larry said. "Why'd you come out with me if you didn't want to have a good time?"

Then Skye appeared in the entrance, searching the room for her, and Caro felt light and easy. For the first time since they had arrived at Toby's, she smiled with the particular radiance that was her hallmark. "I can't imagine," she said. "Then you'll be as glad as I am that the evening is over. There's my stepbrother, Skye, come to take me home. If you'll excuse me—" She rose, evening bag in hand, and maneuvered her way across the dance floor, weaving between the moving bodies, her eyes fixed on Skye's face. She heard Larry exclaim something as he pushed through the crowd that closed the path behind her, and quickened her pace.

"Hurry, Skye, he's right behind me," she said, grabbing Skye's arm and spinning him around.

Skye took one look at the man bearing down on them and thrust Caro through the padded leather doors, quickly hustling her down the steps. "The car's over there. Watch your step, now. That rain left puddles."

The night air was fresh, its chill texture unblemished by odors of cigarettes and highly spiced food. Caro took a deep breath and squeezed Skye's arm. "Thanks for coming, Skye."

"What are you doing going out with a guy like that?"

"He seemed all right when I met him. Acted like butter wouldn't melt in his mouth."

"Until he put you on his menu," Skye said.

"Don't let's fuss." Caro lifted her arms high and moved in a wide circle away from him, turning slowly to the music of the band inside the thick brick walls. The night had a life of its own; a pulse made up of the all-night bars and honky-tonks that straddled parish lines, where jazz pianos alternated with zydeco musicians, creating complicated rhythms that ruled the night.

Suddenly Larry burst through the entrance and stood on the steps, fists clenched in front of him.

"Oh, God," Caro said. She stopped in mid-turn, and her arms dropped to her sides like small wings.

"You come back here, Caro Hamilton," Jordan called to her. He came toward them with the rocking motion of a man whose blood is fueled by alcohol.

"She's going home, Mr. Jordan," Skye said, stepping between Caro and Larry. "Something I think you'd better do too."

"I don't know who the hell you think you are, sonny. Step aside so I can corral my date."

"I'm Skye Langlinais, Mr. Jordan. Caro's stepbrother. We—her brothers and I—are sort of under orders to take her home when she calls. Nothing personal. She just wants to go home."

"And is too high and mighty to let me take her," Jordan said. He was close enough so that Skye could see his eyes; even in the dim light they looked mean, drunk-mean, and Skye closed his hands into fists.

"Get in the car, Caro," he said. "Lock the doors."

He heard the door open, then slam shut. "I'm taking her home," he said.

"Damned if that's so," Jordan answered. He lurched a step closer, hands raised. Skye's muscles tensed, and he felt a quick adrenaline charge. Then Jordan swung. His first punch connected with Skye's shoulder; the second caught his upraised arm. Skye danced back and began to circle, looking for an opening. But even though Jordan was unsteady, and swung wildly, Skye sensed that Jordan had boxed too. Jordan's rage made him reckless; he moved in on Skye, jabbing at him in a barrage of blows, some of which caught only empty air, a few of which landed solidly.

The hell with this, Skye thought, reeling back from Jordan's heavy fists. This is no ring; this is a drunken brawl, and the sooner I get out of it, the better. He backed off, retreating out of Jordan's range, then lowered his head and ran forward, making his body a battering ram. He felt his skull make contact with Jordan's abdomen, and heard the gush of air as it rushed from Jordan's lungs. Skye backed off and hit Jordan with two short jabs. He felt the big body give, and then Jordan staggered away, collapsing over the hood of a nearby car.

Skye followed him and stood over him. "Sorry, Jordan. But nobody gets drunk when he's with my sister."

"Little so-and-so," Jordan gasped. He grabbed the edge of the hood and raised himself up. "You better look out for me."

"You better look out for yourself," Skye said. "Now, have you had enough or are we going to start up again?" He stood balanced on the balls of his feet, hands ready. The slight breeze ruffled his light brown hair, and Jordan could see confidence in Skye's eyes, in the way he held his body.

"Enough," Jordan said. "This time."

Skye threw back his head and laughed. "Mr. Jordan, you don't know Caro very well. There won't be a next time. One chance is all you get—and you threw that one away."

"There's still you, sonny."

"Okay. Come on down to Baton Rouge. We can stage a rematch anytime you like."

For one long moment their eyes met and held. Then Jordan turned away. "Wouldn't waste my time," he said, and lurched away toward the nightclub door.

Skye waited until Jordan had gone back inside and then went to his car. Caro's face was pressed against the window, a pale blur behind the frosted glass. He caught sight of his own face in the side view mirror as he opened the car door, and pushed the wave of brown hair back from his forehead.

"Oh, Skye, did he hurt you?" Caro asked as he got in beside her. She reached out and touched his jaw, then traced the firm chin that appeared in every generation of Langlinaises. She knew Skye's face as well as she knew her own; she had sketched it countless times, shading his gray eyes with quick sure strokes, brushing blond highlights into his brown hair. "I'm sorry, Skye. What a mess."

Skye started the motor and backed the car, turning it in a tight circle and heading out of the lot. "I didn't exactly play by the Marquis of Queensberry rules, but Jordan's a fair boxer, even drunk. It could have taken a while to take him out."

"I hate to see people get themselves into that state," Caro said. She settled back against the seat, pulling her fox jacket around her. "I can handle a sober date. But a drunk one? Spare me!"

Skye shot a glance at Caro. She had lit a cigarette; its smoke filtered through the air between them. The smoke inside and the mist rising from dew-wet fields outside made a veil; Skye suddenly felt that he could not see into Caro's world, nor could she see into his.

"He's a jerk," Skye said.

"So many are," Caro said. She saw the way Skye looked at her, and smiled. "Not really. I've met some nice boys in New Orleans. Only—only no one special, you know?" She shook her head. "I don't know. All the evenings are beginning to run together. All the faces."

"Good Lord, Caro," Skye said. "Don't give up yet." He reached over and patted her hand. "Don't worry. You'll meet someone wonderful. You're only eighteen!"

"So are you," she shot back. "And you've got Rosalind Nasser—so don't tell me to be patient."

Rosalind! They were to go out tomorrow evening. The sound of her name alone was enough to arouse Skye's passion. He still remembered the first time he'd noticed her, at a summer swimming party two weeks after high school graduation. She had walked out onto the end of the diving board, posing for a moment before arching into a perfect back dive. Her two-piece bathing suit had done little to hide the voluptuous fullness of her sun-tanned figure. In that moment he had fallen for her as he had never fallen for a girl before.

They had begun dating soon after; by the time she left for her freshman year at Dominican College in New Orleans, and Skye had left for LSU, Rosalind was his girl. And if he sometimes wondered if Rosalind really meant the promises her eyes made, if he sometimes doubted that she could flirt so provocatively and not really understand her effect on him, he was careful to put such doubts firmly aside.

The car crossed into the path of light cast by the two tall lanterns topping the Langlinais gateposts. A light frost had touched the grass. As Skye pulled the car into the parking area near the huge family house, he heard the long, cold cry of a train chugging through empty canefields beyond their pastures. "I forget how quiet it is out here," he said, helping Caro out. "My dorm at LSU never settles down."

"I know," Caro said. She stood hugging her coat around her; she could see her breath in the chill air. "It's the same at Newcomb—New Orleans is a hard place to be alone. When I get to feeling too closed in, I think of the farm. And Beau Chêne."

Skye took her hand in his and felt the silent communion. Caro felt the same way about Beau Chêne as he did about the Langlinais farm; it was in every painting she made of the place, in every line she drew. As they went up the steps and into the house, he had a sudden insight. Maybe the men Caro met sensed that there were things other than themselves that she held dear. Maybe, when they heard her speak of her family, of Beau Chêne, when they learned how many hours she spent in the studio, wrapped in her own private vision, they decided that as beautiful as Caro Hamilton was, as delightful to be with, too many other things had a hold on her for them to even try to compete.

Caro and her brothers Raoul and Henri had easily slipped into life at the Langlinais farm when her mother married Beau Langlinais five years ago. The fact that their own family's home, Beau Chêne, lay but a mile away through the woods helped establish a link, continuity between their old life and their new one. The arrival of their half-brother André, born a year after Beau and Caroline married, had been the final mortar that solidified the family.

After they had said good night, Skye sat in his room smoking. There was no use going back to sleep. Soon he would hear the light tap at the door that meant his father was awake and ready to go. They would drink coffee in the large, silent kitchen and then drive into St. Martinville for the three-A.M. hunters' Mass, joining other bleary-eyed men who would blink through the service before going out into the marshes to hunt. Skye and Beau would pole through the labyrinth of water that crisscrossed their land to the blind. They would watch the mallards and geese wing in, coasting down the cold, dark sky.

Sitting there with smoke curling around him, Skye could feel the breadth of the land that stretched toward the horizon: three square leagues for the Langlinais farm, three square leagues for Beau Chêne. When the two families first arrived, Beau Chêne had raised sugar, while the Langlinaises grew rich from the bounty of the swamps. Then oil was struck on both lands, and now the steady pumps made a stream of money that, as Beau Langlinais said, at one and the same time freed them and bound them tight.

Skye wasn't sure he understood that. He saw how money could free a man. He was not sure he saw how it could bind him. He crushed out his cigarette. Tonight was not a time for such serious thoughts. He heard a tap at his door and went to meet his father.

* * *

"Careful, André—that ornament is older than I am," Caro said as she handed him a glittering pine-cone ornament to hang on a low branch of the towering Christmas fir that filled one corner of the long Langlinais living room.

André looked up at Raoul, who was balanced on the top step of a small ladder, testing bulbs in the strings of lights he had hung on the tree. "Did you have Santa Claus when you were little?" he asked.

Émilie, one of the twins, looked up from the icicles she was sorting. "Of course we did," she said.

Gennie, the other twin, picked up a cranberry, thrust her needle through it, and pushed it down next to the kernel of popcorn she had just threaded on the long red-and-white string. "There. A few more and I think this will be long enough. My fingers feel like pincushions."

"Where is Skye, anyway?" Henri asked. He, Raoul and Caro had driven in from New Orleans yesterday for the annual decorating of the tree. College or no college, it was the family's new traditional ushering-in of the Christmas season.

"Out gathering pine and holly," Caro said.

She turned to Henri. "Come help me set up the crèche, Henri." They knelt near the tree, placing the tiny figures carefully in a wooden stable Henri had made the first Christmas they had celebrated together.

"Now, André," Émilie said. "We have a very serious decision to make. Where shall we hang Santa Claus?"

"On top of the tree!" André said.

"All right," Émilie laughed, swooping him up.

Suddenly they saw Skye in the doorway with a load of pine and holly in his arms. "Looks like you're about done," he said, looking at the tree. He set his burden of branches near the hearth. "Hey, I'm beginning to get in the Christmas spirit. How about some music?"

"I've got the song sheets right here," Caro said. She opened the piano and ran her fingers over the keys as the others gathered around. Henri handed out song sheets.

In a moment, as Caro struck the first chords of "Jingle Bells," seven voices rose as one as they entered into the spirit of the holiday season. Raoul picked up a set of bells and began jingling them in time to the music.

Caroline Langlinais, preparing dinner in the kitchen at the end of the hall, heard the caroling and smiled over at Beau, who sat at the kitchen table shelling pecans.

"Listen," she said. "Doesn't that remind you of the Christmas Eve we finally proposed to each other?" She went to him and kissed him. "Has it really been six years?"

"No," he said, pulling her onto his lap. "It's been a day. And it's been forever."

"I was sent to get you." Raoul smiled, standing in the doorway.

"I'm just putting the ham in the oven," Caroline said. "Would you turn on the radio in the living room? WWL is going to broadcast *The Messiah* at two o'clock."

"Sure," Raoul said, looking at his watch. "It's just about two now."

Caroline sprinkled brown sugar over the ham, moistened it with pineapple juice, and put it in the oven. "There!" she said. "*That* should be enough to feed this crew."

"Have you *ever* run out of food?" Beau said. He put the last of the pecans into the bowl and got up, brushing the bits of shell from his trousers. "If any of them dares touch those, I'll skin 'em alive. I'm saving those for Christmas pralines."

Caroline watched him scrub the pecan stains from his hands. "I'm glad the Louisiana House is not in session now," she said. "I miss you, even if you are just over in Baton Rouge."

"It's always good to be home," Beau said, drying his hands. "If I had my druthers, I'd never leave."

She snuggled against him, feeling the strength that had been her shield for more years than she could remember. She knew better than to say: "Stay home. If you never worked another day in your life, the money would continue to flow in." Beau Langlinais understood what his son Skye as yet did not—that if a man is decent and responsible, the freedom wealth brings leads to other choices just as binding in their way as the jobs of poorer men.

Beau and Caroline reached the threshold of the living room just as the singers launched into "Hark, the Herald Angels Sing." They paused, surveying the scene before them. "Oh, Beau, get the camera, will you?" Caroline said. "I want a picture."

At the end of the carol the children, grumbling, laughing, jostling, took their places. Caro, her blond hair caught back with an emerald ribbon, sat in the center of a low velvet sofa, Émilie and Gennie on either side, their dark hair in stark contrast with Caro's blond features. The boys stood behind them: Skye in the center, looking like a younger model of his father, his easy smile masking an intense nature few people outside the family were aware of; Henri, standing rather stiffly, light hair brushed severely across his forehead; Raoul, the tallest of the three, seeming to lounge even as he stood erect, his body graceful, lithe, seemingly in motion, as though hurrying to catch up with life. André knelt in front, his blue eyes fixed on his father's face, hand resting on Caro's knee. The bulb exploded. For a moment Caroline saw them as they would appear in the photograph—Raoul with his lazy smile, Skye's typically earnest expression, Henri looking serious, Caro laughing, the twins flirting with the camera, André blinking as the bulb went off. Then she stepped back, and felt her foot strike something on the floor.

"Those are my soldiers," André said, getting up and coming to her. "They're having a parade."

Caroline looked at the neat lines of lead soldiers, tiny weapons molded into place. The picture of her children hung before her eyes and she blinked, and brushed it away. "Maybe you should pick them up," she said, "so they won't get stepped on."

"Here, I'll help you, son," Beau said. He knelt beside André and began putting the soldiers into their wooden box. In the paper this morning he'd read that across the world, German and Russian armies were locked in a real war, fighting for Moscow. And far to the south of Russia's frozen steppes, the British Eighth Army had confronted Rommel and his tank corps. Beau looked again at his youngest son, playing war. You can't get away from it, he thought. Not here, not anywhere. Increasingly, as he met other representatives conducting the business of the Louisiana legislature, they voiced the same worried thoughts. The small, private reality of the Langlinais farm, of Beau Chêne beyond it, seemed suddenly ephemeral, as though in dealing with that larger world he might not be able to hang on to this one.

He shook off the mood that threatened to engulf him. "That tree is the prettiest we've ever had," he said.

"You say that every year," Émilie said.

"It's true every year," Beau said.

Raoul looked at his watch and turned up the volume on the radio. The music of Handel's *Messiah* swelled around them.

Moments later, the front door opened and a blast of cold air invaded the room.

"We were about to give up on you," Beau said to his parents, going forward to help his mother take off her coat.

"Your father got a phone call at the last minute," Alice Langlinais said. The chill air of December clung to her clothes and her lips as she circled the room, kissing her grandchildren. Claude carried a basket piled high with grapefruit and oranges.

"The Christmas bounty has begun," he said, setting the basket down and kissing Caroline. "Gulf Oil sent this and a case of champagne, and I don't know what all's cluttering up the office."

"I'm sure we'll manage to put it to good use," Caroline said. "Thank you, Papa Claude."

Alice settled on the sofa, André in her lap. Claude and Beau stood in the doorway talking in low voices while the others sprawled on the floor near the fire. Handel's music soared, seeming to take in the spirit of the room.

And then, it abruptly stopped.

"What on earth?" Raoul said. He slid over to the radio, hand outstretched.

"Ladies and gentlemen," an announcer began. "We interrupt this broadcast with an announcement from the White House. President Roosevelt has had word that early this morning, Japanese forces attacked Pearl Harbor."

They stared at one another, and saw their own shock in each other's faces.

"Pearl Harbor?" Caro said. "Where is that?"

"Hawaii," Skye said. "It's the base for our entire Pacific fleet." He went to the radio and turned the volume up. The announcer explained that the station would not finish the *Messiah* broadcast, but would join the network for coverage of the attack.

Caro turned to Beau. "Père, does this mean . . . we're at war?"

"I'm afraid we are," he said. "Or will be."

The network marshaled an array of commentators to discuss the attack, switching from New York to correspondents in London and other points abroad. Despite all the talk, there was little substantive information, but the speculations about the magnitude of the disaster let fear into the room that, like the chill of December that had followed Claude and Alice, seemed to change the very air. As the static-punctured voices went on, broadcasting from Singapore, from Paris, from Washington, from the West Coast, where already panicking citizens were arming themselves against the threat of Japanese invasion, they all responded to that change. They looked, almost involuntarily, at the tranquil scene beyond the windows. The sun was lower now, and shadows crossed the front lawn in lengthening steps, shading the browning grass and still-blooming roses, darkening the tints of the flowers on the camellia bushes that grew in profusion around the circular drive.

Skye saw the fear in his family's faces, and he knew that, like him, they were envisioning silent figures, armed with rifles and machine guns in terrible mockery of the lead soldiers scattered across the rug, slipping out of the woods, ducking low to run across the pasture and surround the house. He knew that the others, like him, were imagining the sound of airplane engines overhead, were waiting for the explosion of gunfire and bombs. The images from countless newsreels rose before him; roads flooded with the human debris of war, fields rutted by bomb craters, towns gutted by fire.

"But they can't reach America, can they?" Émilie cried.

The entire family seemed to stir, suddenly restless, needing an outlet for the anxiety Émilie had put into words. The gathering hung by one slender thread; the next heavy slice from a commentator's voice would cut it, letting it shatter against the hard edge of war.

"Now, please," Caroline said quietly. "We don't know anything yet. As of right now, there's absolutely nothing we can do. I think we should use this afternoon the way we meant to. As much as we possibly can."

"You're right," Alice Langlinais said. She looked at each of the grandchildren assembled before her. "No one knows what lies ahead. But you all come from strong people, people who have been part of this land for almost two hundred years. People who have known what it is to be threatened with its loss—and who have had to defend it against enemies. I want to tell you something—you young people are going to have to deal with this war much more than Claude and I, Beau and Caroline. You won't change anything by fearing it. Nor by resenting all the ways in which this war will interrupt your lives. Sometimes—when what we're facing is very big—it tends to overwhelm us. Makes us lose sight of—well, the gift of each day." Alice took a deep breath and reached out to take Claude's hand. "What I really want to say is this—no matter what happens, remember that there is joy and beauty in every day. If you don't find it—well, you just haven't looked." Her eyes lingered on each young face, the tender affection in them like a kiss. Then she smiled. "Now I will admit—there are days when you have to shovel a lot of mud before you find them."

"I think we've got a lot of good shovelers here," Claude said.

"You're right, Grandmère," Skye said, coming forward to kiss her. "We're going to make the most of today. Why don't we start by having some of Mère's famous eggnog?"

"I'll handle that," Caroline said, beckoning to Beau and Claude. "Come on, Beau. You and Papa Claude can beat the egg whites."

The Sunday afternoon slipped past violence and back into a rhythm that was almost normal. Only the crackling of the radio, turned down below the volume of their talk, made a staccato beat that drummed war.

"I know a lot of boys who will enlist," Caro said, thinking of the ways her world would soon change. Her eyes flew to the atlas, the great blue wash that was the Pacific Ocean splashed against the deep colors of the rug.

Skye stood near the mantle, his body tense. He was only eighteen—he wouldn't be allowed to enlist yet. He was both upset and relieved. He shivered and turned to hold his hands out to the fire. The troops at Pearl Harbor had hardly had time to be scared. But if you knew you were going into battle—if you knew that men were waiting to kill you? Again he shivered, an involuntary denial of the fear that rode him. He thought of Rosalind, sitting in her room at Dominican College, working on a term paper. He wanted to call her, to hear her voice. With a rush of honesty, he admitted to himself that maybe it wasn't so bad to be only eighteen. He had time. Time to become braver, time to be with Rosalind.

"It's as though we lived in a silver ball," Caro said. "And then out of the blue something shatters it. And nothing is ever the same again."

Skye thought of his family's power, its immense wealth. But against the world war that terrorized the globe, their small empire seemed puny, defenseless. For the first time in his life, it seemed that being a Langlinais was not enough.

2

JANUARY 1942

Caro walked briskly down the steps of St. Louis Cathedral, pushed along by the throng leaving the eleven-o'clock high mass. She glanced at her watch and calculated how long she could idle in Jackson Square before joining her friends at Brennan's. Enough time to walk at least once around the wrought-iron fence and view the paintings and watercolors hanging there, she thought. She crossed the brick street to the broad pavement where artists sat sketching and peddling their wares.

It was warm for January, and before she had walked a hundred paces she had shrugged off her light coat and taken off her small felt hat, baring her hair to the sun. Many of the paintings were repetitive: the same magnolias, the same swamps, the same views of the same churches. But occasionally something more original appeared; an artist with a real vision that shot through the collage of calendar art like a beacon from a lighthouse. It was in this hope that Caro frequented Jackson Square.

She found one such artist on a stretch of fence near Café du Monde, and stood mesmerized before his work, a mixture of pen-an-ink and charcoal. His use of white space intrigued her, and she became lost in a world of technique and craft, forgetting everything but the work before her.

"Is it really that good?" a voice said, followed by a low, easy laugh.

She turned to see a tall young man, black hair curling low over his forehead, dark brows sheltering blue eyes lit with amusement. And something else that made a spark leap between them—admiration and interest.

"It's a great deal better than most of this," she said carefully, keeping her voice in the proper balance between civility and distance. "I'm no expert, but there are several things here that are quite good."

"You look like an expert," the young man said. "I've been watching you. You walk past some of these pictures as though they're just another part of the fence. I have to stop and consider every one of them, and then I'm still not sure whether they're worth what the artist is asking."

"Are you interested in buying something?" Caro asked. She would not let herself think about the fact that he had been watching her, or of the way he had looked at her. This is not a pickup, she told herself. It's Sunday morning in Jackson Square, and the rules are a little different here. You can speak to a stranger, and then go on about your business with no harm done.

"My mother's birthday is in a couple of weeks," he said. He seemed nearer now, though she didn't think he had actually moved toward her. Maybe the way his body seemed to fill her vision, the way he seemed to take up all the space—she shifted her weight and took a tentative step backward, as though to look more closely at the sketch she had been studying. "She's never been to New Orleans, and I thought it might be nice to send her a typical scene. I don't want her to think her favorite son lives in a subtropical sinkhole."

"Is that what she thinks of New Orleans?" Caro asked.

"She's lived in Manhattan all of her life. I guess she suffers from the peculiar, rather sophisticated provincialism of many New Yorkers."

Caro laughed, a sudden burst of spontaneous sound that obviously startled him. "Well," he said. "So you're human after all." He put out his hand to silence her protest. "I'm sorry. I just meant—you seemed to be trying to maintain a kind of tour-guide tone. And to tell you the truth, you were making me feel terribly . . . isolated."

The blue eyes looking into hers changed; for a moment she saw a kind of lost vulnerability that echoed the way she herself sometimes felt. She involuntarily reached out her own hand and took his. "I'm sorry," she said. "I didn't mean to be . . . cold. I just—"

"Your mother has told you, and very rightly, too, never to talk to strangers. Exactly what my three sisters have always been told." He smiled, and she found herself tracing the line of his lips with her eyes, and then blushing because he saw her doing it. "Look," he said, letting go of her hand. "I really do want to buy my mother a picture. And I don't want to send her something that is just a pastiche. Could I possibly impose on you to help me?" He saw her look at her watch. "I'm sorry. Am I keeping you from something?"

"Yes—no, nothing that won't still be going on when I get there," she said. "I'll make a deal with you. Let's go have coffee and beignets and you can give me an idea of your mother's taste. Then we'll tour the square and find something."

"I'd love that," he said. "But I'm not sure my mother would approve of my having coffee with a young lady whose name I don't know." He bowed formally. "I'm David Selbin," he said. "Dr. David Selbin."

"Caro Hamilton," she said. The name, uttered all by itself, sounded strange even as she spoke it, as though it belonged to someone else. She realized that except for the casual introductions she and her Newcomb classmates performed when meeting on campus, she had never before in her life introduced herself to anyone. Certainly not to an attractive man. Dr. David Selbin. He must be quite a bit older than she was—and much more knowledgeable.

"What kind of doctor are you?" she asked when they were seated in the crowded café.

"Internal medicine," he said. He looked around, taking in the scurrying white-jacketed waiters, the buzz of talk, the pervasive aroma of rich café au lait and beignets. "This place is so typically New Orleans," he said. "Big silver sugar bowls along the counter inside—yet chained down so no one can take them." He smiled, and Caro felt a funny catch in her heart. "French romance and pragmatism," he said. "I'm beginning to think it's an irresistible combination."

"My father was a doctor," Caro said. She needed to slow this conversation down; it seemed to want to rush them along, carry them into territory better explored more slowly. "A country doctor, I guess you'd call him. In Lafayette. I suppose you don't know where that is."

"I do," David said. He sipped his coffee and bit into a beignet. "Charity Hospital has a unit over there. I've been to Lafayette a number of times."

"So you're at Charity?"

"Doing a residency in tropical medicine," he said. A cloud of powdered sugar from his beignet sifted over his dark suit, and he brushed at it. His fingers were long, slender; Caro could almost feel them touching her, stroking her, and for the first time since she had encountered him, she felt afraid. He had completed his residency in internal medicine at a hospital in San Francisco the previous year, she heard him explain, and had decided to take one more specialized residency before entering practice. She heard herself making the appropriate responses, punctuating his replies with interested questions. But all the time they talked, she felt her emotions taking a course all their own, and becoming a growing river of desire.

He must know, she thought, stealing looks at him from under her lashes. Does my face show what I'm feeling? But his face remained calm, placid. And slowly, by forcing herself to listen to what he was saying, by concentrating on all the physical details around her, Caro got herself under control. By the time they left the café to find David's picture, she was herself again, able to walk calmly alongside him talking about art, telling him about her studies at Newcomb.

"A college girl!" he said.

She heard the surprise in his voice and felt a sudden despair; why hadn't she lied?

"A very new college girl," she said. "I'm a freshman."

"A freshman," he said slowly. "But you seem so . . . mature." He seemed disturbed, and her heart caught again. "I had hoped—I want to see you again, Caro."

"I'd like that too," she said. She looked up at him, trying to appear composed. "Is there—is there any reason why we can't?"

His eyes cleared, and he smiled back at her. "None at all," he said.

She ducked away from the quick intensity in his blue eyes, and said hurriedly, "The next artist has some fairly solid work. Would your mother prefer a landscape or a street scene, do you think?"

"Maybe a little of both," David said. He pointed out a painting that showed a French Quarter patio, wrought-iron railings, and lush foliage casting an exotic air. "What do you think of that one?"

"Actually," Caro said, studying the painting, "it's quite good. The use of light and shadow, the way he repeats the touch of crimson from the brickwork in the pot of flowers—you have a better eye than you think you do, Dr. Selbin."

"Oh, there's nothing wrong with my eye," David said, and again Caro looked away from his intense look.

"That's a fair price, too," she said. "Unless you want to look further, I think this one is very nice."

"Sold," David said. He paid the artist, and while the man wrapped the painting, pulled out a small notebook and opened it. "I've got a horrendous schedule, but I don't imagine I need to tell a doctor's daughter about that. Are you free Wednesday night?"

She couldn't focus on Wednesday; her calendar might be filled from dawn to dusk, but she could remember none of it. "Yes," she said.

"Could you—would you have dinner with me?"

"Yes," she said.

"I'll call you," he said. He held his pen poised while she gave him the number. "Is there a time that's best to reach you?"

"I'm in class until three Monday, Wednesday, and Friday," she said. "And from nine to eleven on Tuesday, Thursday, and Saturday."

He tucked the book back into his pocket. Caro had a strange feeling that he had tucked part of herself inside him; suddenly she wanted him to touch her, hold her, and again she stepped away skittishly. "And I suppose you have all sorts of extracurricular things to do," he said. His eyes teased her, and she blushed.

"The usual amount," she said. She deliberately pushed back her sleeve and looked at her watch. "I'm unconscionably late," she said. "Thank heavens I'm lunching at a restaurant—if it was a private home, I'd have been terribly rude."

"May I walk with you?" he asked. He sensed her hesitation, and she saw that vulnerable loneliness in his eyes. "Sorry," he said. "I don't mean to intrude."

"Nonsense," she said. "If you're heading that way—I'm going to Brennan's."

David shifted the painting to his other hand and held out his free arm to Caro. She took it, and fell into step beside him. All at once, everything seemed to fall into place: the warmth of the sun on her head and back; the way his arm steadied her as they walked over the uneven bricks; the way he was just enough taller than she was so that she could meet his eyes by simply lifting hers. Goodness, she thought to herself, is this what love is like?

When he bid her good-bye at Brennan's entrance, Caro went to meet her friends feeling much different than she had when she walked out of St. Louis Cathedral an hour and a half before.

The heavy knife sliced skillfully between the locked edges of the oyster shell, twisting it open to reveal the plump gray flesh. Grinning, the man slid the shell containing the oyster onto the tray in front of Skye. "That makes four dozen," he said. "Keep on that way and you'll break your papa's record."

"I don't think anyone can eat as many oysters as Papa," Skye said. He hefted the frosty mug of draft beer and drank. Wiping the foam from his lips, he looked at Raoul and laughed. "But if you two don't get your appetites back, I'm going to win this bet and you're going to pay for supper."

"I'd rather pay up than throw up," Raoul said, shoving the tray in front of him away. "I don't mind admitting I've eaten as much as I can—more than I can, probably."

"I'll have another dozen," Henri said.

"Your funeral," Raoul said. He got off the high bar stool and went over to the slot machine standing in the corner. "I'll give you guys as much time as it takes to get rid of my loose change. Then I'm heading out."

Skye dipped the last of his oysters into the sauce and held a cracker under it. This last one didn't taste quite as good as the first; he let it slip down his throat with a feeling of relief, and went to join Raoul. "We're ready when you are," he called to Henri, as he watched the line of lemons form in the machine.

"No one has ever been known to hit the jackpot on this machine," he told Raoul. "Papa's been coming here since he was my age, and all it ever pays is a couple of dollars."

"Thank God I have better sense than to try to make money on the slot machines," Raoul said. He fed another quarter into it, watched while three apples came up, and put his hand in front of the funnel at the bottom of the machine where a small shower of silver fell. "Just about broke even," he said, looking at the money in his hand. "Let's collect Henri. He's forcing himself to eat that last dozen—hell, I'll pay off the bet just to get us moving."

"I already told Joe Glorioso to put it on Papa's tab," Skye said. "Stupid bet, anyhow." He went up behind Henri and slapped him on the shoulder. "Come on, Henri, we've got dates waiting."

Henri turned and started at them. His face was covered with sweat, and his eyes bulged against a pasty forehead. "I—" he began, and then, hand shoved against his mouth, leapt from his stool and dashed toward the outside door.

Skye started after him, but Raoul's hand stopped him. "Let him get it over, Skye," Raoul said. "Henri gets madder than a stirred-up bull if anyone tries to help him."

"But he's sick."

"Sure. Probably very sick." Raoul turned to Joe Glorioso, who was opening oysters at the other end of the counter. "Let me have some ice in a towel, would you please, Joe?"

They found Henri sitting on the steps, head between his knees, hands hanging limp. "I'll cover this mess," Skye said as he scooped up leaves from the piles drifted by winter winds and made a thick layer over Henri's vomit, kicking shells from the parking lot on top of them. Raoul held the cold towel against Henri's neck, a grim expression making his mouth tight.

"I'm all right now," Henri said, trying to twist his head away from Raoul's hand.

"Stay still another couple of minutes," Raoul said. He held a large piece of ice in front of Henri's face. "Here. Melt this in your mouth and then spit it out. I've got some gum you can chew to get rid of that taste." He looked at Skye and winked. "Good thing you've got a blind date tonight. If it was someone you planned to kiss, you'd be in big trouble."

"I'm all right!" Henri said. He thrust Raoul's hand away and stood up, the ice still in his hand.

"Okay," Raoul said. "Then let's get going."

They waited until Henri rinsed his mouth; he climbed into the back of Skye's car and leaned back against the seat, eyes closed, his face set in what they had long ago started calling "Henri's sulk."

"I hope he snaps out of it before we pick the girls up," Raoul whispered to Skye. "Henri can be a lot of fun—but when he gets into one of his moods—"

"We can count on Henri," Skye said. He turned his head slightly. "Listen, Henri, I know just how you feel. Last week at the Phi Delt house a guy challenged me to chugalug beer. I spent the rest of the night in the john."

"Somehow, Skye," Henri said, "when you make a fool of yourself, you manage to do it with grace."

They drove the rest of the way to Rosalind's house in silence. The triple date, with the stop at Joe's for raw oysters beforehand, had seemed the perfect antidote for what Raoul called the January blahs. Now, Skye thought, turning into the Nasser driveway, he wished he had not offered to ask Rosalind to get dates for the others. He saw Rosalind rarely enough as it was; he certainly didn't want to have to spend the evening cheering Henri up. The hell with it, he thought. Henri's a big boy. He can either behave himself or not, as he pleases. I'm going to enjoy myself.

"Wow!" Raoul said, peering out at the Nasser's house. "This place looks like something out of the Arabian Nights!"

"I guess it does at that," Skye said, looking at the mass of vine-covered stucco looming at the end of the sidewalk. A sense of the Nasser house, its burnt red and deep gold and burnished-looking brown rugs thrown over tile floors, its air permeated with the scent of saffron and mace, coriander and rosemary, came over him. Rosalind's house affected him much the same way she did; exotic and sensual, both enveloped him in an unfamiliar, exciting world.

"They're very rich, you know," Henri said, unfolding himself from the back seat. "For a family that got here after all the land was gone."

"Brains, my boy," Raoul said cheerfully. "Brains and energy will do it every time."

"The Nassars aren't any different from anyone else," Skye said.

"They're just—" He struggled to put the thought into words. "They're just . . . interesting."

"I hope my date is as . . . interesting as Rosalind is," Raoul teased. He saw Skye's frown and stopped. "I'm just kidding around, Skye. It's darn nice of you to include Henri and me—we won't embarrass you."

Raoul's tactful inclusion of himself had an immediate effect on Henri. "Right. This is going to be a perfect evening if I have anything to say about it."

Throughout the flurry of introductions, Skye could not keep his eyes off Rosalind. She wore a dress that swirled around her; soft drapes, floating panels, a skirt that clung and moved with a life of its own. "This is Skye Langlinais," she said, presenting Skye to two girls sitting on a brocade sofa in the living room.

"And these are my stepbrothers, Raoul and Henri Hamilton," Skye said. "This is Rosalind—" He looked at the two other girls questioningly.

"Felice and Sarah Ashy," Rosalind said. "Two of my cousins."

"Beauty is certainly a family trait," Raoul said, approaching Felice and taking the hand she held out.

"And flattery runs in ours," Henri said, coming forward. "But in the present instance, what might be flattery becomes the truth."

"Well, for heaven's sake, Skye," Rosalind said. "You didn't tell me your stepbrothers had such silver tongues."

"They don't talk to me like that," Skye said, laughing. Sarah and Felice were pretty, even if they didn't match Rosalind's particular appeal. The two couples seemed to be hitting it off well.

"I hope you all have your dancing shoes on," he said. "There's a great band at Chag's tonight. We're all ready to give them a test."

"I'll just tell Mama good night," Rosalind said.

The January night was unseasonably warm and humid; they drove with the windows down, the girls' hair blowing back from their faces. Skye had left the radio on, and when Rosalind leaned forward to turn it up, she came in on an update of the war news.

"Oh, can we change the station?" Felice said. "That's all my father ever listens to. My oldest brother's in flight training, so I understand how Dad feels—but I'm sick of it!"

"Where's your brother training?" Skye asked.

"Pensacola. He's in the Navy."

"Navy Reserve's the best I can manage," Raoul said gloomily. "I checked at the recruiting office, but they said this close to medical school, to forget active duty. You wouldn't mind dating a reserve officer, would you?" he said to Felice, looking into her eyes.

"How about you, Henri?" Sarah asked, holding her cigarette to the lighter he held. She puffed until the flame glowed, then said, "Are you like everyone else, champing at the bit to get in?"

"I won't be twenty until May," Henri said, raising his voice slightly. "Thank goodness they've lowered the enlistment age. I can join up after finishing the term at Loyola."

"What branch are you thinking of?" Sarah asked.

"The Army," Henri said. The decisiveness in his voice made Skye turn to look at him. Henri was sitting with his back against the side of the car to make room for the others; his profile showed sharply against the glow of passing streetlights. "I've been thinking about the tank corps."

"Tanks!" Sarah said. "But they're in the front lines."

"No point in joining up if you're not going to fight," Henri said. Something about his voice alerted Skye. Henri sounded the way he did when he was talking about hunting; although he joined them on their hunts, it was the camaraderie, the time spent in the peace of the swamp, that he enjoyed. The only shooting Henri did was with his camera. Still, when he talked to girls about it, though he did not say so, the impression he left was that he was a master shot who set the pace for them all.

"The Germans have a crack tank corps," Raoul said. "If that's your druthers, little brother, you'll have your chance at glory."

"Or I might apply for intelligence," Henri said. His pupils were dilated, the corner of his mouth twitched, and there was an urgency about the way Henri spoke that made Skye wonder who it was Henri was trying to convince. "Pitting yourself against danger, ferreting out the enemy's secrets, being at the hidden center of the war effort—" He stopped suddenly, as though their silence had interrupted him.

"I read that spies are tortured if they're caught," Felice said. She shuddered. "I can't even think about it."

"So far," Raoul said, "this conversation is all academic. Henri can't join anything until May—and poor Skye here won't get in for two years yet, unless they lower the age limit again."

"I wish I could figure a way around that."

"Don't you dare," Rosalind said. Her hand crossed the space between them and touched Skye's leg. He took one hand off the steering wheel and covered hers. "Why are you all in such a rush to get into the war, anyway? You talk as though it's just another team you're trying out for."

"Maybe that's the appeal," Henri said. "The toughest team of all." He sounded more himself again; less forced, less deliberately seeking center stage. "The call to the primitive male lurking in us. The call to test ourselves against dark forces. A chance to answer the age-old questions: How strong are my beliefs? How much will I sacrifice for them?"

His voice rang through his listeners, and although neither Raoul nor Skye said anything, they both responded to what Henri had said. Maybe Henri was a little grandiose. Maybe he did fudge a little on his exploits. Maybe he could act the fool. But by God, he'd put his finger on it. The war was a chance for them to stop beating their heads against what college professors said were the tests civilization presented each new generation—and go challenge the only one that mattered.

"Hear, hear," Raoul said softly.

Then an Artie Shaw standard, "Begin the Beguine," began playing on the radio, and their mood lightened. Skye turned into the almost full parking lot at Chag's and looked at his watch. "They said they'd hold the table until eight-thirty. We just made it."

"Oh, I don't think they'd have given you any problem," Rosalind said as he helped her from the car.

"Why not?" Skye asked, piloting her toward the nightclub. "Do they know my father?"

"No," Rosalind said, going ahead of him through the door and nodding to the man standing just inside. "They know mine. My father owns Chag's." She moved forward and spoke to the maître d'. "Did you give us a good table, Chuck? We'd love to be near the band."

"I didn't know you were in this party, Miss Nasser," the maître d' said. He looked flustered and ran his finger over the reservation list. "I'll make a switch right away," he said.

"Good," Rosalind said. "We'll wait here while you do."

From their vantage point Skye could see the maître d' speaking to a party seated at a table close to the band. At first they protested, but then he leaned forward and whispered something to them. The people turned and stared toward where Rosalind and Skye stood, the other couples clustered behind. Then the table's occupants began gathering up their belongings, preparing to move. Chuck beckoned to a waiter, who loaded the party's drinks onto a tray and carried it to a table in a corner of the room.

"It's all fixed, Miss Nasser," the maître d' said as he strode toward Rosalind, beaming. "By the time you get to your table, they'll have fresh settings."

"Thank you," Rosalind said. She followed the host as he led their group forward, her head high, looking neither to the left nor to the right.

Skye was accustomed to favors being given him, favors he very often did not even ask for. He was accustomed to preferential treatment. But he was not accustomed to taking it at the expense of someone else.

"I wish you hadn't done that, Rosalind."

"What?" Rosalind asked. Her fingers drummed on the tabletop in time to the music, and she kept her eyes fixed on the bandleader.

"Made that other party move. They were here first."

She turned her green eyes on him. "If Chuck had known I was in your party, he'd have given you this table from the beginning."

"But he didn't," Skye said. He made himself face the pull of those compelling eyes. "He gave this table to someone else."

"So he corrected the error," Rosalind said. "Skye, my father owns this place. When I come here, I should be able to sit where I want." She sounded bored; before Skye could marshal another argument, Henri spoke.

"Of course you should!" he interjected. "What's the point in having such a nice place if you can't enjoy it?"

"My point exactly," Rosalind said. She leaned toward Skye and smiled, her green eyes becoming soft, seductive. "Anyway, if it will make you feel better—Chuck knows to give them their drinks on the house."

"That's fair," Henri said. He had totally recovered from his earlier bad humor, and turned to Sarah, a pleased smile on his face. "Let's dance, shall we?"

Raoul and Felice followed Henri and Sarah onto the dance floor. Skye stood up and held out his arms to Rosalind. "Dance?" he asked, and heard a small remnant of irritation in his voice.

"Are you going to fuss at me some more?" she asked, rising to meet him.

For one short moment, before her body melted against him, Skye's irritation held. And then, as he touched her, it was gone, all thought of her high-handedness dispelled as they moved onto the floor.

The moment became something he wanted to hold on to: this song, Rosalind. He wished the world could stay the way it was now: he wanted to go on attending LSU, exploring the avenues it opened. Already the ranks of his fraternity were being decimated. Almost all Phi Delta Theta's seniors and some of the juniors were gone, and just last week, a classmate had been killed in action. At the memorial service, no one knew quite what to do or where to look.

As a matter of fact, the chugalug contest in which he'd disgraced himself had been held after that service. They'd sought a release for their discomfort in drink, and he at least had learned a lesson. Booze might make you feel better if you were already in a good mood, but it was a poor companion for sorrow.

"Penny?" Rosalind said, whirling expertly back into his arms at the end of a long swing.

"I was just thinking," Skye said. "When I do join up—I'll have the prettiest girl in the United States waiting for me."

"Just the United States?" Rosalind said. She threw her head back to look at him; her throat made a long, creamy curve that ended in the sweetheart neckline of her deep-green dress.

"The world," Skye said.

"That's better," she said, laughing. But as he swung her out again, watched her skirt swirl up around her long, slim legs, watched her feet fly in their deep-green velvet pumps, he remembered that she had said nothing about the other half of his thought—that she would be waiting for him.

3

MAY 1942

"Aunt Annette is going to love you," Caro said to David as they walked up Calliope Street. "You're exactly her sort of person."

"And what sort is that?" he said. He had a rare weekend off; they had spent Saturday sailing, stayed up until two in the morning dancing at the Blue Room, and now he had collected her to go to her aunt's for Sunday lunch.

"Sophisticated. Cosmopolitan. Aunt Annette can forgive people almost anything—but if they bore her, watch out!"

"Let me get the relationship straight again. This is your mother's aunt?"

"Yes. Her father's sister. Mama and Père used to meet at Aunt Annette's house."

David's eyebrows rose. "That sounds rather . . . sub-rosa."

"It was. Mama's parents didn't want her to marry Père—their romance got all mixed up with politics and money and even Beau Chêne itself . . ." Caro shook her head. "Anyway, they used to meet at Aunt Annette's until Mama had to give Père up."

"Very Byzantine," David said. "Here I thought you had a simple, uncomplicated background."

"There are all kinds of depths you haven't explored," Caro said, laughing. She saw the quick passion in David's eyes and turned away. "Here we are. Oh, bother, we're not the only people here." She sighed. "I warn you. Aunt Annette can collect some pretty strange guests."

As they went up the steps to the front porch, a babble of voices greeted them. Although the scene was familiar—men and women in their Sunday best sipping drinks and making conversation—something was not quite right. Only when they came upon Annette standing in the doorway did Caro realize what it was. Although there must have been almost a dozen people gathered on the porch, not one of them was speaking English.

"Bonjour chérie!" Annette said, kissing Caro swiftly on both cheeks. *"Qui est-ce que ce beau homme?"*

"Aunt Annette, this is Dr. David Selbin. David, my Aunt Annette Livaudais."

"Mademoiselle Livaudais," David said, bowing over Annette's hand. *"Je suis enchanté."*

"Oh, for heaven's sake!" Caro said. "Aunt Annette, who are all these people?"

"Pardonnez-moi," Annette said to the guest she had been talking with. *"Viens-ici,"* she said to Caro and David, beckoning them inside. "I'm sorry," she said. "I got my dates mixed. I would have told you not to come."

"But who are these people?" Caro said again. She took the Dubonnet her aunt handed her and sipped it. "They look so . . . foreign."

"Well, they are," Annette said. "Refugees, every one of them."

"Refugees!"

"There is a war going on, Caro," Annette said. "One that is overrunning a great deal of Europe. These people, thank God, were able to get out. I'm working with one of the organizations that helps them get settled—and naturally, I want to be hospitable."

"I think that's admirable," David said. The warmth in his voice startled Caro, and she looked at him to see if he were joking. "I imagine what many of these people miss the most is just this sort of occasion. It's very good of you to open your home to strangers, Miss Livaudais."

Annette's gaze swung to David, and she studied him for a moment before taking his hand in hers. "You're a good man, Dr. David Selbin. I like you." She looked at Caro sharply. "I didn't know you had enough sense to date a man like this, Caro."

Caro suddenly felt as though she were five years old, caught between two grown-ups. "Aunt Annette, I really am not just a silly college girl. I'm sorry if I seemed . . . rude about your guests. It's just—well, I didn't know anyone else was going to be here. I wanted you to get to know David."

Her aunt's eyes softened. "So that's the way it is," she said gently. "Tell you what—you help me get the buffet out, and after everyone is served, the three of us can find a quiet spot to chat. All right?"

"All right," Caro said. She turned her head from David; she did not want to see what that brief moment of revelation had told him. She put down her glass and followed Annette into the kitchen, David on their heels.

"I'm an old hand at fixing platters," David said when Annette pulled packages of cold cuts and cheese from the refrigerator. "One of my uncles owns a delicatessen. I had my first summer job there." He began arranging meat on a plate while Annette and Caro put potato salad and coleslaw in serving bowls. They worked quickly, with an ease that seemed natural, and by the time Annette went to call her guests, Caro felt that the first hurdle had been passed—a member of her family had met David, and they liked each other.

The guests spread over the porch, the front parlor, and the dining room with their filled plates; Annette led Caro and David to a small table set in a bay window with enough room for three chairs. An old woman was standing on the empty hearth. When she saw Annette, she came to them, fixing her eyes on Annette's face. They were brown, and the color seemed to have run, as though made from a cheap dye. She swiveled her head, looking about the room. The motion twisted the wrinkled skin that hung loosely away from her throat; for an instant there was one smooth line. "Why do you have all my things?" she said.

"It is to keep them safe for you," Annette said. She rose and took the old woman's hand. "Wouldn't you like some food now?" Then a man approached them, his face expressing his apologies.

"Mama, come," he said. "I have fixed you a plate. Come eat." He leaned close to Annette. "She is a little distraught this morning. I am sorry if she bothers you."

"Not at all," Annette said. "Here, let me help you get her settled."

"We are fine," he said. "Please, do not disturb yourself." He put his arm around his mother's shoulders and led her away, taking her to a chair placed near a lamp table. Caro watched him seat her, patiently unfold her napkin, and hand her a fork. The woman listened to something her son said, looked at her fork, then picked it up and put it in her purse. Then, while they watched, she picked up her plate and tilted its contents forward into her open bag.

David half-rose, his face mirroring the son's horror. And then the old woman stood up and began to scream. As though it were a well-honed knife, the high, shrill sound cut through the room, slicing its easy ambience into sharp, thin bits. The screams continued, higher and higher, holding them immobile. Then David moved, almost running across the room to the old woman's side. He said something to her son, and the two of them bent over her. Then her son picked her up and carried her out of the room.

"I must see about her," Annette said. "Caro, get things quiet, will you, *chérie?*" She went up to David, and the two of them disappeared into the hall.

I can't do this, Caro thought. All around her people were stirring, talking in low voices, eyeing her uncertainly. She felt alien, as though the calm of her own experience separated her from them, and she realized, with a new kind of sorrow, that the other guests felt responsible, as though it were their fault the old woman could not bear whatever awful burdens she carried. She forced herself to stand up, to move into the center of the room. "Please," she said. "She's going to be fine. Dr. Selbin will take care of her. Please, continue your meal. Aunt Annette would be so unhappy if she thought this would upset your dinner."

She felt the ridiculousness of her words. Politeness was a fragile defense against that kind of tortured suffering. Although the old woman had stopped screaming, the echo of those sounds filled the room, and Caro found it difficult to believe that anyone there still had an appetite.

But first one person and then another turned back to his plate, and in a few minutes the room was as it had been, with only the clink of cutlery against china and the buzz of voices disturbing its calm. Caro went back to her own place and toyed with her food. It seemed ages before David and Annette returned; they came alone, and when they entered the room, Annette, instead of coming back to the table, moved from one cluster of guests to another, speaking in quiet tones. David sank back into his chair and began to cut his meat, eyes intent on his plate. He seemed agitated, barely under control, and Caro heard the woman's scream again, that terrible sound that had torn a hole in the day.

"Is . . . is she all right?"

"She is for now," David said. He still did not look at her, but ate steadily, methodically, in a way not at all like himself. It came to her that he was eating the same way the refugees had eaten after she had urged them to continue their meal, as though he, too, had suffered some great shock.

"Are *you* all right?" she said.

He looked at her briefly, then down at his plate. But in that brief instant she had seen such an intensification of the vulnerability she saw in their closest moments that she suddenly panicked.

"David—what's wrong?"

"Later," he said. "Look—I told your aunt we'd probably cut out of here as soon as the ambulance came. Is that all right?"

"Ambulance? David, is she that bad off?"

"Your aunt had a sedative on hand. I gave her that. But she needs psychiatric care—at least for a while." He smiled, a kind of angry twist. "Her son can hardly take her to De Paul's on the streetcar."

"Do you—do you want to go with her?" She felt bleak, lost, and a little angry.

David shook his head. "I talked to a guy named Fournet. He's in charge of the organization that's taking care of them. He's seeing about having her admitted."

"Not Walter Fournet?"

"Yes, that's his name." He looked at her, and for the first time since he had come back into the room, his eyes were almost clear, almost normal. "Do you know him?"

"He's a cousin of a girl I know. I've met him a couple of times. That's funny. I didn't know he was in refugee work."

"Anyway," David said. "If you don't mind—I'd like to spend the rest of the afternoon . . . somewhere else."

"Of course," she said. She rose and took their plates. There was a commotion on the porch, and then one of the guests came in, followed by a white-uniformed man.

"There's the ambulance," David said. "This will be over in a jiffy, Caro." He went down the hall and Caro carried their plates to the kitchen, scraping them and putting them in the sink to soak. She imagined the attendants carrying the small woman out on the stretcher as she clung fearfully to her son, to David. Caro was overcome with tears at the evidence of what the destruction of that woman's world had done to her.

David found her still sobbing, her head down on the smooth porcelain kitchen table.

"Hey," he said, kneeling beside her and holding her in his arms. "What's all this about?"

"I'm sorry," she said. She leaned against his shoulder, letting his solid warmth envelop her. "It's just—"

"Shh," he said. "I understand." He pulled a handkerchief out of his pocket and tucked it into her hand. "Listen, I have a wonderful idea. Why don't we spend the afternoon at the zoo?"

"The zoo?" A sob caught in her throat, became a hiccup.

"Sure," he said, getting up and helping her to her feet. "Sunny afternoon, lots of things to see—one of my favorite things to do."

"Yes," she said. "That's a great idea. I'll say good-bye to Aunt Annette—"

"I already have," he said. "We can just duck out the back way, okay?"

She suddenly couldn't wait to leave Annette's behind her. "I need my purse—"

"I have it," David said, pointing to the counter.

They left the kitchen through the back entry, coming out onto the small square back porch that led through a garden to a tall fence. Once they were through the gate and standing in the alley, Caro again felt she could breathe. "I don't know why I feel as though I've just escaped," she said. "It's silly. Nothing happened to me. But I felt—I don't know—threatened."

David took her hand. "It's all that fear," he said. They walked slowly toward the street, hands linked, steps matched. "Get that many people in a room who have been through hell—you get a kind of collective anxiety."

"Is that what upset you?"

They reached the street corner, and stood waiting for the streetcar. The warm May afternoon was cooled by a breeze from the river that played with the leaves on the poplars and tossed veils of wisteria over a nearby arbor. "In a way," David said. He gripped her hand more tightly. "I'll . . . I'll tell you about it a little later."

Not until they had reached Audubon Park and were walking through the zoo did he answer her question. "What upset me," he said, stopping in front of the low wall that surrounded the moat that separated the elephants from their audience, "was that I kept imagining my own family as refugees. I kept hearing my own relatives scream."

"I don't understand—"

"You know I'm Jewish," he said. His eyes looked darker than usual, as though the events of the afternoon had permanently shadowed them. He had told her he was Jewish soon after they began dating. The distinction did not mean much to Caro; there were Jewish girls at Newcomb, any number of them. They seemed to have their own groups, just as girls who had gone to high school together, to Sacred Heart or Louise McGehee's, maintained their own circles. David did not fit her vague image of what a patriarchal Jew was like—long dark beard, spectacles, somber clothes. David was David. He never talked about going to the synagogue; never, in fact, talked about religion at all.

"I don't see what you're getting at," she said.

"Let's sit down," he said. They found a bench sheltered by a great shady oak. David began shelling the peanuts he'd bought for the monkeys, dropping them among the pigeons that cooed and fluttered at their feet.

"My mother's people are originally from Warsaw," he said. "My father's family arrived in America from Austria, a small village outside of Vienna, at the turn of the century. My paternal grandfather began as a tailor, and ended up owning one of the biggest factories in the garment district. My mother's father was a teacher." David smiled, a gentle smile somehow so fragile, so vulnerable, that Caro wanted to hold him as he had held her in Annette's kitchen. "I guess he was the one who pushed those of my generation into the professions—I'm one of five doctors among the cousins, we have a couple of lawyers, and one or two Ph.D.'s."

"It sounds as though your family has done very well," Caro said. She was feeling her way carefully, uncertain where this was going. David's people had been in America less than fifty years. In a way, that seemed unbelievable. Her family had arrived in the eighteenth century—on this one small ground, she suddenly felt the elder.

"They have," David said. "We have. Of course, not everyone came over. We've lots of relatives in Europe—my family went to visit them in 1928, when I was twelve." He shook his head. "It was an amazing experience, meeting family I'd never known before. One cousin was almost my mirror image."

"Are they still there?" She thought of the headlines, the context in which those cities' names appeared. Warsaw. Vienna. She shivered and took his hand.

"I don't know," he said. When he looked at her, she realized the source of his vulnerability, his private sufferings. "We . . . we can't find out. For a long time now—letters come back marked 'Address unknown,' " he said. His toneless voice sounded as though it were produced in a perfectly fabricated cylinder that obliterated all resonance.

"But, David—all of them? Don't you know if any of your family is safe?"

The despair in his eyes invited her into his abyss. "A few came over in 1933, a few more in 1935. The others . . . decided to stay—even after the laws in Germany kept changing for the Jews."

"What do you mean, the laws changed for Jews?"

"Regulations on how much money you could take out of Germany. How many household goods you could take if you left. Public identification as Jews." There was no change in his voice, nor in the flatness of his expression, but she could feel tension emanating from him, as though his taut body had charged the space between them.

"But that wasn't happening in Poland, was it? Or Austria?"

"It was just a matter of time," David said. "My father kept writing them, begging them to come. We had room, he said." David's hands came up in front of him, palms open, defenseless. "They didn't . . . listen. They didn't come."

"But there must be some way to find out where they are. What's happened to them." She leaned forward, taking his hand and gripping it tightly. "Père knows a lot of people in Washington. Perhaps he can find something out. Or the Red Cross—they can find out, can't they?"

"Caro," he said. "You don't have any idea what it's like in Europe now."

His voice widened the distance between them, and she saw that it was not age alone that separated them. David stood on the other side of a chasm carved by suffering, suffering she had neither experienced nor could really understand. Against the pain he bore, her own foolish words seemed worse than useless; she felt lost, inadequate, as though she had arrived at a battle where her opponents were armed with machine guns and she carried only a spear.

"I'm sorry," she said. Unconsciously, her head lifted as she fought to regain her poise. "I'm afraid I'm so used to Père working magic . . ." Her voice trailed into silence.

"Look," David said. "You've nothing to be sorry for. Knowing you care—" He stopped talking and looked down at their intertwined hands. "I'm the one who should be sorry. I didn't mean to let all this—ruin our day."

She brought his hand to her lips and kissed it. "It's not possible for a day I spend with you to be ruined," she said. "I . . . I'm very honored that you told me, David. Really, I am."

She saw the light in his eyes, the smile that softened his tense features. "If I'm not careful, Caro Hamilton, I'm afraid I might just fall in love with you."

"Is that a warning?" she said lightly. "Or a promise?"

"I'm not sure," he said. He bent toward her, and again she felt his encompassing presence. "Which do you want it to be?"

Far down the sidewalk, a bell tinkled, and Caro took the diversion and jumped to her feet. "The ice-cream cart!" she exclaimed. "Could I talk you into buying me a Fudgsicle?"

"You can talk me into anything you want," David said. She read the meaning in his eyes clearly, but it was more than she was willing to deal with.

"You're lucky then," she said, very carefully keeping her eyes from meeting his. "Right now all I want is a Fudgsicle. That should be easy enough."

"Too easy," he said. He caught at her arm. "Caro, when you want more than that—you will tell me?"

Again she felt the chasm between them, one that this time she had created. David suddenly seemed far away from her, and she knew that there was really only one bridge. But she was not yet ready to build that bridge with her body. And as she walked alongside him toward the ice-cream man, she wondered—would she ever be?

Since that Sunday afternoon earlier in the month, David had not mentioned his family again, but she could no longer read the war news, or look at the maps used to illustrate it, without seeing faces very much like David's superimposed on the grim lines, eyes imploring her. Girls at school were losing brothers, beaux, uncles, cousins. Gold stars shone from windows; memorial plaques in churches and school grew longer. When she read that German U-boats had been sighted in the Gulf of Mexico, and that nets had been strung across the Mississippi River to keep German submarines away from the booming oil refineries and industries along its banks, she finally was immersed in a total realization of how close to home the war had come.

Finally she made up her mind. She would no longer just read the classified ads begging for war workers. She would act.

Caro waited until Sunday dinner, when they were all gathered together, before telling her family her plans. It was the first family meal they'd had since Easter vacation, and the table buzzed with talk and laughter. Only Henri was quiet, sunk in one of his moods that they had all learned to ignore. She waited for the right moment to tell them, but the flood of talk never stopped. Finally, when there was a small pause, she leapt into it. "I have something I want to tell you all," she said.

She saw Émilie's eyes go to her left hand, and then look at her, puzzled. "I'm not engaged," Caro said, shaking her head. "I'm—quitting school."

"You're what?" her mother said. "Caro—"

"Mother, please. I can't just sit by while . . . while this war keeps on eating at our lives. I have to do something."

"Caro, what are you talking about?" Caroline set her face to receive bad news, and Beau, watching her from the other end of the table, felt his heart go out to her.

"Now, don't jump to any conclusions, Mama," Caro said. "I'm not going to run off and become an Army nurse or anything like that. I would if I thought I could do it, but I don't." She took a steadying breath and looked into her mother's eyes, forcing Caroline to acknowledge the depth of her conviction. "What I'm going to do—I'm going to go out to the shipyards in New Orleans next week and get a job. Not just for the summer. For the duration."

"The shipyards!" If Caro had said she was going to become an exotic dancer in the French Quarter, Caroline could not have sounded more astounded or horrified. "Caro, darling. What in the world do you know about building ships?"

"I can learn," Caro said stubbornly. "Mama, those shipyards run twenty-four hours a day now, seven days a week. They're begging for workers. I guess they can find something for me to do."

"But, Caro—surely there are other things you can do to help the war effort. This is admirable—but, darling . . . I just can't see you in a factory!"

"I can't see myself continuing what I've been doing," Caro said. "There just isn't any sense anymore in painting pretty little watercolors and oils."

"Your work is more than that, Caro," Caroline said. "You've got a real gift, everyone says so."

Caro raised her eyes to her mother's; the depth of the commitment in them shocked Caroline, and she covered Caro's hand with hers. "Darling—does it mean so much?"

"Yes," Caro said. "I have to do something to contribute. I can't sit idly by anymore." She looked down at her lap to hide the quick mist of tears. "Mama, I don't mean to be stopped."

Caroline's eyes, too, filled with tears. "All right, love," she said. "I hope I'd have made the same choice at your age. I . . . I'm very proud of you." Caro's eyes came up to meet her mother's. They stared at each other, a private resolve passing between them.

"Me, too," Émilie said. She picked up her goblet. "I propose a toast—to Caro the war worker!"

"Please," Caro said, smiling now. "It's not that big a thing."

"Sure it is," Henri said. "I wish my own news were as good."

They looked at him warily. His silence throughout the meal had not been unusual; when they left Henri alone, he normally came around by himself. But his voice now warned them that there was worse to come.

"I have a rather significant birthday coming up in a few days," he said.

"Of course you do, darling," Caroline said. "We haven't forgotten."

"Oh, I'm sure you haven't forgotten," Henri said. He sounded bitter, and something else that Skye, sitting next to him, could not quite put his finger on. "But you seem to have forgotten, all of you, that I will be twenty. Old enough to serve."

"Henri—" Caroline's voice sounded as though it were being strained through the heavy linen napkin she clutched in one hand.

"I decided to get the preliminaries out of the way," Henri went on. "Be able to make a grand announcement on the day itself." He stood up, his face rigid, his body taut. "So I went to the Army recruitment office in

New Orleans the day I finished my last exam. Told them I wanted to join up. They wanted me to come back when I was actually twenty, but I did get them to at least give me the physical."

Skye was aware of the tension in the room, the way all their attention met and centered on Henri. "I failed it," he said. "They turned me down."

"Failed it! Henri, what's wrong?" Caroline was out of her chair in an instant and grasped Henri by his shoulders.

"I have a heart murmur," he said slowly, watching his mother's face. "Not enough to make much trouble. But enough to keep me out."

They crowded around him then, offering the familiar catchwords of sympathy and concern. But Skye, even as he offered his sympathy to Henri, felt part of himself standing aside. Something about Henri's face wasn't right, he thought. And then it came to him. Part of Henri was enjoying this. In some strange, crazy way, Henri was enjoying his moment of attention.

"What a day," Beau said to Skye that evening. Henri's rigid calm had broken soon enough; his brief moment in the spotlight had given way to reality, and he had treated them all to a full-fledged display of his bitter rage. "Be a man, for God's sake!" Beau had shouted, and he could not forget the sudden twist of self-disgust that had transformed Henri's face before he subsided into sullen apologies.

"I shouldn't have yelled at him," he told Skye.

"He'll get over it," Skye said. "He's not the only man turned down. He was willing to go; he's not a coward."

"Don't think it's so easy, Skye. If *you* get turned down—"

"I'll just have to handle it, Papa. Aren't you the one who's always saying you can't ask for another hand, you can only play the cards you've got as well as you can?"

"Yes," Beau said. "But do you mind, Skye?"

"Mind what?"

"That the hand you were dealt has a war in it."

Skye shrugged. "What choice do we have? Besides—" He waved at the land that surrounded them. "This is worth fighting for."

"Yes," Beau said. His part in the fight was neither as dangerous nor as exhilarating as what waited for Skye. Long meetings, exhausting discussions, brain-wearying days in Washington when he needed to be here minding the store. His part in the fight was that which belonged to the old stallions, while the young ones like Skye bore the banners into the fray. How many years, how many sorrows, would they see before they all gathered here again? he wondered. He reached out a hand to Skye and felt his son's strong, warm touch. "Yes," he said again. "If anything is worth fighting for, this land is."

And later, in the early hours of the morning, when only the night birds and mists possessed the lawn, Beau left the bed where Caroline slept and went out to the porch, watching the night. Sitting there with the night wind caressing his land, he thought of those sleeping in the house at his back, now secure, but with their futures also possessed by the mist of uncertainty. He felt out of kilter, and knew that his body rhythm had changed. He was on the alert now. He would not sleep really soundly again until the war was over and his family was safe once more. He settled back against the rocker, watching the moon's cold white presence in the sky, and waited for the dawn.

4

SEPTEMBER 1942

Arnaud's was crowded. Like other fine restaurants across America, it was faced with a wartime situation in which the increasing difficulty in obtaining supplies seemed to be in direct proportion to the increasing number of patrons, whose war-fed incomes allowed them to dine in such places for the first time. But when David and Caro arrived to meet her parents for dinner, the headwaiter moved smoothly through the dining room, removing a Reserved sign from a choice table with one hand and holding Caro's chair with the other.

"Your father called, Miss Hamilton. They're running a little late. He said to order a drink and they'll join you shortly."

"This place is a madhouse," Caro said, looking around the room. "Is it always this full?"

The headwaiter sniffed. His head made a small swing; his eyes were like a cold light searching out and labeling the diners he did not know. "Too many of the people who can afford to eat here now don't know the difference between a properly prepared béchamel sauce and a bottle of catsup," he said. "The chef keeps his interest up only by knowing that we still get our old customers."

"Well," Caro said, "if rationing doesn't keep him up to the mark, I don't know what will. The rumor is that meat will be the next thing rationed—I'm going to order beef tournedos while they're still on the menu."

She looked up and saw her parents standing in the entrance to the dining room. "Oh, there they are," she said, turning to David. "They're going to like you so much."

"I hope so," he said, rising; a waiter, followed by Caroline and Beau, came toward them.

During the flurry of introductions and ordering drinks, Caro watched her mother study David. She tried to picture David as her mother saw him: the steady blue eyes, the fair skin, the thick black hair like a thatch across his forehead. Not really handsome, she could hear her mother saying. But attractive. Very attractive. At that moment, her mother's eyes met hers, and Caro read the message there. But he's too old for you! Caroline's eyes said. Attractive—but much too old.

"This is a real pleasure, Dr. Selbin," Beau said. "We've heard a great deal about you, and have certainly looked forward to meeting you."

Caro threw a grateful glance at Beau. Good old Père! You could always count on him to calm things down, make things go well. "I've told David a lot about you, too," she said. "I've talked about the farm and Beau Chêne so much that I imagine David feels as if he's been there."

"Caro will have to bring you out sometime," Beau said. "Do you hunt? Duck season starts in a few weeks."

David laughed, a sound so warm and open that Caroline was drawn to him despite her anxiety. "There aren't many ducks over Fifth Avenue, Mr. Langlinais. I probably couldn't hit anything, but I'd like to try."

"Good," Beau said. "We'll set something up."

Their drinks arrived, and the talk turned to other subjects.

"She's drawing me out, you know," David said, after Caro asked a question about a new writer David had gone to Columbia University with. "She's helping me put my best foot forward."

"David!" Caro said.

Caroline leaned forward and touched David's hand. "Dr. Selbin, I really don't think you need any help. You're everything Caro said you were, and I'm delighted to meet you."

Beau heard the small rush of Caro's breath; he felt her sigh release all of them, and the conversation changed, becoming more personal.

"I'm going to turn this spotlight on Caro for a while," David said. "Did you know that she was part of a team that launched a 10,500-ton Liberty ship in record time? Four days, 15½ hours after its keel was laid!"

"Caro, that's wonderful!" Caroline said. "I can't begin to fathom what that really means—your work absolutely baffles me—but I know something impressive when I hear it."

"I have to admit we were all very proud," Caro said. "You spend days and days doing the same thing. Something like this gives you a real boost."

"I still worry about you," Caroline said. "All those men!"

"Oh, Mother, for heaven's sake," Caro said. "As if anyone would find me attractive in my work slacks—and with my hair all tied up in a bandanna! Our assembly line's about as glamorous as a bunch of farmhands. But I'll tell you one thing," she said, her cheeks suddenly coloring. "The foreman told our unit the other day that we were every bit as good as the male workers—and that he was glad we were there!" She held both hands out in front of her. The nails were filed down even with the fingertips; Caroline looked at her daughter's hands and had a vision of how Caro must appear as she reported to work. Body encased in workshirt and long, nondescript pants. Hair concealed beneath a scarf. No jewelry. Nothing loose that could be caught by a flying, whirling machine. Only the rouged cheeks and lips of the younger women signaled their femininity, bright personal flags in a sea of dun.

"It's amazing what Arnaud's kitchen can still produce despite wartime shortages," Caroline said as she surveyed the plates their waiter served them. "This looks wonderful. And I'm really hungry. I spent the afternoon at the hospital with Annette, and had only a cup of soup for lunch."

"How is Aunt Annette?" Caro asked. She turned to David. "Remember I told you she'd fallen last week and broken her hip?"

"Feisty as ever," Caroline said. "But I'm worried about her—she doesn't look at all well."

And then the conversation turned to other subjects, and all concentrated on the exquisite dishes before them.

"I'm going to bundle your mother off to bed," Beau said, following dinner. "I hope you two will excuse us."

"Certainly, sir," David said, rising as Beau stood. "I enjoyed dinner very much. Thank you for asking me."

"My pleasure," Beau said. He bent over and kissed Caro. "Have fun, sweetheart."

"Thanks, Père. We will."

Caroline leaned over Caro and kissed her. "You look tired, darling," she said. "Don't stay out too late."

"I'm going to hold you to that hunt," Beau said, shaking David's hand.

"We can't promise ducks," Caroline said, turning to David and extending her hand. "But we can promise you a warm welcome."

"I'd love to come," David said. "If Caro and I ever get the same days off, I'll be down there like a shot."

They watched Beau and Caroline move across the room, stopped at nearly every step by someone who wanted to speak to them.

"Your stepfather's pretty important around here, isn't he?" David said.

"Yes, he is," Caro said. "I forget about it sometimes. I mean—he's just Père, you know?"

"And yet you told me that day, remember? You were so convinced of his magic you thought he could even break through Hitler's curtain of silence."

She did not have to ask what day he meant. Since the afternoon he had told her about his family, everything between them had changed. When they were in a group, she would think: I know something about him that no one else knows. It was a little the way she imagined it must be when you had made love with someone a long, long time. All the places on their body that were secret from everyone else. Yet she resisted the analogy. Because if she continued to feel so close to David emotionally—how long could she put off the physical closeness that so naturally followed?

"That's a tough act to follow," David said.

She looked up quickly, and saw the wariness in David's eyes.

"What do you mean?"

"Not everyone has his money, his position," David said.

"I don't expect them to."

"But it's what you've grown up with. Gotten used to. Could you do without it?"

"Of course I could!" She tossed her head to shake the heavy wave of hair from her forehead. "Or do you think I'm some kind of spoiled debutante who can't manage on her own?"

"I think it's difficult sometimes to give up things that have become part of us," David said slowly. "There are things that are part of me, too, things I don't even think about that govern a lot of what I do."

"Then you understand some of what I'm up against," she said.

"What we're up against," he said.

Her eyes met his, then looked away. "Look, I don't know about you, but I'd like to go hear some jazz. Are you game?"

"Are you changing the subject?"

"What subject is that?" she said, now looking straight into his eyes.

"We can't delay the issue forever, Caro," he said. He rose and held her chair. "All right. Where would you like to go?"

"Preservation Hall," Caro said. "The place is a dump, but the music's the best in New Orleans."

"Good," David said, holding out his arm. "Maybe it will distract me."

The streets of the Quarter were filled with sailors from the ships that put into New Orleans' ports and soldiers from the reactivated Army base. As David and Caro pushed their way past the clusters of people in front of strip joints and jazz bars, there were more men in uniform than in civvies, and Caro was aware of the critical way the men looked at David.

"Does it bother you the way they look at you?" she asked. "Wondering why you're not in uniform?"

"It used to," David said. "I'm willing to serve where I'm needed, and so far, I'm still needed here. I know that, and it really doesn't matter to me who else does." He glanced down at Caro, not certain as to how she would react to his next words. "I think, though, that as soon as my residency is finished I may be moved up the list."

"David!"

"Tropical medicine's a hot specialty right now, Caro. Disease is as much an enemy as the Japanese in the Pacific. Malaria and dysentery take almost as many casualties as snipers."

"I don't want to think about it," Caro said. "At least, not right now."

They reached Preservation Hall and joined the line of people waiting for the set to end. A sudden burst of applause was followed by a surge in the crowd, and Caro and David pushed forward to find places on the low wooden benches placed in tiers around the wall of the small room. A black woman at the piano fingered the keys softly, finding chords, sending rippling harmonies against the low ceiling. A drummer stood smoking near his instruments, and the bass player sat in an open window sipping a highball. Smoke was thick, the smell of beer and bourbon pervasive.

David took off his coat and loosened his tie; late September, and it was as hot as high summer. He looked at Caro: her body curved toward the musicians, as though she were offering it to them to play on. Her well-cut silk dress defined the lift of her breasts, the fullness of her hips. David wanted her then as he had wanted no other woman he had ever known. She turned to him and smiled, and he was lost.

He put his arm around her and pulled her closer. "You must be a witch," he said. "A lovely, magical witch."

"No," Caro said. "It's New Orleans voodoo. I've put a charm on you, and I'm not going to set you free."

"Thank God for that," David said.

The piano chords became an invitation to the others; one by one, the musicians drifted into the fabric the pianist wove, making their own fine lines across its texture, and David and Caro became part of its golden thread.

The bus lurched through the rain, its windshield wipers making great sweeps across the oil-filmed windows. Caro ran the last few yards to the corner and took her place at the end of the line of boarding passengers. Her lunch box banged against her hip as she struggled to close her umbrella. Water collected in its folds gushed down her trouser legs, and she felt the instant chill as the cold air hit the wet cloth.

"You almost didn't make it today," one of the regular passengers said. The woman looked around the crowded bus. "Missed getting a seat, anyway." She shifted position so that Caro could brace her body against her seat. "I'll hold your gear if you want."

"Thanks," Caro said. She handed her lunch box to the woman and hooked her umbrella over the back of the seat. Hands free, she clung with one to an overhead bar, with the other to the metal seat frame. The potholed streets were an obstacle course, one that seemed worse every morning. She set her shoulders against the jolts, and let her mind leave the close confines of the bus, drifting back to the night before.

She had overslept because she had been with David until one in the morning. David had had a rare evening free, an evening they had spent at her new home. Annette had died in early October, willing her house to Caroline, who offered to let Caro and two of her friends live there. Cousin Robert had produced a Miss Jennings to serve as chaperon and chatelaine, and for the past six weeks they had been settling in. Last night had been something of a housewarming; David had located two rib-eye steaks, and Caro had opened a bottle of Annette's Mouton Rothschild Bordeaux. Ruth Carrithers and Babs Longwood, her housemates, were out, and Miss Jennings agreeably had retired early with a slight cold and a hot toddy Caro pressed into her not altogether reluctant hands.

Caro could still feel David's body, as though already she were bonded to him. His hand seemed still to be on her neck, stroking it. His lips seemed still to be on hers, his tongue probing her mouth. Sitting on the jolting bus, Caro felt again the steady pulse of passion that had beat through her last night. And then, with a mental wrench, she made herself turn the images off, as she had made herself pull back from David's hands and lips, shifting to the other end of the sofa almost violently, staring at him as though what she were looking at was her own surprising response. It had taken her a while to get her breath back, to slow her racing blood. Nor had David made it easier.

"Christ!" he had said. "Caro, do you have any idea at all what happens to me when you kiss me the way you just did?"

"No," she had said. And then, because she could not lie to him, "Maybe I don't—think about it."

"Maybe you don't," he said. He lit two cigarettes and passed one to her. "You're going to have to make up your mind, you know. This business of being a grown woman in full charge of her emotions one minute and a debutante who plays games the next is more than I can take, Caro."

"I don't play games!" she cried.

"Maybe not intentionally. But, dammit, Caro, I'm not some little college boy you can kiss a couple of times and then send back to his room to suffer."

"I don't mean to do that, David. I . . . I'm sorry. I've never gone out with anyone like you before. I don't know how to act."

He had come to her, put his arms around her, and laughed. "You damn well do know how to act. That's what's driving me crazy."

"It's driving me crazy too, David," she had said.

For a long moment he had looked at her. Then he had bent down and kissed her, a slow, gentle kiss. "Good," he said. "Then I can hope."

Now Caro thought of all the hours, days, maybe, that must pass before she saw David again. "Damn!" she said aloud.

They were nearing the Higgins Shipyard, and the bus slowed, getting in line behind other buses discharging workers at the guard posts to have their identification checked. Caro looked down at her badge, pinned securely to her overalls. "Caroline Annette Hamilton. 5′5½″, 117 lbs., 343 Calliope Street, New Orleans, Louisiana." As she followed the crowd off the bus, she peered at her picture, mounted in one corner of the card. Was it the picture of an independent woman, or a child? For the first time, she realized that only she could make the choice; that she in fact did have a choice. The easy path to womanhood had been detoured. The terrain she now covered had no markers, no maps. David had offered himself as a guide—perhaps the real question, then, was whether or not she could trust him to make it a safe passage.

Caro went swiftly to her place in the assembly line. She was working on Higgins' Eureka landing boats now, one of the two boats Andrew Jackson Higgins had designed. The Eureka was a thirty-six-foot motorboat with a bow like a spoonbill, its propeller protected by a half-pipe-like projection so it could land on beaches without being damaged. The other boat the shipyard built was a motor torpedo boat, nicknamed "mosquito" boats by the British. The torpedo boats, seventy to eighty feet long, could maintain speeds up to forty-five miles an hour, carrying an impressive arsenal of weapons including two antiaircraft guns, a gun that could pierce armor, four torpedo tubes, and eight depth charges. The Liberty ship Caro had helped build last July had been the first and last one built at Higgins Shipyard; the contract had been canceled in late summer, and the yard was now full steam ahead on the smaller boats.

It made no difference to Caro whether she built cargo ships, torpedo boats, or landing craft. The realization that men she knew might be on a craft she helped build kept her going. Like war workers all over America, her will to work well had been given an enormous boost when it was reported that during the attack on Guadalcanal, a seaman whose ship went down survived because of a life belt that had been inspected, packed, and stamped by his own mother at a factory in his hometown.

The last notes of "The Star-Spangled Banner" blared over the loudspeakers set high above the assembly line, and the noises of the machinery took over.

"What are we celebrating?" the girl next to Caro asked.

"What?" Caro spoke without turning her head; absolute attention to the task at hand was an imperative of the job, and she had resolved early on that her work would never have to be sent to the special group of benches where poorly performed jobs were redone.

"The music," the girl said. " 'The Star-Spangled Banner.' "

"They play it at the beginning of every shift," Caro said. There was a small pause in the flow of work toward her, and she looked quickly at her neighbor. "You're new," she said.

"First day," the girl said.

"If you need anything, ask me," Caro said, and then lost herself in the roar of motors, the steady whine of the tool in her hands.

At first break, her neighbor followed her to the rest room. "At least it's clean," the girl said. "Is that Higgins' idea of decoration?" She jerked her thumb at a picture of Hitler taped to one wall. Its caption read: "Come on in, sister. Take it easy. Every minute you loaf here helps us plenty."

Caro felt a surge of dislike for her companion. Although she had been half-kidding when she described her new workplace to David, now she heard herself saying coldly, "If thousands of workers waste even one minute every break, that adds up to a lot of hours."

"Say," the new girl said. "It's okay by me. I don't care what the old man puts on his walls as long as he puts good money in my pay envelope." She took off her scarf and fluffed her hair. "I hate wearing this rag on my head. Makes me look like my ma."

"Better leave it on," Caro said. "They check constantly—there are enough accidents as it is without asking for one."

"Pretty tough, aren't you?" the girl said. She looked at Caro. "You talk kind of funny. What are you, one of those coeds out to see how the real world lives?"

"I'm no different from anybody," Caro said. She put out her cigarette and headed for the door.

"Those shoes you have on must have cost a pretty penny," the girl said, catching up with her. "I used to work at the Imperial Shoe Store. I can spot Italian leather at ten paces."

Caro said nothing. She had gone through this, and worse, time and time again since she had gotten the job at Higgins. First from the hiring office, which refused to believe that an art student at Newcomb had any serious intention of staying on an assembly line long enough to justify hiring and training her. She had found herself explaining to the man interviewing her that men should not make the only sacrifices; the passion in her voice had embarrassed both of them, and to this day she was unsure whether her interview or a reference to her stepfather was the reason she was finally hired.

No matter what the reason, she had been hired. She had survived training. She had survived harassment from male workers. She had survived the suspicions of fellow female workers, who, in the days before gasoline and tire rationing, had seen her driving up to the yard in her little blue convertible, top down and radio blaring. Even now, remembering those mindless days made her blush.

As did a memory she could not rid herself of. A morning when she'd been working at Higgins about two months, long enough to feel almost like an old hand. A bunch of them were sitting together eating lunch. Caro had opened her lunch box and taken out the cloth napkin she always brought to spread her food on. She had been unaware of the special quality of the silence around her until a voice said, "So what's Miss Society got for lunch today? Pheasant under glass? Caviar and champagne?"

When she realized the woman was talking about her, she had looked up, thin-sliced sandwich in her hand. The ring of eyes around her was like a ring of steel; she saw expressions ranging from the mildly negative to the openly hostile, and panic closed in on her. Then she had gotten angry.

"I work as hard as any of you," she said. "Stop picking on me."

"But why do you work?" the ringleader said. "You're just taking a job someone else could use, Miss Society."

"Don't call me that!" Caro cried. Her face was a furious red, and she felt thirteen years old, the new girl being hazed by the inner circle.

"What else should we call you? Read your name in the *Times-Picayune* just last Sunday," the woman drawled. " 'Miss Caroline Hamilton, daughter of Mrs. Claude Louis "Beau" Langlinais, stepdaughter of Representative "Beau" Langlinais.' Something about a tea dance at the Southern Yacht Club on Saturday. I've never been to a tea dance," the woman said. "Most of the time, my day off, I'm doing the washing and cooking up enough food to feed the kids during the week while I'm out here. So tell us about it, why don't you? Let us know how the other half lives."

Caro had gathered up her lunch and fled, followed by laughter that she knew she would not soon forget. It had taken all her will to go back to the assembly line after lunch, all her will to ignore the stream of gibes the woman, who worked two positions down from her, kept up. When she went out to her car at the end of the shift, someone had broken a dozen eggs into it, where they had hardened on the leather upholstery, cooked by the August sun.

And then she had gotten mad. Defiantly she had marched to the guard post and asked for the newspaper lying on the bench. She had spread the newspaper over the upholstery and gotten into her car, starting the engine and switching the radio to top volume. She had taken time to light a cigarette, and then, head high, had taken off across the parking lot in a satisfyingly dramatic spray of gravel.

Her anger stayed white-hot all the way back to Calliope Street. She flung herself through the door and entered the parlor, where Ruth and Babs sat with Miss Jennings, putting liquid makeup on their legs. "Those witches!" Caro said, pouring out her story. She took the lemonade Miss Jennings offered her and sat down, ready to be indulged and comforted. Ruth and Babs listened, but said little. Only Miss Jennings was properly horrified, agreeing with Caro that the woman had shown her low breeding, her lack of manners.

Unable to let the matter drop, Caro pushed. "Ruth, do the women where you work treat you like that?" Ruth worked at one of the refineries on the river, Babs at a rubber plant near it. Neither had ever reported the slightest incident at work, but Caro had concluded, when she thought about it at all, that they worked with a nicer class of people than she did.

"No, they don't," Ruth said. She stretched out her leg and examined it. "Is that even?"

Caro inspected the makeup they all used to spare their irreplaceable nylons. "Looks fine to me," she said. "Anyway, it'll be dark, who's going to notice? But listen," she said, "why do they pick on me?"

Ruth exchanged a look with Babs, a look that closed Caro out.

"Why don't you and Babs run into the teasing—the malice, even—that I do?"

Again that look. Then Ruth said, rushing over the words, glancing at Babs, "Babs and I don't drive cute little convertibles to work, Caro. Convertibles our stepfather gave us. We don't have a stepfather everybody's heard of. We don't come from an old New Orleans family, so not only do we not get our pictures and names in the paper, we hope to heaven we never do, because the only time we would get that attention, other than when we marry, is if we'd done something awful. We don't bring lunches that cost more than what most of the women at work can spend on food for a week. We don't wear handmade Italian shoes." She stopped. "I guess that's why."

There had been a long silence in the pleasant, cluttered parlor. Miss Jennings had been suddenly absorbed in the blouse she was mending, Babs was intent on drawing a seam along the back of her leg. Ruth went to the phonograph and began sorting through the records stacked there.

"You mean I'm a spoiled brat," Caro said slowly. Her throat felt dry, and she sipped her lemonade, feeling the sharp cold bathe her parched mouth.

"I didn't say that, Caro," Ruth said. She turned on the player and slipped a record over the spindle. "Look, Caro, you're not spoiled." She laughed. "Well, no more spoiled than any girl with your money and family position. But, Caro, there are not many girls like you working at Higgins, have you ever thought of that? I mean, do you have any idea what the lives of the women you work with are like? Really?"

For one moment of intense anger, Caro wanted to throw the contents of her glass in Ruth's earnest face. Throw Ruth out of her house, for that matter. Ruth and Babs had a pretty good deal, as they were the first to admit. The rent they insisted on paying was low, lower than a single room in their old boardinghouse. Here each had her own room; they had as much run of the rest of the house as Caro, and Beau and Caroline paid Miss Jennings, insisting that they were the ones who were worried, and that there was no reason for Ruth and Babs to take on any part of that expense.

Then the anger died. "No," she said slowly. "I don't. Of course I don't. How could I?"

"That's right," Babs said. "How could you? But they have an idea of your life, Caro, and whether it's correct or not, it's what they've gathered from the society pages, and from hearing you talk—" She smiled at Caro. "It's not fair, it shouldn't matter to anyone how any of us live away from the job—"

"That's not the point," Caro said, remembering her casual comments, her innocent questions to her coworkers. Had they seen the new Hepburn and Tracy movie, *Woman of the Year*? Was anyone going to the Hazel Scott concert, the classical pianist who combined Beethoven and Count Basie, Bach and boogie-woogie? Her cheeks grew hot, remembering the times she had announced that such-and-such a store had gotten in a shipment of rare cosmetics, in case anyone wanted to try to get there after work. "I've . . . I've been really dumb," she said. "Dumb and insensitive." Fired with contrition, she added, "I'll tell them so, tomorrow. Apologize."

Again Ruth and Babs exchanged glances, but this time they came to her, and put their arms around her. "Honey," Ruth said. "Don't."

"What would you say?" Babs asked.

"I—" Caro fell silent. Of course, there was nothing she could say. "But what will I do? I can't just let things go on like this."

"Well," Ruth said, smiling at her. "I think you're just going to have to use your artistic talent and blend into the scenery a little, Caro. Beginning with leaving that cute little car of yours at home."

The first day Caro had appeared on the bus heading for Higgins Shipyard, there had been catcalls and comments. That same day, when her lunch box revealed nothing more interesting than egg-salad sandwiches and store-bought cookies, the other women said plenty. But she said nothing. Somehow she fought down the retorts that clung to her mouth like peanut butter, somehow she kept her hands steady and her eyes on her work. She stopped tying her hair up in bright silk print scarves and wore ones she found at the dime store. She attacked Montgomery Ward's and bought overalls and workshirts, khaki trousers and a boy's windbreaker. She could not find a pair of the tough lace-up shoes the other women wore to fit her. "Foot's too narrow, ma'am," the clerks said. "You'd have blisters in one day." She decided that the Italian leather walking shoes weren't that conspicuous, particularly since they were half-covered by her trousers. And she stopped wearing makeup, making this last concession with the greatest reluctance of all. But finally, she was accepted. At lunch one day someone offered her a piece of devil's-food cake made from bits of rationed sugar hoarded against a birthday feast. At break, someone offered her a cigarette. Fighting down her tears was as hard as fighting down her anger had been, but she managed. And went back to her machine feeling better than she had felt even when her charcoal drawing of André had taken a blue ribbon at Newcomb's Spring Art Show.

5

NOVEMBER 1942

The noise in the stadium was like a wall. Thousands of LSU-Tulane fans stood in a solid block of people and sound. The LSU cheerleaders running along the sidelines didn't have to urge the crowd to yell; it chanted, shouted, cheered the Tigers on as though it were urging on the LSU men now fighting in North Africa.

"This is unbelievable!" Rosalind said, putting her hands over her ears as a roar rose and threatened to overwhelm them.

"Just wait until the end," Skye shouted. "Way LSU's ahead, they'll probably tear down the goalposts."

Rosalind's eyes telegraphed her disbelief. Her family had sent her to Dominican College in New Orleans; safe behind its sheltering walls, Rosalind lived in a world where escorts were thoroughly checked out by her housemother upon arrival, and where her hours off-campus were extremely limited and narrowly defined. "It's like being a pampered poodle on an elegant but very short leash," she had told Skye. Had the LSU-Tulane game not taken place on the Saturday after Thanksgiving, while she was home for the holiday, she almost certainly would not have been allowed to check out for a weekend in Baton Rouge.

Rosalind had explained the rules to Skye the first time he had called her at school, her voice sounding reasonable, almost maternal. "I've used up all my time off-campus this week. If you want to come visit me here, I can see you for an hour in the main parlor." Her dorm did have a few smaller parlors, where the older students could go with their dates and have semiprivacy—as long as the doors were kept widely ajar. But Rosalind and the other freshmen entertained their dates in the living room of the dorm. After his first experience there, Skye had immediately reserved every free off-campus hour Rosalind had for the next month.

"But how can you drive down that often?" Rosalind said. "Tires are rationed, gas is rationed—Skye, that's purely crazy!"

"I'll buy up other guys' gas," Skye said. "Listen, I'm going to be here every minute I can." He had looked around the parlor, filled with couples dancing, playing the piano, stealing surreptitious kisses. "Not all the boys in New Orleans have gone to war. And I don't want any of the ones left getting ideas about you."

"What kind of ideas would that be, Skye?" Rosalind asked. Her green eyes could burn as clear as brilliant emeralds—or they could flash green fire, cold sparks that cut places in Skye's heart he had not even known were there.

"Ideas about you being their girl," he said. "You're my girl, Rosalind, and I want everyone to know it." Involuntarily, his eyes had gone to her finger. She had taken his ring, but she didn't wear it unless she was with him. Even then, more often than not she slipped the ring onto a golden chain, dropping it over her head and letting the ring itself disappear into the crevice beneath her neckline.

"Why don't you want to wear it where people can see it? What's the point of having it if—"

"If no one can see the ring in my nose?" she said. "I know I have it. You know I have it. Why does everyone else have to know?"

"But I want them to, Rosalind."

"And I don't," she said. She had gone into his arms, and that evening, when his hand drifted to her breast, drawn there simply because it could not stay away, she had not pushed it away. He could caress her through all the cloth that covered her; so far, that was all.

The gun signaling the end of the game went off, and the LSU fans standing at the sidelines poured onto the field as the two teams ran off. The scoreboard showed the final score: LSU 18, Tulane 6. Not an overwhelming victory, but that autumn of 1942, any victory at all triggered an exuberant response. With a mighty crack, the purple-and-gold-wrapped goalposts fell under the fans' enthusiastic onslaught, while in the stands the LSU marching band played one more triumphant fight song.

"Let's get out of here," Skye said. He piloted Rosalind through the jostling crowd, spotting Émilie and Gennie with their dates several rows below them. He knew his father and stepmother were somewhere in the crowd that surged and snaked down the stadium ramps.

There was a party at the Phi Delt house; the brothers had built up a war chest which they had blown on hiring a good band to replace the usual jukebox. Besieged with cries for help, most mothers had come through with packages of food, and except for the fact that the only liquor was hidden in coat closets or under car seats, to be slipped into the punch or glass of Coke when the housemother wasn't looking, it promised to be one hell of a victory party.

"You've been looking like that famous cat that swallowed the canary all evening," Rosalind said to Skye as they mixed with his fraternity brothers and their dates at the party. They had scarcely left the dance floor as the band played one hit after another without a pause. "When are you going to let that bird out?"

Skye pulled slightly back so that he could look at her face. "Have I told you you look especially gorgeous tonight?" he said.

She shook her head. "If you did, I've forgotten. Tell me again." He whispered in her ear, and watched the slow blush stain her ivory skin.

"Skye Langlinais, for heaven's sake!" she said, but there was a gleam of satisfaction in her eyes.

Her green wool suit made her eyes and her figure stand out so seductively that if the football players had been able to see her, Skye thought, not one of them would have been able to keep his mind on the game. When she walked, her legs swung all the way from her slightly rolling hips. Her outthrust breasts curved from the line of her throat into their full swell, and Skye, looking at her, thought: Thank God she's in a girls' school. He swung her into a deep dip, letting her hang over his arm for a moment, her weight suspended on his strength. He pictured himself over her in bed, her green eyes changing from that misty calm to sudden fire.

"You're not going to pull curfew on me tonight, are you?" he whispered as he drew her up again.

Rosalind tossed back one loose lock of hair that had fallen forward from the sleek black helmet of hair capping her head like a single piece of shimmering black silk.

"I'm staying with my aunt, Skye. She'll expect me home at a decent hour."

"What's a decent hour?"

"One o'clock," Rosalind said. He saw the smallest gleam of fire in her eyes. "I told her the party here went on late."

He let his breath out, his mind running over possible parking spots. "All right, then," he said. "Let's get out of here."

He waited until he had the car parked, facing one of the university lakes, and the radio tuned to a station that played romantic music. Then he took her in his arms and kissed her long and hard. He felt her lips grow softer, her body alive in his arms. His hand went to her breast; the layer of coat jacket, added to her blouse and underthings, was too much of a barrier. He slipped his hand beneath the coat and felt the soft silk that molded the lines of her breast. He could feel her nipple stiffen against his probing fingers. "Unbutton your blouse," he said in a hoarse, urgent voice that he barely recognized as his.

"No," Rosalind said. She sat up, pushing him away. She looked at him appraisingly, a look that carried her miles away. "Give me a cigarette, Skye."

He lit two and handed one to her, fighting to make himself calm. But the tense, hard anger would not leave him. "I'm joining the Air Force right after Christmas," he said harshly. "I thought you should be the first to know."

"Joining the Air Force!"

Her shock pleased him: he wished he could see the expression in her eyes.

"You're not old enough, Skye. You won't be twenty until next April."

"Last week the Senate passed a bill lowering the draft age to eighteen. It's already been passed by the House, and there's no question but that the President will sign it. So I'm plenty old enough, Rosalind."

Her hand crossed the space between them and touched his arm. God, what one touch could do to him! "Wait to be drafted, Skye. Don't enlist."

"Wallow around in the mud?" Skye said. "Fight out in the Pacific jungles where you can't see six inches in front of you? Dig in some foxhole and stay there waiting for air cover, artillery fire? That's not my style, Rosalind. I want to fly." His voice took on a quality she had not heard before, and she realized for the first time that there were some parts of Skye Langlinais still unknown to her. "I want to fly a P-37, or a bomber. I want to look out of my cockpit and see nothing but clouds and sky—"

"And enemy fighters," Rosalind said. "Enemy antiaircraft guns."

"You don't fight a war without risking dying," Skye said. "But if I'm going to take that risk, it's going to be one I want to take."

"Don't they have rigid standards for pilots, Skye? How do you know you'll get in?" Something had shifted in her world, something that surprised her. Skye must mean more to her than she had thought. Now, that was something to think about.

"I've already taken the physical," he said. "I passed with no problem." He turned to her and swept her into his arms. She knew the exuberance he felt had nothing to do with her—the excitement in his voice, even the fierce passion of his kiss, was fueled by something else. She felt his lips, felt his arms, the quick tension in his body, and sighed. Whether she liked it or not, Skye was involved in another kind of war now, one that in no way would be her ally.

Henri followed his mother and Beau up the sidewalk, scuffing at the leaves scattered over it. He had come to Baton Rouge to see the LSU-Tulane game. Skye had gotten him a date, and he should have been at the Phi Delt house this very minute, instead of tagging along behind his parents. But his date had called early in the morning, clearly in tears, to say that her grandmother had died and she had to cancel their plans. It had been too late to get another date—it was, after all, the biggest game of the season. And although Skye had urged him to come to the game along with him and Rosalind, and to go on to the Phi Delt party afterward, Henri had declined. It was one thing to double-date with Skye when Henri himself had a date, and quite another to be the odd man out at someone else's frat party. So when his mother had pressed him to sit in their box on the fifty-yard line, Henri had agreed. The fun of sitting in so prominent a place was somewhat diluted by the fact that he was surrounded by older people, none of whom paid much attention to him. By the time he had been to four after-game parties with Beau and Caroline, his nose was definitely out of joint, and he had gotten out of the car to attend this one feeling very much the martyr.

"Now, tell me again who the Mitchells are," Caroline said, pausing on the steps leading to the porch. "With all these business parties, it's getting so I can't tell the players without a program."

"Mitch came down with Standard Oil," Beau said, turning his head to include Henri in the conversation. His eyes seemed to fire a warning at Henri: mind your manners and don't embarrass yourself in front of your mother. "He's a consultant on the pipeline, though he's always got a lot of other deals brewing—one of those energetic Yankees. His wife is a former opera singer—supposed to have had quite a creditable career."

"Twenty minutes," Caroline said. "And then we can go to the Theriots and relax."

"I told Mitch we could only look in," Beau said. He smiled at Henri. "The Theriots have two daughters, Henri. I think there'll be more people your age there."

Beau meant to be kind. He didn't care for the way Henri allowed himself to sulk when things didn't go his way, but he had a certain amount of sympathy for the boy. But to Henri, Beau sounded condescending, the stepfather who had it all, handing out crumbs to the beggar at the gate. He followed his mother up the steps of the unprepossessing cottage feeling angrier by the moment, determined to cut out on his own as soon as they left.

A large jovial man with ruddy cheeks greeted them at the door. "Come on in," he said. "We've got a hell of a party going.."

"Caroline, this is Mitch Mitchell. Mitch, my wife, Caroline," Beau said. "And this is Caroline's son, Henri."

They moved past Mitch into a surprisingly charming room; although the Mitchells had rented it furnished, sight unseen, like many others who poured into Baton Rouge, Mitch's wife, Sallie, had obviously brought enough of her own things to give the house some flair. "Sallie's over there," Mitch said, gesturing to a sun porch that opened off the living room. "Mrs. Langlinais, why don't you and your son go introduce yourselves, and I'll show Beau where the bar is."

Sallie Mitchell, standing in the arch between the living room and the sun porch, suddenly turned, and Henri caught his breath. Her red hair swooped over her pale forehead in a wave; her eyes, highlighted by long dark lashes, were so deep and brilliant a green that Henri felt a physical shock. The neckline of her gold jersey dress plunged into the cleft between her breasts, and her skirt clung seductively to her hips before swirling out over long, slender legs. She laughed and moved toward them, both hands outstretched.

"I'm Sallie Mitchell," she said. "You're Caroline Langlinais, aren't you? I saw you come in with Beau." She cocked her head at Henri. "But I can't imagine who this good-looking young man is—"

"This is my son," Caroline said. "Mrs. Mitchell, Henri Hamilton."

"How nice," Sallie said. Her hands closed over the hand Henri extended. "How very nice to have young blood in the house. I was just going to sing a little," she said, her hands still holding Henri's. "Come on and listen."

Beau came up behind them, bearing drinks. "Did I hear the promise of a performance?" he said. "We came at the right time."

Caroline shot Beau a glance that seemed to say, "Remember, we're not staying long"—a glance which Sallie caught. Sallie had read Caroline the minute she entered the room; the well-cut wool dress with the matching coat, the almost regal posture, told Sallie as clearly as if she had known Caroline for years that here was the real article, a product of years of breeding and good taste. But something else had thrown the glove between them before all else. Sallie was accustomed to being easily the most attractive woman in any gathering. Although she was not a conventionally pretty woman, the vitality in her face and the frank sensuality of her body, combined with the effect of her red hair and green eyes, put other women in shadow. She rarely ran up against a woman like Caroline Langlinais, who had not only the charm and grace of a well-bred lady but also an aura of unconscious sexuality whose effect on a man meeting

Caroline for the first time Sallie could see as her husband had greeted the Langlinaises. The natural resentment Sallie felt toward any competitor, any rival, rose to the surface. When she caught the small exchange between Caroline and Beau, her resentment changed to thorough dislike. Since the day Mitch first brought Beau Langlinais home for a drink, Sallie had had her eye on him. She had imagined Beau married to the kind of dull little country wife that made husbands eager for excitement elsewhere. But watching him with Caroline, she knew that although Beau might well catch all the signals Sallie broadcast, he would never acknowledge them. She felt humiliated, angry, determined to get her own back at whatever cost. She decided to begin by keeping them there, holding them against their will. Swiftly she turned to Henri. "Come turn the pages for me, Henri. I'll signal you when to turn."

Henri felt himself suddenly the center of attention. His mother gave him a look that told him to say no, that they could not stay that long. Looking away, he smiled at Sallie. "You're taking a risk, Mrs. Mitchell. The extent of my musical ability lies in putting a record on the phonograph."

"That's a risk I'm willing to take," Sallie said. "Come on."

She led the way to the sun porch, which she had turned into a music room. A baby-grand piano, with a Spanish shawl thrown over it, stood at one end. Multicolored silk cushions spilling from the Victorian wicker chairs and settees and bright rugs scattered over the black tile floor completed the room. Sallie opened the piano, and, spreading her golden jersey skirts around her, patted the seat beside her. Henri sat down slowly, his eyes on Sallie's face. He did not understand the tension that had entered the room, he did not fully comprehend why his mother held herself so straight, her chin tilted in the way that meant she was ready for a fight. He supposed his mother was finally tired of all these business parties, and that Père was sorry he had put her through them. Then he felt Sallie Mitchell's soft hand on his, and he stopped thinking about his parents. After all, they had asked him to come along, hadn't they? They had wanted him to be polite, enter into things, hadn't they? What could be more polite than helping his hostess entertain her guests?

Sallie's red-tipped fingers ran over the keys, teasing chords from them. Then she lifted her head, exposing the long line of throat, and began to sing. Caroline recognized the song immediately as a French art song, a romantic potboiler, and she made a small moue of distaste. But one look at her son's face changed distaste to alarm.

Henri couldn't take his eyes off Sallie Mitchell. He watched the body that seemed to swell with the music, as though each breath pumped her firm breasts even fuller. The deep-cut neckline of her dress fell away from her cleavage as she leaned forward; sitting so near her, Henri could see the creamy lace that edged her slip. Her eyes were on her audience, but Henri felt the slight pressure of her body next to his, and he turned the pages at her signal without being aware that his hand was moving.

When the song series was over, Sallie waited until the applause died and then closed the piano. "Thank you, Henri," she said, giving him a long, cool look in which the ice was just beginning to melt. "You're better at that than you thought you were."

Henri felt himself blushing and got up quickly, suddenly ready to get away from this disturbing woman, who, though younger than his mother, was certainly much, much older than he. "I enjoyed it," he said, sounding stiff even to himself. "You sing very well, Mrs. Mitchell."

Sallie rose too, her mouth curved in a teasing smile. " 'Mrs. Mitchell'? I'm not that much older than you are, Henri. My name is Sallie. Come by someday soon and we'll play again."

Beau turned to Mitch, who stood beside him. "I'll call you about that deal on Monday," he said. "In fact, I think I may have Henri work on it with you. Thanks for the party."

Henri followed them through the crowd and out into the deepening night. The street was quiet, and the air, after the thick closeness of the Mitchell house, was crisp, fresh.

"Well, Henri," Caroline said as he held the door for her. "You certainly seemed to be having a good time."

He heard the crossness in her voice, and an instinct wiser than thought made him laugh carelessly as he got into the back seat. "At least there was a floor show," he said. "Mrs. Mitchell has a good voice. But I'm not sure she's as good as she thinks she is." He looked at his mother and smiled. "I guess she's pretty well past her prime, don't you?"

"Oh, I imagine she has a few years left," Caroline said. Seeing nothing in her son's face but polite interest, she felt reassured. But just to test the waters, just to make sure her men had not really been taken in by Sallie, she turned to Beau. "You didn't tell me Sallie Mitchell is so attractive," she said.

Beau leaned across the space between them and kissed her, then took her hand and squeezed it. "It's Mitch I do business with," he said. "I've only seen Sallie once or twice—" He shrugged, dismissing her. "She's pretty enough, I suppose. A little hard." Henri saw the way Père smiled at his mother, and the back seat felt suddenly large and lonely. He saw his mother move across the seat so that she was sitting close to Père, very, very close. And although she whispered, putting her mouth next to Père's ear so that Henri could not hear, he caught the sense: ". . . not stay too long . . . get back to the hotel."

The small glimpse of the adult world piqued his curiosity; he settled back and thought about Sallie Mitchell.

As though to underscore the fact that the world had turned topsy-turvy, Christmas week was perversely warm; roses bloomed in profusion, and mosquitoes swarmed up from the swamp, while the tall fir tree and pine and holly branches decorating the farm and Beau Chêne wilted in the heat.

David and Caro wangled three days off and arrived two days before Christmas. David thought he had been prepared for the Langlinais household, but it was late Christmas Eve before he had sorted everyone out and begun to feel at ease. Caro, sensing that the whole clan had been a bit too much, declared that they would steal some time alone, and had taken him into the living room after lunch while the rest of the family scattered on last-minute Christmas errands.

"Hand me that blue plaid stocking, will you?" she said.

David set down the photo album he was looking through and held out André's stocking to her. One of Beau's hunting socks had already been nailed up for David; when he had said mildly that as a Jew he didn't celebrate Christmas, Caro had told him he could call it a Hanukkah stocking if he wanted to, but that no guest in their house went without presents at Christmas.

He glanced at the array of stockings on the mantel. Catching sight of a familiar-looking candelabrum, he got up and approached it for a closer look.

"Is this a menorah?" he said, his voice showing his disbelief.

Caro regarded the bronze candelabrum and smiled. "A lovely old couple gave that to Père and Mama for their wedding. It had been in their family for years.

"A Jewish couple?"

"Well, yes," she said. She gave the tack one more firm tap with the hammer and smiled again. "David—there are any number of Jewish people around here. I hate to disappoint you, but you are not the rarity in my life you think you are."

"I damn well better be," he said. He spun her toward him and kissed her, testing a different quality in her response. "You're different down here, you know that?"

"How?" she said.

"I don't think you need me as much here," he said.

"We're on holiday!" she said.

"What difference does that make?"

She reached out and straightened a tassel hanging from a stocking.

"David—this is my family. When I'm with them—well, I know I can rely on them. No matter what. I feel . . . safe."

He sat on the sofa and pulled her down beside him. "Don't I make you feel safe?"

"It's not the same thing at all," she said.

"Then explain it for me," he said. "Explain why I feel that the New Orleans Caro has run away somewhere—and that I'm facing a girl I hardly know."

"I guess everyone reverts a little when they go home," she said. He saw her quick tension, her instant defensiveness. "Is it so unusual for me to enjoy being pampered again?"

"It's not just that," he said. "I'm enjoying the pampering myself. It's—I don't know. You almost seem larger than life down here. I'm suddenly aware of all the ancestors crowding your blood."

"Oh, David!" she said, and laughed. "What a way to put it!" She took his hand in hers and began tracing the lines in his palm. "As if you don't come from a family with a long heritage yourself."

"I suppose I'd forgotten how families pick up traditions and rituals," he said. "At lunch today, no one would start eating until you remembered exactly whose turn it was to read the last prayers of Advent."

"This is an important season," she said. "From a religious point of view, of course—but for our family, too. Anyway," she burst out, "doesn't your family have traditions? You of all people should understand."

"I do. But understanding them doesn't keep me from feeling . . . shut out."

There was a silence neither knew how to end; then Caro said, keeping her voice even, "You don't have to go to Midnight Mass with us. I don't want you to be . . . unhappy."

"I want to," he said. "You know I want to."

"Well, then?" she said, keeping her voice light.

"Well, then," he said. He stood up and held out his hand. "You promised to show me Beau Chêne. Is now a good time?"

"As good as any," she said. She took his hand, but her touch was cool, and she released it as soon as she was on her feet.

"Caro," he said. "Don't be angry."

"I'm not angry," she said. "I . . . I don't understand, David. Everyone has made you welcome. Everyone likes you." Her lips were trembling, and he was reminded how very young Caro really was. In New Orleans, working at the shipyard, living in the house on Calliope Street, she seemed—she *was*—much older. Here, where she was petted and fussed over, she reverted to her true age, an age he had almost been able to forget. With a kind of sorrow he realized the strain her job and her seemingly adult existence imposed on Caro; no wonder she took to being at home again, where she was cushioned by familial love and ritual.

"And I like them," he said. "I'm sorry, I'm being churlish. If I feel left out—it's not because your family hasn't made me feel at home." He stopped talking and bent to kiss her. Again he felt that different quality, a certain restraint that he could no longer put down to Caro's fear that someone would walk in on them. No, this visit home reaffirmed Caro's beliefs, her commitment to the code that allowed them to kiss each other long and often, but always stopped before it went much farther. More than once he had told himself he was too old to court a girl who adhered to such a rigid code. But, code or no code, the attraction he felt for Caro Hamilton went beyond physical desire, and the reason he kept seeing her, no matter how frustrated he became, was that he could not seem to help it.

"We'll walk," she said. "It's only a mile through the woods, and you can see something of the land."

Her voice made the word "land" special; walking over it to Beau Chêne, listening to her describe it, he thought of the narrow brownstone he had grown up in, the apartment that seemed spacious because it had occupied the entire floor, and every one of the four children had his or her own room. He tried to see the woods they walked through with Caro's eyes: oaks the Langlinaises and DeClouets had owned for almost two hundred years, the path made by the feet of generations of the two families, crossing back and forth to share one another's lives.

When they came to the house, he realized with a feeling of loss that Caro's religion and moral code were not the only things that distanced them. Standing in the parlor under the portrait of Hélène DeForet DeClouet, the first ancestress to reach Louisiana, Caro told him how her mother had sacrificed her love for Beau Langlinais to keep Beau Chêne for future generations. "It was so fine of her," Caro said, eyes intent on the painting. "She told me she could have given up Beau Chêne for herself—but she couldn't give it up for generations to come."

"And you," David said, coming closer and taking her hand. "Could you give it up?"

"It won't be mine to give," Caro said.

"Why not?"

"I imagine one of the boys will have it." She tossed her hair back out of her face. "I don't want to think about it. That's years off."

"But it means a lot to you," he persisted. "This house. This land."

"It's home," she said.

"Yes," he agreed. He looked up at the portrait. "That's nice. Who painted it?"

"Her son," Caro said. "I like to think I'm maintaining the family tradition."

David started to speak, then stopped. Caro talked about her ancestor as though he were only recently dead, rather than seven or eight generations away. In the short time he had been down here, David had become aware of how alive all the DeClouet and Langlinais ancestors were to this family. It was natural, he supposed, to pass on family stories. His own family did that too. But somehow, this was different, as though Caro's people could not bear to let anyone go. Following Caro back to the farm, he felt a small chill; if her family had such a hold on the dead, how tight was their hold on the living?

Christmas dinner was festive, with everyone in an exuberant mood. Raoul had begun doing volunteer work with Walter Fournet's refugee organization; once a week he took medical histories, gave inoculations, and helped out in the clinic Walter had established. "He asks about you all the time," he said to Caro. "Said to tell you that he has open house at his apartment on Royal every Sunday afternoon, if you ever care to go."

"I often work on Sunday," Caro said. "And when I am off—" She looked at David. "I'm usually busy."

"Walter's all right," Henri said. "I've been to a few of his parties. He comes across as a dilettante bon vivant—but then there's something about him. He reminds me a little of that aristocratic detective fellow of Dorothy Sayers's—what's his name?"

"Lord Peter Wimsey," Raoul said. "You know, you're right, Henri. Walter looks as though he doesn't have anything on his mind more serious than the wine he's going to open for dinner—and then he pulls off something like this refugee-relief organization.

"I'm about to pull off something myself," Skye said. He looked around the table. This wasn't exactly the opening he had been waiting for, but he had a feeling there would never be a better one. "I'm going to join the Air Force this week."

Their heads jerked to attention, as though his words had tightened a string run through all their necks. Skye did not hear distinctly what everyone said, the chairs scraping as family members got up—he saw only his father's face. One quick flash of fear in the gray eyes. Then pride. Admiration. And respect. Beau got up and came to Skye, taking his hand and gripping it tightly. Against his back, Beau felt the tension in the room. Picking up the burgundy, Beau went around the table, filling their glasses. Then he lifted his own high. "I'd like to propose a toast," he said. They raised their glasses, waiting for him to speak. "To Skye, and to all the young men he will join, to whose courageous hearts and patriotic spirit we owe the very preservation of freedom and dignity for all mankind."

The solemnity of his words had the effect of lifting everyone out of their first fearful reactions onto a higher plane, one that would, Beau hoped, get them through the rest of the meal. Time enough, when Skye was really and truly gone, for his sisters to add his name to the litany they remembered in their prayers. Time enough for André to choose a colored pin that would represent Skye, a pin that would move on the big map fastened to his room wall from the safety of a Stateside training base to the unknown skies that waited for him. Time enough for the family to come to terms with this closer reality of war. And time enough for himself to accept the fact that his firstborn son was gone to war.

Then David spoke, his eyes on Caro, but his voice taking all of them in. "I . . . I have an announcement of my own, if it's all right," he said. "My own family is too far away—" He felt Caro's hand on his arm, saw her eyes grow large and dark with fear.

"I've been on the Navy reserve list since the war broke out," he said. "Now that my residency is finished—they want me on active duty. I report to San Diego right after the first of the year."

He saw fear devour Caro's face, her eyes fill with tears. Again there was a babble of sound: encouragement, praise. Then Beau again pulled the moment together. "I'd like to offer a kind of . . . blessing," Beau said. "One I think is especially appropriate today, for all of us." Listening to the quiet resonance of Beau's voice, its confidence and strength, David understood something of the strength that reverberated through every beam in this house. As he bent his head with the others, he thought: There's a man I'd like to know better. And when he heard the blessing Beau had chosen, from Genesis, he felt the circle of belonging close around him, and thought helplessly how very like life it was to offer a gift with one hand and dash it to the ground with the other.

" 'The Lord watch between me and thee, when we are absent from one another,' " Beau said.

"Amen," they all said.

Then Caro stood and pulled David up. "Mama—if you'll excuse us for a minute—we'll be right back for dessert."

Caroline watched them disappear into the hall, heard the soft murmurs—and then silence. She looked down the table at Beau and signaled him with her eyebrow.

"Well," Beau said. "I don't know about anyone else, but I'm still hungry. Skye, don't tell me you're going to turn down another helping."

"I should say not," Skye said, handing his plate to Beau. He felt newly important, suddenly much older. He looked out the window, his eye drawn by the flight of a cardinal that had come too close to the panes and then suddenly veered away. His eye followed the bird as it arced away up the sky. I'm going to be doing that, he exulted. I'm going to be soaring up into that blue. "Listen," he said to Émilie, "if I'm assigned to basic training at Keesler, you and Gennie can come over and see me. The Gulf Coast is jumping."

Beau, hearing enthusiasm charge Skye's voice like air pumping up a Benjamin rifle, felt a moment of wistful longing, even envy. He had been too young for the first world war, too old for this one. He had shared hunts with men, deep-sea-fishing trips. Battles in the legislature. Fights in boardrooms. He had never shared that ultimate experience of putting your lives on the line together. Then a shaft of sunlight poured over the room, catching them all in its silent gold. You idiot, he chided himself. If grown men with your experience still glamorize war, when the hell will they ever stop?

"Why didn't you tell me?" Caro demanded. After the first flurried exchange, the first long kiss, she had pulled him down beside her on the broad bottom step of the hall staircase, still clinging to his hand.

"I haven't known anything definite very long," he said. "Only found out for sure two days before we came down here."

"Why didn't you tell me then?"

He bent nearer her, staring into her eyes, forcing her to remember. "That was the night of our last date in New Orleans," he said. "Think, Caro."

Her face flooded with color, and she looked away. They had gone to a movie, and had returned to her house to find everyone asleep, the place theirs. The bounds she usually put on their lovemaking had seemed to hold. Then, all at once, David's hands were under her sweater, unhooking her bra, coming around to cup her breasts. For one long moment she had given herself to him. Then she broke away and fled, running down the hall to the safety of her room. There she had made herself take deep breaths, straightened her clothes with impersonal fingers, and tried to forget the way his hands felt on her flesh. She had brushed her hair and fixed her makeup. When she returned to the parlor, David was reading a magazine as though he had no other interest in the world. He had left shortly afterward. It was she who had kissed him good night; he had not responded, only giving her a funny little smile and striding away into the dark.

"I don't understand," she said. "Why didn't you tell me?"

"It might have been the thing that tipped the balance," he said. "You want to make love with me—we both know that. But you can't let yourself because of the Church and because of your upbringing. I thought if I told you I was leaving so soon—" He smiled, the same funny little smile she remembered. "You might have lost your argument."

"David!" His concern overwhelmed her; she felt suddenly very young, very ignorant. "But I would have thought you'd—"

"I don't take advantage of people I love Caro," David said. He sounded almost harsh, as though he should not have to explain that; in her confusion, she almost missed what he had said.

Then the words hit her, and she stared at him, her eyes dark. "David—you said you love me."

"I do," he said.

Caro felt caught in a tumult of emotions. David had said he loved her. And then suddenly she realized that she loved him too. She went into his arms and whispered the words in his ear, saying them over and over again as though repetition could form an amulet against the forces that swept over them, forces she could neither control nor understand. "I love you," she said. "Oh, David, I love you!"

Even as she spoke, a sense of desolation dimmed her happiness. How little it mattered, she thought, what her feelings for David were, his for her. In a little over a week he would be gone, and the question of whether or not to make love with him would be academic only. She felt dizzy, almost faint, and as she leaned against him, felt his heart beating beneath her cheek, she confronted a new reality: how very little command men and women have over their own lives, even the most intimate and private parts.

6

MARCH 1943

The barracks door slammed violently and Skye looked up from his book. Red Tucker, a fellow pilot trainee, stood squarely in front of the door, hands on hips, jaw set. "Man, that mess hall is plumb full of spades," he said. He took his cap off and threw it onto his bed disgustedly. "If they think I'm having my supper with a bunch of niggers, they're crazy." Red flung himself on his bed and stared at Skye. "Sportin' around the base with their little gold wings on their collars, acting like they damn near own the place." He propped himself up on one elbow and thrust his face nearer Skye. "Few of us think they ought to be taught a lesson, Langlinais. You in?"

Skye closed his book, keeping his place with one finger. "Take it easy, Red. We've got enough to do learning to fly without starting a lot of trouble. Those men aren't bothering anybody."

"Sure they are," Red drawled. "They're bothering me." His lips widened in a grin, exposing misshapen teeth. "Every time I see one of those niggers, I want to hit his smart-ass face." He made a fist of his right hand and pounded his left palm. "Get one of those cocky spades and just beat the shit out of him."

Skye got off his bed, book still in his hand. "I'm going to eat," he said. "You can sit here and starve if you want to—that makes as much sense as everything you've just said." He put the book in his locker and started toward the door. Just as his hand touched the knob, he felt his shirt grabbed from behind.

"Nigger lover," Red's voice said. The hand that held Skye spun him around. Red's face was in his, eyes narrowed, lips drawn back. "What's the matter? You Cajuns live so far back in the swamp you ain't never heard that white men don't eat with niggers?"

The fury that Skye had held in abeyance ever since the all-Negro Ninety-ninth Pursuit Squadron had arrived at Keesler Field for maneuvers could be checked no longer. His right hand broke Red's grip as his left hand grasped Red's throat. His knuckles whitened as he tightened his hold. His thumb was pressed against Red's Adam's apple; with Red's air cut off, his face began to change color, going from its normal ruddiness to an unhealthy blue-red. Red's mouth worked frantically, but no sound emerged. The thick tongue wobbled, as though it were loose at both ends and could roll forward any moment.

"I don't think I heard that last thing you said, Red," Skye said grimly. "Something about someone not eating with someone else?" He leaned forward, head cocked, as though trying to understand. "Maybe what you meant to say was that decent men don't eat with scum like you. Is that it, Red?" He increased the pressure slowly, and then nodded his own head. "You might just try moving your head a little, Red. Let me know that's what you meant."

He saw yellow hatred in Red's eyes. A vein bulged at one side of Red's head. And then he saw the struggling motion as Red slowly forced his head to jerk first up, then down. Skye let up the pressure and watched the enlarged vein begin to subside. "All right," he said. "Fine." He released Red and then moved back, feet slightly apart, hands held hip-height, ready to ward off any sudden move Red might make. "Couple of things you need to understand, Red," Skye said, his voice even. "First thing—nobody calls me any kind of name. Second thing—nobody starts a fight with me just because I don't agree with him." He looked at his watch. "Third thing—don't take a seat at a table where I'm sitting, Red. Not today, not this week, not ever. Because while I don't mind sitting in the mess hall with those Negro pilots, I sure as hell do mind sitting with you." He turned and opened the door, the memory of Red's hate-filled face going with him.

Now you've done it, he told himself, walking swiftly across the quadrangle toward the mess hall. You've tried to lie low and not rile that dumb redneck ever since you got here—now you've made the worst kind of enemy, one who's as mean as he is bigoted. Until the Ninety-ninth Pursuit Squadron arrived, Red had picked on the smallest, scrawniest, least likely fellow trainees, making their lives miserable with a constant stream of verbal abuse and practical jokes. Skye had remained aloof from the proceedings, neither defending Red's victims nor joining in the laughter at their discomfort. His first impulse was to stop Red in his tracks with a couple of well-placed blows to that bigoted jaw. But he remembered what his father had told him about getting involved in other men's battles. "When a man has put himself into a situation he needs to get the best of, better let him try to fight it out by himself, son, so long as he's not in danger of losing anything vital." So far, Red's victims had lost nothing but a little face—and Skye could see that some of them were beginning to fight back, thus gaining some necessary toughness.

Skye paused and took a deep breath. A huge sweet-olive bush blooming near the door of the mess hall made the air smell like home. Masses of live oaks, their moss veils moving gently in the soft night breeze off the Mississippi Sound, loomed at the corners of the quadrangle, and azaleas made patches of color that contrasted with the khaki uniforms that filled the square daily. He knew that the mere presence of Negroes in the Air Force caused continual debate; he and his father had discussed the issue before Skye enlisted, with Beau pointing out all the ways in which Skye's experience with Negroes was different from that of many other Southerners, and certainly different from that of any Northerner.

"The Langlinaises never owned slaves, for one thing," Beau said. "Our family never was into sugar the way the DeClouets were—we didn't believe in slavery, and any help we had were free people. That's one difference, Skye. Another one is that people in our part of Louisiana don't set themselves above others. We're close to the soil. We're all hostages to the same nature, all victims of the same floods, the same droughts."

"But our schools are segregated," Skye said. "We do treat Negroes differently, Papa. They sit in the back pews at Mass—and we damn sure didn't have any Negroes at St. Peter's."

Skye remembered the way his father's eyes had looked. Sad, and a little angry. Hurt, almost. "I know, son," Beau said. "I know." He had taken Skye's hand, held it tightly in his. "Something else I know, too. If I'm going to see my oldest son off to war, then that war had damn well better bring a world in which there's no foolishness about a man's worth being based on the color of his skin. Or the way his last name sounds. Or the kind of church he goes to."

Skye had understood the anger, but he had not understood the sorrow or the hurt until he'd reached Keesler Field and found out that to many of his fellow trainees, a man with a name like Langlinais, who came from some little town in Louisiana they'd never heard of, and who went to Mass every Sunday, was more than a little peculiar—of a species not quite human, more than one barracks mate had made clear. Two men who had been at Dartmouth together had baited Skye, getting him to talk to them and tell them stories about St. Martinville. He had never met prejudice before; he did not know what it was, nor did he recognize the amusement he saw in their eyes as laughter at him instead of with him—until the night he heard one of them mimicking him for the benefit of a group of men drinking beer in one of the many bars they frequented when they had time off-base.

Even now, weeks later, the memory of that Eastern voice attempting to capture the lilting rhythms of Skye's speech made him furious. Tom Conrad was telling one of the stories Skye had given them, but he was telling it all wrong, making it seem stupid and mean instead of funny. Skye waited until the laughter started, forcing himself to hear the scorn, the derision.

Then he stepped into the center of the group. "Pardon me," he said. "You missed the point of that story."

Tom Conrad looked at him, a long, slow glance that measured every inch of Skye and ended with a slow, insolent shaking of the head, as though Skye had been found wanting. "I didn't think it had a point," Tom said. "Maybe I'm just not sufficiently . . . educated in what you people find humorous."

"Maybe you're not sufficiently educated in what my people find courteous," Skye said. His fists were clenched at his sides, his neck was taut, and he could barely open his stiff lips.

"I beg your pardon," Tom Conrad said. His voice was openly insulting, and his eyes invited the men around them to join in his mockery. "From what I've heard about your part of Louisiana, it's even more ignorant than the rest of the state—and as far as manners go, what kind of manners can a place have when it's got as many snakes and alligators as it has people?" He laughed and poked Skye's chest. "But if you think I owe you an apology—" He looked at the men circling them. "I'm sorry I messed up your story. Maybe you should tell it, all right?"

For one tense moment Skye thought he was going to lose control and leap upon the man in front of him with both fists flying. Words cascaded into his mouth—he wanted to fling his family's money, power, land, squarely in that scoffing face. He thought of his father, praised in editorial after editorial for his stance in the legislature, his efforts to better the state. He thought of his grandfather, consulted by businessmen and politicians from every corner of Louisiana on any decision of significance. And then he remembered that the spurs he was about to put on his boots had been earned by other men. He let out his breath and made his fists relax. He made himself put one foot on the bar rail, signal to the bartender for a beer. He made his mouth smile slightly as he turned to face his tormentor. "I think maybe it lost something in the translation. My stories aren't accustomed to finding themselves in Yankee mouths." He managed to put the merest insulting inflection on the word "Yankee."

Skye saw the quick blaze of anger in Tom's eyes and smiled. He could feel his blood racing, and closed the small space between them. "Maybe you need a lesson in storytelling," he said. "If you ask me nicely enough, I'll give you one."

The men around them laughed, but this time the laughter was not at Skye. Skye laughed too. "We've got a saying back home," he said. "*'Prendre garde veax mieux que demandre pardon.'* In case you don't understand Cajun French, it means 'It is better to take care beforehand than to ask pardon afterward.' So mind your manners to begin with, Yankee, and you won't have to make so many apologies."

"If I didn't know we'd both end up in the stockade, you'd be on the floor, Langlinais," Conrad said. He hurried the syllables together so that the name sounded alien, even to Skye. "But I'll catch you somewhere, someday, when there're no MPs around. And then we'll finish this."

Skye sipped his beer, watching Conrad over the rim of his mug. "Man, don't you know a grudge is the heaviest thing a man can carry? Gets heavier every day until all you can do is carry it—don't have strength for anything else."

"I imagine I can manage," Tom Conrad said. He set his own mug on the counter. "Come on," he said to his companions. "Let's find a place that's a little more discriminating in its clientele."

Skye had managed to let that comment pass. He had managed to hang on to his temper time after time when he and Tom Conrad crossed each other's paths. He told himself it was a discipline he must impose on himself, just one more of the many obstacles that lay between him and his dream of earning his wings.

Now, entering the mess hall, he quickly checked the men gathered there. It was Sunday, a quiet day, and many of the men were still off the base, using passes to go to a movie in Biloxi or Gulfport. A group of Negro pilots were seated at a table at one end of the room, talking quietly, heads turned into a tight circle. Men Skye knew were scattered around the mess hall; he got his tray and joined two trainees from his squadron.

"A long time ago somebody told me if I didn't like the weather in New Orleans, to wait five minutes and it would change," one of the men was saying as Skye came up. "Seems like that's true on the Gulf Coast, too. Day before yesterday I damn near froze, and tonight it's almost hot."

"That's March for you," Skye said. He grinned. "But don't begin thinking this is hot. It's not even warm. Wait until August. You won't believe that heat."

"You think we'll still be hanging around Biloxi in August?" the man said. "Hell, Skye, they're going to get us trained, sit us in a plane, and send us over."

"I hope so," Skye said. He began cutting his meat. "I want combat so bad I can taste it." He heard the young eagerness in his voice and blushed at his own boyish enthusiasm.

"If they give you your druthers, Langlinais—what do you want to fly?"

"A bomber," Skye said. He thought of the huge B-17's, the even heavier B-25's. His hands twitched, and he picked up a mug of coffee and closed his fingers around it.

"That's like flying a tractor," one of the men said. "Me, I want to fly a fighter—a P-37, now that's a plane."

Skye knew the conversation would become technical, with each of them dredging up everything he knew about his pet aircraft. During the month he had been at Keesler, he had absorbed flying through every pore; he had recognized the bull sessions devoted to planes for what they were—boning up, trying to become as expert as they possibly could, because the country needed them now, and could not afford to keep them Stateside very long. He shot a glance at the Negro pilots in the corner of the room. "They'll be going over soon," he said. "Scuttlebutt is they're headed for North Africa."

"Hope we've won by then," one of the men said, lighting a cigarette. "God knows a bunch of jigs won't be any help."

"Aw, keep it to yourself," another man said. He was big, Irish Catholic, from a mining family in Pennsylvania. His world was totally black and totally white; he had been put down enough for being poor, Irish, and Catholic in his own home state, and had complete sympathy for any other group equally oppressed. "I guess if the Air Force says a man can fly, he can fly."

"I was thinking about guts," the first man began.

"You wasn't thinking, period," the big Irishman said. "Listen, fellow, I didn't come all the way down here from Pennsylvania to listen to a bunch of crap like that. All right?"

"All right," the other man said and ducked his head over his coffee.

Irish looked at Skye and grinned. "Can't digest my food proper when there's argument going on," he said. "Come on, Frenchy, let's take a walk by the seawall."

The waters of the Mississippi Sound lapped against the seawall, the tiny wavelets lined with silver by the moon. Dark long shapes, wooden piers reaching out into the water, were strung at their far ends with netting and strands of barbed wire to prevent saboteurs in small boats from using them as easy access to the land.

"Nice out here, ain't it?" Irish said. Neither smoked; blackout rules demanded that no cigarette be smoked in the open where its glowing tip could guide an enemy. The air had the same faint tang of salt as the swamps back home; the Sound opened into the Gulf, so its water was brackish, part fresh, part salt, supporting crabs and flounder and the sharp-toothed gar which could bite through a man's leg. "You really want to drop bombs, Frenchy?"

"It's not a matter of wanting to—" Skye stopped. He and his father had talked about that, too. About what it meant to be in the Air Force.

"Unless you're assigned to fly transports—or be on reconnaissance—you're going to have to come to terms with the kind of killing you'll be doing, son," Beau had said. His face had been worried; nothing in his own experience had prepared him to counsel his son now. One death only was he responsible for, and that one long ago, when he was a hotheaded young man who bit off a larger piece of experience than he was quite ready for—and had had to grow up to it in one black night.

"Whatever I fly into combat, whether it's a fighter or a bomber, I'll be killing men I don't know."

"Some people seem to feel that makes it better," Beau said.

"Maybe they mean easier," Skye said.

Beau had gripped Skye's shoulders and looked long into his face. "Problem with that, son, is that Langlinaises haven't ever been too crazy about something being easier—instead of right."

And now, when he had actually seen the bombers he might one day fly, when he had actually seen military films of bombing raids, seen the plumes of fire and smoke marking the path of the planes as though the earth were a giant cake and the bombs had lit candles, now he was more uncertain than before. Not that he could fly a bomber. But how he was going to deal with what that bomber did.

They heard footsteps behind them and turned to see three of the Negro pilots walking toward them.

" 'Evening," one of them said as they passed Irish and Skye, heading past them down the seawall.

" 'Evening," Irish said, and Skye echoed him.

They were silent then, standing breathing in the fresh wind from the Gulf, listening to the small plop leaping fish made, watching the moon sparkle on the dull water.

A sudden shout broke the silence. It was followed by another one, and then the sound of scuffling. They looked to their right and saw a fight in progress.

"They've jumped the spades," Irish said, and began running, Skye on his heels.

Just as they reached the melee, Skye saw the flash of metal in a man's hand. Automatically he thrust his hand toward the man's wrist and gripped it, jerking the man's other arm behind him. "Drop it," Skye commanded. A face twisted by hatred swung around. It was Red. Skye tightened his hold. "Drop that knife, Red."

"Goddammit, Langlinais, can't you keep from poking your nose in where it doesn't belong?" Red's eyes glittered, and Skye knew that he was included in the target of that mad rage.

"Drop the knife," Skye said again, and saw Red's fingers relax and the knife fall to the grass.

"Got it," Irish said, scooping it up. "Damn, you meant business!" he said, holding the knife up in the moonlight so Skye could see its brutal edge.

While Skye had disarmed Red, Irish and the Negro pilots had turned the tide on the attackers, who now lay sprawled on the ground. "Take off their ties, Skye," Irish said. "We'll tie 'em up and leave 'em here—let them explain themselves when they're found."

Irish worked quickly, efficiently trussing each of the three men in his own tie and shoelaces. He rose from the last man and looked at his watch. "I make it five minutes before bed check," he said. "Let's make tracks." He turned to the three Negroes. "You men okay?"

"Fine," one of them said. "Man, thanks."

"It's okay," Irish said. He slapped the nearest Negro on the back. "See ya around," he said, and then grabbed Skye's arm. "Come on, Frenchy," he said. "I can explain a few bruises on my knuckles, but I can't explain being late." His grin in the moonlight was big, and relaxed. "Land in the stockade and I'll never get my wings."

It was the next afternoon before Skye learned Red and his friends had talked their way out of the stockade. He ran into one of the Negro pilots on his way to the base post office, and after an awkward greeting, fell into step beside him. "Say, have you heard what happened to those men last night?"

The Negro's eyes were deep brown, blazing now with a fire Skye didn't understand at first. "Sure, I heard. Was called in to testify."

"You mean about them jumping you?"

"I mean about the story they cooked up. Said they'd been jumped by some . . . Negroes from in town here. People coming to see me and my friends. So we were called in to verify their story." The heavy anger in the man's voice made each word leaden.

"Damn," Skye said. "So nothing's going to happen to them at all?"

He watched a smile cut through the dark mask of the Negro's face. "Oh, man, I didn't say that. I didn't say nothing's going to happen to them."

Skye let the silence develop between them. Then he smiled back. "You want some help sometime, you let me know." He held out his hand. "I'm Skye Langlinais."

The Negro looked from Skye's face to Skye's hand, then slowly reached out and took it. "George Washington Harris," he said. "One guess as to who I'm named for."

"Well," Skye said. "My real name—my baptismal name—is Claude Louis Langlinais. But that's my father's name, too, though he's got a nickname. And my grandfather's name. And every single firstborn male in my family for a long way back. So when I was a baby, they called me by my initials—C.L. That makes a word in French."

"Ciel," George Harris said. "Sky."

"Yes," Skye stammered, hating the surprise he heard in his voice. "We put an E on the end. So it's spelled S-k-y-e."

Harris laughed, but the laughter was friendly. "Surprised I know French, Langlinais?"

Skye relaxed. "A little, I guess."

"I'm from Nashville," Harris said. "My father's head of an insurance company there. I actually went to a school that had textbooks and whose teachers knew something about what they taught." Harris sounded mocking again, and looking at the neatly uniformed man in front of him, dark curly hair cropped under the cap, smooth brown skin emerging from the crisply starched sleeves and collar, Skye had a sudden memory of Negroes at home, in the fields. Torn overalls without a shirt. Bare feet. Bad teeth. Children with stick legs and round bellies. He shook the memory off. It was getting mixed up now with his memory of Red's sharp, ferret face. Of Tom Conrad's scoffing superiority. Of Irish's wading into the fight.

"I'm glad," he said. "Look, I just got a package from home. You like fudge?"

"I hear you," George Harris said. "I'll trade you some oatmeal cookies . . . Skye."

Later, writing to Rosalind, Skye found that he could not put any of it into words. He tried to tell her about Red, about Tom Conrad, about Irish. About the fight, and meeting George Washington Harris. The words made sense to him, but reading over what he had written, thinking of Rosalind, sitting in the open window of her dormitory room at Dominican College, he felt that they would not make the same kind of sense to her. He ripped up the pages he had filled and tossed them away. Then, pulling a blank sheet of paper toward him, he began writing. "Dear Rosalind, I miss you. Life is different here, but what is the same is that I think about you all the time." He read over those words. Was something wrong with them? And then, as he continued writing the same sort of phrases, he knew. Rosalind would read this letter, and it would make perfect sense to her. It was, he felt, precisely the sort of letter she expected to get from him. But as he sealed it and stamped it, he thought, with a kind of strange pang, that that was really not the sort of letter he had wanted to write at all.

"What you need is a bastard file," Caro said, leaning over and looking at the tools in front of the girl next to her. She heard a gasp, and looked up. The girl's mouth made a perfect O, and her eyes were two wide circles of shock. "What?" Caro said. Then she remembered her own reaction the first time the foreman had told her to go to the tool clerk and get a bastard file. "Sorry," she said, and smiled. "That's its name. It's a very coarse file. You'll need to go to the tool clerk to get one."

"I couldn't," the girl said. She was small, blond and pretty; her fluffy bangs stuck out of her bright scarf, and her tiny hands seemed ridiculously inadequate next to the heavy tools on the worktable in front of her. "I couldn't use that word in front of a man."

That's the least of what you're going to have to learn to do, Caro thought. But remembering how long it had taken her to adjust, she smiled again and patted the new girl's hand. "Okay. I need something anyway, I'll get your file, too." As she walked down the assembly line toward the corridor that led to the toolroom, she remembered those fluffy bangs making a curly trap across the new girl's head. She started to turn back, and then went on more quickly. She'd warn her when she got back, tell her that she musn't allow the slightest bit of hair to protrude from her scarf, or the least bit of loose strap or belt to hang away from the smooth lines of her overalls.

Absorbed in her thoughts, Caro forgot to take an essential precaution herself; she walked past a dark nook in the corridor that had been called "Wolf's corner" by the girls in this part of the shipyard, because certain male workers lurked there to pounce on passing women. Not until she felt a hand close on her arm and felt herself pulled into darkness did she remember; by that time, a thick, meaty hand had come over her mouth, and a thick, heavy body was pressing her back into a corner.

"Well, if it isn't the debutante," the man said. She could not see his face in the darkness, but she recognized his voice. This was one of the roughest men on the line, an ex-prizefighter, who, it was rumored, had lost his title because of involvement with racketeers. Someone had asked him once, and only once, why a big man like him wasn't in the military. The prizefighter had delivered a broken nose and a split lip with two quickly placed blows, and had then announced that there was something wrong with his heart, but if anyone else wanted to test his fists, they had his invitation to do so. He was also a womanizer of the worst kind; more than once, girls had slipped back onto the line after a lunch break with red cheeks and frightened eyes, and though not one ever opened her mouth, all the other women knew that he had somehow persuaded them to accompany him to one of the many hideouts on the premises where couples had quick encounters. He had been saying things to Caro every time she had to walk past him, things she had ignored with her head held high and her face set in forced calm. Lately, what he had been saying had gotten worse. And now, hearing that voice in her ear, feeling his hand on her mouth and his tight grip on her arm, she went weak with panic.

She had no doubt that he would rape her, right here and right now. His voiced droned on, telling her that he was going to take his hand away from her mouth, but reminding her that if she screamed, he would simply say she had induced him to follow her, had agreed to have sex with him. His hand slowly left her mouth, instantly replaced by his lips. Now the free hand was unbuttoning her shirt, quickly laying it open to the waist and pulling it from her shoulders. When she felt the hand began to pull at the strap of her bra, Caro thought she would faint. If he touches me, she thought, I won't be able to stand it. She closed her lips against the assault of his tongue, but he forced it between them. And then, just when he pushed her bra down and his hand was moving from her throat to her breast, a high, shrill scream cut through the heavy darkness, stopping everything.

At first Caro thought that somehow, she was screaming. His lips were motionless on hers, his tongue still. The screams came again, and then a chorus of screams, a discord of shouts. Pounding feet. A whistle blowing. "Shit!" he said. He stood away from her. "Get yourself together, girlie. Don't want anyone else seeing what's under all that ice." He turned and vanished into the corridor, where people were running. Dazed, Caro pulled her bra up and buttoned her shirt. Two men carrying a stretcher raced by the opening of the nook where she stood, with a nurse carrying a medical bag running behind them. Caro stepped out into the corridor and followed them.

They were heading for the part of the yard where she worked; people were clustered around something, their faces white with shock. They're where I work, Caro thought, moving forward. Something has happened where I work. She made her way through the crowd, murmuring, "That's where I work. Let me through, please. That's where I work."

The crowd swayed, made a path for the stretcher and nurse, a path Caro slipped through. And then she was at the edge of the circle, staring down. The new girl lay on the hard concrete floor, blood covering her. It spilled from the top of her head down over her face, masking it thickly. It cascaded over her shirt, soaking it, darkening it, making a pool on the gray concrete beneath her. But something was funny about the head, with the blood pouring from it. Something strange. Then Caro knew. There was no scarf on that head. There was no hair. Her eyes went up to the massive machine that loomed behind the line. She already knew what they would find. A bloody scarf. A scalp, with curly blond bangs fluttering like a small yellow flag. Her eyes closed and her knees buckled. She felt hands come up under her elbows, felt something hard jammed under her nose, and smelled the strong, bitter ammonia. She jerked her head away from it. "Head between knees now, come on," a woman said, forcing Caro onto a bench, forcing her head down.

She fought the nausea that rolled over her. She fought the memory of that bloody head, that bloody scarf, those silly blood-spattered curls. She kept her eyes closed until the woman said, "She's gone now. They've taken her away. They're cleaning up now." Then Caro lifted her head and opened her eyes, blinking at the sudden bright light. Two men were swabbing down the concrete floor. Another one was walking quickly away, carrying a bloody bag. That held the scarf, Caro thought. That held . . . it. She swallowed hard. She would not throw up. She would not faint. She stood up. "Okay now?" the woman asked. A whistle blew, and the woman looked upward. "Back to work," she said, moving toward her place. "They're sending someone in to take over her job," she said. A long, hard look at Caro. "You going to be able to work?"

Caro thought of David, now in San Diego, of Skye, getting ready for combat. "Sure," she said. She went back to the line and went to work. And not until that night did she allow herself to think of that poor girl for even one moment. She kept her mind on her work and her eyes on the job in front of her. It was only when she got home, and drew a hot bath, and brewed a cup of tea and took it into the tub with her, that she allowed herself to deal with what happened. The girl's young, silly face. The silly yellow bangs. The way she couldn't ask the tool clerk for a bastard file. I should have made her go, Caro thought, squeezing a sponge full of warm water over her back. Someone should have made her tuck that hair up—or I should have. Then the sponge stopped in midair. But if that silly young new girl had gone to the tool clerk, gone down that dark corridor, been pulled into "Wolf's Corner" by that terrible thick meaty hand—she would have been raped. Caro shut her eyes. She could almost see him violating that small, fragile body. See the shock in the silly little girl's eyes change to pain. Panic. And then go blank? Lose consciousness? She shook her head, her face taut. Her hand on the sponge gripped it more tightly, and cooling water gushed from it. She began to shake, sitting in the big claw-footed tub in her safe house on Calliope Street. Her stomach churned, and she was suddenly sick. Because it had become clear to her, for the first time that terrible day, that she herself had been saved by one thing, and one thing only. A horrible accident that had killed another human being.

She rose out of the tub and hung over the toilet, retching and heaving until only bitter bile came up. Weakly she sank to the bath rug and leaned against the tub. There had to be something she could do. There must be someone in the shipyard who cared that some of the men preyed on the women, took their harassment beyond mere verbal insults and occasional quick feels to active violence.

She sat there on the floor for a long, long time, while the water in the tub cooled and her tea became tepid. She sat there until she was chilled and the hard edge of the tub made a hurting mark across her back. Then she got up and pulled a nightgown over her head and tied a thick robe around her. She brushed her teeth and gargled away the taste of bile in her mouth. She brushed her hair and rubbed cream on her face. And then she went quietly down the hall into the library of this safe house, where she lifted down a small watercolor of a French Quarter scene to reveal a metal door. Quickly she spun the dial. When the door swung open, she reached her hand in past boxes holding jewelry, back to the darkest recess of the cavity. Her hand closed on something hard and smooth, and she pulled it out carefully. Then, the tiny revolver snugly in her hand, she turned off the light and went back down the hall to her room. As she got into bed and settled into sleep, she thought with satisfaction of how neatly the little gun fit into the deep pocket in her trousers. And how quickly she would be able to remove it, should the occasion ever arise.

7

MAY 1943

Skye stopped the car in front of the Nassers' house and sat for a moment, letting the peace of the May evening wash over him. Sweet olives and roses, lemony magnolias and gardenias made layers of scent in the air, and for the first time since he had arrived home six hours ago, he began to relax. Although he had not yet announced that he would be shipping out when he returned to Keesler, the look in his father's eyes when he met Skye in New Orleans told him that the military-training timetable was engraved in his father's head, and that now that Skye was wearing two tiny gold wings on his collar, his father knew there was nothing left for Skye to do in Biloxi.

The past six hours had been a whirlwind, with everyone talking at once; by the time he left to drive to New Iberia, feeling a little self-conscious in his uniform, his head was literally spinning. The thought of Rosalind, waiting for him inside, added its power to the emotional load he was already carrying; he got out of the car slowly, afraid that if he did not pace himself, he would grab her and unleash on her all the past months of denial in one passionate burst.

Hold on, he cautioned himself. Get control of yourself. But when she opened the door and flung herself into his arms, he realized this was not the girl who had let him kiss her but who had so rarely been stirred herself. He was surprised at the passion he felt in that one quick kiss, and he held her away from him, taking in the low-cut neckline, the clinging skirt of her pale green silk dress, the thin straps of her high-heeled sandals. "You look like a million dollars," he said. "Better than any pinup girl."

"Maybe I should pose for one of those pictures," she said, getting her purse. "To give to you, I mean."

"I don't want other guys ogling you," Skye said. He pushed down the questions that rose to his lips. He had never asked Rosalind, either in letters or during one of their infrequent telephone conversations, if she dated anyone in New Orleans. She had a way of vaguely referring to parties where "a bunch of us" went, or talking about a movie she had seen with "friends." Skye had decided he could live with anonymous 4-Fer's who were no more threatening to him than one of Rosalind's own brothers would have been, and he never asked for details. Now he took her arm possessively. "You're my girl, and no one but me needs to look at you."

She looked up at him from under her thick lashes; the fire in her eyes had died, and they were cool again. "Is that an order, sir?" she said. She reached up and touched one of the wings. "You're an officer now, aren't you, Skye? Lieutenant Skye Langlinais! That sounds wonderful."

"It does sound pretty good, doesn't it?" he said. He was suddenly proud of his uniform, proud to be wearing it, to be showing it off in this familiar town with pretty Rosalind on his arm. "Where would you like to go?" He grasped at names. "Toby's? Chag's?"

"I have a key to my uncle's *garçonnière,*" she said. Her voice was as bland as though she had announced that she had two tickets to the movies.

Skye stared at her blankly. "You have what?"

"My Uncle Tobi has a *garçonnière* at the back of his property. You can get to it from the back alley. He's in New York. And I have a key."

She can't mean what it sounds as though she means, Skye thought. He put the key in the ignition and started the car. He waited for her to say something else, to say she had planned a party for him, and that their old crowd was waiting there.

She looked up, her green gaze enveloping him. "You know where Uncle Tobi lives. Let's go."

She leaned forward and clicked on the radio, fiddling with the dial until she found the station she wanted. Glenn Miller's "String of Pearls" swirled around them, and Rosalind tapped her foot against the floorboard, her silk-sheathed body swaying rhythmically.

"Nice to listen to music like this with a girl again," Skye said. "Listening to big-band music in a barracks full of men just isn't the same."

Rosalind's head jerked around and she stared at him. "But there must be girls?"

"In Biloxi? I guess."

"There must be plenty of girls. Are you telling me you haven't gone out with anyone the whole time you've been gone?"

"I've gone to a few private parties," he said. "Families of guys I knew at LSU. I've met some girls, sure." He shrugged. "But I wasn't interested in them. Why would I be? I have you."

"That's not what I meant," she said. She shifted position so that her back was against the car door and she was facing Skye. "I go out, Skye."

"You wrote about parties—movies—I didn't think it was always just girls, Rosalind." He gave the steering wheel a hard turn. "But I didn't think there was anyone I had to worry about."

"What would worry you?" Rosalind said. "I can take care of myself."

He couldn't read her tone—it sounded rough, almost coarse. "That's not what I meant," he began. And then the entrance to her uncle's place loomed before them. The property was bounded by huge bamboo clumps so old that silt and rotting leaves had sifted down into their base to a height of several feet, making an impenetrable wall.

"Keep going," Rosalind said. "The back drive is around the corner."

He turned and saw the second opening, a narrow passage between two enormous stands of bamboo. He guided the car through, and saw a two-story dovecote illuminated in the car headlights.

"Park under that big oak, Skye," Rosalind said.

"Look," he said, trying to make his voice light. "May a rather slow-witted pilot ask a dumb question?"

"Certainly," Rosalind said.

"Why are we here?"

The moon had come up, rising high enough above the trees to light the car's interior so they could read each other's eyes.

"He's got a stocked bar, a good record collection—" Rosalind said. "A little privacy, Skye. Isn't that what you want?"

"It's not a question of what I want. What do you—" He shook his head. "Look, Rosalind. I know how many guys use that 'I'm shipping out tomorrow, can't you give me one night to remember?' bit."

"Are you shipping out?" she asked, staring at him.

"As a matter of fact—yes, I am."

A smile that seemed to match the calculating tone in her voice altered her face; it seemed to darken, as though the shaft of moonlight had moved on. "Is this your last night?" she said, taking his hand in hers and beginning to trace the lines in his palm. Her skin was cool, soft, smooth, and the passion he had struggled to control woke and fired him. He pulled her to him and kissed her, and for the first time since they had begun dating allowed his tongue to seek her mouth. He felt her lips open, felt her tongue touching his, her hands on him, all over him. His hand went to the zipper of her dress and began to work it down. Then she was undressing him, too, pulling his shirt out of his trousers, unbuckling his belt.

"Let's go in, Skye," she said. "Now."

They stumbled from the car, clothes in disarray, hands still touching, stroking. Rosalind managed to unlock the *garçonnière* and they almost fell over the doorstep, staggering forward and collapsing on a leather couch. Then Rosalind stood up and began to take off her clothes, letting the dress fall to her feet, pulling her slip over her head. At last she unfastened her bra and let it fall forward. Skye, his shirt already off, lay on the couch watching her. The moon lit the room, picking up the smooth ivory of Rosalind's skin, making her dark hair mysterious. His eyes devoured her; they reached her right hand and stopped. It was bare, empty.

"Where's my ring?" he asked. He did not recognize his voice; it was hoarse, strained. "Rosalind, where's my ring?"

She lifted her hand and looked at it. Her body was smooth lines, round curves, a carving in old ivory gleaming in the gentle light of the moon. And then she moved, and came toward him. "I guess I forgot to put it on," she said.

"I thought you wrote that you wore it all the time," he said.

She shrugged, the movement rippling from her shoulders to her breasts, those soft mounds he had been obsessed with for so long.

"I do," she said. "When I remember."

Suddenly he felt terribly naked, and embarrassed. He reached for his shirt and began to put it on. "I don't think this is a good idea," he said. "I . . . I don't imagine you really do, either." She looked at him and for the first time since he had picked her up, her mask was gone, and she was transformed again into the old Rosalind, exotic, amusing, sophisticated, but somehow vulnerable. He got up and went to her, handing her her slip. "Put this on, Rosalind. And we can talk about . . . about all this."

She picked up the rest of her clothes and went to the corner of the room, where she dressed swiftly. By the time she turned around, Skye was dressed too, standing at a mirror tying his tie.

"I'd rather we didn't talk about it, if you don't mind," she said.

"All right."

She waved her hand in the direction of the bar. "Do you want a drink?"

"Sure," he said. He knew they were as safe now as though five chaperons were sitting in the room with them. There was in fact a presence in the room so powerful it might as well have been human. And although he could not put a name to it, no more than he had been able to put a name to that calculating tone in Rosalind's voice when she asked him if this were his last night, he felt that same sense of alienation he so often felt at the airfield in Biloxi. It was as though everyone he met had a passport to this strange new territory, and only he had crossed the border with no papers.

The next night, when he took Rosalind home after a party in New Iberia, they kissed as they always had, and Skye's hands remained carefully on Rosalind's shoulders. She was wearing his ring, but he did not comment on it. Driving back home through the mist that rose up from the ponds and bayous that laced the land like silver threads, he felt as though the evening he had just spent with her already belonged to the dim and distant past, as though what they felt for each other had constraints that kept it apart from everything else that was happening in their lives.

As he got ready for bed that night, he caught sight of his body in the mirror above his chest of drawers. For a moment he was startled. Was that tall, lean, muscled body really his? He remembered the way Rosalind had looked at him when he stood naked before her. He had not understood that look then; he had been too confused, too torn with his own passion. But now, seeing the cool way he surveyed himself, he recognized the look as the one he had seen in Rosalind's eyes. Measuring. Appraising.

The breeze blowing in through his open windows teased him, light fingers down his spine. He made himself remember the minutes when he and Rosalind had not held back, but had let their feelings hold sway. He thought of the barracks talk, the constant dirty jokes, the stream of sexual innuendos. He couldn't reconcile the way he felt about Rosalind with the way he wanted her; for a long time he had subscribed to the ideas he had been taught, that some girls must be protected against themselves—and certainly against Skye's own desire.

Until this weekend, he would have put Rosalind Nasser in that category. Now—he wasn't so sure.

Caro put down David's letter and kicked her foot against the floor, setting the swing in motion. Sitting in this end of the porch, she was screened from the street by a heavy web of wisteria; deep purple, pale lavender, and white blossoms fell in thick clusters, embroidering the air with scent and color. She felt closed in, almost stifled, by the warm, humid air, the sweet perfume. She picked up the letter and read it again. "There isn't anything definite, of course—but somehow, I have a feeling I'm not going to be hanging around San Diego much longer." And then the last sentences. "I want you to come out here, Caro." Followed by an entreaty. "Please. I love you."

The letter had arrived two days before; the very next morning, Caro had spoken to her foreman about time off. "I want to go see someone off who's . . . shipping out," she said. The foreman's face had not changed. Caro's request was no different from the ones he heard regularly; as he checked her records and made a decision, she realized that he did not even know if she were married or not, engaged or not, or if this might be a brother she wanted to say good-bye to. He found four days for her, Friday through Monday of the following week. And so the first obstacle was overcome. A call to the travel agency knocked over the second one; she could get flights on those days, if she made the reservations right away. The ticket to San Diego was propped up now on her dressing table, a reminder that the final, and most substantial, obstacle was still to be crossed.

If she went to San Diego, she would have to make love to David. She could not possibly fly all the way out there and not go to bed with him. It would be not only ridiculous, but a lie. The word made her sit bolt upright. She turned it over in her mind, letting herself finally admit how dishonest her behavior was, what a betrayal of her true feelings. She loved David. Against the knowledge that he was shipping out, that it might be years before she saw him again, the codes of her childhood seemed small.

I want to make love with David. I want that more than anything, she thought. She leaned back against the swing and pushed it, the easy swaying motion accompanying her thoughts. She had slept with him many times in her dreams, had lain beneath him a hundred times, imagining how it would be. If she really believed everything the nuns at Mt. Carmel had told her as she was growing up, she had already sinned; it was supposed to be as bad to think about lust as to act on it. Somehow, she had never been able to accept that. It had always seemed to her that there must be some credit for resisting, some credit for not carrying out the dark acts spawned in an active brain.

Oddly enough, it was Henri who had given her a different perspective on her dilemma. They had been to see a movie, and had gone to the Camellia Grill for hamburgers and coffee afterward. Caro felt compelled to keep bringing the talk back to the heroine of the movie and her conflicts—although she herself hardly repressed her emotions as the sheltered Charlotte Vale did; she sympathized with the strictures her world put upon her, strictures Caro felt confined by herself.

"A lot of fuss over nothing," Henri said, peering at her over the rim of his cup.

"That's not what the Church says," Caro said.

"Most morality originated for practical reasons," Henri said. He signaled the waiter for more coffee, pausing until their cups were filled.

"Look at it this way. If married women play around, the wrong person might inherit property, titles."

"Henri!"

"It's true," he said. "Read history. Even," he added, smiling cynically, "the history of the Church."

"I can't make decisions based on—" she began. And then realized what she had said, and stopped, her face fiery red.

Henri's hand closed over hers. "Caro. If you want to sleep with David—sleep with him. If you don't, and anything happens to him while he's overseas, you'll regret it the rest of your life."

She had let the veil slip from her eyes, had let her confusion show. "Do you think I will?"

"Caro, the world's blowing up! Who the hell cares if you sleep with David or not?"

The thing was, she cared. She had to know whether the easy lip service she gave to principle meant anything. Or whether the principles themselves meant anything. When David had left for San Diego, she thought the issue had been put on hold "for the duration." But now it was here, embodied in an airline ticket and an invitation. She wished there were someone she could talk to, someone she could ask. What would her mother say, she wondered, if she asked her? That would be silly; she couldn't ask Mama for permission to make love with David. And then, as though David were sitting next to her, she seemed to hear him say, with that tender voice that made her feel so loved, so cared for: "Caro. You don't ask other adults for permission to live your life. If you're old enough to fly to me, to love me—you're old enough to make your own decision."

She stood up and walked slowly inside. She did not have to decide just yet. She had almost a week before the plane left, almost a week to come to terms with two alternatives: the possibility that she would regret sleeping with David—and the equal possibility that she would regret it more if she did not.

Raoul dropped by the next evening, full of news about his coursework, talking knowledgeably about IV's and blood tests, casually wearing a white lab coat with a stethoscope jammed in one pocket. She let his words drift over her, glad he was there to occupy her, sorry she could not ask him what he thought. And then she thought of a way he could help her, a practical question he could answer that she did not think she could ever ask David. If she decided to go.

"Raoul, in medical school, do they—well, do they teach you about . . . about contraceptives?" She found that she could not look at him, had to keep her eyes on the skirt she was hemming. The quality of Raoul's silence told her he saw through her question, and she thought she might as well get a bulletin out to all of them, announcing that she was considering having sex with David Selbin.

"Sure," he said. She waited to hear what else he would say, but nothing else came. After a minute or two he said, his voice soft, "Is that all you wanted to know?"

"Yes," she said. But when he left, she hugged him and kissed his cheek. "Thanks, Raoul."

"Sure," he said, and went off down the walk whistling.

And so she put all the bits and pieces together and decided to go. She had not yet fully decided just what kind of sin she would be committing: the Church said it was a mortal sin, but it also said just entertaining the idea was a mortal sin, and she could not buy that. She couldn't. David was simply too much a part of her. How could she not think of him that way? Anyway, she would take the risk that she would live long enough to make her peace with the Church. There was a careful distinction in her mind between God and the Church. God, she felt, had his hands full with the war. Only the part of the Church that carried on in safe America had time to worry about whether Caro Hamilton and David Selbin made love to each other. At least that is what she told herself.

Caro shifted the strap of her shoulder bag higher and stood on tiptoe to see past the people jammed in front of her. Where was David? The San Diego airport was a mass of blue Navy uniforms, with an occasional khaki appearing momentarily before being swallowed up again in the mass of blue. Of course I'm five hours late, she thought, trying to ignore the crick in her neck and the dull ache across her instep where someone's heavy foot had stepped. He may have had to go back to the base. If I can just get to the airline counter . . .

That seemed as impossible as the cross-country trip. She had been bumped off her flight in Dallas, and had to wait three hours before getting another one. Both planes had been crowded to capacity; screaming infants, weary mothers, lonely military personnel winging their way home on leave or returning to their bases—the stewards and stewardesses had spent the entire time dispensing comfort and reassurance. But airplanes were not only means of getting to some glamorous destination like New York or Paris. Like the great ocean liners that had been converted to troop ships, no plane flew that did not somehow further ultimate victory.

And then there had been the soldiers and sailors who had wanted to talk with her, buy her drinks. Even, during that wait in the Dallas airport, sleep with her. Except that was not the term the soldier had used. The term he used was quite direct and very explicit; no one watching them could know what he was saying, but Caro had finally had to give up the precious seat she had found in the crowded airport and flee to the ladies' room, which was more crowded, and smelled awful to boot, because there was no way facilities constructed for peacetime travel could possibly meet the needs of masses of women and children traveling for days, and who used public rest rooms for everything from sponge baths to laundry rooms to places to nurse babies.

Caro felt now as though she had the grime of weeks ground into her hair, her skin, her clothes. If she could have a shower. If she could wash her hair. If she could see David.

She felt surrounded by a wall of bodies; she stopped struggling to make a path through it, and let herself be carried along, the bag banging against her.

And then, suddenly, there was a hand on her arm, and a familiar voice in her ear. She turned. For one instant, all she saw was David's face: the curly black hair, the straight eyebrows, the blue eyes devouring her, the curve of his lips as he spoke her name. There were new hollows in his cheek, and a faint line of stubble on his jaw. And then she fell against him, crying his name over and over again, a litany to replace the old litanies she had left behind.

"God, you look wonderful!" he said, holding her against him.

"I look a mess," she said as she brushed her hair from her face. "I feel as though I crossed by wagon train."

"I'll bet," David said, making a path through the crowd. "I've been here most of the day myself, pestering the airline about when your plane would arrive."

She clung to his arm and let him lead the way; she felt that she had done everything there was for her to do. She was in his hands now, and she simply had to trust that he would take care of her.

David had a car outside, a battered convertible that ran on sheer hope, he said; he stowed her bag in the back seat, and after tucking her into the front, said, "Now, let's get the hell out of here."

"Where am I staying?" she asked. He had said, when she phoned to tell him she was coming, to leave that to him. "San Diego is an absolute madhouse," he had said. "You'd never find anything trying to make reservations from New Orleans."

"Friend of mine is letting us use his apartment," David said. "The hotel situation is ridiculous—overcrowded and overpriced. This way we've got a couple of rooms and a kitchen—and a great view of the ocean."

"Letting *us* use it," she said slowly, feeling each word as though it were a hot iron on her tongue.

"Caro. I thought that was resolved. We're not going to go through all that again, are we?"

He sounded weary, so weary that her own fatigue dropped away.

"No," she said. "We're not."

"Good," he said. "You know how I feel. How much I love you. How much I want you."

"Oh, David," she said, "you do, don't you?"

"So much it frightens me," he said.

"I thought I was the only one who was scared," she said.

The look he gave her seemed to come from a place inside him she did not yet know. "Darling. It's going to be fine."

"Yes," she said.

He swung off the main road into a byway that took them toward the water. Houses clustered thickly, their yards blooming with hibiscus and roses. They were built mostly of stucco, with arched doorways and leaded windowpanes, or with Spanish-looking tiles and turreted chimneys. Caro's own columned, shuttered world seemed very far away. Blue water glinted at the end of the street; small boats lined the dock, and the smell of sea air made her feel as though she had plunged into a cleansing pool.

David stopped the car at the last house on the street, a two-story house with windows facing the water. She wondered which ones were theirs. She lifted her arms overhead and stretched. "I can't remember when I've felt so grimy," she said.

"That's easily fixed," David said. She was suddenly conscious of the rooms upstairs—the waiting bedroom, the bath. Her heart beat harder, keeping pace with the fear that again seized her.

"I really am scared," she said.

"I know," David said. She heard passion roughening his voice, saw the sudden blaze in his eyes as he looked at her. His hands reached for her, pulled her close. "Let's get upstairs," he said, his mouth caressing her ear.

Then, as though some latch deep inside her had sprung, the door it locked suddenly free and open, she felt a rush of emotion so strong it broke through the last of her reluctance. All the denials, all the silly halts fell away, and nothing was left but her desire for him. "Yes," she breathed.

She stood on the threshold of the apartment, knowing that once she crossed its boundaries, she would be in a territory that she did not have to explore alone. They would explore it together, and whatever happened, she knew she would never forget it. David gave her a guiding nudge and she stepped into the room.

"Are you hungry?" David said. "I stocked up on stuff—"

"Yes," she said. "And I want a bath."

"I'll fix something while you bathe," he said.

She went into the bedroom and closed the door. The bed drew her eye; she found it difficult to believe that in a little while, she and David would be in it, and all the things she imagined would be happening. She shivered and began to undress, pulling off her travel-stained blouse, shrugging out of her skirt. She filled the tub almost to the brim, and let the water soothe her. She squeezed soapsuds over her, watching them spill down her breasts and fill the hollow of her stomach.

As she bathed, she imagined David's hands on her breasts, on her body. When she heard him in the bedroom, she hurried out of the tub, patted herself dry with a huge towel, and twisted it around her sarong-fashion. David looked up when she opened the bathroom door. He was holding a tray in his hands. He set the tray on the dresser and came to her, hands outstretched. Just as he reached her, he undid the knot that held the towel around her. It fell in a puddle of blue at her feet.

Then his mouth came down on hers, tongue probing. One hand cupped her breasts, while the other roved over her body. She couldn't believe the tide of passion rolling over her: she couldn't believe that it was she, Caro Hamilton, tugging at David's clothes, thrusting her tongue deep into his mouth. "You have too many clothes on," she said huskily, struggling to get the words out.

"Give me a minute," he said. He moved away from her and began to undress, never taking his eyes off her. Then he was naked too, yanking the spread from the bed, tumbling her onto it. She pulled him on top of her, pressing her body against his. Moments later, as he entered her, she thought, in a last flash of absolute certainty, how very right she was to come.

By the end of the second day, when they had gotten up only for food, when they had spent every hour discovering each other's secrets, each other's bodies, Caro turned in his arms and laughed softly. "I was thinking," she said.

"What?" David said, bending to kiss her.

"I'd better get some postcards so I can describe San Diego when I get back." She laughed again, a teasing, conspiratorial sound. "I'd hate to admit that all I saw was the airport and this room.

8

JULY 1943

Thick dust roiled up from the ditches that lay between the canefields and the gravel road, adding yet another layer to the dirt that covered the convoy of trucks carrying German prisoners of war to St. Martinville. They were headed to the prison camp set up at the old Conservation Corps camp in Evangeline Park on the outskirts of town. As the trucks entered the town and began winding through it, people came out of their houses and stood silently watching the prisoners go by. A parade without drumbeats, a victory without flags. It was noon, and as the trucks passed the church, the Angelus began to toll. All over town, heads bowed and hands made the sign of the Cross. And in the trucks, heads bowed also, and more than one prisoner heard the bells with a sense of being once again in a world that possessed continuity.

In a makeshift office at the camp, Caroline and Émilie Langlinais waited along with other Red Cross personnel to receive the prisoners. This day marked the end of weeks of negotiations with the commanding officer at Camp Polk in Leesville, one of the three main POW camps in Louisiana. The prisoners were received there, then assigned to one of the side camps being set up across the state. More than one farmer who had stood staring at fields of cane, or cotton, or rice, wondering how in hell he was ever going to get it harvested, hoped to be saved by the POWs who spread through rural Louisiana that summer of 1943, taking up the terrible slack left by men who had gone to war.

The machine put together by General Dwight David Eisenhower and the British General Bernard Montgomery to sweep Field Marshal Rommel from North Africa had worked; it had swept three hundred thousand of his Afrika Corps into ships heading for America. It was part of this great flood of men which now reached St. Martinville.

Caroline rose and went to the open door, looking out at the rows of empty barracks in front of her. They could accommodate as many as six hundred men for the harvest peak in the fall; this first group would be about two hundred. That two hundred would constitute the year-round complement. Year-round complement? she thought. Good God in heaven, were these men really settled here for the duration? What kind of crazy world was it, when your deadly enemies tilled your fields? The Angelus bell's toll floated to her across the still air, and she began to recite the familiar words. "The Angel of the Lord declared unto Mary, and she conceived of the Holy Spirit. Hail, Mary, full of Grace—"

And then she saw the first of the trucks, its headlamps making circles of light against the thick dust that blanketed the July day. She grasped the doorpost. These men were not her enemy; they had families—fathers who loved them, mothers who worried about them, wives who were lonely for them, children who wanted them home. She pushed the screen door wide. An American officer leapt from the first truck and approached her. "Mrs. Langlinais?"

"Yes," she said. "We're ready."

As she went back to her place in the line of workers, she looked at the others quickly. The women's faces declared their personal involvement in the war, she thought. Those with no immediate relative fighting in America's armed forces looked curious, a little excited at this break in summer's tedium. Those who had men in the war were tense, holding themselves together rigidly, as though when they had buttoned themselves into their stiffly starched dresses they had buttoned their flesh too.

By late afternoon the routine had numbed them all. A gray line of men marched through the door in front of Caroline, stopped at her desk to be registered, and then passed on down the line of tables to receive ditty bags Girl Scout troops and Junior Red Cross members had been putting together for weeks. A steady line of men, feet scuffing across the floor, men dusty, sweaty, pale with fatigue, or flushed with the oppressive heat, blond, dark-haired, tall, short, fat, lean. And the eyes. Always the eyes. Anxious. Cold. And only occasionally, a question, a hesitant greeting in German, or French, or English. Once in a while, a low-voiced comment to a fellow prisoner. A sudden shock of laughter. A tremble of fear went down the line of women as they were confronted with a hostility far older than war.

Men denied women, Caroline thought, looking at them again. She mentally checked over the list of activities the committee had arranged, everything from concerts to amateur theatrics. She thought of the plantations stretching on either side of the camp, waiting for the work these men could provide. She thought of the scarcity of guards, the isolation of the houses. And she resolved to keep Émilie busy at the farm or in town at the office. But not here. And not at her beloved—and now dangerous—Beau Chêne.

It had begun to rain on the last leg of the transatlantic flight, a driving rain that buffeted the plane and fell off its wings in cloaks of gray. Skye, perched on one of the benches that ran the length of the transport, twisted around and watched the gray rain merge with the gray waters of the Atlantic Ocean. He was one of the first to catch a glimpse of England; looking at that rain-veiled shore, he remembered his first trip here, the summer of 1936, when his father and Mère had taken all six of their children to Europe to celebrate their wedding.

That trip had been a montage of cathedrals and museums, five-star hotels and quiet country inns. He remembered how, in the early days of the war, he, or Henri, or Raoul, or one of the girls would come across a familiar name in a news story and turn and say, "Remember that little village in France where we had lunch with a real marquise in her château? It was bombed yesterday." And he remembered how hard it was for them to look at the photo album crammed with pictures: all of them frolicking on a beach now barricaded with barbed wire, or posing in front of the Eiffel tower in what was now Nazi-occupied Parris. At least, he thought, as the transport began her lumbering descent, I've never been out into the English countryside. I won't have any memories attached to my new base.

He was no more certain of the exact location of the air base than any of the other men on the transport; somewhere between Brighton and Portsmouth, they had decided. Since the British Bomber Command and the American Eighth Air Force had begun their combined Bomber Offensive, the air power of both nations had been concentrated in the south of England.

Skye was sure that if each American pilot on that transport had been quizzed before he left the plane about the history of the Eighth Air Force, and its military objectives, he could have recited them as easily as his own name: created early in 1942 for the specific purpose of daylight bombing; the first contingent had arrived in the British Isles in May 1942. Because the U.S. Army Air Force had commitments in the Pacific and in North Africa, its arm in England remained at less than full strength for a considerable period of time. At the end of 1942, the

Eighth Air Force had only one hundred heavy bombers operating from its bases in Huntingdonshire and East Anglia.

One hundred was not nearly enough. Daylight bombing was particularly hazardous because the fighter planes which normally escorted bombers did not have as long a flight range; in order for American heavy bombers—the Liberators and the Flying Fortresses—to bomb German territory effectively without escorts, the Americans needed a base force of seven hundred bombers, with three hundred of those able to fly on any one raid. Only by sheer numbers could the American bombers survive German antiaircraft batteries and the desperate skill of the Luftwaffe.

Now, with the war in North Africa over, some air power could be deflected to England, and to the air war against Germany. On June 10, the "Pointblank" directive had been issued: the British and American air forces would work in tandem. By night, German targets would be hit by the British heavy bomber, the Lancaster, whose way was marked by Pathfinders, planes that flew low over the target area and dropped bright red flares. By day, American B-17's, the Flying Fortresses, and B-24's, the Liberators, would fly en masse over the same target. The primary objective of Pointblank was to destroy and dislocate the German military, industrial, and economic system, at the same time undermining the morale of the German people. Targets were prioritized; first, the German submarine-construction yards and pens, followed by the aircraft industry, transportation systems, oil plants, and other key factories in the German war industry.

"Going to really get a taste of it," one of Skye's fellow pilots had said after their last briefing before leaving for England. "Daylight bombing, now that's a hell of a thing. Nothing between us and them but a few clouds—I should have signed on with the limeys when I had the chance."

"Our heavy bombers can fly higher than the flak," Skye said. "And our gunners can take out the Luftwaffe."

"So they say. I'd still feel better if the fighters could stay with us the whole way—gets kind of lonesome up there when you see them heading back, even in maneuvers. What the hell's it going to feel like when it's the real thing?"

Now, watching the runway come up to meet the plane, feeling the hard bounce as the tires hit the tarmac, Skye felt the sour taste of fear in his mouth. He could see the wisdom behind a plan to pound German targets day and night. But thinking of films he had seen of those lightning-fast Luftwaffe fighters, thinking of the broad expanse of metal belly a heavy bomber exposed, he was reminded of the way he had once felt when he was swimming in Bayou Teche; Gennie had cried sharply that there was a 'gator in the water, and he had hightailed for shore, arms flailing, legs kicking frantically. He could still remember how his stomach muscles tensed, as though to make some kind of shield against the sharp teeth and crushing jaws that lay somewhere in the murky water below him. But you got away, he told himself. You swam in that bayou a thousand times more, and you always came home safe.

And then the door was open, and he was hefting his duffel bag and following the line of men out into the rain. A small cluster of RAF pilots waited at the foot of the ladder, holding out their hands and greeting each American as he walked by. At the far end of the field stood a group of buildings; their bulk loomed through the rain, and Skye let fatigue wash over him. What he needed was a drink, some food, and a bed, in just that order. As though reading his mind, one of the RAF pilots fell into step beside him.

"Tony Harrington," he said, offering his hand. "Welcome to England."

"Skye Langlinais," Skye said. "I don't suppose you'd know where there's such a thing as a drink?"

"What I'm here to tell you," Harrington said. "We're throwing a little party in the officers' quarters—came out to ask you Yanks to join us."

"You're stationed here?" Skye asked. "Isn't this an American base?"

"Liaison," Harrington answered. "Working out the details of this Combined Bomber Offensive." Harrington seemed hardly able to contain a kind of jubilance that charged his voice and energized his body. When they joined the others, and the new arrivals had been given drinks, Skye learned the reason for Harrington's elation. Two nights before, on July 24, the British Bomber Command had made its first raid against Hamburg. Seven hundred and ninety-one planes, all but seventy-three of them four-engine bombers, had made the run, and all but twelve returned safely. The raid had incorporated a new radar-jamming technique called "Window"; strips of aluminum-coated paper ten and a half inches long had been dropped in the air over Germany in large quantities, clouding or jamming the radar that directed German flak and night fighters.

And the next day, 252 American bombers had hit Hamburg, fighting their way through clouds of smoke that obscured their primary targets, a submarine yard and an aircraft-engine factory. "Some of the smoke was from fires the Germans set for just that purpose," Harrington said. "And of course some of it was from targets we'd hit the night before." He refilled Skye's glass. "It'll take a while to get this one-two punch going. But we're damn glad to have you aboard."

Questions flooded Skye's lips, but he drowned them with a swallow of whiskey. What's it like? he wanted to ask. How do you feel when you see a city in flames? Looking around the small, close room, he was struck by the difference in the faces of the British fliers and the newly arrived Americans. Harrington and his fellows had the sharp-honed look of men who work without enough sleep, with little release from tension, with little letup from strain.

Skye and the others still looked fresh, rested. Untried. He shivered and turned the collar of his jacket up. July, and still chilly. A lot to get used to, he thought.

". . . about three hundred and forty miles now. And they're working on increasing that."

"What's that?" Skye said, moving closer to the central group.

"Our Thunderbolts can take us in as far as three hundred and forty miles from the takeoff point, Langlinais. They're adding gasoline tanks anywhere they can bolt 'em."

Within minutes they were all talking shop. Remembering those early bull sessions back at Keesler, Skye had a vision of himself then. Young, so terribly young. And ignorant, my God, how ignorant! Thought all there was to being a pilot was a little knowledge and a lot of guts. He nodded at Harrington, who was holding out the bottle. Now he was only a little older, in terms of days, weeks—but far less ignorant. He could listen to this discussion of evasion tactics, and follow the maneuvers in his head. He could listen to a debate about the relative merits of the British Lancaster versus the American Liberator and understand the arguments on both sides.

He drifted toward a curtained window that gave onto the edge of the airfield. The window had black cloth tacked over it, as did every window on the base. This close to the coast, shells from submarines were as much a threat as bombs from planes; when Skye began to explore the countryside around the base, he would discover that road signs had been taken down and that the roads he traveled were a maze for the uninitiated. If saboteurs landed, they would not be able to simply read where they were.

Standing there, watching the others, listening, measuring, he was aware that he was doing just what his father had taught him to do when he was hunting on unfamiliar ground: "Get your directions straight so you'll know exactly where you are. Read the signs so you'll know what else is in the woods with you." Good advice, Skye thought. Advice that had served him well more than once. Whether it would prove useful in the skies over Germany remained to be seen.

And then from above him came a steady, throbbing sound, the sound of planes flying steadily through the dark. The sound grew until it dominated the room, and everyone stopped talking, eyes staring up through the ceiling as though to see the hundreds of planes overhead.

"Hamburg again," Harrington said, looking at his watch. His eyes met Skye's. "If they leave any of it, you might get to make that run yourself."

The 787 bombers that hit Hamburg that night of July 27, 1943, did not in fact leave much. More than twelve hundred tons of incendiaries were dropped with high precision and unusual concentration; the result was a firestorm that appeared within half an hour of the first bombing wave—an airman told Skye later that the clouds, illuminated by that towering blaze, looked like "cotton dipped in blood." And although it would be a long time before the Battle of Hamburg had its full effect, its immediate effect, coupled with the fall from power of Italy's Benito Mussolini on July 25, was to shake the German High Command badly. Air Marshal Goering was stunned; his Führer's reaction was characteristic. Greeting an emissary from the new Italian leader, Marshal Pietro Badoglio, several days after the July 27 strike, Hitler said, "The day will come, maybe three hundred years from now, when we will be able to avenge ourselves."

But for Skye Langlinais, and hundreds of American pilots like him, Hamburg meant only one thing—carrying the war into the heart of Germany on wings whose greatest power was the courage of the men who flew them.

The small oscillating fan set on a file cabinet across from Henri's desk moved listlessly from side to side, barely stirring the hot, humid air. It riffled the edges of papers stacked all over the desk, and on the credenza behind it, occasionally managing to lift one and send it wafting to the floor.

But the fan was not responsible for the chill that gripped Henri and made the sweat on his forehead cold. His eyes were fixed on the letter in his hand; already its edges were damp, and he had a sensation that it was melting into his flesh, its words becoming part of him, something he had to live with the rest of his days.

For the first time since he had talked Beau into letting him run Carolina Oil, a small production company Beau had put together just before the war started, he regretted it. He tried to remember how he had felt a few minutes ago, before he had opened this letter. He tried to remember the pride he'd had, reading Carolina Oil's latest production figures. In 1941, the United States oil industry, already the producer of two-thirds of the world's petroleum, broke all previous records with a total of approximately 1.4 billion barrels of crude oil. And by the first day of this hot July of 1943, private industry had completed 63 percent of its wartime expansion plans. The fact that part of that production was 100-octane gas gave the Allies an edge their enemies did not have. Forty thousand barrels of high-octane gas per day flowed fom American plants to the fighters and bombers manning Pacific and European defense and offense; high-octane gas gave planes more power, greater takeoff speed, greater climbing speed, a higher ceiling, and the capacity for a longer range and a heavier load. The crucial role oil played in the Allied war machine made well owners rich, and Henri had watched Carolina Oil's profits grow with a real sense of achievement. That pride did him good; when he met other businessmen for lunch at Mike and Tony's or the Italian Gardens, they no longer joked about ordering milk for the baby, but listened to him and made him one of them.

The letter changed all that. Once this got out, no one would ever want to have lunch with him. Père would bundle him back to Loyola, saying that the decision he'd made in January to let Henri leave college for a while and help on the home front was obviously premature. He read the letter again, as though hoping he'd misread the words. But no, they still said the same incredible thing, still sounded the same awful knell: three payments on a note securing the loan covering the purchase of a synthetic-rubber factory had been missed; in the absence of payment from Mr. Mitchell, Mr. Henri Hamilton of Carolina Oil, as cosigner, was obligated for the entire amount.

How could this be? He had signed nothing. When Henri had gone to Beau, who as chairman of the board of Carolina Oil had the final say, four months ago with Mitch's proposal, Beau had listened carefully, making detailed notes. "Mitch has narrowed the process down to butyl," Henri said. "There're four ways to make synthetic rubber, and a lot of people go for Buna-S, because it's the best-known process. But butyl is easier, it's quicker—and the raw materials for it are cheaper."

"Is it as useful as Buna-S? If butyl's too limited—"

"It's every bit as flexible," Henri said. "They're using it a lot to make inner tubes. Fact is, Mitch says if we sign the papers this week, we can be selling the stuff in a month."

"I didn't know things had gotten that far," Beau said.

"Mitch said you told him to call me," Henri countered.

Beau recognized the exchange for what it was: Henri was pitting his own experience and acumen against Beau's, determined to prove to Beau how capable and grown-up he was. But I already know how bright Henri is, Beau thought. He's able to grasp details of business that escape many men with more experience, and sharp in a way that's a good match for the demands of his job. If I could only convince Henri of that, our troubles would be over. But no one's opinion means a damn thing if you don't think well of yourself—and for some reason, Henri was not impressed with Henri.

"I did tell him to call you," Beau said, making his voice easy. "But surely he's given you a prospectus. I told him, as I've told you—I'm not going to sink a lot of money into a project without looking at some actual figures."

"He said they mailed it last week," Henri said. His voice sounded defensive, and his lips began to slip into the familiar pout. "You know how long it takes mail to get delivered now. If we have to wait around for that, the whole deal could fall apart. The factory's been on the market almost five weeks now. Mitch has the inside track—but we have to move fast, or they'll find another buyer."

"We'll just have to take that chance, Henri. I'm sorry, but we're talking about a lot of money. I have to use the same rules in every deal I get into. And I've never invested that kind of money without seeing a prospectus—at the very least."

"It's an awfully good deal," Henri said.

"It sounds like an awfully good deal," Beau said, putting the slightest stress on "sounds." "I'm extremely pleased with the way you've handled the preliminaries, Henri. You've done very well. Still, Mitch can't expect us to close the deal without solid information to go on." Beau looked at Henri, his voice still easy. "As a matter of fact, it surprises me Mitch would propose this without having done his homework."

"I guess he thinks you trust him," Henri muttered.

"That really doesn't have anything to do with it," Beau said.

Henri opened his mouth, then closed it. "All right. I'll tell Mitch he's got to get that prospectus to us, or the whole deal's off."

"There are always other deals, Henri," Beau said. "When word gets out what a good businessman you are, you're going to have more things to consider than you can handle."

"More things to investigate for *you* to consider," Henri said.

"For you to consider, too," Beau said. "After all, I don't expect to hear about anything you don't think is a good idea. And remember, Carolina Oil is half your mother's. You'll own part of it someday—which means the profits you make for it are yours, too."

"I forget that sometimes," Henri said, looking more cheerful. "Okay, I'll tell Mitch what we decided."

And he had. He was sure he had.

Frantically he reviewed his last meeting with Mitch Mitchell in

March. Mitch had not come up with a prospectus, and Beau's "no deal" had stood firm. Mitch had listened, saying nothing, only his eyes betraying his anger. Fumbling through the papers in his briefcase, Mitch handed Henri a long, closely written sheaf of documents. "You'll need to sign this release," he said. "It relieves you of any precontract commitments."

Henri had not really understood what Mitch was talking about; he had begun reading the papers when Sallie Mitchell had come in with a tray of highballs. One highball had become two, then three. He had tucked the papers aside to take home and read later, and had spent the rest of the evening drinking and listening to Sallie sing. It had made him feel better about the whole thing that the Mitchells were still friendly; he had fallen into the habit of dropping by the cottage on Oleander Street these first months in Baton Rouge. His small apartment wasn't very homey, and with Skye gone, he really didn't know many people. The Mitchells were fun, not that much older than he was—and Sallie made him feel wonderful.

Mitch had disappeared at some point, murmuring something about work, and things were foggy after that. He thought he remembered sitting on the sofa with Sallie, he thought he even remembered kissing her. That memory always made him squirm; when he woke the next morning, he couldn't remember whether he had read the papers and signed them, or just left them near his chair. He decided he'd wait for Mitch to call; when Mitch didn't, Henri decided he must have read the papers after all, and signed them when he was still sober.

He didn't drop by the Mitchells' house for some time after that. Beau had dropped a couple of other deals in his lap, and by the time he'd looked into them and completed negotiations, he'd met some people his own age. He kept thinking he would run into Mitch somewhere; for months, he had hardly gone anywhere without seeing that familiar bulk, hearing that raucous laughter. But then he forgot all about the Mitchells, put his back into his work, and had the satisfaction of seeing Carolina Oil flourish.

Until now.

Time after time, his hand reached for his telephone, and time after time, it drew back. Finally he snatched the receiver from its cradle and dialed the operator. "I want to place a person-to-person call to Mr. Conrad Johnson at the First National Bank in Greenville, Ohio," he said, reading off the bank's number from Johnson's letter. "I'll hold until you get through."

It took close to fifteen minutes, minutes Henri spent smoking and staring through his open window at the traffic on Third Street. Two girls with wide-brimmed straw hats and white gloves strolled down the sidewalk, looking at the displays in Dalton's windows, idling away a summer afternoon. A couple of airmen from Harding Field stopped near the girls, ostensibly looking in the same windows. Damn. What he'd give to be one of those men, his uniform announcing his patriotism, making his way for him. What he'd give to be anywhere else, be anyone else but Henri Hamilton, gripping a slippery telephone and wishing for a miracle.

When Johnson finally came on the line, Henri could barely speak. "Henri Hamilton here," he said. "With Carolina Oil. I got your letter today. And I have to tell you that that was the first I knew of any loan. We . . . I turned down that deal with Mitchell. I'm not in it at all."

"That's not what the records say," Johnson said. "We've got a complete file on this loan. Your signature is on several documents—a financial statement about Carolina Oil, an assignment of its assets as collateral—"

"Collateral!" The word exploded from Henri's lips, blowing away the cobwebs that shrouded his brain. "Mr. Johnson, I don't know what you've got, but if you have a document giving Carolina Oil as collateral for that loan, I know damn well I didn't sign it. For that matter, you must know I didn't sign it. I would have to have come to Ohio, come to the bank."

There was a silence at the other end of the wire, and Henri thought that this whole bad dream was over. Whatever the error was, he hadn't made it. Who ever heard of a bank lending money on the signature of an unseen partner?

"I'm afraid that's not the case," Johnson said. "We ran a thorough check on you, on Carolina Oil—and one of our officers assured me that he had spoken to you on the telephone several times, in the presence of Mr. Mitchell, to affirm that what you said in writing was true. In fact, I have written memos describing every one of those calls in case you need to refresh your memory."

"There's nothing wrong with my memory," Henri said, forcing the fragments of that night in March back into the dark. "Maybe you'd better send someone down here with those papers you say you've got."

The silence was longer now, and then Johnson spoke. "You're putting yourself in a pretty untenable position, Mr. Hamilton. This bank is well within its rights to start proceedings to take over Carolina Oil."

"I wouldn't do that until you've sent someone down here," Henri said. "Look, let's talk to each other as though we're on the same side, all right? Because if Mitchell went to all the trouble he apparently did, he must have gotten something out of it."

"He got the money for the factory, that's what he got out of it," Johnson said.

"Then why isn't the factory collateral? Wouldn't that be the normal procedure?"

"The factory isn't operative yet," Johnson said.

"Mitch told me it was ready to go!" Henri exploded.

"So you are aware of this deal," Johnson said, his voice cold.

"We discussed it. I told him no," Henri answered.

"But I hold a document naming Carolina Oil as the interim collateral. We want our money, Mr. Hamilton."

"There is a factory?"

"Of course there's a factory! Our officers inspected it—what do you take us for, Mr. Hamilton?"

"It's what Mitch Mitchell takes us both for, I'm afraid," Henri said. "I'm sure there is a factory—but I'd be very surprised if Mitch Mitchell owns it. Look—I'm going to get hold of Mitchell—and in the meantime, you better get someone down here. If you start proceedings to take over Carolina Oil without being sure of your ground, you could be in a countersuit that would ruin you." He slammed the phone down without waiting to hear Johnson's response. Christ, what a mess! He lit a cigarette and walked to the window. The girls and airmen were gone, whether together or separately, he didn't know. His sense of security was gone, too, as was his sense of power. He stood watching his smoke drift straight out into the heavy air, making a small gray ribbon. He waited for his mind to provide an answer, but none came. Call Mitch, he told himself. He'll explain. But as he watched the cigarette burn to the end, he knew that when he called Mitch, he would find no one there, and that there would be only one explanation that fit all the facts. Somehow, Mitch had tricked him. Somehow, Mitch had made him his dupe.

The memory of that night in March returned, but now it was sharp and clear, brought into focus by his fear. He could see himself lounging against those rich silk pillows, Sallie bending over him, red hair shimmering in the glow of one small lamp. Sallie putting a pen in his hand, holding the paper while he traced his name. Traced it once. Not several times. Not on several documents. Only once.

So that was how Mitch had done it. Gotten one signature, forged the others. As for the man the bank officer had spoken to—it could have been anyone. Henri ground out his cigarette and picked up the telephone once more. He dialed the operator, heard her come on the line. He almost gave her his stepfather's office in Washington, and then thought better of it, and hung up. Beau would get him out of this, he knew that. But if he did . . . Henri shook his head. The consequences of having to run to Père were far worse than the consequences the bank president had outlined. No, he'd figure this one out for himself. But the first thing he'd do was to find Mitch Mitchell.

It did not take many phone calls to learn that no one knew where Mitch Mitchell was; when, later that afternoon, Henri drove by the house on Oleander Street before going home, it had a closed look. Grass grew up over the sidewalk, and a few rain-stained newspapers clustered at the bottom of the steps. Funny, he thought, a line of fear marching down his spine, how a place that looked so cozy in March looked so alien now. His stomach seemed to plummet, and his heart began beating very fast. He forced himself to breathe calmly as he got back in his car and drove slowly home. That evening he sat alone in his darkened apartment, staring out into the night, beginning to plan.

9

SEPTEMBER 1943

Caro pushed her way past the couples dancing in the space cleared between a massive walnut armoire at one end of the small living room and a marble-manteled fireplace at the other, coming out breathlessly to stand on the balcony overlooking Royal Street. "Whew!" she said, leaning against the wrought-iron rail and fanning herself vigorously. "One more Buddy Rich number, and I'm gone."

"I don't believe it for a minute," Walter Fournet said, following her and handing her a glass. "You're the best dancer in New Orleans, Caro Hamilton. It'll take more than Buddy Rich to make you sit down."

"That Sinatra record is more my speed," Caro said, nodding toward the living room. Henri had put on "I'll Never Smile Again"; the intimacy of Sinatra's voice and the lateness of the hour made couples huddle, swaying, almost not moving; how many of them will end up in bed, Caro thought, feeling the quick tightening of her pelvis, the sudden awful ache for David. She sipped her drink and looked up at Walter.

"Would you believe that I still have stuff my grandfather laid down before Prohibition? He must have had enough stashed away to float a yacht."

"Glad he did," Henri said, joining them. "You certainly know how to give parties, Walter." He looked back into the apartment, furnished with a tasteful blend of family pieces and what Walter called his finds. "This is probably the nicest apartment in the Quarter. I know people who would kill for this."

"So do I," Walter said. "If you ever need a place to hang your hat—I'm out of town a lot, you're welcome to stay here."

"I might take you up on that sometime," Henri said. "Cousin Robert is always glad to have me—but since he believes in retiring at ten, and expects his guests to do the same, I don't mind admitting staying there cramps my style."

Thank heaven, Caro thought, Henri was in a good mood. The few times she had seen him during the summer, he seemed worried about something, more withdrawn and irritable than he had been in a long time. When Gennie had called to tell her she was joining a USO troupe leaving New Orleans the first weekend of September, and that they were all gathering for a farewell celebration, Caro had almost hoped Henri wouldn't show up. It would be too bad, she thought, if his still-tender feelings about not being in the service himself marred Gennie's sendoff.

But Henri had blown in full of goodwill and high spirits. By the time they had put Gennie on the plane earlier today, Caro was convinced that leaving college and getting into the business world was the best thing that could have happened to Henri. She saw the way Père turned the conversation to Henri's achievements, heard her mother underscore how vital Carolina Oil's production was to the war effort, and watched Henri bask in their obvious approval.

Walter and Henri began discussing the effects of having All-American football players drawn to the Tulane campus by the Navy ROTC program on the upcoming football season, and Caro stood idly watching the street below. It was past midnight, and although the noise from Bourbon Street was as loud as though the evening were just beginning, Royal Street had closed its shutters and gone to bed. Only a few lights in a few apartments were still lit, and except for the music floating out from Walter's party, the only sounds on the street were an occasional late-partying couple and a rare automobile passing by.

So when an open-topped convertible drove past, Caro leaned over and looked at the couple inside. The car itself was long and black, a piece of ebony shining under the streetlights. The interior was deep crimson; the girl sitting so near the driver wore a white dress, and its skirt spilled over the red seat like a bandage across a field of blood. The man had his arm around the girl's shoulder. Like so many wartime couples, he was much older. His hair was silver, hers jet black. Then the girl laughed, throwing her head back and opening her mouth wide. And Caro, standing almost directly above her, saw with an ugly jolt who the girl sitting in that car was. Rosalind Nasser. Skye's girl.

"Anything wrong?" Walter said, seeing her turn abruptly away.

"Nothing," Caro said. She held out her glass. "Can you give me some more of that wonderful gin, Walter? And I think you're right—I'm well up to Buddy Rich and any other drummer who wants to take me on."

"That's my girl," Walter said, steering her toward the living room.

"I'm heading out," Henri said. "Thanks for the party, Walter. Caro, I'll say good-bye now. I'm going back to Baton Rouge first thing tomorrow."

"Don't make me think about tomorrow," Caro said. "It's going to arrive entirely too soon as it is."

"I can let myself out," Henri said, shaking Walter's hand and kissing Caro. Then he wove swiftly through the crowd, suddenly fearful he would be late for his appointment with Mitch Mitchell.

Just when he had thought he could no longer keep Père from learning what a mess he was in, the long-prayed-for miracle had happened. Mitch Mitchell had called him, full of apologies and swearing that everything was fine. "It's a long story," Mitch said. "I got sent out of the country—can't say where or what—and Sallie went home to visit her family. But I'll be in New Orleans this weekend, and we'll get this thing straight."

"Johnson sent a man down with the documents, Mitch," Henri said. "I met with him three weeks ago. My name's all over the damn place."

"Now, hold your horses," Mitch said, the big voice flowing like the bonded bourbon he poured in such generous measures. "I said it was a long story—it's also a damn fantastic one. But you just trust Mitch, Henri. You're going to be just fine."

Since that call, Henri had hung suspended between hope and doubt, but the combination of his early belief in Mitch and the fast-paced family weekend had swung his mood to the positive side, and as he swung down the sidewalk, heading toward the address Mitch had given him, he began to whistle. The whistle changed to a low, drawn-out sound of dismay when he found the hotel on Dauphine. Although he didn't have much experience, if he had to guess, he'd say this was a hot-sheet joint, one of the places so low that even adventure-seeking college boys stayed away from it. He walked around the block twice, coming back to stand before the door, staring at it as though that would bring Mitch out to him.

The fact that Mitch was actually staying here alarmed him; what kind of man would bring his wife to a joint like this? A flood of memories, each one of which underscored the fact that he and Mitch were from very different worlds, filled his mind. Doubt that Mitch could straighten this mess out undermined his failing confidence, and his heart began a rapid, irregular beat. He stood fighting the impulse to run, held in place only by the praise Père and his mother had heaped on him earlier that day. Was it only twelve hours ago that he had sat at the table at the Caribbean Room, modestly disclaiming the achievements they praised?

A woman came up from behind him and put her face close to his. "Wanna go upstairs?" she asked. Her powder had worn away, and her forehead and nose shone like patches of moisture in the dim light. Only the deep wrinkles in her cheeks were powdered, and here it was like a layer of dust filling in crevices in the soil. A ruin of a face, a ruin of an evening. A ruin of a life, Henri thought, and felt a surge of energy. He had to go up and see what Mitch had to say; instead of standing here in a blue funk, he should be charging up the stairs, eager to get this thing over. He shoved the woman aside and darted into the hotel, blinking his eyes to accustom them to darkness deeper than that of the street outside. He saw a red light glowing, with numbers showing faintly underneath, and went toward the elevator with his face averted from the desk, where a clerk snored loudly. God, what a dump! His spirits rose. If Mitch were in such desperate circumstances that he could afford nothing better than this place, Henri might be able to get this mess worked out after all. No man this poor had much behind him. Thinking of the money and power he had at his command, Henri smiled.

His sureness increased as he left the elevator and walked down the hall toward the room number Mitch had given him. The ceiling was low, the walls disfigured with cracks and stains. The carpet beneath Henri's feet was so thin that he could feel the uneven floorboards under it. He knocked on the door marked 318 loudly, making each rap an announcement of his confidence.

Mitch opened the door and stood there, his bulk almost filling the doorway. Then he stepped aside. Henri had a blurred view of a dressing table with powder spilled across its surface, of hair caught in combs and brushes. Lingerie, the straps and lace dingy and gray, was thrown carelessly over chairs, and a pair of stockings made a silken snake on the floor. He could hear his mother admonishing Caro—"No one should ever know a lady has even been in a dressing room or a bathroom. She doesn't leave a single trace." Well, if that were so, Sallie Mitchell was no lady.

And then he saw her, flying toward him, stripped naked. He felt Mitch grab him and rip his coat off, yank his shirt open. Sallie unbuckled his belt, jerked his trousers down, and reached inside his shorts. He felt Mitch throw him across the bed, and Sallie jumped on top of him, her moist skin rubbing against him, her breath hot on his face. Something else was going on, an insistent light that flashed and flashed and flashed—my God, a camera. He gathered his strength and forced her from him, thrusting her away while he stumbled from the bed. A small man holding a camera tucked it under his arm and fled out the door Mitch held for him. Then the door slammed, and he was gone.

"Well," Sallie said, putting on a bright green Japanese silk kimono and taking the lighted cigarette Mitch handed her. "Sorry you weren't more interested, Henri. Long as you're paying the price, you might as well have gotten your money's worth."

"What do you want?" Henri said angrily as he pulled up his pants and buttoned his shirt.

"We have what we want," Mitch said, sitting heavily on the bed. "Leastways, we will when those pictures are developed." He blew smoke toward Henri. "Those pictures are insurance, Henri. Insurance that you'll drop the trouble you're making and behave yourself."

"Trouble I'm making! Listen, Mitch, you forged my name—"

Mitch held up a broad, flat hand. "Save it, Henri. I'm not interested in all that."

"You'd better be interested! I talked to a lawyer—we can prove those signatures are forgeries—and you know it."

"As I said, I'm not interested. Whatever you thought you were going to do before tonight, I'm sure you won't do it now."

"And why not?" Henri demanded. But as though he had been holding the camera, the pictures of him and Sallie flashed through his brain.

"I don't think you want your mother—or your stepfather—to see those pictures. Matter of fact, they might not see them—first. Maybe some of your illustrious stepfather's political enemies would get their hands on them. Or some of your mother's lady friends."

Henri knew the futility of his protest as soon as he uttered it. Of course Mitch would do just what he was threatening. He found a last scrap of dignity and faced Mitch squarely. "All right. What do you want?"

"That's better," Mitch said. "Sallie, fix me a drink. You want one, Henri?"

"Thank you, no," Henri said. His legs trembled and he wanted to sit down, but he would not give Mitch—nor that woman—the satisfaction of seeing him give way. He locked his knees and made himself stand straight.

"Now, as I understand it, you have to pay that Ohio bank, isn't that the case?"

"Those documents are forged—"

"But those pictures validate them," Mitch said.

"I won't let them take Carolina Oil, Mitch. You're out of your mind if you think I will."

"You don't have to let them take Carolina Oil. You only have to pay the debt."

"And where in the hell would I get that kind of money?"

"You control Carolina Oil's stock, don't you?"

"What are you getting at?"

"If you sold me, say, three-eighths of the stock—I'd pay you enough to satisfy the loan."

"Three-eighths! You're crazy! That's a family corporation! I can't—"

"You can, Henri. So far, you won't. But I imagine by tomorrow afternoon, when you see those pictures, and the envelopes all ready to mail them in—you'll change your mind." Mitch crushed out his cigarette and got off the bed. His big hand closed on Henri's collar. "You're nothing but a spoiled pup who hasn't had his nose rubbed in his own messes enough to grow up. Maybe you'll grow up now, Hamilton. Knowing Beau Langlinais the way I do, I reckon he'd think this was cheap enough, if it makes a man of you."

Mitch's contempt finished him. Henri picked up his coat and found his way out the door, feeling their eyes on his back. He staggered to the elevator and leaned on the button to summon it, fingers of fire and ice chasing each other over his body. He felt sick, sicker than any illness had ever made him.

Somehow he found his way to the street, somehow he found a cab; he even managed to walk into the Pontchartrain lobby with a firm step and a calm face. He thanked God all the way up to the suite that his room opened onto the hall and that he need face none of the family. Not, he thought, looking at his watch, that anyone would be up.

Henri slept badly; he awoke to a ringing telephone and to Walter Fournet's cool voice. "I have something here that belongs to you," Walter said. "If you have time before you leave for Baton Rouge, you might pop around and pick it up."

"What—" Henri shook his head to clear it. He had a headache, still felt half-ill, and he peered in astonishment at the clock beside him.

"My God!" he said. "It's five-thirty in the morning."

"Sorry," Walter said in the same cool voice. "I keep wretched hours. But I think this is something you'd very much like to have possession of. I'm leaving for Washington in a couple of hours—I'd be obliged if you could come over now."

"What is it?" Henri said. A suspicion crossed his mind, but he could hardly dare hope that Walter Fournet had somehow gotten those pictures.

"Oh, I'd hate to describe it over the telephone," Walter said. "It's not exactly material for polite conversation."

"Okay," Henri said. "I'll be there as fast as I can."

He dressed, his mind turning over all the ways by which Walter might possibly have gotten hold of those pictrures. No solution presented itself, and he slipped out of his room and down to get a taxi, still baffled.

He could smell bacon and eggs cooking when Walter opened the door to his apartment, and gratefully took the chair Walter ushered him to. "Breakfast will be ready in a minute," Walter said, going into the kitchen. "Help yourself to coffee. And you might just look at the contents of that envelope."

Hastily Henri dumped the glossy prints and strip of negatives onto the tablecloth. The images leapt at him, images he thought he would never be able to forget. He picked up the photographs and was about to rip them up when Walter's hand stopped him. "That's evidence," Walter said. "If you don't mind."

"Evidence! Are these going to court?"

Walter replaced the pictures and negatives, tucked them into his pocket. "No," he said. He went to the kitchen to get their plates.

"But you said evidence—"

"Trust me," Walter said as he sat down to eat. He gestured toward Henri's plate. "Don't let your eggs get cold." He smiled. "You're already looking better than you did when you came in. Eat that, and you'll be a new man."

"Walter—"

"Later," Walter said. "I never discuss business on an empty stomach."

Over cigarettes and coffee, Walter got the whole story out of him. At first Henri attempted to be objective, to make it sound like any business deal gone wrong. Then all the fear and worry of the last few months took over; he paced up and down the dining room, growing more and more agitated. It was as though once he began, he had to dredge up every detail and place it before Walter's microscopic view. He talked on and on, hardly conscious of his listener. Finally, exhausted, he threw himself down in his chair. "What I can't stand is thinking about Père finding out. He's been so pleased with me—"

"For good reason," Walter said. "Look, Henri, you were up against some real con artists. Anyone could have been taken in."

"Père wasn't. No prospectus, no deal."

"But you told them that," Walter said reasonably.

"Yeah. But I didn't really see how significant it was that Mitch didn't come up with one. And I damn sure made a fool of myself when I—when I drank too much and signed that paper."

"If you insist on being hard on yourself, there's nothing I can say," Walter said. "Let's get on to the real question—what next?"

"What next?" Henri stared at his host. "Why—without the pictures—Mitch doesn't have a leg to stand on."

"But you're going to have to move very fast. It won't take him long to know he's been double-crossed. I don't imagine he'll hang around."

"How did you get those pictures, Walter?"

"Never mind," Walter said. "What are you going to do to stop Mitchell?"

"I don't know. What can I do?"

"Call your stepfather, for starters," Walter said. "Tell him the whole story. I imagine he'll have the D.A. signing a warrant for Mitchell's arrest within the hour."

"Tell Père!" Henri's face took on the haggard look it had had when he had arrived at Walter's. "That's the last thing I want to do!"

"Why? Don't you think he's ever made a mistake? He struck me as a pretty decent sort when I met him yesterday."

"But, Walter—"

"Can you solve this without him?"

"I can't. But you could." Henri did not know the source of Walter's contacts and power. But if he had pulled off one miracle, surely one more was not impossible.

"Sorry," Walter said. "I've really done all I can."

"Then I'm sunk," Henri said. "Père will take Carolina Oil away from me in a minute if he finds this out."

"That's a risk you'll have to take," Walter said. "At least it will still be in the family." There was a small cutting edge on the last words, and Henri looked up quickly. Walter's face was smooth again, but Henri had caught a small twist of distaste, and felt that despite Walter's friendliness and concern, at bottom Walter thought this was a mess that could have been avoided.

"All right," he said, hating the stiffness he heard in his voice. He stood up. "I . . . I'll go talk to him right now."

"Good," Walter said. "I think that's by far the best thing to do." When Henri left, he went to the telephone and placed his own call to Beau Langlinais. Their conversation was rapid and to the point: when Beau asked, as Henri had, how Walter had gotten hold of the pictures, Walter said tersely, "One of my employees came across them. He has instructions to bring things like that to me."

"You have strange employees," Beau said.

"I do," Walter agreed.

"Maybe we should talk about that sometime," Beau said.

"Maybe."

"In the meantime—thanks. And thanks for the call. I don't want to cave in on Henri. At the same time—"

"He's being pretty hard on himself, Mr. Langlinais. It's none of my affair—but he's probably harder on himself than you could ever be."

"I'll think about it," Beau said. "Bourré players and businessmen know better than to drink when the stakes are high."

"I believe Henri's learned that," Walter said.

"We'll see," Beau said. "And my name is Beau."

After they hung up, Walter went to pack. As he filled up his small case, he thought again of the events of the past few hours. Henri was not the only one who had taken a risk. In the usual course of events, Walter would have thrown the pictures of Henri and Sallie Mitchell back to his informant without another glance. The fish he was after were much larger, and much more important to the United States, than a boy being taken in by a scam. Had Henri not been Caro Hamilton's brother, he probably would still be over that very difficult barrel. He has you to thank, Caro, Walter silently addressed Caro. You and no one else.

Later that morning, as his plane left New Orleans, climbing above the lake before it turned to head east, he looked down on the sprawling city. Somewhere down there, Caro was working at her position on the assembly line. And thinking, as Walter very well knew, not of him, but of David Selbin, serving on a destroyer somewhere in the Pacific.

10

NOVEMBER 1943–JANUARY 1944

A cold wind blew in from the English Channel, ruffling the water and making spray dance over the rocky shore. Skye turned up his collar and pulled his soft wool cap lower on his head; there was a warm fire and a hot cup of tea waiting at the end, but he needed the strength of the wind and waves to blow the cobwebs out, the isolation of this winter beach to get his thoughts straight.

The first excitement of being on active duty had carried him through August and September, had borne him up even when it became increasingly obvious that daylight bombing was not going to work—not, that is, without severe losses. His first major raid had taken place on August 17. He had flown one of 376 B-17's whose targets were the ball-bearing facilities at Schweinfurt and the Messerschmitt factory at Regensburg, both deep in Germany. Swarms of German fighters had surrounded them as soon as their shorter-ranged fighter escorts turned back. The bombers, despite heavy armor and guns, were in an untenable position. Sixty Fortresses were shot down. Although Skye made it back safely, he was aware that neither skill nor courage nor American know-how protected him, but only that most fragile of all human resources, Lady Luck.

He had not been sorry when, during the next five weeks, the American bombers struck targets nearer the French coast. There was a tremendous difference, he quickly learned, in how safe he felt when looking out of the cockpit at the comforting presence of P-39's and P-47's ready to take on the Luftwaffe, and when there was nothing between him and those hornetlike planes but blue and empty air.

But then, from October 9 through October 14, the Eighth Air Force had once again experimented with deep daylight penetrations into German airspace. There had been four missions during those days: Skye's plane had been one of the 291 that flew in two groups toward Schweinfurt on the last mission. Standing on the dark, wet sand, staring mindlessly at the black waves, he could remember every moment of that flight. The pit that developed where his stomach had been when the fighter escorts turned back over Aachen became a pit that swallowed courage and threw back fear. No sooner had the last of the American fighters made its turn, dipping its wings in salute to the long-range bombers forging ahead, than wave after wave of German fighters appeared in the sky. There was no end to them; they seemed spawned by the clouds. The air was ripped by explosions from the fighters' rockets as they tried to blow the Flying Fortresses out of the sky.

Even now, Skye could feel the way the plane shook under the impact of the attack. He remembered how he gripped the wheel, making himself think of nothing but his duty—to get his plane over the target, and keep it there until the bombardier had completed his job. And then the flak began, great bursts of fire coming at them from the earth until there was no friendly place anywhere, only a world on fire, a world owned by men intent on killing him.

He watched planes fall; he did not know until later how many the Germans got. They dropped from the sky trailing black smoke, as though they were awkwardly made kites with too-heavy tails. Somehow he had gotten to Schweinfurt, had kept his plane on course until the bombs were dropped. And he had gotten them home again. But when he climbed out of the cockpit, he stepped onto an airstrip desolate with death and loss. One bomber in five had not returned; when the losses for the week were totaled, the results staggered them. One hundred and forty-eight Fortresses had been lost. No matter how accurate their bombing, how successfully they destroyed their targets, the Eighth Air Force could not afford to pay such a devastating price. For the time being, they were told, no more such raids would be made into the Reich.

Skye hated the relief with which he greeted that announcement. He hated the relief with which he flew the closer, safer runs. What he hated most, however, was the fact that he might be a coward.

Tony Harrington suspected Skye's mood and tried to reassure him, delicately talking around the subject, but nevertheless making his point. "Someone made an idiot decision, sending you fellows that far into Jerry's turf with no protection," he'd said, carefully not watching Skye's face. "It's always that way—someone sitting safe and sound behind a desk who wants to test a theory. Then, when he finds out it won't work, he changes his mind, see, and does what he should've done to begin with."

"But then a lot of men have been killed," Skye said. "And a lot of planes lost."

Tony shrugged. "Men and matériel always are lost when new strategies are being tested." He leaned forward and clasped Skye's hand. "Try not to think about it, Skye. Look at flying as just something you do a couple of times a week—and then it's over until the next time."

"That's kind of hard," Skye said. "Even if I'm not flying—buddies are." Some of the men he had trained with were already gone, plummeting to earth in flaming planes or floating helplessly to earth on the silk wings of parachutes. And every time one of them was lost, he had to confront all over again the fact that he had been saved one more time. He thought that should mean something. But if it did, he didn't know what it was.

"You've got a weekend pass due you," Tony reminded him. "Take it and get away from here. Go up to London."

"I don't know anyone in London," Skye said. "Besides, I saw London before the war. I'm not sure I want to see London again right now. I'd rather go to someplace quiet—someplace where I won't have to think about airplanes and bombings for a while."

And so Tony had proposed this small seaside inn, promising Skye a place so remote and so little-advertised that he might well find himself the only guest. Until this afternoon, he had been. The woman who ran the inn had welcomed him last night with a hot meal and then had shown him his room and left him blessedly alone. He had closed the door of the small square room, breathing in the luxury of having a door to close, reveling in the unfamiliar solitude. He had touched everything in the room: the curtains, the woven rugs on the floor, the rocking chair with its cushioned bottom. He had held the conch shell that served as a doorstop to his ear to hear the ocean; he had shaken the small round globe with a tiny bride and groom inside to see the miniature rose petals whirl around them. He had let the ordinariness of the room pervade his spirit, and he had begun to believe again that if he went home—when he went home—it would all be there.

His room would be there, with all the old trophies, all the mementos of summer camp, of his Boy Scout days. His tennis racket. His shotgun. And when he stepped out of his room at home, he would be able to go downstairs, and they would all be there. Papa. Mère. Émilie and Gennie. André. He felt tears start, and brushed them angrily away. Not because he was ashamed to cry, or because he thought it unmanly to miss his home and family. But because he was afraid that once he gave in, he would never be able to close off the hollowness again. And he had a terrible feeling that the pit called homesickness and loneliness was a far deeper, and more dangerous one, than the one called fear.

Instead he had gotten into bed and pulled the down comforter around him and sunk into an almost drugged sleep. When he awoke, he saw that he had slept twelve hours, and went down to breakfast ravenous.

He spent the next day roaming the fields that ran alongside the narrow beach. The innkeeper had packed cheese and bread and apples for him, and tucked two bottles of beer in with them. Tony's prescription was just right; by that afternoon, Skye felt almost normal again, the terrible tension of the past weeks drained from him with every stride he took.

He had passed near the inn on his way down to this point of the beach and seen a car pulling up into the parking yard. Another guest was expected, he had been told, and he found himself regretting his loss of solitude. You don't have to chat them up, he thought, unconsciously using one of Tony's expressions. But it would be difficult, having tea in that tiny parlor, to ignore another person. If the new guest turns out to be a dragon, or a bore, I'll just carry my tea up to my room, he promised himself, turning finally and heading back toward the inn.

"I was just going out to call you in," the landlady said as he came through the door. "Our new guest is here. She went up to wash; as soon as she's down, I'll bring tea."

A woman, Skye thought. Oh, well, a little polite conversation and he could excuse himself. Tony had recommended a nearby pub for dinner; he'd walk over and dine, and by the time he got back, he'd be ready for another night of that dreamless, restorative sleep.

He went into the parlor and took one of the chairs drawn up near the fire, closing his eyes and letting the smell of woodsmoke carry him home. He could almost see his dog Marq's great golden head, the way his fur glowed in the firelight at home. He could almost smell Mère's favorite perfume. He sniffed. He *could* smell Mère's favorite perfume. He opened his eyes to find a young woman standing in front of him, warming her hands at the fire.

"Is that Shalimar?" he asked.

She turned, her face in shadow. "I beg your pardon?"

Blushing, Skye rose. "I'm sorry. I was dozing—and I smelled your perfume. It . . . it reminded me of my stepmother's favorite. Shalimar."

"Yes, that's what I have on," she said. She hesitated, then held out her hand. "Natalie Watkins," she said.

"Skye Langlinais," Skye said. Her hand was slender, but her clasp was firm. There was a row of small calluses across the top of her palm; he wondered what caused them. "You're American," he said.

"Are you disappointed?" she said, sitting in the chair opposite his.

"No," he said, backing into his chair. "It's just that I haven't seen an American girl since I got here."

"How long have you been here?"

"I arrived in July—or do you mean here, at the inn? I arrived here yesterday."

"It seems very nice."

"A friend suggested it. He said it was a great place for peace and quiet."

She moved forward, as though to rise. "I didn't mean to disturb you—"

"Oh, you're not. Please—"

"I really have been looking forward to tea by the fire," she said. "I had rather a long drive."

"Well, have you two met?" their landlady asked, bustling in pushing a tea cart. "I thought with two of you, I'd do a little extra. Make it like a party."

"Mrs. Phillips, if you ever find yourself in Louisiana, I'll expect to repay your hospitality," Skye said. "Your inn more than lives up to everything Tony Harrington said about it."

"Oh, do you know Tony?" Natalie said, her hand poised over the rose-sprigged teapot.

"Yes. He's a liaison officer at my base," Skye said. "As well as my guardian angel, I guess. Tony's sort of taken me under his wing. But you know Tony too?"

"He comes up to London a lot, sits in on meetings with my boss. He's a nice guy." She saw the question in Skye's eyes and gestured at her uniform. "I'm a WAAF. I drive for Lieutenant Colonel Hap Morris." Natalie caught Skye's quick glance at her hands. "That accounts for the calluses. I should wear gloves—they're part of the uniform—but I think I've lost the right hand to about two dozen pairs!"

Now the last restraint between them slipped away, melted by the warmth of the fire, the soothing tea, the easy manner of the girl sitting opposite him. She's not really pretty, Skye thought. Though attractive, very attractive: her hair a thick, deep gold with auburn lights. Her eyes brown, a dark rim circling the pupils and making them seem bigger than they actually were: neither dark nor fair, but something in between. Her skin is almost golden, he decided, as though she had tanned so deeply during the summer that even the gray autumn had not taken away all her color.

"Where in Louisiana are you from?" Natalie asked. "I have an uncle who lives just outside of St. Francisville."

"That's about thirty-five miles north of Baton Rouge," Skye said. "I'm from St. Martinville—fifty miles due west and then about twenty-five miles south of Baton Rouge."

"I do know where Baton Rouge is," Natalie said. "I grew up in Virginia. During all the hurrah when Huey Long was governor, my uncle was up to his neck fighting him. Dad used to read every word he could find on the whole debacle." She paused and looked directly into Skye's face. "Sorry. Maybe your family supported Long."

"Fought him tooth and nail," Skye said. "If your uncle was a dyed-in-the-wool anti-Longite, my father and grandfather probably know him."

"His name is Paul Watkins," Natalie said. "He was in the legislature for a long time."

"So was my grandfather," Skye said. "As is my father now."

The warmth between them solidified and made a place they could stand together. Skye took the scone Natalie passed to him and spread it liberally with raspberry jam. "Say, would you like to have dinner with me? Tony said the local pub does reasonably well."

She refilled both their cups before answering. "Look, this is probably a little too direct. But nine times out of ten, it saves trouble later. I'm engaged to a Navy lieutenant—he's on a ship somewhere in the Pacific." She met his eyes again, and he thought that he had never seen a more honest look in a woman's face. "So although I would very much like to have dinner with you—that's really all." For a moment, Skye said nothing, and Natalie's expression changed, becoming anxious. "I'm sorry. I do just blurt things out. Make assumptions." She leaned forward, the firelight glinting in her hair. "But there are a lot of Americans who are in London for one hectic weekend and some of the time—a lot of the time, even—they want me to be part of . . . well, part of that weekend." She shook her head. "I'd rather risk offending a gentleman than encourage a bounder."

Skye laughed happily. He felt suddenly free, free and wonderful. "I'm sure that nine times out of ten that little speech is necessary. I think it's great you can make it. But I'm the tenth case. I have a girl back home myself—someone who means a lot to me."

"So do a lot of the guys I meet in London," Natalie said. "It doesn't seem to stop them."

"I don't play games with people's feelings," Skye said. "And I'm sure you don't either."

"No," she said. "I don't. So—shall we have dinner?"

"Yes," he said. "A late one, I should think, after all this."

"I have some letters to write," Natalie said. "And I've been thinking about that long tub and a hot bath since I got here."

"Why don't I meet you down here about eight?" Skye said.

"Fine. And now, I'll just take this cart out to Mrs. Phillips," Natalie said. "Better eat the last scone, Skye. For luck."

He went upstairs, wondering why his name sounded different when Natalie spoke it. As though he were hearing it for the first time. Or as though he had heard her use it so often that she had given it an inflection all her own.

His feeling of having stumbled on an old friend increased over their dinner together; the coincidence of her uncle's and his father's political experience was only the first discovery in a series that revealed mutual interests ranging from a passion for Dashiell Hammett to a fondness for Gilbert and Sullivan.

"You're in the right country if you're a Gilbert-and-Sullivan admirer," Natalie said. "You'll have to come up to London sometime—I'll get tickets to a D'Oyly Carte production."

"Thanks. I'd like to," Skye said. "Some of that wonderful foolishness might drive the cobwebs away."

He didn't tell her how many cobwebs were being dispelled by her breezy humor, her easy poise. He felt comfortable with Natalie Watkins, easy and lighthearted, and he found himself prolonging the evening as long as he could. Before saying good night, they agreed to walk into the village for church services on Sunday. "I'm sure it's High Church enough to make you feel at home," Natalie assured him. "Your pope won't mind, will he?"

"I doubt I'll be excommunicated for attending an Anglican service," Skye laughed.

The next morning Skye found that Natalie was right: the prayers, the order of worship, the incense, the altar boys, even some of the hymns were the same as the Catholic services in St. Martinville; if he closed his eyes, he might almost be at home. Except, of course, for the clipped English accents that made the most familiar prayer sound different, and the absence of statues that filled the church at home. But he did feel more as though as he belonged, and when they filed out of the church with the rest of the congregation, he smiled back at the villagers and shook hands heartily with the attending priest.

"I suppose one problem is that people from my part of Louisiana feel strange even in other parts of the state," he said. "We've kept to ourselves too long, I suppose—live in a kind of cultural enclave."

"A very nice enclave, if it produces people like you," Natalie said. "I hope you will get up to London, Skye. I've had a very good time."

"So have I," he said. The morning seemed to be eaten up by the clock; in no time, he was helping Natalie into her car, tucking in the packet of sandwiches Mrs. Phillips had prepared, and watching her drive off. He didn't have to leave until midafternoon, but the fire on the hearth was not nearly as cozy with no one to share it, nor the final walk along the beach nearly so bracing.

"I met a friend of yours," he reported to Tony when he arrived back at the base. "Natalie Watkins."

"Really?" Tony said. "Fancy you two being down there together." Something about the way Tony grinned made Skye suddenly suspicious; had Tony arranged so that he and Natalie would meet? He immediately dismissed the thought. Tony had certainly heard Skye talk about Rosalind, had seen her picture. And if he knew Natalie, he knew she, too, was involved.

The weekend and its momentary peace were immediately forgotten amid new bombing missions. November became December. He did go to up to London to see *Pirates of Penzance* with Natalie; for the rest of the weekend, they broke into snatches of the patter songs, each filling in lines the other forgot. He found himself thinking about Natalie a lot, but because most of the time when he thought of her he began laughing, he considered her nothing more than a good buddy. They were fellow Americans, out of their normal time, out of their normal place.

Toward the end of January, Tony invited Skye to his house in the country for a long weekend; he mentioned casually that his wife, Alicia, had included Natalie among the guests. "It will be nice to see her again," Skye said, just as casually. He managed to deny the leap of his heart that said just how nice it would be.

"Four spades," Natalie said, and winked at Skye.

"Double," Alicia Harrington responded.

"Redouble," Skye said, grinning back at Natalie.

"Foolhardy Americans," Tony said, surveying his hand. "I won't take you out of it. Pass."

"All right," Natalie said. "Skye, I hope you weren't bluffing when you raised me."

"Don't let the girl blame you," Tony said. "She's the one who took you to game."

"And I'm the one who redoubled," Skye said. "But I have complete confidence in Natalie. Prepare to eat that double, Harrington."

"My lead," Alicia said, studying her hand carefully. "Now give me a minute. I want to absolutely devastate you with this lead."

The warmth and solid peace of the room closed them in from the January cold outside. A huge fire burned steadily on the hearth, melting the chill in the room. Alicia had drawn heavy draperies over the mullioned windows of the card room as they sat down to play. It was as though she had drawn a drapery over their minds, too, so that no one would think of the world beyond. Even the military guests had relaxed their dress code, and their comfortable tweeds and soft sweaters contributed to the carefree ambience of the afternoon.

The size and stateliness of Tony's home had surprised Skye from the moment he turned into Hedgeforth's gates. The house towered at the end of the long drive, surrounded by formal lawns and acres of park. Tony and Alicia welcomed him as warmly as if he were a familiar guest, and by the time dinner was over that first evening, he and the other guests had coalesced into a compatible group.

Natalie made it plain she was as glad to see Skye as he was to see her; when a bridge game was gotten up after lunch on Saturday, they laughingly announced that as the only bridge-playing Americans present, they would take on any and all British teams. Natalie's game proved to be as bold as Skye's. She bid her hands to their limit, and then played them coolly, taking her losses calmly and her successes with a pleased little smile.

Suddenly the door behind Natalie burst open, and Bill Collins, another American officer, walked in with a London *Times* in his hands. "It's easy to forget a war's on out here," he said. "Until you see something like this." He held the newspaper out so they could see the black headlines: "ALLIES LAND AT ANZIO UNDER HEAVY BOMBARDMENT."

"Oh, God," Tony said, scanning the story. He handed the paper to Skye. "Those poor bastards. They've run into a hell of a lot more opposition than they expected—the Germans are dug in safe as houses on the hillsides, and our men are caught on that damn beach like so many fish in a barrel."

"You'd have thought we'd have bombed the hell out of the German gun emplacements before we hit the damn beach," Bill said.

"Sometimes I think the Germans are like Medusa," Skye said. "Cut off one part of their strength and it grows back ten times stronger. Hell, the German air defenses are stronger now than when we began joint operations against them last fall."

"Well," came a lazy voice from a corner of the room, "since the Ninety-ninth Pursuit Squadron was supposed to be part of the offensive against Italy, I'm not surprised to hear that so many of the enemy were left."

"I don't understand," Alicia Harrington said, turning toward the man who sat reading in a big leather chair pulled up near the fire.

"It's simple," Ted Compton said, putting down his book and rising.

"The Ninety-ninth Pursuit Squadron is made up of Negro pilots—who have proven to be more yellow than they are black."

"That's a filthy thing to say," Skye said, his blood instantly heating up.

"Why?" Compton said. He had come up to the table and stood looking down at them, his mouth twisted in a small smile. "Were you with them in North Africa when they turned tail and ran back to the base the first time they came under enemy fire?"

"Were you?" Skye shot back.

"No. But I have friends who were. The Ninety-ninth's performance is a disgrace to the entire Air Force. It's being investigated right now—"

"Does that make you feel btter?" Skye said. Nantalie's head jerked up, and she fixed her eyes on him intently. Something in his tone made her curious, and she wondered, for the first time since she had met him: was there something of substance beneath that confident, lighthearted exterior?

"What?" Compton said.

"Maligning fellow American fliers."

"Now, don't put me in the same boat with—"

Skye rose and stood before Compton. "With fellow Americans who, although they don't have the same size stake in this war as you do, think the very small stake they have is worth fighting for."

"What the hell are you talking about, Langlinais?"

Skye could feel the tension in the room. He knew that he should stop, should change the subject and sit down and finish the game. He knew that he should not disrupt the precious tranquillity Tony and Alicia had provided for them. But one more look at Ted Compton's arrogant, scornful face and his hands itched. "I'm talking about the fact that almost no black pilot or serviceman has as much to fight for personally as, say, you and I do. Because you and I, Compton, and our fellow *white* men, truly *are* fighting for all the good things. Liberty. The right to own and protect property. Decent schools. The right, for God's sake, to be the same kind of free Americans you and I are."

"Are you some kind of pinko nut?" Compton asked. His tone made it clear: the only man here making a fool of himself was Skye Langlinais.

Tony Harrington spoke up then, speaking as casually as though simply joining a conversation that interested him. "Compton, I happen to have seen some reports on the Ninety-ninth's performance up at London headquarters, and they're nothing to be ashamed of." He smiled to soften his next words. "Anyway, there's a motto written over the door of this house that we try to live up to—" He glanced across the table at his wife, and she recited with him gently: " 'For a man's house is his castle, and one's home is the safest refuge to everyone.' "

"Which means," Alicia said, "that while we are aware of the terrible conflicts and tensions beyond Hedgeforth's gates—we try not to bring them here."

"I apologize," Skye said quickly. "To everyone. I've got a quick temper and I don't always think before I speak." He held out his hand to Ted Compton. "I happened to be at Keesler Field when the Ninety-ninth was on maneuvers there before they went to North Africa. Made a friend of one of the pilots. I got into a fight over them there, too, come to think of it. I guess I have a personal bias."

"I guess I do, too," Compton said. They settled back to their bridge game, and Bill Collins took Ted Compton off for a walk in the park surrounding Hedgeforth.

"I think the rest are mine," Natalie said, and Skye heard the quiet triumph in her voice. She spread her cards out on the table. "The ace of diamonds is good, the king of hearts covers your queen, Alicia—I trump your ace of clubs—and the rest of the spades are good."

"Ouch," Alicia said. "That's game and rubber. Tony, we're going to have to hock the family silver to pay off this little score."

"We'll settle for the use of your lawn and a tall whiskey when we get back," Skye said. "Come on, Natalie, all this mental concentration has worn me out. I need some fresh air."

The terriers dozing by the fire looked up, ears cocked.

"You said the magic words," Alicia said. "Fresh air. Would you mind awfully if they ran with you?"

"We'd love it," Natalie said. She knelt and took one of the terriers in her arms. "I miss my own dog so much."

"Come down and play with these anytime you want," Alicia said. She looked at Skye. "You too, Skye. We love having you."

He felt a moment of unity, an instant when he and Natalie, Tony and Alicia, made one tight group. He moved slightly, breaking the spell, and went upstairs to get his coat, telling himself the warmth he felt, the happiness, was due to the entire weekend, and not just one girl.

The air was sharp and clear, the ground hard with frost. They struck away from the house, walking rapidly with the three terriers racing ahead until they reached the end of the terraced lawns and were on the edge of the park. Far at the end of an alley of linwood trees they could see Bill Collins and Ted Compton standing near a marble bench smoking.

"Takes all kinds, I guess," he said.

"Compton, you mean?"

"Kind of shot his mouth off in there," Skye said. "Guess I did too."

"You stood up for what you believed," Natalie said. Her cheeks were glowing with the color the cold air stirred, and her eyes sparkled with the energy of her conviction. "You made me really proud."

"Talk is easy," Skye said. He shook his head. "But when you're in the cockpit of a bomber—" He fell silent, but he could see by the intensity of Natalie's gaze that she understood what he was feeling. He thought of the way he felt when he climbed into the cockpit of his Flying Fortress and waited for the signal to take off. The first quick rush of adrenaline turned to exhilaration as the shoreline of England vanished and there was nothing beneath him but the dark choppy Channel, waves licking at the sky as though to swallow it. It was easy then to feel only the throb of the motors, only the pulse of his ship as he steered her toward Germany. But when the Messerschmitts leapt out of the clouds, guns blazing, the exhilaration became fear, a fear mingled with his own sense of waiting death. A second adrenaline rush when American fighters swarmed forward, engaging the German fliers in duels whose scars would be more lasting than a line across an aristocratic cheek. And then the prayers, breathed each and every time he flew a mission. That by some miracle of accuracy, the bombs fell on military targets only. That no mother was scrabbling through the rubble his bombs left, weeping for her dead children. That no family was standing numb before the ruins of their home. He could tell himself, over and over again, that the German people were his enemy. But he knew, at another level, that the German people were not a block, were not a mass to be treated with the anonymity of a crowd. They were individuals, as he and Natalie were individuals. They had private dreams, secret fears, onerous burdens, and willingly accepted duties. They had, if it came to that, souls.

"I guess the view from a bomber is always different," he said. "But even there, what I think of is that when it's all over, I hope to heaven all of us—no matter who we are, or where we live—can own our own souls."

For a long moment she stood and looked at him. Then he saw tears form, a mist making her eyes look like agates under glass. She leaned toward him and gently kissed his cheek. "I'm glad I know you, Skye Langlinais," she said. Then she stepped back and looked at the dogs sitting panting at their feet. "Let's give these lazy animals a run they won't forget," she said. "Bet I can beat all of you back to the house."

He raced after her, hearing her laughter float back over her shoulder. She ran well, a steady, even pace that reminded him of what she had told him about herself—a girlhood spent on a plantation in Virginia, where her father had taught her to hunt alongside him and her brothers, and where she had learned to ride before she went to kindergarten. A feeling of well-being filled him. He had brought a new Frank Sinatra album Émilie had sent him; after dinner, he'd put it on the phonograph and they'd have dancing. And before dinner he'd write to Rosalind. It would be good to have something to write about other than the military routine, most of which he could not write about anyway. He could describe the house, and tell her about the ghost alleged to haunt the picture gallery. He caught up with Natalie just as she reached the doorstep, and stood laughing with her as they recovered their breath. But he probably wouldn't tell Rosalind about his new friend. Distance could distort things; he wasn't sure that Rosalind, who seemed to think only one kind of relationship possible between a man and a woman, would understand his friendship with Natalie at all.

Come to think of it, he thought as he went up to his room, Rosalind was still pretty much of a schoolgirl. So of course such a friendship would be out of her ballpark altogether. He sat at the desk and pulled a piece of stationery toward him. It had the Harrington crest at the top, with Hedgeforth, and the address, beneath. She's going to love this, Skye thought. "Dear Rosalind," he wrote. "I am writing in a bedroom of a house built when Queen Elizabeth was reigning. I'm the guest of Tony and Alicia Harrington—" His pen stopped, and he stared at the paper. He could not bring Rosalind's face into his mind. He could not see her at all. His hand went to his pocket, and he pulled out the small leather folio where he kept her picture. Opening it, he propped it in front of him and stared at it. Yes, there she was. The green eyes gazed out at him from under her thin, arched eyebrows. The mouth made a small, sultry pout. The cheeks had the faintest blush. Rosalind Nasser. His girl. From the hall outside, he heard the chime of a clock. God, he'd better hurry or he'd be late for dinner. He picked up his pen and began writing rapidly. "The house is enormous—I'd have to stay here a month to see it all. . . ."

He wrote without thinking, filling four pages before he stopped. When he came to a close, he wrote that without thinking, too. "I think of you every minute and I can't wait until I can hold you and kiss you and be with you forever. All my love. Skye." As he folded the pages and tucked them into an envelope, his eye fell on those last words. Forever. He thought of the days he flew a mission, when life was counted by hours, by minutes over the target. No one could mean forever, not anymore.

He began to get dressed, letting his thoughts wander to the evening ahead. As he left the room, the new Sinatra record under his arm, his eyes fell on his letter to Rosalind, sitting on his desk. Forever. Well, of course, that was just something you said. But as he started down the hall to the great curving stairs, a thought nagged at him. What about all the rest of it? Didn't he mean that, either?

II

MARCH 1944

Caro stepped away from the painting to get a better perspective, narrowing her eyes slightly. "It's very good, isn't it?" she said to Walter. "In fact, it's one of the best things I've seen in a long time. Who is the artist? The name's not familiar—"

"Actually, she's very new," Walter said. "And quite young. Ann Baron, from someplace in Texas. Making something of a reputation for herself."

Caro laughed, trying to keep the bitter edge from showing. "I'm beginning to hate her," she said.

"You don't paint at all anymore?"

"When?" she demanded. She turned away and headed toward the gallery door, then stopped, looking out into the dreary afternoon. "Sorry," she said when Walter came after her. "I haven't slept well the last couple of nights—and gallery hopping hasn't turned out to be such a good idea after all."

"I'm at your disposal," Walter said. "Anywhere you want to go."

"Let's go to Gin's and eat Chinese food," Caro said. "And then hear some Dixieland."

Walter waited until they were settled over their meal before turning the conversation back to art. "If I'd thought seeing Ann Baron's work would upset you, I'd never have taken you there," he said.

"I know that. I feel like a fool. No one has me chained to that job. If I wanted to paint all day, I'd be doing it."

"No, you wouldn't," Walter said. "You're one of those who will always put first what she thinks she *should* do—not what she wants to do."

"Not always," Caro said, thinking of her visit to San Diego. God, that seemed like a century ago!

"Most of the time," Walter insisted. He reached across the table and took one of her hands. "Has it ever occurred to you that your painting might have so much merit that it is more valuable than running a machine in a shipyard?"

"Paintings don't drop bombs," Caro said. "Watercolors don't carry troops. I could no more sit in front of an easel now . . . To tell you the truth, I'm still angry that Ann Baron can. Why isn't she helping out in the war effort?"

Walter shrugged. "Maybe she is. Her own private war—"

"Spare me from private wars," Caro said. "We've got one big one going right now, and until it's over—well, you won't find me doing much painting."

"It won't last forever, you know," Walter persisted. "Then what?"

She put down her chopsticks and stared at him. "If I'd known this was quiz-Caro night, I'd have stayed home. Goodness, Walter, how do I know?"

"Are you going to marry Selbin?"

The question startled her, as did Walter's direct gaze. He usually talked around things, rarely coming out with exactly what was on his mind. Her answer must be important. . . . She looked down at her food, as though trying to decide what to pick up next.

"I've no idea," she said.

"But you have thought about it," he said. Then, before she could answer, he drew back. "Sorry. I'm being very rude. Absolutely none of my business, of course."

She suddenly wanted to talk to him about David, wanted to test some of her own feelings against Walter's perception of the world he and she had both grown up in. "Nonsense. There's nothing wrong with asking. And anyway, now that you've brought it up, I can't help wondering—do you think that's a preposterous idea?"

"You marrying David?"

"Yes."

Walter shrugged and signaled the waiter for a fresh pot of tea. "My dear Caro. I have no earthly idea of what you might want out of marriage, or what Selbin might want out of marriage. I can hardly say whether the idea is preposterous or not."

"I want the usual things—" she said.

But Walter's raised eyebrow cut her off. "The usual things? Oh, I think not," he said. "Or perhaps you and he should decide if his 'usual things' are the same as yours."

"Because he's Jewish and I'm Catholic."

"And because he's from New York and you're from New Orleans."

"That's not so important—"

Again the eyebrow curved, questioning her.

"Oh, all right. There are a lot of differences. So many I sometimes—" She broke off again, thinking now of some of the ways she and David were alike. How, when she was with him, none of the differences mattered. She smiled at Walter. "The whole thing is academic. David's somewhere in the Pacific, I'm here. Until the war is over—there's no decision to make."

"And for that reason," Walter said, "a great many people will be sorry when the war is over."

She didn't respond to his statement, nor did she dwell on it. She counted on Walter to take her out of herself, to spin her away into a world where it was still possible to be a little frivolous, have a little fun.

The Famous Door was packed when they got there. But a twenty-dollar bill got them a table, and another twenty got them a better one. The tables were pushed up to the edge of the narrow stage; people lined the walls and stood in doorways. Layers of smoke hovered in the thick air, its smell mingling with the smell of old liquor and fresh sweat. And over all of it, the sure, insistent music of the Dukes of Dixieland. Their black faces shone under the layer of moisture that covered them; black fingers flew over brass instruments, black hands made drumsticks beat and roll and crash. The five musicians became the focal point in the hot, smoke-filled room. Their rhythms became the rhythm of the crowd; every pulse beat with theirs, every head nodded, every body swayed, every foot tapped with theirs.

The music unwound Caro as though she stood on a music box slowly turning, slowly coming to a halt. She lost herself in it, and when a hand clasped her shoulder and a voice called her name, she barely recognized the person in front of her as her brother.

"Hey, Caro, Walter. It's great to run into you," Henri said. He nodded to Walter, who gestured at the empty chair at their table.

"Please sit down," Caro said, raising her voice to be heard over the music. "I haven't seen you in ages. What are you doing in town?"

"I registered at school today," Henri said. "Going back to Loyola." He pulled the chair out and sat down. "I've thought it over—I need to get my degree if I'm going to do anything when the war's over." He smiled a little. "May as well do it now before the campuses are flooded with returning heroes."

"You both sound as though the war were going to end tomorrow," Caro said.

"Not tomorrow," Walter said carefully. "But the tide is turning. It most definitely is turning."

"What about Carolina Oil?" Caro said.

Henri flushed, and looked away so that Walter would not see it. Père's been helping me with that for a while," he said. "It got kind of . . . complicated. A little bit more than I could handle, I guess. I'll still take care of my end—but it's not a full-time job,, not by any means."

"It'll be good to have you in New Orleans again," Caro said. There was an odd pause during which both Walter and Henri seemed to look anywhere but at each other. When no explanation was forthcoming, Caro dismissed it. Walter, as she had learned on more than one occasion, could be extremely secretive. At one time she had thought Walter really had something to hide, but she later decided this was just the way Walter was, a personal trait as natural to him as his easy manners and talk. "Raoul is buried in his work. I hardly ever see him."

The set ended and the musicians left to take a break. Walter looked at his watch and then at Caro. "Would you mind terribly if we made this an early evening? I've got an appointment at the crack of dawn, and I'll need my wits about me."

"I don't have any business being out any later, either," Caro said. "We're laying keels for a new kind of landing craft tomorrow." She was sorry the instant she had spoken. It had become second nature for her never to mention anything about her work, and although she couldn't imagine that either Walter or Henri would spread company secrets, still, caution bred of discipline made her search for a way to smooth over her gaffe. I'll only make it worse, she thought, and went on to other things.

Halfway down the block to Walter's car, they were accosted by three enlisted men whose drab khaki uniforms were enlivened by rows of ribbons on their chests. They did not make room for the trio to pass, but stood solidly blocking the sidewalk, staring belligerently ahead.

"Excuse us, please," Walter said, moving forward.

"What's the password?" demanded one of the servicemen.

"I'd like to get by," Walter replied.

"That's not it," another one said. He looked at his cohorts. "What should we do with this guy? Doesn't know the password, out of uniform—" He paused, as though the thought had just struck him. "Say, wait a minute. Maybe I'm doing you an injustice. Maybe the reason you're out of uniform is that you were never in uniform."

"Maybe," Walter said. "Now, may we please get by?"

"What about your friend?" the serviceman asked, pointing at Henri. "Did he forget to wear his uniform too? Or doesn't he have one either?"

"I'd drop this whole thing if I were you," Walter said.

"I'll drop you," one of his opponents said. The three closed in suddenly. One of them grabbed Caro and pushed her out of the way as the other two moved in on Henri and Walter.

Caro cowered against the sheltering brick wall, her vision blocked by the bulk of the man who held her. She heard the sound of fists, the grunts of the combatants, the heavy panting as they fought for air. Then she heard someone hit the ground; flesh hitting flesh, and a thin, high scream. She fought against the man holding her, but his grip was too tight for her to break. Someone hit the ground, then someone else. And then the man holding her seemed to spring away from her, flying through the air, and Walter stood before her dusting off his gloved hands.

Henri sat up, putting his hand to his bloody mouth. He looked dazed. The three servicemen lay where Walter had dumped them; one seemed to be unconscious, the other two half-stunned.

"Are you all right?" Walter asked Caro.

"I—yes, I'm fine," she said. "Henri—" She opened her purse and took out her handkerchief. "Here," she said, extending it to Henri. "Put this on your mouth."

Henri ignored the handkerchief and also Walter's hand, stretched out to help him up. "A lot of help I turned out to be," he said. "What'd you do to those guys, Walter?" He struggled up, still refusing Walter's hand. The servicemen were rousing themselves; Walter's attack, combined with the liquor they already carried, had taken the fight out of them, and once on their feet, they staggered off down the pavement without a backward glance.

"Used judo," Walter said. "Are you really all right?" he said to Caro. "That was a nasty experience—"

"They didn't do anything to me," Caro said. "Henri, let me look at your mouth—" She saw white fragments on the sidewalk and bent over. "Henri! Did they break your tooth?"

"It feels like it," Henri said. When Caro came nearer, he backed off. "Look, Caro—I can take care of it. I may not be much use in a fight—but I guess I can get my wounds fixed up without big sis hovering over me."

"No one's hovering—" Caro said.

The look on Henri's face stopped her. The strange tension between Henri and Walter was stronger than ever. She felt as if a wall separated her and Walter from where Henri stood.

"It's not your fault—" she began. That was even worse. Henri gave her one angry look and turned on his heel, walking away as quickly as his bruised leg would let him.

"Poor Henri," she said to Walter. She was suddenly exhausted. If she didn't get to sleep in about one minute, she thought she would collapse where she stood. "He expects such great things of himself—"

"You can't do anything about that," Walter said. "Now, let's get you home."

"Do you care about those men?" she said abruptly as he helped her into his car. "Taunting you because you're not . . . in uniform."

"I do what I do, they do what they do," he said. "We serve one and the same country." He heard his words with more than a little dismay. Maybe Caro was too tired, maybe she hadn't picked up on them—

"How do you serve your country?" she said. "I've wondered about that."

"The refugee organization—" he said.

She shook her head. "That's private. That was started by people right here in New Orleans. And it doesn't pay you a cent."

"Not everyone has to work for money," he said. "You don't."

"Walter. What do you do for your country?"

"Something very tedious that would bore you to death," he said. He put his finger over his lips, mimicking the Uncle Sam posters that warned against careless talk. "Trust me. You wouldn't want to know."

Of course, she did. But discipline took over; if Walter did not want to tell her, she did not need to know.

Skye ran across the open ground back to his quarters, a sheaf of letters in his hand. This was one of the good days, when a whole packet of letters arrived at the same time, as though every member of his family had decided to write to him at once.

There was a letter from Rosalind in the batch, a letter whose first half apologized for not writing more often, and whose second half promised to do better. Her excuses seemed fragile, unreal. Classes, tests, papers due—what the hell did all that mean? How long did it take to scrawl a few words on a V-mail form and send it off? If Caro had time to write the long letters that amused him with their funny stories and clever pen-and-ink sketches, certainly Rosalind had time for more than this schoolgirlish missive. He allowed himself to be angry with her, to disallow her plea that she had never been any good at writing letters, but that she thought about him all the time. Hell, a lot of people were doing things in this war that they had never been very good at. Doing them because they were their duty. And, by God, learning to do them well.

He reread Rosalind's leter, then tore it into small pieces and dropped it in the wastebasket. She should see what he saw whenever he went to London. The courage of the people living in its rubble. The staunchness of their faith that their nation would not only survive but also triumph. The gallantry with which they bore the loss of homes, family—everything. And still had enough humanity left to be courteous to Yanks. Opening their homes to them. Opening their hearts. Sharing a "cuppa," no matter how tight their rations. Grateful for the chocolate, the cigarettes, the soap Skye and other Americans shared in return. Rosalind doesn't know what it's all about, he thought.

He tried to tell himself that there was no way she could, living in her sheltered world. Physically protected by Dominican's walls and rules. Mentally protected by her ignorance of what this war was really like. Emotionally protected by her innocence. Even that seductress scene she'd put on his last time home had a kind of innocence about it, he thought. As though she believed that what she offered to do with Skye could exist outside of time, outside of the life she normally lived. He did not for a moment imagine that she had offered herself to him for any reason but that she thought it was what he wanted. He did not for a moment imagine she would offer herself to anyone else.

Soothed, he pulled paper toward him and began to write. "Dear Rosalind, It was good to hear from you. Just the sight of your handwriting makes me miss you and want you. . . ." There, he thought, that's what she wants to hear. In anticipating pleasing her, he managed to lose his own disappointment. And by the time he had finished writing all the things he believed a young girl at college in New Orleans would want to hear from a beau so far away, so involved in another world, he had convinced himself all over again that Rosalind was his love, his only love, and that he could hardly wait to get back to her.

He shoved the letters through the mail slot on his way to the field the next morning. Standing outside his plane buckling on his flight helmet, he sniffed the air and thought of the coming spring. At home the cypresses would be putting out their feathery leaves, the soft new green contrasting with the tougher green of the pines and live oaks. The fields would still be bare, but in a matter of weeks, farmers would wake to a green haze that promised summer's bounty. There would be new calves in the pastures, new foals in the stables. New kittens in the haylofts. He ached with wanting to be home, and he turned his head from the crew assembled around him so that they would not see the yearning in his face, the misted eyes that betrayed him.

"Another milk run," his copilot said. "But you won't hear me complaining." He jerked his thumb at the fighter planes warming up, propellers spinning. "With those little beauties riding shotgun, our job's a piece of cake."

The fighters had finally caught up with the bombers; now when Skye flew, he had American Mustangs swooping and diving and somersaulting all around him; the Luftwaffe was being blasted out of the air. The Germans could fight back no longer against the Americans' persistent bombing of the railroads and highways and side roads that laced France like leather thongs.

A sense of exultation, of victory, held the Allied forces; since January, one word had dominated every meeting and haunted every mission: Overlord, the code word for the Allied invasion of the continent of Europe. General Dwight David Eisenhower had been named Supreme Commander of the Allied invasion forces by the Combined Chiefs of Staff of the U.S. and Britain. His orders were simple: "You will enter the continent of Europe, and, in conjunction with the other United Nations, undertake operations aimed at the heart of Germany and the destruction of her armed forces." In response to that directive, men, tanks, ships, and planes were being assembled in southeast England. Every time Skye flew over the English coast, he saw the massive gathering of battleships, destroyers, cruisers, and landing craft. They lined the docks and filled the harbors, their painted camouflage blending them into an indistinct mass that rode gently on the ebb and flow of the tide. And as though also borne by one great tide that was sweeping armies from across the face of the earth to this one small island, men gathered on the shore, making ready for one of the boldest military campaigns of all time.

Skye had early grown weary of the arguments that raged on every side in these preinvasion months. Like most Americans, he wanted to hit Hitler's Fortress Europe with everything they had. A relatively brief history, and one with scant experience of all-out, large-scale international war, added to a faith in American industrial might that proved to be not at all naive, led Americans from President Roosevelt on down to believe that an assault on Europe could end in only one way—with a total Allied victory.

The British, with a much longer history and a much deeper experience with war, remembered Dunkirk, that almost fatal battle early in the war, when Britain and her European allies still stood alone. Had it not been for the daring feats of British civilians who worked along with the British Navy, adding their sloops and yachts, tugs and speedboats, paddle steamers and car ferries to more ordinary vessels, and sailed across the English Channel under heavy German attack to take more than 300,000 British, Belgian, and French troops off those death-ridden beaches, that one defeat would have spelled the end of the British Expeditionary Force—and the end of any hope of halting Hitler's juggernaut.

The British were haunted, too, by the terrible campaigns in France thirty years before, when the first act of this world conflagration took place. They remembered troops who died by the tens of thousands on Flanders' fields, ripped apart by gunfire, drowned in the mud, suffocated by poison gas. They knew that Hitler must be met in Europe, and their will to do it was not lacking. But when Prime Minister Winston Churchill wrote to President Franklin D. Roosevelt, when Overlord was in its earliest planning stages, "My dear friend, this is much the greatest thing we have ever attempted," and then later, to American General George Marshall, "We are carrying out our contract, but pray God it does not cost us dear," he was echoing the sentiments of many of his countrymen, who had learned, over centuries of defending their island, and then their empire, that courage without discretion had lost more than one battle.

The immense capacity of American industry to provide the materials for such a bold plan, and the determination of the American military to see it through, swung the British: the will and might of two old Allies became one, and the sword that would sever Nazi power was forged.

The planes of the Eighth Air Force were the cutting edge of that sword; their assignment was to level the transportation system that brought German men and matériel to the exposed coasts of France and Belgium. They were to leave no bridge standing on the Seine and Loire rivers; with each bridge that was bombed into uselessness the German dream of conquest became more fragile.

"They must know we're going to invade Europe," Skye said more than once as they turned toward home, leaving pillars of fire supporting girders of flame.

"But they don't know where. And they don't know when," his copilot answered. "No more do we."

Sometimes, as on this March morning, Skye felt that for the rest of his life he would climb into the cockpit of this B-17, roll her forward into her place in line, and then take her into the low-ceilinged sky. Sometimes he thought that he would make these bomb runs forever, as though he had forgotten how to do anything else. They had become routine, and the relief he felt that he was bombing bridges and railroads and highways, cleared of human life by the warning sirens, made them almost dull. He took off, he made his run, he came home, he landed. Until the next time.

And so, when an engine coughed, and then stopped running, he felt nothing more than mild annoyance. Three engines were more than enough to get home on; he was only a few miles from his target, there was no sense in turning back.

A second engine died soon after the bombs had been dropped. And despite the Mustangs clinging to him, warding off the occasional Messerschmitt that still challenged them, a shell found yet another engine, and he was left with one.

"I'd better take her down," he said, speaking into the intercom. Smoke plumed around the plane; in his earphones he could hear the crew reporting on the damage the shell had done, and he heard the copilot exclaim roughly, "Take her down! You mean bail out. This thing could go up any minute, Skye. Tell 'em to prepare to bail out, it's our only hope."

The pilot of the Mustang on his left wing broke in. "It looks bad, fellow. We'll ride you down—but you'd better get the hell out of that plane."

And then the minutes collapsed upon one another; one minute he was strapped into his seat, and the next minute he was standing at the open doorway of the plane, his hand gripping the rip cord of his parachute. Below him, members of the crew floated down the sky, guarded from the German fighters by a pair of Mustangs. He took a breath and fell forward as he had been trained to do, making himself count, making himself wait until he was clear of the plane before pulling the cord. He felt the sudden jerk as the parachute bloomed above him. And then he was swaying, held in the cradle of his harness, surrounded by cloud-mists and filled with a consuming fear.

The roar of the Mustangs was all he could hear; the brightness of the morning sky was all he could see. He felt nothing, he thought nothing, wrapped in his cocoon of terror. And then the ground came up to meet him, and he was rolling across it, the parachute dragging in his wake. He heard shouts a short distance away. The words were indistinct, but the tone was clear. Someone was giving a command.

He stood and looked in the direction of the shouts. A small squad of German soldiers was marching toward him, his crew members banded together in their midst. He saw the rifles trained on him, the flash of sunlight on a bare bayonet. Name, rank, and serial number, he told himself. That's all I have to tell them. He braced himself, made himself stand tall. A finger of sweet air caressed him; he looked at his feet and saw a small blue flower. If he closed his eyes, this could be the sweet air of home.

The men were closer now; one advanced toward him, a pistol in his hand. He gestured toward the holster that held Skye's gun; Skye pulled the gun and threw it on the ground. "My name is Claude Louis Langlinais," he said. "I am a captain. My serial number is . . ." Behind him, he heard a dove's low sweet call. As he fell in with the others, he thought of how easily that small bird could lift her body, could fly from this field to another far away. To an English field, a place of safety. It wasn't possible that this earth he had soared above so freely was now his prison. It wasn't possible that the wings he commanded had failed. He felt dizzy, as though he had not eaten for many hours. Light-headed, as though waking from having too much beer. They had marched almost a mile before he made himself face what lay ahead. He was now one of war's casualties. He was now a prisoner. Something stirred in him, an instinct he had not known he had. He began to take note of the terrain around him. He began to figure, from the distance they had flown from the target, just where they might be. He began to plan to escape.

12

APRIL–JUNE 1944

The first shock hit Caro's assembly line before the flames shot up. She reeled back, clutching the edge of her worktable, blinking her eyes behind the protective glass of her goggles. The wall at the end of the shop suddenly burst into bright orange flame, a sheet of fire that seemed to devour men and machines. Then the sirens began to wail, and workers fell into place, automatically forming the lines that would take them to safety.

Crews carrying limp fire hoses ran toward the flames; even as the first massive burst of water hit them, there was another explosion, one that shattered the fire and sent it into the air in brilliant torchlike pieces.

Caro followed the others blindly, her heart pounding. She could see nothing but the backs and head-coverings of the workers ahead of her, hear nothing but the sirens and shouting of the crowd, feel nothing but a kind of numb terror. Had the explosion occurred only five minutes earlier, she would have been caught in it, bent over the bench where defective work was sent.

She had a sudden vision of herself being blown to bits and pieces. She fought for control, fought to keep from pushing past those ahead of her. "Please, God. Please, God." As with many of her prayers these days, she did not say what it was she wanted. Mostly she wanted this moment to be over.

And then it was. They burst out into the factory yard, moving quickly away from the building to crowd the perimeters near the fence and stand staring back at the fire. Caro leaned against the fence, her breath still coming hard. "Cigarette?" the woman standing next to her said, offering a crumpled pack of Luckies.

"Thanks," Caro said.

"I guess poor Nancy's bought it," the woman said.

Caro thought of the woman she had been helping not half an hour ago. She bit her lips and swallowed back the bile in her throat. "I was down there myself," she said. The words seemed thick; they filled her mouth, and she stopped, stifled.

"I know," the woman said. She patted Caro's arm. "Doesn't do to think about it."

"No," Caro agreed. "It doesn't."

When the all-clear sounded an hour later, she marched back inside with the others. The debris had been cleared away, Nancy's body carried off, and the five injured workers taken to the hospital. Two landing craft ready to go had been severely damaged, three others needed extensive repairs. When volunteers were called for to work extra shifts to get the yard back on schedule, Caro raised her hand. She would not sleep more than a few hours anyway—she might as well be here.

Toward midafternoon, she took a break, standing in an open doorway and absorbing the soft April afternoon. It did not seem right, somehow, that the spring sky was still this particular shade of whitewashed blue, that the new leaves on the pecan trees were as feathery as they always were, that the air could still caress her skin. The world should be harsh, made of sharp lines and deep shadows, glaring reds and threatening blacks. The world should match the way she felt.

They had gotten word in late March that Skye was missing in action; a week ago they had had news that he was in a POW camp somewhere in Germany. Skye was somewhere in Germany. David was somewhere in the Pacific. She had not had a letter from him for almost two months, and although she told herself that the Pacific fleet had more important things to do than to see that mail got delivered, that did not comfort her. She was tired of anxiety, weary of fear. She was lonely. She saw none of the girls she went to school with, only Babs and Ruth, and then only when their schedules coincided. Raoul rotated between school and hospital; he might as well not exist. Henri seemed always busy. He had finally found a group of people he liked, and who liked him, and where before Caro nagged at him to find friends of his own, now she nagged him to spend more time with her. That left Walter, who was away from New Orleans more than he was here.

Self-pity is probably the most unattractive emotion there is, she told herself. Shape up, Caro, and stop feeling sorry for yourself. There are millions of people all over the world who would give everything they have left to be safe and sound in the United States. She went over all the things she had to be grateful for, all the reasons she should thank God she was in this place at this time. Today, none worked.

She ground out her cigarette and prepared to go back to work, still in the doldrums. I need the country, she decided. I need the farm. And Beau Chêne. Père was in Washington, but Mama and André and Émilie were in St. Martinville, keeping both places going and doing war work besides. I'll do these extra shifts this week, she thought. And then next weekend I'll go down there. Just thinking about it cheered her up, and by the time the whistle that ended the shift blew, she was almost on an even keel again.

Then another whistle sounded, two short blasts followed by a long one that meant there was an announcement to be made. Caro stood quietly, listening to the crowd of workers gradually settle into silence. "We have every reason to believe that the explosion which caused one fatality, five casualties, and damaged five landing craft was the work of saboteurs. Security is investigating. You are asked to cooperate with them, and to answer any questions to the fullest extent of your knowledge. You are further requested to remember that *nothing* you hear within these walls is to be repeated to *anyone* on the outside."

It was not until Caro's bus was almost to the corner of Calliope that she remembered that several weeks ago, just before this batch of landing craft was begun—hadn't she said something about it to someone? She racked her brain, trying to put the memory into a context. And then, as she swung off the bus and began walking up her street, she remembered. The Famous Door. Walter and Henri. She stopped, trying to remember what it was she had said. Nothing much, nothing either of them paid any attention to. You're really letting your nerves get out of control, she told herself, starting to walk again. After all, even if you did say something about laying keels for a new kind of landing craft—Henri is your brother, for heaven's sake. And Walter is one of your best friends.

The whistle blew shrilly, cutting over the whir of machinery, the throb of engines, the rat-a-tat of the rivet guns. Two short blasts and a long one—the signal to listen to the loudspeaker. Caro shut off her drill and relaxed her shoulder muscles, forcing them into a straight line and lifting her body into the same alignment. She reached up and rubbed the back of her neck, which always first showed the effect of standing in one position for hours. There was a burst of music over the loudspeakers throughout the yard, and then a familiar voice. The President. She looked at her watch. Eleven o'clock in the morning. Automatically, without thinking, she said a quick prayer. "Please, God, whatever it is, make it not bad."

"My fellow Americans," the President said. "In this poignant hour I ask you to join with me in prayer: Almighty God: Our sons, pride of our nation, this day have set upon a mighty endeavor, a struggle to preserve our republic, our religion, and our civilization, and to set free a struggling humanity. Lead them straight and true; give strength to their arms, stoutness to their hearts, steadfastness in their faith. . . ."

Comprehension dawned on the faces of the workers around her. D-Day. The President's message continued, but no one could hear it. Their shouts and cheers created a mass of sound that rose to the metal roof high above them and ricocheted back. And then the workers began singing, one voice after the other taking up the tune. "God bless America, land that I love . . ." Caro's eyes misted, and she could no longer clearly see her neighbors or the machines that loomed around them. "Stand beside her, and guide her, through the night with the light from above." Her voice lifted and she brushed the tears from her eyes. "God bless America, my home, sweet home . . ." As she went back to work, she stared at the rivet gun in her hand. It suddenly seemed separate from her, something she really could lay down and walk away from when the war was over.

When the war was over. They had been using those words so long that they had lost their meaning. But now they meant something. This invasion was the beginning of the end. David would come back to her. And Skye would be set free. Even now, it was difficult to think of Skye. The memory of Père's face when they got word that Skye was missing in action could still hurt, even though the pain was softened by the knowledge that he was at least alive. Père had gone into her mother's arms making sounds Caro realized were sobs. She had never heard a man cry, nor had she ever heard a grief as desolate as this. She had watched her mother stroke Père's hair, kiss his cheeks, his forehead, the hands that clung to her. And then Caro had fled, to shed her own tears and pray for Skye. She prayed for him now. "Keep him safe," she murmured. "Bring him home."

Then, resolutely, she went back to work. She knew that weeks from now, she and other Americans would see newsreels of the action taking place so far away. She knew that when she left work and picked up the afternoon *States-Item,* black headlines would shriek tales of valor, tales of glory. Tales of death. These hours were a bridge, a time when all she knew was that the invasion had begun. She would use them, she thought, almost as a respite. Because once she read about it, her mind would never be free of it. She would follow those armies mile by mile, village by village. She would read names of old cities and monasteries, places that housed the great treasures of European civilization. She would weep at their destruction, bothered by the thought that she might be the sort of person who mourned the loss of a Rembrandt more than the loss of unknown lives.

At lunchtime she called Walter's office, intending to remind him of his promise. "I've got the last of my grandfather's champagne that I'm saving for the day we invade Europe," he'd said. "And you have the first dibs."

Walter's secretary answered, against a tumult of sound in the background that made it difficult for Caro to make out her words.

"Sorry about all the noise," the girl shouted into the phone. "We're overcome with a flood of refugees—they're so happy we've invaded Europe, they're already planning to go home."

"Is Mr. Fournet there?" Caro asked. The jubilation on the other end of the line made her feel more isolated, and she desperately wanted to hear a friendly voice.

"I'm sorry. He's away," the girl said. "Is there a message?"

"No," Caro said, and hung up. As she went back to work, she decided she'd try to get hold of Henri. There really was no fun in drinking champagne alone, she thought, even on the day the Allies raised the curtain on the final act of this long and exhausting war.

In the days that followed, newspaper and radio accounts deluged eager Americans with details of D-Day. Each fresh story was greeted with elation, each yard advanced taken as a step toward victory. The mood of the country was high, and everyone from farmers to war workers went back to his task with fresh vigor.

There were other reactions. In St. Martinville, as in POW camps all over America, the news that the Allies had landed in Europe caused a wide range of response. At one extreme were those openly relieved that perhaps Hitler would soon be deposed, and sane Germans would once more rule Germany. At the other were those who fanatically held that Hitler would throw the Allied armies back where they came from, and then follow them to England's shores. But in the main, in the days after the invasion, the camp as a whole became lethargic, apathetic, as though the men hung suspended between one state of being and another.

Their lethargy was furthered by their isolation; the cane grew in dense rows, green blades woven into an almost impenetrable mass. Between the stands, narrow paths of dark, rich soil led to the outer reaches of the canefields that stretched for miles in every direction around Beau Chêne. Caroline's fields met those of the Billeauds; their fields met someone else's, until the entire region was covered with slender blades, and the gentle movement the wind made as it crossed over them made a sound like the earth sighing.

In late June the cane was only half as high as it would be at harvest in October, and the guards who patrolled the fields where the German prisoners worked could see them easily, and watch as they hoed their way down one endless row after the other. Negro hands worked in the fields too, and a camaraderie had sprung up between the two groups of workers, a feeling based on their mutual awareness of the limitations of their lives. The few prisoners who had tried to escape in the year they had been at St. Martinville had found refuge in field hands' cabins, from which they were soon flushed and returned to the base camp at Fort Polk.

Escape, as German prisoners all across Louisiana learned, was not as easy as the laxness of the guards and the lack of fences around the fields made it appear to be. While it was simple enough to hide behind the cane, to make one's way along a row to a drainage ditch, to follow the ditch to the railroad, and then to walk along the track, what they had not first realized was the isolation, the distance from cities the rural areas in which they lived were. The tracks led nowhere helpful for miles and miles. The camp grapevine reported attempted escapes, and a favorite topic for conversation centered on devising new means to get away. Some held that if they could just reach the Gulf of Mexico, a tantalizing thirty miles due south, they could be picked up by a German U-boat. Others wanted to go north, to lose themselves in the population of a large northern city. But no cities lay within close proximity to the north, and the thirty miles to the south led through uncharted swamp. When word came that a group of POWs from another camp had indeed begun a walk through a swamp, but had been picked up covered with mosquito bites, with more than a few suffering from snakebite, the POWs changed their minds about which direction to head off in, and, if they thought about escape, thought no further than the gleaming railroad tracks leading outward.

Like other American POW camps, the camp at St. Martinville was as comfortable as the joint efforts of those running it and those who were imprisoned could make it. The core of educated prisoners worked with the Red Cross staff to provide entertainment; even though the complement of prisoners was small, there were enough musicians to get up a small chamber orchestra, and many a spring and summer evening found the people of St. Martinville seated on blankets just beyond the prison fence listening to Viennese waltzes and other light classical programs.

The people who came into contact with the prisoners—planters, townspeople—made it a rule never to discuss politics with any of them. The mood of the camp was positive from the beginning, and they wanted nothing to change that. On the whole, they respected these Germans, all of whom were regular army who had served in the North Afrika Corps. The same insouciance that lightened the Cajun attitude toward many of life's complexities helped them deal with the POWs in their midst.

At least one planter threw a party for the prisoners in gratitude for their work, and as the unusual became familiar, the sight of a POW having a quiet dinner out with the family he worked for became, if not the rule, at least not an unacceptable exception. It was precisely this ease between prisoners and captors that made a Swedish inspector, on a tour of duty with the Red Cross, write that the POW camp at St. Martinville was the "loveliest of any in the United States."

And Beau, who held on to a kind of superstitious belief that if he observed to the hilt the rules of the Geneva Convention dealing with prisoners, if, in fact, he went beyond that, then his own son would be treated well, continued to support all efforts to make this experiment work.

"It's a way to test our own capacity for good, I suppose," he told Émilie one afternoon. "We do a good turn for those poor fellows . . ."

"And breathe a prayer someone is doing one for Skye," she said, catching her father's hand and holding it tightly. "I know. Oh, Papa, I know. But sometimes, when I'm at the camp, organizing an entertainment, or giving an English lesson, I—well, I get so *discouraged*. As if it's all for nothing. Goodwill between men, that kind of thing. Because the world's already done this, Papa. It's *had* this war. And what good is it doing?"

"I'm not sure a war does good," Beau said. "We hope it will prevent further evil."

"I wish I thought I were doing something useful," Émilie said. "I think of Gennie, entertaining in hospitals—of Caro, building ships. Of Skye—" Émilie fell sobbing against his shoulder. "Oh, Papa, do you think he's all right?"

"We have to hope so. And pray so," Beau said. Now that the war was on European soil, the channels that had gotten mail through were less effective; what comfort could be gained from a letter dated months before it was received? He held Émilie close. She was only twenty-two, but the years of responsibility in the office and on the farm had matured her; although her hazel eyes still sparkled with laughter, and although she still loved to go out dancing or throw impromptu parties, there was a seriousness beneath her gaiety that was just one more legacy of the war. Beau had learned just the week before that Émilie had imposed on herself the duty of calling regularly on local families who had lost sons in the war.

Thinking of that trail of grief, and of her courage in choosing to walk it with the mourners, he kissed her tenderly. "You've no idea what it means to me—to Mère—to have you here. To have life in the house—your friends coming in—some semblance of normalcy."

She saw the pain he usually hid from them, and swallowed her tears. "What you're saying is that 'they also serve who only stand and wait,' " she said, smiling a little.

"Sometimes that's the hardest part," he said. It was the closest Beau had come to saying what he felt—that to have his oldest son held captive, and to be able to do absolutely nothing about it, was the most difficult test of his life. A test of his belief in his own power, of his ability to keep those he loved safe. "Well," he said, turning his face and blinking rapidly, "let's take a break from all this. Let's collect André and go for a swim, okay?"

"Okay!" Émilie said.

Later, stretched out on the bank near the swimming hole, watching André swim, Beau realized that in his struggle for power, what he really wanted was not an empire, but a fence. A moat. Something that would keep his land and his family safe.

A Lady Banksia rosebush almost covered the library windows at Beau Chêne, yellow blossoms making a curtain between the room and the green world outside. A mockingbird sat on the rim of the birdbath, singing along with the cardinals flitting near their nest. A lawn mower sounded in the distance, the clack-clack of its blades a soothing counterpoint to the familiar hum of insects and sounds of birds. Émilie pushed her pillow more comfortably behind her back and bent over the book in her hand. She had walked over to Beau Chêne after lunch on this slumberous summer day, thinking to spend a quiet hour with one of the old books that filled the towering mahogany shelves.

This place never feels empty, she thought, feeling the cool house around her. The shutters on the west side of the house were closed against the afternoon sun, but the shutters and windows facing east and north were open, and the sunbeams danced into rooms, lighting up faded brocades and touching old portraits with a sudden gleam of gold. She liked to think of all the people who had lived here, all the hands that had taken books off these very shelves, settled into this very window seat, spent the same kind of lazy afternoon.

She did not know what made her look up from her book, head lifted as though she were sniffing the wind. Then she saw a quick movement in the shadows at the end of the room where the big desk was, and as she watched, her body rigid, a man stepped toward her, a machete grasped in his hand.

She felt her heart beating, a rapid pounding that seemed so loud she could hear nothing else, not even the slight noise the man made as he walked toward her across the Tabriz rug that covered the library floor. It's one of the prisoners, she thought. Did she know this man? Was he someone she had worked with at the camp? But the dullness in his eyes denied recognition; as far as he was concerned, Émilie was only an obstacle, someone in his way.

"What do you want?" she said, swinging her feet down to the floor. Her hand gripped the book tightly while her mind worked. If she could distract him, shout to whoever manned that lawn mower . . . She sat up straight, her eyes never leaving the man's face.

"Don't move," he said. "And don't scream." He was almost up to her now, and she could smell his sweat and see the field mud that clung to his shoes.

"What to you want?" she said again.

"Money," he said. "Clothes."

"There's no money here," she said. "Not really any clothes."

"This so fine house has no money? The people have no clothes?"

"No one really lives here—" Émilie said, and then, when she saw the way he smiled, knew what a terrible mistake she had made.

"No one lives here," he said. "You mean—there is no one in the house."

"No," she said. Her lips were dry, she could almost feel the skin cracking, and she licked them. She saw him watching her tongue, saw an expression she did not understand come into his eyes.

"So there is no money, and no clothes."

"That's right," she said. A burst of courage helped her add, "You can't escape, you know you can't. There's nowhere for you to go, don't you know that?"

The prisoner's posture did not change; he still held the machete high, the long curved blade glittering along its sharp edge. "You think I should go back to the fields, is that it?"

"Isn't that the sensible thing to do?" She was encouraged now; maybe he would give way, turn and docilely march back where he came from. "I won't—I won't say anything."

That was the second mistake. He moved toward her and his free hand flashed out, gripping her wrist. His eyes flicked over her. "You are not as beautiful as my woman at home. But you have all that I need."

She didn't understand his coldness, the lack of passion, the evenness of his voice, and the stillness of his body. It was like confronting a robot, or a marionette, from which any human element had long since been extracted. She made herself look into the cold eyes staring at her, made herself aware of the steel in his grip on her wrist. She would say nothing, she would not waste her strength on useless talk. She would have to go from one minute to the next, concentrating on the only thing of any importance—saving her life.

"Kneel down," the man told her.

She looked at him, uncomprehending. He put his hand on her head and shoved her toward the floor. "Kneel down," he repeated roughly. "Open my pants."

She fell to the floor and then struggled to her knees, staring at the sweat-stained legs in front of her. She could not imagine what it was he wanted her to do, but the sour odor of his clothing, the thick roughness of his voice, sickened her, and she clenched her hands in front of her body, lips closed against the bile that rose in her throat.

"Don't act as though you don't know what I want," he said. His hand took a twist of her hair, and he yanked it viciously. "Or do you want me to put it in you?" A stream of obscenities hit her, as though he were vomiting hatred and lust. "I wouldn't dirty myself with your filth." His other hand jerked the zipper of his pants down; he thrust the hand inside, and then pulled his organ out. "Now, take it in your mouth," he said. "Now. Or I'll kill you."

She shut her eyes. He would kill her anyway. He would have to. She shut her lips more tightly, bent her head as though to receive the blade.

And then she heard a grunt, and several quick blows. "Get the hell out of here, Émilie," her father cried, and she opened her eyes to see him smashing his fist into the German, one solid blow after the other, until the man fell and Beau fell on top of him, beating his head furiously against the floor. "Get out, Émilie," her father cried again. She got to her feet and stumbled to the door, unable to take her eyes from the scene. The prisoner's face was covered with blood, his eyes dull and sightless. Her father's hands moved to the man's throat, and she saw him take it and begin to squeeze.

Father's going to kill him, she thought. Then the haze terror had put between her and reality parted, and she ran forward, crying, "Papa—don't! Stop!"

Beau's hands faltered. He looked up at her, and she did not recognize his face. "Papa. I'm all right. I'm not hurt. Papa—he's been stopped. It's enough."

She saw reason return; Beau's grip relaxed, and he sat back on the unconscious prisoner's chest, breathing hard. "All right," he said finally.

"All right." He got up and found heavy cord in the desk and tied the man's hands behind his back. "I'll call the sheriff," he said. "He can take this man to Fort Polk. They can do anything they want to him there—but if he stays in St. Martin Parish even one night, I won't be held responsible for what I do to him."

"How did you know to come?" Émilie asked. She couldn't look at the man lying on the floor; she couldn't think about what had almost happened. She braced herself against one of the big wing chairs. "Could I—do you have a cigarette?"

"Actually," her father said, taking out two cigarettes and giving her one, "it was a piece of luck." He was watching her closely, waiting to see which direction her nerves would take her. "I felt sluggish after lunch, thought I'd never be able to stay awake this afternoon unless I had a walk. Took the old path over here out of habit, I guess, and then decided to come on up and check the house." He took her face in his hands. "Are you really all right, baby?"

"Well," Émilie said, "it's nothing I'd want to repeat." The thought of the blade, of that thin, shining edge, and the memory of his forcing her down, of the stench from his trousers, broke through her bravado. She began to shiver; her face contorted, and the hard sobs came. She felt her father's arms open around her, and she bent her head against his shoulder. She knew she was "all right" if that meant all her parts were still in place. That she would get back her nerve. She would wait with her father for the sheriff to come; they might even sit in the kitchen sipping coffee with the prisoner safely trussed and locked in the storeroom outside. But when she pulled away from her father and looked up into his face, she knew that in one way, she was not "all right." And would not be, ever again.

"Promise me something, Papa. That you won't tell Mère. Or anyone. Can't you just say . . . he was stealing?"

The wisdom in Émilie's eyes made Beau want to weep. Even as he gave his promise, he knew whose innocence Émilie was protecting. "You're a brave soldier," he said, and kissed her cheek. He felt the tiny withdrawal, the slightest flinch, and chalked up one more scar to this wretched war.

13

LATE JUNE–SEPTEMBER 1944

Guy Loring's king jumped over four of his opponent's remaining checkers, leaving him with one unprotected king. "Your move," Loring said, sitting back on his haunches.

"I have no moves," his opponent said. "Your game, Loring."

Guy, realigning the checkers, turned to Skye. "You're on, Langlinais."

Skye took the other side of the board. Guy Loring had not been in the camp long, but already he commanded respect. He was a Commando; he had been among the first Americans to hit the beaches in North Africa, and he had been captured alive, it was rumored, only because he had been wounded and unconscious when he was picked up. His training had been vastly different from that which infantrymen received. He needed no weapon to kill but his bare hands; he kept himself in shape by disciplined exercise. Since he'd arrived in camp in April, he had kept mostly to himself, maintaining his distance from the other prisoners.

There had been rumors at first that Loring might be a German spy placed in the camp to ferret out plans for escape. Skye had not been in prison long before he had heard of "escape" attempts that were traps arranged by prisoners working for the Nazis. He had taken his own measure of Loring and had decided that Loring was his own man. Skye could not name a reason for this trust; some instinct, some gut-level feeling that seemed able to identify men whose honor was more important than their lives.

The game became an even contest, one that promised to take a long time to resolve, and the few kibitzers drifted off to other parts of the prison yard. "I've been watching you, Langlinais," Loring said. "There's something I want to talk to you about."

Skye felt the skin at the back of his neck tingle. He knew even before Loring spoke what the "something" was. He decided to take a risk equal to Loring's. "Are you going to try to escape?" he asked, his eyes on the board.

Out of the corner of his eye, he could see Loring's grim smile. "I'm not going to try. I'm going to do it," Loring said. "I've got four others—I can take one more. Are you in?

"How will you do it?" Skye asked, carefully moving a king out of Loring's reach.

"I can't tell you that. You'll have to trust me. But it will work. Now, are you in?" Loring surveyed the board, and then looked up to meet Skye's eyes. "You have twelve hours to decide," he said. "I don't blame you if you're not sure you trust me—but maybe the fact that I trust you says something."

Skye did not wait twelve hours before seeking Guy Loring out and agreeing to be part of the plan. After all, didn't his grandmother always say that to a bold man, fortune holds out her hand? Better the risk than to rot here waiting for the war to end.

Loring's plan involved digging a tunnel under their barracks out past the fence and under the open fields surrounding the camp until it emerged in the screen of a small woods beyond. "That's all you need to know right now," he told the men he had chosen at his first meeting. "It's not safe for you to know what happens when we get out."

No one could argue with that. If the Germans discovered the tunnel and questioned them—well, no matter what methods they used to give their questions force, a man could not tell what he did not know.

They began to dig that week. Skye, along with the others, took his turn scooping out dirt with his hands or with a rough tool fashioned from a spoon stolen from the camp kitchen. He hit the dirt in his pockets or put it in pouches tied to his legs, later dumping it into the latrine or scattering it over the hard prison ground. When he was sent on a work party out of the camp, he could sometimes smuggle out larger amounts of dirt; but always, when he passed beneath the guard towers flanking the gates, he felt the terrible rigidity of his spine bracing him against the bullets he lived in fear of.

The days were marked now by the length of the tunnel. Loring had chosen an angle that traveled the shortest distance to the woods; he calculated they had to dig just over a hundred yards to reach its cover. And although the amount of dirt each of the six of them managed to remove from each shift seemed small, Loring was pleased. The days might seem to drag into each other, but he assured them their progress was good.

Then one day in June Guy came to Skye, body tense, face fighting for control. He had learned through his Resistance contacts that the Allies had landed in Europe. For the first time, Skye felt the tunnel was real and that escape was not just a dream to keep him going. The knowledge that their armies were actually on European soil served as a powerful fuel for all of them, and day by day, handfuls of dirt at a time, the tunnel reached toward freedom.

Although Loring could speak German, he kept the fact to himself. He was able to piece together, from bits of news gleaned from conversations among the guards and prison staff, that the Normandy invasion had shaken the German High Command badly—not because they had not known the invasion was coming, but because they had been so completely deceived. The first few days after D-Day, this confusion aided the Allies who had it all their own way. But then the Allied armies slowed their pace just enough to give the Germans time to rush their best panzer divisions to the western front, where a slogging foot-by-foot, yard-by-yard battle developed.

The progress of the tunnel seemed paced to that same slow struggle. The weeks crawled by, with only the thought that the tunnel would soon be done to buoy Skye through days of increasing tension and fatigue. When he was very weary, Skye found it almost impossible to keep a third emotion from weighting him—fear. Loring pointed out, in that calm way he had, that as things got worse for the Germans, discipline would start falling apart—and American prisoners could well become scapegoats for their anger and frustration. The thought of being helpless against the rage of his captors spurred Skye to work harder. Put in that perspective, the risk of escape looked more attractive than staying where he was.

And then one day they broke through into the copse of woods beyond the field. The tunnel was complete. Not long after that came the night they had all been waiting for, a night late in August when the moon was at its darkest. Loring gave his group the word after the evening meal, when they were standing in clusters around the prison yard. They would begin leaving at 0200, going into the tunnel at five-minute intervals. Once they were through the tunnel, Loring said, members of the French Resistance would meet them. By sunrise they should be on French soil.

His eyes, glittering with excitement, belied the quiet tone in which he spoke. Skye felt a moment of exultation: by this time tomorrow he would be a free man.

Never had an evening been so long, nor so filled with tension. If Skye happened to be near one of the other five, he immediately moved away, so that nothing in their faces would betray them. Then he worried that by moving, he was calling attention to himself. He was partially relieved when Guy told him that the camp staff was having a party, celebrating the commander's birthday. "They'll be full of schnapps and beer," Guy said. "Sound asleep, most of them, and only the regular guards to worry about."

As a rule, the guards patrolled on schedule. They had not varied the routine for weeks; although the routine itself changed, once a change was made, they could count on guards checking the barracks at the same time every night. The present schedule had been in effect only three days; it was the congruence of a new schedule, a dark moon, and something to divert the staff that made Loring choose this as the night to effect the escape.

Skye did not expect to sleep, nor did he want to. He must be on the alert; he lay in the dark barracks, testing sounds, almost sniffing the air for danger. And then it was 0200, and he knew that in fifteen minutes his turn to leave would come.

At 0215 he stealthily slipped from his cot to the floor, crawling across it to the door. The mouth of the tunnel was behind a corner of the barracks, concealed by the concrete piers which lifted the barracks floor off the ground. Each man was to leave the barracks individually, making his way to the tunnel and beginning the long journey alone, not knowing if the others were in the tunnel with him or not. Although Skye had strained his ears, he had not heard the other two leaving their bunks. As he ducked through the barracks door, he wondered if the others had left. Or was this a trap? Was Loring even now sitting in the camp headquarters while German guards waited at the tunnel entrance to snatch them?

He lay on the ground and began wriggling under the barracks, using his elbows to propel him forward to the tunnel entrance. It was absolutely black; even the light from the guard towers did not penetrate here, and when something scurried over his legs, he had to bite his lips to keep from crying out. And then he was at the tunnel entrance. He reached into it and felt the cool, black emptiness. For a moment he clung to the tunnel's edge, fear crowding all other emotions. Then he made himself enter. He remembered the timetable. Another man would be entering the tunnel at 0220; he had better be well on his way.

He moved forward, trying to keep his mind on the goal and to ignore the claustrophobia that assailed him. The walls of the tunnel closed around him like an earthen coffin as he crawled on his stomach into the blackness. Before he had gone ten yards, his clothes were covered with dirt and his fingers were bleeding from root ends and stones that tore at them. Skye lost all track of both time and distance: although at first he had tried to keep count of both, it suddenly seemed pointless. In this dark world, neither time nor space existed. He shut off all thoughts, and pushed blindly forward.

At times he thought he heard someone ahead of him, someone behind him. But most of the time he felt as though he were the only person alive on earth, burrowing through this wet, dark tomb toward freedom. He would not let himself think of the other possibilities. But despite his best efforts, images of death rose before him in the dark. He had seen prisoners' bodies hanging on the barbed wire surrounding their compound. He had seen prisoners' bodies left all day in the fields around the camp, bloody reminders of what happened to those who tried to escape. He knew that no rules of international law would stay his captors' hands; the fall of Paris days ago had had almost more effect on German morale than had the invasion itself, and though the guards were partying tonight, the mood of the camp command was ugly.

Just when he was beginning to believe that he would never reach the tunnel's end, Skye smelled fresh air. The scent of field grasses sweetened it; he struggled forward, tears streaming down his cheeks. The tunnel's mouth was just inside the covering woods. As he climbed out, a figure emerged out of the dark, and he heard Loring's voice. "Stay low. Crawl forward past me. It'll be all right to stand up then." When Skye finally stood next to Loring, he looked through the screen of trees to the brilliantly lit camp. Guards manned the watchtowers, and the searchlight beams made a circle of danger all around them.

"If everyone's on schedule, we'll be almost safe before the guards find out we're gone," Loring said. "I'll stay here. You go on through the woods—a French Resistance member is stationed near a stream just beyond the woods." Loring seemed to melt into the black woods, leaving Skye once more alone. He followed the path Loring had indicated; it was not really a path, just a sort of trail that animals might make going to the stream to drink. Just as he saw water gleaming in the starshine, a hand touched his arm as another one came over his mouth.

" 'The Diamond Necklace,' " a voice hissed in his ear, and Skye relaxed. This was the password Guy had chosen; it was the title of a story by Guy de Maupassant.

" 'All that glitters is not real,' " Skye answered. He suddenly wanted to laugh. The escape was an adventure, a game like those he and Henri and Raoul used to play during the long summer days of their youth. He saw something flash in the man's hand; the sharp length of the knife cut through his fantasies, and he took the rope the man handed him and, following his instructions, tied it around his waist.

"Follow the stream," the maquis said. "There will be another of us waiting for you. Keep your head underwater until you are signaled to take a breath. It is very dangerous here."

Skye slid into the water and ducked his head beneath its murky surface. The rope tied to his waist floated behind him, to be anchored by the weight of the next man; it stretched before him, connected to the man ahead. He held his breath and forced himself to be calm. The stream was not deep, and his back felt like a broad, open target. He hunched lower, as though two more inches of water could protect him from the tearing bullets of a machine gun. In a few moments he felt as though his lungs were bursting. There was no air left in them; if he could not raise his head and take in air, he would suffocate. He could feel his eyes bulging, feel the urgency to open his mouth and take in anything—water that would drown him, mud that would engorge his lungs—anything. Even with his eyes open, he could see nothing. His legs were numb, he could not feel his hands. And then came a tug, one short followed by a long. The signal that he could come up for air.

His head shot through the water, and he opened his mouth, taking in oxygen in great gulps. Ahead of him, he could just make out one of the others, barely poking his head from the covering stream. Reeds clustered thickly on either bank, and when he stared beyond them, he saw stars glimmering high above.

And then his head was underwater again, and he was moving forward, the sodden rope clasped in his hand. He lost count of the number of times they stopped and gulped air. He lost count of the number of rocks that cut his knees and bruised his hands. He lost count of the number of prayers he said, or the times he seemed to lose consciousness. Finally came the signal he had thought would never come. Three short tugs. We are there.

He poked his head above water, weak with disbelief. The men ahead of him were already climbing up the muddy bank of the stream, reaching their hands to those behind to help them over the slick surface. Skye stood and staggered forward. Hands grabbed him, hauled him up. Quickly he left the stream and they moved into the cover of a clump of trees, where three men waited for them. In a few minutes Loring and the other two men arrived; for a moment they stood in a loose circle, breathing hard, their common exertion and emotion bonding them. One of the maquis spoke to Guy, and Skye caught a word or two—a boat was waiting to take them across the Rhine. Hurry.

He followed the others through the woods, ignoring the branches that lashed him. He climbed into the small launch moored at the foot of the woods, and sat immobile, his breath coming in short, quick gasps. Every muscle was taut, every nerve stretched. He heard the motor catch and braced himself. Surely the Germans would pour from those quiet woods now, and make the night a cacophony of gunfire. Surely a shell would arc over this solid river of glass, shattering its surface and making a hole their boat would vanish through. But nothing broke the stillness except the low roar of the motor and an occasional murmur from one of the men. The night air blew against him, making his wet clothes clammy on his skin. It's no worse than a hunt, he told himself as he began to shiver. You've gone overboard many a time, and laughed about it. His teeth chattered and he huddled into a tighter ball. So cold. So tired. Numb with it. Dead with it.

Minutes later the boat bumped against the far shore, and the motor cut off. Skye stumbled along the boat and climbed over the bow, wading through the shallow water until his feet reached dry land. He could see a cluster of people ahead of him, and he staggered toward them. He no longer cared whether they were French or not, friend or foe. Where there were people there must be a fire. Food. Something to sleep on. Something struck his foot and he fell forward over the root that protruded in his path. His head hit something hard, and he let go of consciousness. As though he were still underwater, as though his senses were distanced from the world around him, he felt himself lifted and borne forward. He felt a hand on his cheek, a hand that felt soft and smooth. He heard a voice, low and sweet. "*Pauvre homme,*" the voice said. "*Apportez-lui avec précaution.*"

When Skye awoke, it was to the same low voice, a girl singing softly by the fire. He lay back looking at her. She was young, so very young. Large brown eyes, black hair pulled back in a bun at the nape of her neck. A man's shirt belted over pants that hung loosely on her slender body. Feet thrust into heavy socks that brushed quietly against the cottage floor. He recognized the song as an old lullaby his grandmother had sung to him when he was small. He felt exhausted tears fill his eyes; he sobbed helplessly and heard a stir as the girl left her seat and came to him. "You are awake," she said in English. She touched his face. "You are safe for now," she said. "Later they will take you to where your armies are."

"Where am I now?"

She shook her head. "It is better that you do not know. The Germans do not bother us anymore—they are too busy fighting. But still—it is better."

"My name is Skye," he said.

"You may call me Adèle," she said. "Now I will get you something to eat."

Guy Loring appeared later in the afternoon. He wore a large gray smock and had a beret pulled down over his face. "We'll move out after dark," he said. "Toward Paris."

"All of us?"

"Not all at once. In pairs." He paced the small floor, hands clasped behind his back, head erect, voice energetic. "So far, this has been a piece of cake. Just a little more luck—and we'll be back in the war."

Skye threw back the rough blanket that covered him and stood up. The floor rocked beneath his feet, and he willed himself to stand firm. It seemed astonishing that this place of refuge was only a way station, after all, and that they still had so far to go, so much danger to evade.

"How bad is it?" he asked, gesturing toward the door. He saw a flicker of surprise in Guy's eyes, and knew that danger was something Loring lived with, expected—even thrived on.

"It's hard to say. The Allies are breaking though everywhere—so there're pockets of hard fighting—places already liberated—" Loring shrugged. "Mixed bag, I guess." His teeth flashed in the familiar wry grin. "I guess our friends in the Resistance aren't looking to be caught any more than we are." He picked up a smock like his own and handed it to Skye. "One thing for sure—we can't stay here."

"No," Skye said. He looked at Adèle, stirring something in a pot that hung over the fire. The simple peace of the room entered him. Beyond the window, a climbing rose hung out its flags of color as though there were no war. The scent of blended herbs simmering in stock permeated the air; the bed behind him was soft, cushioned by the down of a hundred geese. What magic did she know, this young girl who fought alongside men in an underground war where no rules applied, and where capture meant long torture and agonizing death? How had she held on to it, this clean space, this tranquility in the midst of terror?

He shook his head, as though shaking off his own lethargy. He could not stay here. He was on the first leg of the road back to war. His war. Another plane waited for him, a plane that might be based in England, but could just as easily fly from some airfield carved out of a coral island half a world away. The mental journey back could prove longer than the real one, he thought, stripping off his prisoner's shirt and pulling the smock over his head. He thrust his head through the shirt's neck, and saw Loring watching him. "I'm ready whenever you say," he said, and hoped Loring was more convinced than he was.

"She'll bring you to the meeting place," Guy said, and ducked through the low doorway.

Adèle came to sit on a low stool, a piece of knitting in her hand. "It will take you a while, you know," she said. "It always does."

"A while to do what?"

"To become accustomed to not being in prison anymore." She bent over her work, the smooth crown of her head suddenly reminding Skye of Rosalind. "But it is like everything else. Time passes, and you go to the next thing."

"Is that what you've done?" His imagination flagged; he could not envision what her life must have been like these years since the occupation.

"When one had not what one likes, one must like what one has," she said. She let the knitting rest in her lap and looked up at him. "I do not like the war—only the Boche like war. But I cannot hang my life on a hook until it is over, *n'est-ce pas?* And so I do what I can."

They moved out the next day, Skye and Guy going together. There was a member of the Resistance with them, an old farmer who chewed stolidly on the same plug of tobacco the entire morning, plodding steadily down the narrow dirt roads that crisscrossed the region. This part of the escape seemed anticlimactic; although they heard guns in the distance, and on occasion saw bombers winging their way to some faraway target, they came across no German patrols.

They reached American lines on the third day out. The farmer came to life then, taking the whiskey they were offered, tucking cigarettes and chocolate bars into his clothes. When he finally left them, Skye watched him go almost wistfully. A part of his life that was totally separate, unconnected to anything he had ever known, was finishing. And although he most certainly did not want to repeat it, in an odd way he was reluctant to let it go.

They were to be flown to London in a transport that had just disgorged more Allied troops, there to go through the debriefing given all returning prisoners of war. "Then the real battle will start," Guy Loring told Skye. "We're going to have to fight like hell to get back in this war, you know."

That was something Skye had forgotten all about. There was a rule, one made to protect the French Resistance, that any escaped prisoner was automatically sidelined, because if he were caught again, the Germans would be relentless in their determination to learn how he had escaped.

"But all over France, the Resistance is openly joining the war," Skye said. "Maybe that will make a difference."

"It had better," Loring said. "I've got more than a few scores to settle still."

I do too, Skye thought. But before I do anything else—the minute I finish with all that debriefing business—there's someone I've got to see.

Natalie's face rose before him, the golden eyes crinkling with laughter, the mouth smiling happily. She had seen enough of the war to understand his mood, he thought. She would recognize this kind of limbo he was in. Whereas the family at home—Rosalind—the most they would feel, he knew, was a tremendous relief and thanksgiving that he was free. Not for the first time, he wondered if the scars that did not show might in the long run have greater effect than the ones that did.

Skye hurried up the steps of the gray stone house where Natalie worked. Like many other London residences converted into wartime office space, this one retained some of its domestic character; a fire blazed away in the reception hall, and the portraits lining the walls had a familial rather than an official look. He had debated, ever since the debriefing ended and he had been given a leave, whether to call Natalie or just walk in unannounced. The debate had occupied most of the trip up to London; the lieutenant driving the jeep had maintained a respectful silence, certain that Captain Langlinais was still recovering from his experiences, giving Skye plenty of time to think.

He had imagined the call; how she would sound, what he would say. And then he had realized that she might not be in her office; he might have to leave a message. Constructing that message proved impossible; the longer he thought about having to tell some unknown person that this was Captain Skye Langlinais, calling Miss Watkins to let her know he was free—it finally seemed easier simply to drop in. If she isn't there, he thought, I can write a note.

The closer he got to her office, the more he questioned his emotions. Why this heightened heartbeat? Why this rush of anticipation, so strong it seemed to push him ahead of it? She's only a friend, he told himself. Why are you reacting as though she's something more? At one point, he even turned back, thrusting the bouquet of flowers he'd picked up into the astonished arms of an elderly lady puttering down the sidewalk with her little spaniel on a leash. He was two blocks in the opposite direction before he made himself face his own ambivalence.

"Don't be a damn fool, Langlinais," he told himself, making himself deal with this as he thought the doctor at the debriefing would have. "You're in a period of reentry, that's all. Don't be so cerebral." He decided to ignore what the real problem seemed to be: that far from being cerebral, the thought of Natalie reduced him to a mass of intuitive response, a response that had nothing to do with friendship.

But that's part of it too, he reminded himself, striking off across the street to a flower stand to buy another bouquet. Remember what the good doc said—for a while, every young woman, even those not terribly attractive, can cause the most astonishing desire. The doctor's prescription for the problem had been matter-of-fact; Skye had pushed it down to think about later.

Now he stood before the tall double doors, his breath short as though the flight of steps had been an alpine cliff. He grasped the bronze doorknob and opened the door, thrusting his body forward with the same sense of falling into alien space that he had had when he left his crippled plane. He approached a desk at which an Army sergeant sat, face impassive.

"I'm looking for Miss Natalie Watkins," Skye said. He saw the sergeant's jaw tighten, and reached for his ID. "I'm Captain Langlinais," he said. "Can you—can you call her, please?"

The sergeant's hand went to the telephone in front of him; he picked it up, said something Skye could not understand, and then hung it up again. In a few moments a private came hurrying down the hall, brightly polished shoes tapping briskly on the marble floor. "Follow me, Captain Langlinais," the private said. The main hall had a maze of halls opening off it; it seemed forever before the private stood in front of a small door and said, "In here, sir."

Skye watched the private disappear around a turn in the hall. Then silence closed around him, and he stood staring at the door, flowers clutched in his hand. He brought his free hand up to knock—the sharp sound his knuckles made as they struck the heavy wood startled him, and he followed the first knock up with two lighter ones. He thought he could hear movement, small sounds—and then the door swung open, and Natalie stood before him.

"Yes?" she said.

In the light that shone from the windows behind her, he could see her face turn pale. "Oh, Skye!" She put a hand out as though to take the flowers as he released them, and they cascaded to the floor, a shower of petals and feathery green leaves. She came up to him, and suddenly her arms were around his neck, and she was kissing him. She broke away to murmur his name, and then kissed him again. The low-burning passion he had held at bay all day flared; he pulled her closer, his mouth clinging to hers. He felt her respond, felt her body press closer—and then pull away.

"Skye! My God, you're here! You're all right!" She threw her arms around his neck and kissed him again, but this time her lips were against his cheek. "You gave me such a start!"

"I'm sorry—I should've called—I didn't think," he said.

"It's just that I'm so glad to see you. I thought you were still in Germany. I thought—" She sank into a chair, ducking her head to hide the tears that filled her eyes.

His own began to mist as he knelt in front of her. "Natalie, for God's sake, don't cry. I'm no good at all when women cry. I should have had better sense than to walk in on you—"

"I'm a little shaky," she said. "War nerves, I guess. And then to look up and see you—" She glanced at the flowers spilled over the floor, and for the first time since he had entered the room, she smiled. "Honestly, Skye," she said, getting up. "You're probably the only man I know who would bring a girl flowers when he's just out of a POW camp." She bent down and began to pick them up, and he moved to help her. She looked at him, her eyes filled with concern. "Was it—was it just awful?"

He handed her the last rose and helped her up. "We're not going to talk about it, we're not going to think about it. We're going to celebrate the fact that I'm free, I'm here—and ready to take you to the best restaurant in London tonight. Will you?"

Something flickered in her golden eyes, a memory of her impetuous welcome. "I might make a fool of myself in public," she said. "Do you want to risk that? God, Skye, when I saw you, I was so astonished . . . delighted—" She blushed, then laughed. "I didn't mean to . . . attack you."

"I rather enjoyed it," Skye said. He strove to replace the balance, their easy friendship, their camaraderie. "I figured you were just rehearsing for when you see your fiancé again."

He dropped the word carefully, watched her catch it. "Sure," she said. "I have to keep in practice." She had arranged the flowers in a pitcher of water; now she put them on her desk, breaking off one small carnation and bringing it to him. "Put this in your buttonhole, Skye. This feels like prom night, or graduation, or something equally momentous—" She stopped and stared at him, then came slowly forward, one hand outstretched. He felt her fingers follow the line of his chin, trace their way up his jawline, move lightly over his forehead, down the other cheek. "I'm really very glad to see you, Skye Langlinais," she said.

"I'm really very glad to see you, Natalie Watkins," he said.

She looked at the flower in her hand. "I guess this really isn't allowed with your uniform."

His hand closed over hers. "I'd like to have it anyway," he said, taking the carnation and tucking it into his pocket. And then, because he was almost afraid of what might happen next, he looked at his watch, made up an excuse about an appointment, and almost fled back down the hall to the safety of the street.

When he picked her up that evening, Skye thought he had never seen

Natalie look so beautiful. Even the dinner dresses she had worn at the Harringtons' had not set off her golden hair and amber eyes the way the copper silk she wore tonight did. They went dancing after dinner. It was the first time, he realized, they had ever danced together. Her body was soft, relaxed, easy to hold and guide. She followed his steps as though they had been partners in dancing school; when her hair brushed against his lips, he smelled the familiar Shalimar.

The night was punctuated by music, all the great songs he hadn't heard in what seemed a lifetime. Toward the end of the evening, when the two of them were almost alone on the dance floor, Skye pulled Natalie over to the jukebox and punched the button for "You'll Never Know."

"I've been wanting to hold a beautiful girl in my arms and dance to that song since I got back," he whispered.

She leaned away from him slightly. "Are you going to close your eyes and pretend I'm your girl?"

For a long moment they stared at each other, not speaking, not smiling, not moving. Skye knew the memory of their bodies, closer than skin, burned between them. He pulled her close and began to dance.

Sinatra's voice throbbed around them, the familiar words seeming to speak for them both. "I wonder," Natalie said, "if anyone ever really does know how much someone else cares—"

He caught sight of her face in a mirror behind them. Her head rested on his shoulder, her expression soft, dreamy. But her eyes were wide open, and when she saw him watching her, she tightened her hand on his neck, and her fingers curled into his palm.

They ended the night back at Natalie's flat, scrambling eggs in a chafing dish and eating the last of a country ham Natalie's mother had sent her. "Mother has that Southern conviction that nothing resembling food exists anywhere outside of Virginia," she said. "There's this constant stream of packages—"

It was astonishing, Skye thought. The more he found out about Natalie Watkins, the more he realized that they were exactly alike. And yet that diamond still gleamed on her finger, and Rosalind's picture was still the first thing he saw each day.

Maybe there were women you met and were just friends with all your life. He had never thought of having a girl just as a friend. He felt her stir in his arms, and looked down at the top of her shining head. His own body stirred; damn, he might try to lie to himself and tell himself that Natalie Watkins was just a friend. But if he were going to be honest, he would have to acknowledge that what he really wanted to do was take her to the nearest bed. He couldn't, in the furthest reaches of his imagination, consider doing that with someone who was only a friend. No matter what the base doctor had said.

Walking back to his hotel, he made himself conduct his self-examination even further. Wasn't most of what he'd felt this afternoon, tonight, just plain old lust? Not to be confused with love?

Later, in bed, he lay awake for a long time, thinking of Natalie and her lieutenant, thinking of Rosalind. He really didn't think he and Rosalind knew each other at all anymore. But instead of making it easier to write her breaking it off, it made it harder. He had certainly changed, grown up. My God, after the last few months, he felt sixty years old. And Rosalind must be changing too. When he thought of the promise he had always seen in her, he couldn't bring himself to write that final letter. Because no matter how much he was attracted to Natalie—not just today, but all the time he had known her—he had the sense to know that war was conducive to fast romances and faster letdowns. He also had the sense to know that neither he nor Natalie would ever again be the people they were at this particular point in their lives.

He would never again be so tired, so strung-out on a high wire held at one end by duty and patriotism, and at the other by risk and death. She would never again have to be so constantly brave, so constantly independent—nor would she ever again be so vulnerable, so far from home and all that made her feel secure.

So it would be silly, and destructive, to break off from Rosalind, who was maturing, changing herself into someone better, to chase after Natalie, who was a person she could not possibly continue to be.

Damn. Maybe tomorrow he would go to a different kind of bar and find a different kind of girl. One of the kind the base doctor had almost prescribed.

He drifted to sleep remembering his father's advice, almost an echo of the doctor's. "There's one big difference between sex you pay for and sex you get for 'free,' Skye. The sex you pay for usually costs a lot less in the long run."

Thinking of the price he would have to pay if he worked on Natalie's loneliness, if he transformed simple lust into a kind of love, he realized what his father had meant. It would not be fair to take this attraction, these feelings of compatibility, and blow them up into love. It would not be fair to court her, and distract her from her lieutenant so far away. If he were sure that he meant it . . . But he wasn't. The only thing he was sure of this September night of 1944 was that he was ready to be back on duty, ready to take his bomber up and help end this war. The rules had been changed; now that the Resistance was openly joining the war, even escaped prisoners could fly again. He would see the battle through, see all these complications ended. And then he would be far away from all of it, too far away to even remember what the complications were. He would be going home.

14

JANUARY 1945

The last of the credits faded from the screen, and the house lights came up. Caro sat for a moment, her mind still focused on the movie she had just seen. She looked at her watch. Ginger Rogers and Ray Milland had killed nearly two hours of this slow January Sunday, but there were hours left before she could sleep. She had very carefully timed her arrival at the theater just when the feature was about to start, avoiding the newsreels that she could no longer bear to watch.

It was not possible for her to watch them and not see David on every sinking ship, not see him caught in the gunfire from a kamikaze diving toward the deck on which he stood. She tried not to visualize him kneeling on a coral beach, caring for a dying marine while bullets ripped him apart. But her nerves were losing their resilience; even Skye's escape last fall had offered only temporary respite from the all-encompassing anxiety she lived with. He had been back in battle all autumn, and though of course his family had no way of being sure, they all believed that he had been in the thick of the Ardennes campaign, the weeks-long struggle in Belgium that seemed the last defiant stand of a dying German Army. But that stand had taken a toll that would live in American military history, as would the courage of the American armies who turned the "Battle of the Bulge" from a massive defeat to the beginning of the end for Hitler's Reich. Some 600,000 Americans fought in that battle; of the 81,000 casualties, 19,000 were killed and 15,000 captured. When Caro read that the German SS had killed ninety prisoners of war taken near a small Belgium village a week before Christmas, she had been overcome with despair. It might have been Skye; it could be David.

The amulets didn't work anymore, the rituals had lost their power. It was no longer true that if she worked well, did not waste even a second, that God would reward her, and they would both live. It was no longer true that if she was kind to everyone she met, if she fulfilled even the smallest duties cheerfully and thoroughly, God would reward her and she would once again have a normal life. Now the "Battle of the Bulge" was over; the Germans were being driven back across Europe, and the Russians, whose armies had been at a standstill since late summer of 1944, had finally lurched into motion, moving across Poland to meet the advancing Allies.

Visions of swirling snow and marching men filled her mind; refugees pushing handcarts, war ophans licking Hershey bars. I need some diversion, she thought, coming out into the sunshine. It was one of those mild winter days that mimic spring; camellias bloomed on every side, and someone's rose garden budded valiantly. I'll drop by Walter's and see what he's up to, she decided, and took the St. Charles streetcar down to the Quarter with a feeling of anticipation.

Walter had a knack of dealing with whatever bothered her with one eyebrow quirked, a patient smile on his face. He would listen, and nod, and without saying a word, hand her a mint julep or a Pimm's cup or a milk punch, or something else "medicinal," as he called it, and by the time she had run out of words, and had sipped her drink half down, she would feel deliciously relaxed and in quite another world. Much, she once told him, as though she were Alice and had fallen down Walter's own wonderful rabbit hole.

Royal Street slept, shutters closed and sidewalks empty. There was a somnolent quality in the air, a tranquillity that existed nowhere else in the city. Elsewhere, houses burgeoned at the seams and nerves frazzled by more and more shortages, less and less privacy, longer and longer lines for everything from cigarettes to meat, frayed at the slightest cause. Just Friday, toward the end of her shift, Caro had heard the two women next to her arguing. The argument had begun over something simple; one woman was telling the other about a letter she'd had from her brother, stationed at Fort Benning in Georgia. A woman near the base who owned a chicken farm had converted the coops into bedrooms to rent to soldiers and their wives, and the rough conditions and the ugly utility of the place had reduced his young wife to tears.

"Listen, if that's all your brother has to put up with—people listening while he makes out with his wife—he's got it lucky," the other woman said. "My brother just got both his legs amputated, see?"

The voices had droned on, then become sharper. And then one woman had slapped the other, and the first had hit back. Caro and the other workers had intervened before the foreman came over, but it had been useless and demeaning, and she was sick of it all. Most of all, she thought, standing looking up at Walter's balcony, I am tired of hearing how much better I have it than everyone else because I don't need to work for money. Better because I have enough space. Better because I'm alive. I hate feeling guilty because I'm me, she thought. Walter was the only person she knew who understood that. He was the only one who knew that at one and the same time Caro appreciated her advantages and resented like hell anyone else pointing them out.

"You think you pay your dues," he told her. "And you think that means they'll leave you alone. But they never do, my dear Caro. They never do."

They'll leave me alone this afternoon, she thought. Walter will tell me some funny stories and give me a drink from that absolutely illicit supply of his, and by the time I get home again, I'll feel much better.

She could hear music from behind Walter's door as she reached the top of the stairs. The music was so loud that she thought he might be having a party. But as she approached the heavy front door, she could hear nothing but the insistent beat of drums and the loud cry of a trumpet; one of Walter's jazz records. He must be all alone then, burying himself in his favorites.

Then, above the music, she heard something shrill, a long note quickly cut off. Her hand hovered over the bell. Had someone screamed in there? The Ellington piece was mounting to its finish, and Caro put her ear against the door. The record stopped, and there was a tiny pause before the next one fell into place. In that space Caro heard a man's voice, harsh, deep. A rumble of brutal sounds. And then another cut-off scream, followed by a thud. And then music again, a fast, upbeat Artie Shaw.

She stood quietly, making herself reason this out. There must be an explanation—she just couldn't think of what it was. Yet everything she'd heard warned her that something was wrong. Walter never played music that loud; he said it distorted the purity to have that much volume in so small a space.

And Walter never mixed musicians. He wouldn't go from Ellington to Shaw; especially would he not go from one record to another repeating some of the same songs. He liked programs, programs he carefully put together in his own order. Walter did not have the kind of guests who screamed.

A crash, the sound of something breaking, jolted her. That settled it. Walter did not hurl things about.

She looked around the narrow hall, the quiet foyer. All the other occupants had apparently vanished, either into deep Sunday naps or into other neighborhoods. The building had that stillness which isolates separate units, locking each one into a solid fence of its own. She went to the hall window and looked down into the street. It, too, was empty, quiet under a warm sun. She could not even see a place from which she could telephone. And whom would she telephone? she thought. The police? What would she tell them?

She could imagine the conversation. "I have this friend, Walter Fournet. His life is sort of . . . peculiar. He's up to something, I've always thought he was. Now he's in trouble."

"Sure, lady," the policeman would say. She could imagine his broad wink at a fellow officer, his shrug. In the French Quarter, as nowhere else in New Orleans, it took all kinds to make a world. She tiptoed back to the apartment door and listened again, this time opening her purse and closing her hand around the revolver she carried everywhere she went.

Her hand went to the ornate handle of Walter's bell. She would simply turn it, wait for someone to answer the door. She would have her gun ready; if she didn't like what she saw, she would . . . Her hand dropped. If there really were trouble inside, the last thing she needed to do was to walk into it. And then fear took her, its steel fingers gripping her neck, and she fled away from Walter's door into an alcove further down the hall.

What she wanted to do was leave. She thought of the house on Calliope Street, her familiar room. The half-knit sweater she could work on. The letters she could write. A productive afternoon, after which she would call Walter. "The funniest thing," she would say. "I went by your place this afternoon—but from what I could hear, I decided I'd better leave you alone. So I came home." And then Walter's lazy drawl would explain this strangeness away, and it would be all right that she had left.

But suppose that what she suspected was right? Suppose all the peculiar things that seemed to lie beneath the surface of Walter's life had merged and roared over the ordinary, like one of those red tides that come up from the depths of the sea and toss misshapen animals on the sand? Suppose the cutoff screams and the thud and the crash meant what such things usually meant? If she did not then intervene, there would be nothing she could say that would excuse her. Not to Walter, not to herself.

She crept down the hall to the back of the building. A narrow gallery ran across it, with iron staircases leading into the courtyard below, and apartment service doors opening off it. Walter's door was locked and bolted, and she stood irresolute, wondering how she would get inside. The window next to the back door was open to the mild air; it was small, a tiny square with a screen fixed firmly in place, but it was the only way in. She took out her nail file and loosened the screws that held the screen, praying that the music held and that no one inside could hear her.

Taking her shoes off, she used a heavy flowerpot to stand on, and climbed through the narrow opening, scraping her knees and elbows as she went. In another moment she stood in the tiny utility room, breathing hard and fast. She felt dizzy, as though she were going to black out, and she leaned against the wall behind her, eyes closed, body slack.

Then she heard another sharp sound from the apartment beyond her, a kind of half-scream that ended in one loud cry. This, too, was cut off, but not as quickly as the first one, and it was followed by a heavy jolt that terrified her. She gripped her gun and turned the knob of the utility-room door carefully, pushing it open just enough to allow her to slip through. She stood in Walter's neat kitchen. The sun glinted off the copper-bottomed pots hanging in shining rows on the wall, and Caro wondered how this kitchen could seem so peaceful when she was in such a tumult of fear.

She crossed the tile floor on bare feet, and pressed her body against the wall. There was a mirror in the dining room that gave her a full view of Walter's living room, and what she saw framed in its ornate gold edges made her skin tingle and her hands shake.

Walter was sitting astride one of his Jacobean side chairs, bound and gagged. A huge man stood opposite him, a pistol in his hand. The other hand held a young man whose arms were tied behind his back. The young man jerked his head away from the tip of the pistol as it lashed toward his face, and Caro saw who he was. Henri. My God. Henri. Blood ran down his cheeks from a gash on his forehead and stained his starched white shirt. His eyes were so dark that they seemed to vanish in his head, and his lips were pale, blood-specked where he had bitten through the dry skin.

She could not believe the scene before her was real; it was too much what she had imagined, too much like the vague forms and dark shapes from her nightmare. She heard the blast of the music, saw the stubborn set of Walter's jaw. The man with the gun barked something, a short, sharp command, and she saw Walter's head shake defiantly, a long, final movement from side to side. The man lifted the pistol and held it against Henri's head. And then, as easily as she drew breath, Caro raised her own gun, took careful aim, and fired. She paused and fired again. Two dark spots appeared on the back of the man's shirt, becoming wider and brighter, making rivulets down his spine. He half-turned toward Caro, but the pistol fell from his hand. Then he fell, crashing against a small gilt table, sending its ornaments tumbling to the floor.

For a moment Caro and Walter stared at each other. Then she ran forward and loosened the gag. Henri had slumped onto the sofa, where he lay with his hands still bound.

"Walter—what on earth?"

"I'll fill you in later," he said as she finished untying him. "See to Henri, will you? I've got some calls to make. You know where the brandy is."

He disappeared into his bedroom, where she heard him on the phone. I could use a little brandy myself, she thought as she released Henri. The dead man lay between her and the liquor cabinet; she could not bring herself to step over that still form. She grabbed the Spanish shawl from the piano and threw it over him, refusing to acknowledge what it was she covered.

She took the brandy over to Henri, who sat staring into space, his eyes dazed. "Drink this," she said. Henri's eyes looked awful, so awful that Caro knew his feelings echoed her own: shock, disbelief.

"What happened?" she said.

Henri's hand shook as he brought the snifter to his lips: liquor ran down his chin when he sipped. The blood on his face was beginning to dry, like dirty lace against his still-pallid skin. He took another sip, his hand a little steadier.

"Give me a cigarette, will you?"

She lit two, placing one between his lips. He took several short, rough drags that he released quickly. She sat down beside him and questioned him, making her voice gentle. "Henri, what in the world was going on here?"

He looked at her, and she saw shame burning in his eyes, as though the small glowing tip of his cigarette were a brand burning him. "It . . . it was all my fault," he said. His voice was hoarse, and he stopped speaking.

"Your fault? Henri—"

From behind her she heard Walter's voice. "Don't give yourself so much credit, old man. He would have tumbled onto me sooner or later—"

"I made it sooner," Henri said. He looked at Walter. "I almost got both of us killed."

Walter leaned over Henri and pushed back his hair, exposing the cut that crossed his forehead. It had stopped bleeding, except for a wet place in the middle that glistened thickly. Caro felt her stomach heave, and backed into the chair behind her. "Come with me," Walter said to Henri. "I'll tape it together. You may have to get it stitched later."

Henri stumbled up off the sofa, the cigarette trailing blue smoke. He did not look at Walter, but moved around him to start down the hall toward the bathroom. "Walter?" Caro asked.

"Later," he said. His tension communicated itself to her; he was still on the alert; the danger wasn't over yet. She moved away from the shape under the shawl, taking her brandy with her. The quiet of the apartment settled around her; it seemed thick, as though it took up actual space, leaving no place for her to hide. She went over to the phonograph and turned it off.

When Walter came back alone, she confronted him. "You have to tell me what's going on," she said.

"I made Henri lie down," Walter said evasively. He smiled at her, a shadow of the old wry smile. "I don't know if he needs a little rest, but I can't handle his *mea culpa* right now." He went to the decanter and poured himself some brandy. Then he lifted his glass to Caro. "Well. You certainly appeared in the nick of time."

"Walter! Who was that man? Why did Henri say it was his fault?"

"Later," he said again. He was setting the room to rights, picking up the gilt table and replacing the bibelots that belonged there, returning the heavy statue—the one that must have caused the crash she heard—to its pedestal. He stepped over the silk-covered form on the floor as casually as though it were a permanent fixture in the center of his living room. Caro found herself feeling almost the way she did when Walter told her one of his wild stories or created one of his expeditions that took her out of her daily world.

"Should you be doing that?" she said. "Don't the police always want everything left as it is?"

"The police?"

"Didn't you call them? When you went to phone—"

"No," Walter said, fluffing the pillows on the sofa.

"But, Walter—I killed a man. The police will want to know about it. You have to call them."

She heard footsteps in the hall, and the bright jangle of the doorbell. Walter went to the door to let in three dark-suited men. She curled up in the big wing chair and huddled there, feeling more lost by the minute.

One of the men went straight to the body, pulled back the shawl, and looked intently into the face. Then he covered it again and stood up, nodding at Walter. "I'll send a stretcher in the back way," he said, and disappeared into the hall.

Walter and the two other men went into the dining room and sat at one end of the table, heads close, voices low. Caro leaned against the wing of the chair and closed her eyes. She really didn't want to hear what they were saying, she really didn't want to know.

She heard Henri's name, and opened her eyes. Walter and one of the men were heading toward the bedroom; she supposed they would find out what Henri meant when he said it was his fault, but she was too tired to care, and shut her eyes again.

Then there was a rustling sound, and Walter and the other man stood in front of her. Walter was saying that the man wanted to ask her a few questions, and would she just answer them as fully as she could.

"Jack Morris," the man said, extending his hand. She took the hand, thinking that the name was probably no more real than any of the rest of this. It was hard to concentrate on what Jack Morris asked her; she could hear the rise and fall of voices from down the hall, and she realized that the other man was talking to Henri. It was hard to remember just why she had come here this afternoon, or what made her think something was terribly wrong. But Morris was patient, very patient; she thought that he must do this a lot, and finally she was able to tell him what he wanted to know.

"Let me understand this. You heard what sounded like a scream, and knew—thought—something must be wrong." He smiled, and she thought it looked like the kind of smile practiced in front of a mirror until it is perfect and can be assumed at will. "Now, Miss Hamilton, you really don't strike me as the kind of young lady who would go breaking into someone's apartment—even a friend's apartment—just on the strength of that one little scream."

He seemed to be waiting for Caro to say something else, and she looked at Walter, searching for a cue. "I think perhaps he wonders if there was anything else—anything from another time here, even, that would make you think something could be wrong." Walter's eyes were sending a message, but she couldn't read them, and she thought of the way she had felt standing there, the certainty that Walter led the kind of life in which danger could become alive, could become real. She said slowly, each word dropping like a bead of water from a faucet, "I just thought that Walter is the kind of person strange things happen to. He never finds a penny on the sidewalk. It's always a fifty-cent piece."

She stared at the man questioning her. She wasn't making sense, she knew she wasn't, but the man nodded, and smiled that patient smile again.

"I see. You thought it would not be . . . totally unexpected for Walter to have . . . trouble."

Caro nodded, and she felt Walter relax.

"Now, about the gun," the man said. "Do you always carry a gun, Miss Hamilton?"

He sounded as though he were asking, "Do you always carry a clean handkerchief, Miss Hamilton?" and she thought of her mother pressing fresh linen squares into her hands as she left the house, and began to giggle. The giggles went on and on and turned into sobs, hard, racking sobs that also went on and on, and wouldn't stop. She knew Walter and Jack Morris were looking at her, and at each other, and that they wanted her to stop. She caught a sob back, right in the middle, and swallowed it. Her throat tensed. It hurt, the breath could barely get through, and she took a tiny sniff of air through her nose, then another, and another, until her throat eased and she could let air stream down it.

"I always carry a gun," she said. "I . . . I work at Higgins shipyard. I often come home late."

"I think Miss Hamilton might be willing to talk to you again, Jack," Walter said, "when she's had time to rest."

"Yes," Caro said. "Of course."

Morris pulled his chair closer, until his eyes were looking directly into her face. "Miss Hamilton. I don't need to tell you that you're not to speak of this to anyone, do I? Not anyone."

"No," she whispered. "No, I won't."

"Not anyone," he repeated.

He looked at Walter, and Walter said quickly, "I can vouch for her. She won't say a word."

"All right," Morris said.

His partner had returned from Walter's bedroom alone; he stood examining a watercolor that hung on the fireplace wall.

"I'm ready," Morris said. The other man turned and came forward; his face had no expression at all, but his eyes darted toward Walter, and he said, almost under his breath, "We're going to have to keep an eye on that one." His head moved slightly toward the hall, and Caro knew he was talking about Henri.

Walter shrugged. His hands were thrust in his pockets and he was playing with coins; Caro could hear the faint jingle, and thought he was probably holding the two sixpences he carried for luck.

There were footsteps at the back of the apartment, and then two men carrying a folded stretcher came in, followed by the third man of the original group. They took the Spanish shawl from the body and handed it to Walter, then loaded the man onto the stretcher and covered him with a tarpaulin.

"Did I get blood on your shawl?" Caro asked Walter. Her voice sounded shrill, on the edge of disorder, and she bit her lip and leaned back in her chair.

One of the men with Walter murmured something; she heard "shock" and "doctor," and closed her eyes until they had gone away and Walter came and took her hands and spoke to her.

"Caro," he said.

She opened her eyes and stared at him. His eyes looked clear, calm, but a tiny twitch at one corner of one eyelid and the pulse she saw beating at the base of his throat betrayed him. "I wouldn't have had this happen for the world."

"I wouldn't either," she said. She could not seem to speak above a whisper; it was as though if she gave voice, she would begin to scream.

Henri came into the doorway from the hall, and stood there, his face frozen against them. "They said I could go," he said.

"You can," Walter said.

"They scared the hell out of me. As if I wasn't already. I didn't do it on purpose, Walter."

"No one believes that you did, Henri," Walter said.

Caro struggled forward in her chair. "Did what? What did you do, Henri?"

Henri started into the room, taking a few steps and then stopping again. "Talked out of school. Didn't Walter tell you?"

"No," she said.

"Don't," Walter said.

"She'll have to know—"

"Not yet," Walter said. "They did tell you you'd have to get out of town for a while, didn't they? Since you were the last person seen with him."

"I've got classes—"

"So you'll miss a few weeks," Walter said. "Go to your room and stay there, Henri. I'll be in touch later this evening, all right?"

"Sure you trust me to go home?" Henri said. Caro heard the old sullenness and knew how badly Henri felt. She wanted to go to him, comfort him, but her legs had no strength. She leaned back and waited for whatever would come next.

"Actually," Walter said, smiling a little, "I was getting to that. You're to go out the back way, Henri. Morris has a man there who'll drive you back to the dorm to pack your things. He'll stay with you until we decide where you're going."

"Look, Walter, you can't just dispose of my life—"

"The normal rules of living got suspended this afternoon, Henri. I'm sorry, but we can't take the risk of your being picked up before the rest of that little nest is cleaned out."

Henri's body slumped, and Caro knew the fight had gone out of him. He came over to her chair and looked down at her. "I'm sorry you had to get mixed up in this, Caro. I—look, I owe you my life. I know that."

She waved her hand at him. She did not want to listen, to be reminded of the way she felt when she saw the gun move against his head. "It's all right, Henri. I . . . I'm glad I was here."

He bent over and clutched her, his face suddenly crumpling. "Dammit, Caro, when am I going to learn to keep my mouth shut?"

"It's all right," she said again, patting his head. "Please, Henri—"

"She's about done in, Henri," Walter said. "Why not get a move on, let me see about her?"

"Right," Henri said.

Walter gestured toward the back of the apartment. "If anyone asks—Morris' man is someone your family sent to get you."

"All right," Henri said. He hesitated, then turned and walked quickly from the room. Caro heard footsteps, a door opening and closing—silence.

"What did Henri do?" she said.

Walter knelt before her and began rubbing her hands between his. His skin was cool and dry and smooth, and she thought what a fragile shell it was after all, to hold the complex maze of Walter Fournet's being.

"He talked about me to someone who was already curious," Walter said. "A rather dangerous someone."

"The man I . . . killed?"

Walter nodded.

"But what did he say, what does he know about you, Walter?"

"Nothing much, as it turned out. The only concrete thing he had—well, I managed to retrieve something for him once, something he needed badly. When my name came up in a conversation Henri was having . . . he wanted to let the others know he knew me . . . knew the kind of . . . power I have." Walter's face was suddenly dark, shadowed with some knowledge that seemed to sadden him. "As it happened, the man who came up here with him hangs around bars, joins conversations, plants names—for a purpose a little more sinister than mere . . . boasting. Henri's hard luck, that's all. He was in the wrong place at the wrong time."

"But why was that man after you, Walter?" She thought of the movies, the murky underground world of spies and secret couriers. "Are you a spy?"

"Can you do something for me, Caro?" He was still rubbing her hands, but the regular circular motion did not match the agitation in his eyes. She wanted him to look better; she wanted him to look like the old Walter, the one who could make everything right again, so she nodded.

"Yes," she said.

"Can you just not ask any more questions? Forget this, as much as that's possible?"

Her eyes went to the place where the body had lain. "I killed him, Walter."

He put his finger over her lips. "Shh. Try not to think about it, Caro. Try not to think of him as a . . . person."

"Will you tell me one thing, Walter?"

"If I can."

"Would he—would he probably have been killed sooner or later anyway?"

Walter got up and took two cigarettes from his case. He handed Caro one, lit it for her, and then lit his own before he spoke. "Considering the business he was in, I think it's likely."

"I don't think that's going to help," she said.

"Caro, is there anyone you could . . . talk to? I don't mean tell the whole thing to, but just . . . talk about it?"

For a moment the world seemed empty of such a person. David was further away than he had ever been; besides, how would this one small death, even if she were responsible for it, measure against the scores he witnessed daily? A face floated before her. A strong voice seemed to resonate in her ear. "There's Père," she said. "My stepfather."

"Perfect," Walter said with such warmth she wondered at the impression Père had made. "Where is he?"

"Right now?" She leaned her head back and thought. It was hard to think; thoughts came and went, drifting by as though they could not find a place to stop. "I'm not sure." She dragged her mind out of the shadows it kept fleeing to. "Maybe in Baton Rouge. Isn't the first primary this week?"

"Yes," Walter said. His hands were in his pockets again, and his body appeared relaxed, but the pulse beat more rapidly, and his eyelid twitched like its mirror.

"Then maybe he is in Baton Rouge. I know he's been working with Governor Jones to get Davis elected." Her head sank back against the chair and she closed her eyes. "Mère will know," she said, and gave him the number.

Beau was indeed in Baton Rouge, closeted with the governor and a few others to make final plans for the gubernatorial primary. The sound of Walter Fournet's voice put Beau immediately on his guard; such a call at such an hour from a man like Fournet was not to be taken lightly. He filled in between the lines; something bad had happened involving Caro, and he was needed. Thinking back to his first encounter with Walter Fournet's world, Beau asked no questions. He was being called, he knew, not for explanations, but to help Caro, to absorb some of her shock, and reduce the threat to secrecy her present state made.

"I'll keep her here until you come," Walter said. "I don't think she should be alone."

He persuaded Caro to lie down in his study, on the couch that made up into a bed. She could hear soft sounds beyond the closed door; voices, doors opening and closing, dishes rattling. Then there was silence, and then music. Not jazz now, but Chopin, his ballades, silver notes scattered through the air, making a thin, glittering line that protected her from what had gone before. She nestled her head into the satin-covered pillow and slept.

When she awoke, Père sat next to her, holding her hand. The early-winter dusk had fallen, and the room was dark. He heard her stirring and switched on a lamp near the couch. "Caro? Honey?"

She sat up and fell against him, putting her head on his shoulders and allowing herself finally to cry. No wonder Mère could hardly stand to be away from him, she thought. His arms were like steel bands around her, his chest was the most solid thing she had ever felt, and his voice soothed her, saying over and over again that it was all right, he was here now, it was over, and she never had to think about it again.

"But I killed a man," she said at last, sitting back against the pillows.

"It's what you carried the gun for, Caro," Beau said carefully. He had thought about what he would say to her every mile of the fast drive between Baton Rouge and New Orleans. And he had finally decided that the less said, the better; now was no time for moral statements or ethical judgments. Now was the time for pragmatism; he had to make Caro understand that when she began to carry that gun, for all practical purposes she had already stepped on the bridge she crossed today.

"I carried it for protection—" she said.

"Yes. That's what you used it for."

His eyes were so clear, so sure. Would she ever possess that sureness? she wondered. Would she ever be able to so thoroughly accept the consequences of everything she did?

"And if you had not shot that man, Henri would be dead. And so, in all probability, would Walter." Beau would not think about Henri. Walter's main concern was Caro, but he had said, just before they hung up, "I'll need you to help me plan for Henri." Yes, Beau thought. Poor

Henri, who could not seem to help misstepping, no matter how clearly marked the path appeared to others.

"I never thought I'd have to use it," she said.

He leaned forward and held her, looking into her face with such sad eyes that she could feel herself again on the verge of tears. "I know," he said. "I know, Caro. Somehow, we never do think we'll have to use our guns. Or the moral equivalent of them. We keep hoping, despite all proof to the contrary, that those who are out to get us will suddenly start playing by the rules—only there are no rules for their games, there never have been."

"I'm not sure I'll ever be able to carry that gun again," Caro said.

Beau's eyes flickered, and he remembered the cautious hints Walter had given him, and the clear warning. "I think you'd better carry it, Caro," he said. "For a while, anyway."

She felt fear grip her. "Do you mean—do you mean there might be . . . more?"

"I didn't say that. Walter and I think it would be a good idea if you left New Orleans and went home."

"I won't do that," she said.

"All right. But carry the gun, Caro."

He knew that Walter would have her watched, and that he did not think Caro's role would ever be known to anyone who could harm her. So long as Henri kept his mouth shut. Thinking of the danger Henri's careless boasting had put the three of them in, Beau resolved to have a long talk with him. It was time for Henri to come to terms with his own weaknesses, more than time for him to correct them.

He saw the aimless way Caro's fingers fiddled with her ring, moved her watch up and down her arm. He knew that her nerves would not soon recover from today, and that for a long time to come, every shadow would be menacing and every noise a threat. Sitting here watching the lamplight make her hair glow against the pale blue pillows, seeing her cheeks flushed with sleep, it was hard to believe that the war raging around the world had been able to enter even this room and tear at her with brutal fingers.

"Now," he said, "let me take you home and wait while you get dressed. And then I'll take you to dinner. How does that sound?" He saw reluctance in her eyes. To end this day by having dinner with her stepfather, as though she were still a coed at Newcomb and he was here on a Sunday visit? To sit in the Caribbean Room and make small talk, while somewhere a dark form lay stiff and still, two bullet holes from her gun like bloody fingerprints on its back? Then her eyes changed, and he saw acceptance come. She knew now that it made no difference what they did. There were a certain number of hours to be gotten through, and there were only so many ways to do it. If they were lucky, dinner and small talk might make them forget, for an instant or two, what lay behind them. If they were not lucky, dinner and small talk would at least give their mouths and hands something to do.

"All right," she said. She did not ask him where Henri was going or where Walter had gone. She let him help her down the steps and into the car waiting at the curb. Then, as he drove away, carrying her down the still-slumbering street, she took one long look back at Walter's apartment. The glare of the streetlamp lit up its front; the palms still waved from the balcony, the ironwork still curved like graceful vines across its narrow width. She could imagine Walter standing there, glass in hand, watching the world go by. She thought of the rooms that lay behind the balcony, rooms cushioned with old rugs and garbed with fine furnishings. Rooms rich with silence, protected by wealth. Those rooms had been her hidey-hole, the place she went when the war closed in, and loneliness closed in, and fear held sway. Now those rooms were bare and empty; their charm no longer worked. They had lost their innocence, and in all of New Orleans, there was no place left for her to run.

15

SUMMER 1945

Once the bottleneck called the Battle of the Bulge had been broken, the Allied armies rolled full steam across Europe into Germany. The Germans retreated, blowing up bridges behind them, laying to waste ammunition that had to be abandoned, drawing nearer and nearer to Berlin. By a miracle the Allies could almost not believe, the Remagen bridge across the Rhine was left standing; it served as a gateway over which they poured. American forces met the Russians rushing from the east at the Elbe: General Patton liberated camp after camp where emaciated prisoners and stacks of bones told a tale of horror—and Berlin fell.

At one minute after midnight on May 9, 1945, Fortress Europe's guns had become silent, and her liberated people surged into the streets, the jubilation of their victory a triumphant counterpoint to the deadly silence that cloaked the defeated. And now the stream of men who had sailed across the Atlantic, across the English Channel, up Italy's boot, to become the greatest army ever assembled in the military annals of mankind, would reverse its path. Men would leave their tanks and antiaircraft guns, abandon their bazookas and grenades, and don their uniforms and medals for the long trip home, and for the dreams that awaited them there. They would carry with them the faces of comrades who would not return, the memory of voices they would never hear again, the vision of horrors they knew no one at home would ever understand. But they carried, too, the bright colors of glory, of honor, of duty done. Behind them were years of slogging, deadly war. Before them were ticker-tape parades and marching bands, the girl next door, and kid brothers all grown up.

They would bring back German Lugers and French perfume, a taste for wine, and a smattering of European culture. The war in Europe was over, and America's boys were coming home. And if many of them knew more about death than was good for them, if many of them had seen more of its forms than they had ever known existed, they knew other things too. They had seen the human spirit tested. They had seen it survive. They had helped turn back a scourge that threatened the very existence of civilization, and so their generation would always be touched with glory.

Skye quickly sensed the almost unreal response of the civilians he met when they asked him about his war. His B-17 assumed mythic qualities: he became a hero. Even as he joined in the celebration in the village near the base, he thought: If they give me so much credit for victory, how much of the blame would I have had to bear for defeat?

It had finally become too much for him—the frenetic joy, the wildness that seemed to infect everyone. The first bitter ironies were already being revealed: the soldier killed by a mine fifteen minutes into the peace, the patrol cut off and destroyed before the Germans had word to put down their arms. He listened to all of it, tried to respond to the inevitable questions, become part of the interminable discussions: now that the war is over, what are you going to do? His answer had been easy. "Go back to school. Get my law degree." But that, too, seemed unreal. He felt stale and tired and old, all at once. Restless and anxious and ready to get going. Listless, bored. Eager for a new life to begin.

The sun glinted off the broad face of the river, casting a film of pink light across it. Clouds piled along the horizon, a gossamer bank reflecting the water; water and clouds were edged with gold, and a tall bird stood silhouetted against a band of deep lavender sky.

"This has to be the most beautiful place in the world," Natalie said, dabbling her fingers in the clear, rippling water.

"The most peaceful," Skye said. He poled the canoe swiftly down the river toward the landing where Tony and Alicia Harrington waited with a picnic basket. It had been their idea to gather one last time before Skye was rotated back to the States and Natalie followed Lieutenant Colonel Hap Morris to his post in Washington, D.C.

"I promised Colonel Morris I'd help him make the transition back to the War Department before being discharged," Natalie had said when he asked her what her next step was.

"And then?"

"I'm not sure what I'll do. I had started a journalism major before the war—I might go back and finish that up." Skye's eyes had been riveted to the diamond on the third finger of her left hand, but he had not asked if marrying her lieutenant were not the next logical step on her postwar agenda. During the months since he had come back from prison camp, he had seen her more than a dozen times. Each encounter was the same unsettling blend of casual friendship and compelling desire; he left London on each occasion vowing not to put himself through such an evening again.

"Well, now that the war's over, we can do almost anything we please, can't we?" he had said. And those few words—now that the war's over—rang through every other word, representing all the possibilities that had been put on hold for the duration.

People used them over and over, in every kind of context. "Now that the war's over, I can go back to school." "Now that the war's over, we can get married." "Now that the war's over, I can start up my business." Now that the war's over, we can get on with our lives.

Now that the war is over, he was going home, leaving on a transport plane day after tomorrow. He poled the boat past a cottage, its tiled roof poking through a screen of hedge. He had a week at home before school began; he could not absorb the fact that soon he could be poling his pirogue on Bayou Teche, pushing it past oak trees heavy with moss through the slow, muddy water that drifted under the still August sun. He could not imagine what it would be like to again be able to sleep as late as he liked—all day, if he wanted. Whistle up Marq and go rabbit hunting. Laze on the porch, sipping his father's bourbon. See Rosalind.

He looked at Natalie, sitting quietly in the bow of the canoe. She wore a big straw hat that hid her face, and her skirt of some light fabric rippled gently in the evening breeze. "I can't get used to it being over," he said.

"Neither can I," she said.

"But you're not getting out for a while—you'll be in Washington, won't you?"

"Yes. But after that—I can't seem to make myself think past the next few minutes." She raised her head, and he saw that her face looked sad, and he wondered if there were bad news about her lieutenant she had not shared. "I feel terribly old," she said.

"I guess war ages us," Skye said.

"I don't mean that. It's just—I've already said good-bye to so many people. And I'm only twenty-one years old." She shook her head. "It's as though the people I'll never see again outnumber those I will." She shrugged. "It makes me feel old, Skye."

"Well," he said, waving to the Harringtons, who were setting up the picnic things a few yards ahead. "I'll make you feel a little younger. Let's exchange addresses, promise to get together at some point when we're both settled again."

"I'd like that, Skye," she said.

He tied the canoe to the landing and helped her out, and they joined Alicia and Tony and found places on the blanket and watched the sun go down. The food was good, the wine sparkling. The talk was easy, and a sense of ease finally held him.

Most of what he felt was a carryover from the war. Like his first track meet, early in the season before he had trained properly; his muscles quivered for hours afterward, and he could feel adrenaline keeping his body on edge. He had been on the alert for too many months to let it all go; he had slept with an awareness of danger too many nights to sleep well now. But soon he would be home, and the deep, deep silence of late summer in the country would close around him. The thick dust of country roads would conceal nothing more frightening than an occasional car, a team pulling a wagon. The humid air would make a heavy layer between the farm and a sky empty of any but the most peaceful airplanes. The only gunfire would come from the canefields, where someone blew the head off a cottonmouth. The only schedule would revolve around meals and Mass. And his only duty would be to rest.

"So what's the first thing you're going to do when you get home, Skye?" Tony asked, pouring wine into Skye's glass.

"The first thing? The first thing I'm going to do is see my girl."

Alicia laughed and said something he didn't hear. Nor did he see Natalie quickly duck her head so they could not see her face. He leaned back on one elbow and stared beyond them at the river. He would call Rosalind, and then he'd borrow his father's car and drive over to New Iberia. He'd go right up to the Nasser house and knock on that big door, and when Rosalind opened it, he'd take her in his arms and tell her she was going to marry him. Now, this very month. Before he went back to LSU. She would come with him; they'd find an apartment near the campus, and Rosalind, who had finished college in May, could design interiors to her heart's content all day, so long as she was waiting for him when he came home.

His idea would take their families by surprise. He might have to argue a bit. Be firm. He would have to make them understand that he and Rosalind had lost too much ground; they couldn't find each other on casual dates and hurried weekends. They needed to be near each other, close. They had been distant from each other for a long, long time. But now that thing that had made the distance was over. They would pick up again where they had left off, before this funny time-out called war had happened.

"What I'm mainly going to do," Skye said, gazing out at the river, "what I'm mainly going to do, is marry my girl."

* * *

From the moment he ran across the airfield into his father's arms until the moment he saw Rosalind face-to-face, everything about his homecoming was just as he had dreamed it. The first glimpse of his father and Mère, André, Émilie, Caro, Raoul, and Henri pressed against the rope that held the waiting crowd off the field as the big plane circled and landed. The dinner at the Caribbean Room, waiters hovering by, everyone talking at once, Mère stopping in the middle of a sentence to clutch his hand, his father never taking his eyes off Skye's face.

And then the drive from New Orleans home, across the Atchafalaya Swamp, brimming with life, through fields of corn and sugarcane, past farmhouses needing paint and tractors needed tires. Stopping at the Palace Café in Opelousas, as they always did, to drink cup after cup of rich, dark coffee. Approaching St. Martinville, looking out either side of the car and seeing nothing but row after row of sugarcane.

Luella stood on the porch, waving her apron at him, as they drove up to the house. Her arms came around him, and he smelled baby powder and starch. Marq leapt against him, almost knocking him down, covering his face with his rough, familiar tongue.

Gennie called from New York, promising to make it home for André's birthday the next weekend. Then finally they could let Skye go long enough to make his own calls, his own plans. He gave the operator Rosalind's number and stood waiting for her to come to the phone, his breath suspended. He heard her voice, husky, breathless, too. He did not examine the quality of the happiness he heard. He told her he was coming to see her and that he'd be there within the hour. Then he changed into civilian clothes, a suit he'd worn for high-school graduation. The pants were an inch too short, the shoulders much too tight. "We'll go shopping tomorrow," his father said when Skye came to get the car keys. "Pick up something to hold you until you can get down to New Orleans and let Alcide take care of you."

Since the afternoon he had decided to marry Rosalind, he had not really given the idea a great deal of thought. He had not given much thought to anything in the weeks between that afternoon and now; that had been the dividing line, the line between the "then" of the war and the "now" of peace, and he did not see anything he could use from that other side. Had he stayed home, had he not gone to war, he would have finished LSU this May. He would be entering law school this fall. And that was certainly a good time to marry. The thought of going back, of unreeling his life and setting it on the track where it had been four years ago, wasn't possible. He could only go forward. And so he picked up the accoutrements he had left behind: this suit, that experience, this girl.

When he arrived at the Nasser house, the maid answered and showed Skye into the living room. Although summer blazed away outside, here it was dark and cool, and Skye settled into a silk-covered chair. Rosalind approached him out of the shadows that led into a central hall; when he saw her coming he sprang up and went to her, arms open.

"Rosalind!"

She stopped just beyond the reach of his arms and looked at him uncertainly. "Hello, Skye," she said. Then, before he could put his arms around her, she ducked away and sat in a low chair across from him, feet flat on the floor and hands folded in her lap.

"Rosalind—" And then he saw the diamond on her left hand. It was huge, a marquise-cut solitaire set in a heavy frame of gold.

She followed his gaze. "I'm engaged, Skye," she said. "I'll be married at Christmas." She looked somewhere past him, into the dimness that lurked in the corners of the room. "I would have written you—but I didn't get around to it. I'm sorry."

"What?" he said, shocked practically into silence. A sense of having slipped over the edge of time came over him, and he shook his head as though to clear it. The room looked exactly the same as it had when he entered. The house looked the same. How could the rest of the world look the same when suddenly it was playing tricks, masking itself behind one reality while confronting him with another? "Who? Who is he?" he asked.

"You don't know him," she said. "He's a . . . a distant cousin."

"I can't believe it. I've waited so long—are you in love with him?"

"Of course I'm not," Rosalind said. She brushed a lock of hair from her forehead and he saw the white curve of her arm. He wanted to kiss the inside of her elbow, he wanted to run his lips the length of that smooth white arm. He wanted to possess her. He thought of all the times he had left her, all the frustration and useless denial. He thought of the night they went to her uncle's *garçonnière*. "You don't love him," he said, and saw her flinch from his tone, "but you're going to marry him."

"Yes," she said. Her back was straight, her chin firm. There was no expression in her face; even her eyes were blank. He was suddenly filled with a desire to hurt her, to make her angry, to make her feel something.

"And sleep with him. Sleep with a man you don't love."

She said nothing. There was something at the back of her eyes now, something she hid with a quick veil of dropped lashes.

"All the times I wanted you. And you made me stop."

Her tongue moved across her lips, and she looked up quickly. "There was one time, Skye."

"At your uncle's. Sure. But I had the feeling, all the time we were there, that you had gone off from me. That what you were doing didn't have very much to do with me at all."

She got up and came to him. She wore a pale yellow dress made on simple, almost severe lines. The curve of her breasts and of her hips contrasted with the straight cut; looking at her, he knew that she would always be one of the most exotic, beautiful women he would ever know. "I . . . I was trying to get rid of you, Skye," she said. "I thought if I could get you to . . . to take me, I'd get rid of you."

He rose to meet her and took her hands in his. "What are you saying, Rosalind?"

"I thought if we made love—if we had sex—when we'd had too much to drink and didn't much care who we were with—" She came closer, and he pressed her hands harder. "Well, I thought that if I ruined it for myself, I wouldn't have to spend the rest of my life wondering what it would be like to . . . to do it because you love someone. I'd know it wasn't ever part of love. It was always just . . . lust. Or duty."

"You mean you knew then that you were never going to marry me."

"Yes," she said.

The very lightness of her words gave them weight. She spoke as though this were something they both knew, had always known.

"You sound as though I should have known that too," he said.

"Oh, Skye. We're Syrians. We don't marry outside our people. You're bound to know that."

"Well, dammit, I didn't know it! You were my girl, Rosalind, and you know damn well I didn't know it."

"I was a high-school sweetheart," she said. She sounded very tired; her hands in his were limp, and when he released them she let them drop to her sides as though they were too heavy to hold higher. "No one takes that seriously, Skye."

"I did," he said stubbornly. He had forgotten the times overseas when he sat staring at an empty page, struggling to fill it. He forgot the times he had stared at her picture and wondered who the hell that pretty, smiling girl was. He had been in a disjointed time, a time that curved away from the line his life made, and made a parabola with a continuity all its own. Now he wanted to get back into the mainstream; the fewer decisions he had to make, the faster he could travel. "And you're wrong, Rosalind. Wrong to marry a man you don't love, wrong to mess up your life that way."

The something he had caught a glimpse of earlier blazed up in her eyes and burned her weariness away. "Mess up my life, Skye? On the contrary. I think marrying my cousin Eddie is probably the one thing I can do to keep myself from messing up my life for good."

He felt some dark force in her, something he had seen briefly that night she took him to her uncle's *garçonnière*.

He didn't know her after all. He didn't know if he had ever known her. Maybe he had made her up, spun her out of his own need for a girl who fit his dreams.

"One thing, though, Rosalind. You're wrong about sex. People use it as an act of love all the time."

She shrugged. "Maybe they do. I remember watching your father and stepmother together—and thinking they were probably the exception to the rule. But as far as I'm concerned, sex is never for pleasure. It's a trade, and I'm prepared to make it."

"I'd better go," he said. His hands twitched; did he want to slap her or shake her? Shock her, or shame her out of this view she had, a view that seemed more terrible the longer he thought about it? But there was nothing left to say. He turned and walked steadily across the room, into the hall, out through the foyer, and down the red tile steps into the green-gold of late afternoon. Light shimmered all around his father's car, a heat haze that blinded him. He shut his eyes against the glare and put his hand across his face. When he took it away and opened his eyes, he felt as though he were looking through a lens at things very far away. The house across the street was strange and new; the sidewalk twisting its way over tree roots led to places he had never been. He struggled against a sense of chaos and confusion. Then from far overhead he heard the sound of an airplane, and he shielded his eyes and stared into the sky. A biplane lumbered along through the cotton clouds. For a moment Skye could feel the shuddering motion of his own plane as he took her into a steep bank. He gripped the edge of the car, and felt the hot metal burn into his flesh. Then the plane flew out of hearing, and the world was still.

He got into the car and started the motor. He had a hell of a lot of decisions to make, after all. He drove away without looking again at the Nasser house, his mind turning each thought over carefully as though it hid a truth he had to find. By the time he parked the car at the farm, he was beginning to feel a sense of release. The path ahead of him had seemed clearly laid out, neatly defined. Now it had twists and bends around which he could not see. He went up the steps whistling. Hell, anything could lie beyond the next curve in the road. Anyone.

He hurried down the hall to the kitchen. "Luella, I swear I could smell that pot of fudge icing ten miles back," he said. "Did you save me the pot to lick?"

Luella grinned. "Mr. Skye, I had to fight André off with my big spoon. I told him you was just back from the war, and that pot was yours."

"Give me two spoons, Luella," Skye said. "There's plenty for both of us."

He called André and they sat together on the back steps, digging out the remnants of icing from the sides and bottom of the heavy pot. André sat practically in Skye's lap, asking one question after another about the war. When the pot was empty and they were getting ready to go down to the bayou for a swim, André took Skye's hand and said, his blue eyes dark and serious, "Skye, it's all over now, isn't it? It won't come back anymore?"

"The war, you mean? Sure, André. It's all over now."

And for the first time since Japan had surrendered, ending it, he knew that it really was.

Caro sat in the parlor, a drink on the table near her, a cigarette in her hand. She had gone through almost half a pack in a little over two hours, and the brandy decanter, which had been three-quarters full when she sat down, was now at the halfway mark.

"You are going to feel like hell in the morning," she told herself. She could not remember a time in her life when she had deliberately set out to get drunk. But David's letter, which had arrived this morning, seemed to demand no other response.

"And so I may just have to take Phil up on his offer," David wrote. "I know we've talked most about my going into practice in New Orleans, but the clinic Phil is with is one of the best in San Francisco, and if I go with them, I'll be years ahead of where I'd be starting fresh in New Orleans. San Francisco is an exciting city, so much like New Orleans. I think you'll love it. . . ."

She still hadn't read the rest of the letter. With a beginning like that, it couldn't possibly say what she wanted to hear. Needed to hear. "Caro—all I care about is being with you. That's first. Everything else comes second." The letter didn't say that. In fact, it didn't even consider that she might not want to leave New Orleans. That returning to Newcomb and finishing her degree might be important to her. The letter really didn't consider her at all.

The letter had added to the weight she carried, a leaden weight that seemed centered somewhere in the middle of her chest where she had thought her heart was. Since early in the year, she had not been able to get rid of that weight. Since, to be honest, that Sunday in Walter's apartment when she had killed a man. Walter had tried to help her get over it, and so had Père. A week or so after it happened, Walter had cooked supper for her, broiling steaks he'd gotten God knows where on a little metal grill he set up on the balcony, and producing a bottle of prewar Mouton Rothschild burgundy that blurred the edges of her pain. He had not told her a great deal, but she was not stupid, so he did not have to give her that much for her to piece together what must have happened, what it was she had so fortuitously walked into. Fortuitious, that is, from Walter's viewpoint. And from Henri's. Not, she thought, from the dead man's. Certainly not from hers.

Walter must be a government spy, then, or an agent after spies. Père seemed to know the whole story; he added his appeal to Walter's. Please don't ask any more questions. Please trust us. One question she had demanded an answer to. Had Henri blabbed about the new landing craft? Was it through her that saboteurs had known when to strike? Walter would not add another death to the burden she carried. He had said he honestly did not know. Henri's friends liked to play chess at the Napoleon House, and the people who drifted in and out of the bar were a motley lot—merchant seamen, refugees—who knew who said what, who heard what? They could tell her that it was Henri's loose boasting that had led the man she killed to Walter. That was all. She had had to be satisfied with that.

The year had gone downhill from there. Roosevelt had died, and that had seemed the end of an era. He had been president as long as she could remember; how could he not be president anymore? Then in early May, the war had been over in Europe. And on the heels of that, just when her spirits were picking up again, came the pictures from Dachau. Buchenwald. Auschwitz. She had a folder full of them, and of the eyewitness accounts from men who liberated the camps.

She had had a long, almost incoherent letter from David shortly after the world began to learn about the death camps. The letter was filled with his own agonized conviction that all those relatives his family had lost track of had now been found, and that their bones had been added to the stacks that whitened European soil. She had written back immediately, offering what small hope she could. She had not told him about the folders growing thicker every week. She hoped he did not have access to as many of these articles as she did; she couldn't imagine David, or any other Jew, being able to bear looking at all that. For that matter, she couldn't imagine any person of any humanity being able to bear looking at all that. Which brought the next question: how did people of any humanity do it? All the things the pictures revealed? What had happened over there, anyway?

Her mind skittered away from the folder and the pictures and the articles, but there were new ones, fresh ones every week. Pictures of girls no older than herself, who literally worked their flesh off their bones as slave labor. The pictures from Dachau and Buchenwald and all the other places made the war seem very different from what she had believed it to be; when she thought about those camps, and then about the spies and racketeers here in the States, she felt frightened, and as though an ocean between them were not such an invulnerable barrier after all.

Now Japan had surrendered, beaten into submission by two bombs that had been dropped on Hiroshima and Nagasaki, and the half-million American lives military leaders had calculated would be lost in an invasion of Japan had been saved—those and the millions of Japanese who would have died defending their island. She didn't know what to think about any of it anymore. She didn't feel comfortable with Walter now; she had tried going there a few times after that Sunday, but it didn't work. He knew it didn't work, and she could tell he was sorry. But he had his work to do: his work hadn't stopped just because of that one afternoon, and so she saw less and less of him. Less and less of anybody.

What she had really been doing was waiting for David. She looked at the letter again. Yes, they had talked about his going into practice in New Orleans. In her own mind, they had decided that he would. Her own private film unrolled in her mind, the same film that had kept her sane all these long months. David, setting out in the morning from this house. Herself, leaving for classes at Newcomb. They would both work very hard, and by the time David was established, she would have finished her B.A. She could stay home and make babies and pictures, one form of creativity feeding upon the other.

The film had been like many other films; it had shown only the happy things, only the things that worked. It had ignored the question of whether the babies were to be raised Catholic or Jewish. It had ignored all the ways in which David and Caro were different. It had shown only the ways in which they were alike.

But David was not running the same film. In David's film, what he wanted was more important than what she wanted. She read his words about San Francisco again. "San Francisco is an exciting city, so much like New Orleans. I think you'll love it." Was that a proposal? Or did he think she would just move herself out there for a new kind of duration? She shook her head. He would be back from the war soon; they would meet and talk this through. In the meantime . . . She got up and switched on a lamp. If she kept drinking brandy, she really would be drunk, and she had to decide if that's what she wanted.

She felt something brush the edge of her memory, something unhappy, something that had made her mother cry. What was it? She drew the curtains and sat down again. Then, as she picked up her glass, a sudden beam of light catching it just the right way made her remember. Herself as a child, when her grandmother came to live with them in the house in Lafayette. Her grandmother stayed in her room a lot; she didn't like to eat with them very much, and most of the time, someone took her her meals on a tray. Once in a while Caro took a tray up, if Bea and her mother were both busy. And now she remembered what it was that made her mother cry. Her grandmother sitting at a table with a decanter on it, and a small glass of liquid in her hand. A glass that was only briefly empty, and that she filled again, and again. Her grandmother often couldn't even pick up her fork; when she did, the food fell off and cascaded down the ruffled front of her peignoir. After a while, her mother stopped sending Caro up with her grandmother's trays, and then her grandmother went to live somewhere else, and Caro never saw her again.

Well, damn. She stood up and put the stopper back in the decanter. She felt a little fuzzy, but she was far from being drunk. She'd go make a grilled cheese sandwich and open a can of soup. Then she'd listen to the radio; it was Sunday night, and she could count on Jack Benny and Edgar Bergen to make her laugh. She went to the kitchen and quickly fixed her supper, loading it onto a tray.

She carried her tray down the hall to the small room behind her bedroom. All her art things were in here, easels and sketchpads and oils thrust in hastily when she'd left Newcomb and gone to war. She put her tray on her drafting table and settled herself on the high stool. As she ate, she turned over the pages of a sketchpad, pausing now and then to hold one up to the light. Her interest grew as she flipped through them. I'd no idea I knew that much, she thought, and felt a small glow of excitement begin to warm that leaden weight.

She finished her sandwich and spooned up the last of her soup. Then, shoving the tray to the edge of her work space, she turned to a fresh, blank page and began to draw.

Part II

16

OCTOBER 1948

A wash of golden light poured in through the open French doors, falling on the paintings hung around the room, deepening their colors. A tall, spare woman leaned toward one work, then drew back and studied it intently. Caro Hamilton, standing across the room in the center of a cluster of people, caught her mother's hand. "Oh, heavens. There's Miss Clements."

"She'll be very proud of you, Caro. How many new graduates are asked to hang their work in such a fine gallery?" Caroline said. "A student's success always reflects well on the teacher."

"I can still hardly believe Charles Dupuy asked me to be in this show," Caro said. And then, as the gallery owner bore down on them, she said more loudly, "Oh, Mr. Dupuy, I can't thank you enough for this opportunity—"

"Nonsense," Charles Dupuy said, taking her hand and tucking it under his arm. "Come, let us go speak to Miss Clements." He led her across the room, nodding and smiling to his guests as he drew her along. "When I saw your work at your senior exhibit, I knew I must claim you early, or lose you to one of my rapacious competitors." He stopped to speak to people several times as he made his way across the room, introducing Caro as "a young artist who is going to make a name for herself." "You must become accustomed to center stage, dear child," he murmured in Caro's ear. "You *are* going to make a name for yourself—and, if I have anything to do with it, a nice sum of money for us both."

They came up to Miss Clements, who turned her gaze to Mr. Dupuy, fixing his face as though, Caro thought, she were going to sketch it. "Ah,

Dupuy," she said. "You've placed Caro's work very nicely. It shows to good advantage." She came forward and kissed Caro's cheek. "I had not seen this one. It's marvelous."

"I wasn't sure," Caro said. "I did it over the summer . . ." She felt the old uncertainty, the doubt whether the watercolor in front of her conveyed what she intended. "I thought maybe it was a little . . . derivative."

"Derivative!" Miss Clements looked at the watercolor in front of her, then strolled a few feet further, where two others were hung. "These are the work of an artist who has an original vision. And who is learning quite rapidly how to make that vision true."

"Maybe you can help me convince Caro that this early in her career, she should sell everything patrons want to buy. I've had at least three people ask for a painting Caro is determined to hold on to."

"They can have any of the others," Caro said. "For whatever price you think fair. But not that one."

Mr. Dupuy shrugged. "Then let me go help them choose among the others. Your work is going to increase in value: they will be doing themselves a favor to buy it now."

"Let me be one of Caro's early collectors," Miss Clements said. "I insist on first choice, Dupuy. Now, don't argue!"

"Oh, Miss Clements, you don't have to buy one! I'd love to give you one—goodness, it's the least I can do!" Caro said. "If it weren't for you—and all the encouragement you've given me these last three years—I wouldn't be here today."

"Yes, you would," Miss Clements said. "If you had to paint on cardboard or old planks, you'd be here." She took Caro's hand and looked at her with the familiar stern face. Her eyes were different, though. Instead of the challenging glare that either spurred her students on or sent them out of the studio weeping, Miss Clements' eyes were warm, approving, accepting. The way one artist looks at another, the way one peer views another's work. "Caro. Professionals do not *give* their work away. They sell it. To everyone." A small smile softened her lean features, made her face match her eyes. "Now if, on my birthday, you want to present me with a small sketch—a little pen-and-ink—I would welcome it. But never, *never* let people get in the habit of not paying you."

"My sentiments exactly," Dupuy said. "Now, let's go select yours, my dear Miss Clements, before these avid people quite wipe me out."

"Did you hear that?" Skye said, coming up behind Caro. "I'd better hang on to all those sketches and drawings you've given me over the years—if I fail as a lawyer, I can open a gallery and get rich on your work."

"I wouldn't stop studying yet," Caro said, linking arms with him and sighing happily. "Oh, Skye, I'm beginning to feel like a real artist!"

"Feel like one? You *are* an artist," Skye said. "Wish I were a lawyer. Seems like I've been going to school forever."

"Only two more years," Caro said. "They'll go by like lightning."

"Even that's not fast enough to suit me," Skye said. Then he smiled at her. "Say, I don't mean to be spreading gloom on this festive occasion. Think I'll go bid up the price of your work."

"You may get stuck with it," Caro warned.

"The way Dupuy is talking about it? Not a chance."

He strolled off to where Dupuy was in earnest conversation with a well-dressed couple. Caro turned for another look at the watercolor she refused to sell. She couldn't bear to part with it. Caught now in the full beam of light, its colors glowed as though they had been distilled from the very essence of spring. It was a landscape of the alley of oaks at Beau Chêne from a diagonal perspective, the oaks forming the focal point in the center, while the background dimmed into a green mist and the foreground appeared as a deeper green lawn. The landscape had a mystical, ethereal feeling that contrasted with the concrete reality of trees, lawn, and barely sketched house, putting it, as the *Times-Picayune* art critic previewing the show wrote, "in the stream of impressionistic painting while at the same time conveying an earthiness that brings the viewer back again and again."

Caro turned from the painting, feeling that that one work made all the sacrifice, all the long hours of the past three years worth it.

Suddenly her eyes widened as she saw the man coming through the door at the far end of the room. "David!" she cried, running toward him.

His arms came around her and he bent to kiss her. "I practically got out and pushed the plane," he said. "I was so afraid I'd miss your entire opening."

She became conscious of curious eyes on them and drew away, her hand still clasped in his. "You haven't missed a thing. Mr. Dupuy has been lying like crazy about my work, getting these poor people to buy it—and my whole family is bragging to beat the band. If this is what it's like to show your work, I'm not sure I can do it."

"Nonsense," David said. "You deserve all the praise you get. This is your day, and I defy anyone not to celebrate you to the hilt."

"Now that you're here, I have everything I want," she said. "I wish you could stay longer—it's such a long way for just a few days."

"My patients have a peculiar way of wanting me around," David said. He traced the line of her cheek gently with his forefinger.

"So do I," Caro said.

"Maybe now we can do something about that," David said. He looked around the gallery. "Now that you're on your own—not tied to working with Miss Clements."

"Right," she said, and felt the funny little flutter that warned her away from David's meaning. "Everyone's here," she said, drawing him toward a corner where her family had gathered. "Gennie came down from New York, Fielding and Émilie drove over from St. Francisville, Mama and Père—now you're here too. It's the most wonderful weekend I can imagine."

"As glad as I always am to see your family, Caro—it's you I came to be with." He paused, then looked at her intently. "I didn't make hotel reservations this time."

"David—"

"Darling, I could go along with the hotel room for appearances when you were still in college. But you're all grown up now. There is absolutely no point in my spending a couple of hours in a hotel room just to preserve some fable that we're not sleeping together."

"Not here, David, please."

"All right," he said. "But I have no intention of playing this game any longer, Caro. It's . . . demeaning."

He held out his hand to Beau, who was crossing the room to greet him.

"Glad you could make it," Beau said. "Caro would have been mighty disappointed if you hadn't been able to come."

"This is one of those occasions the proverbial wild horses could not have kept me from," David said.

Beau felt the tension between the two of them and looked at Caro. Her color was high, her eyes bright. "I think Caro has held up pretty well," he said. "But she's had to deal with a lot of people—not all of them especially easy." He laughed and patted Caro's hand. "Most of the people here know art, and even if it's difficult to hear your work judged, at least they know what they're talking about. But there is always at least one like the woman over there in the red hat. She followed Caro around for at least twenty minutes insisting Caro take her brother-in-law's name and address. It seems he works for a firm that makes calendars, and she thought there was every possibility they might buy Caro's work. Of course, she did warn Caro not to expect much at first—maybe five dollars a picture!"

"Speaking of buying paintings," David said, "I want to buy one. Caro, what about that one over there? There's something about it that looks familiar—though I don't really recognize the scene."

"Oh, that's the boat landing at Beau Chêne," Caro said. "I took a little liberty in the way I set the composition."

"Maybe it's the light on the water," David said. He backed off a short distance and studied the work. "Something about it takes me back to quiet times on the ship—" He shook his head. "Whatever it is, I know I have to have it."

"Oh, David, you don't have to buy one! Let me give it to you—"

"I'm no fool," he said. "Years from now, people will envy me having gotten in on the ground floor."

"As soon as you've gotten your painting, why don't you and Caro go on over to Commander's and have a leisurely drink while I get this crew together?" Beau said.

"All right," David said. He, too, had noted the tautness in Caro's face, the way her breath came fast and quick, her words tumbling out while her eyes darted over the crowd. He slipped his arm around her shoulders and guided her over to the painting of the boat landing. "That will look marvelous in my office," he said. "Very soothing to nervous patients." He looked at her anxiously. "Are you all right?"

"I'm fine. Just—well, a little strung-out, I guess. It's been hectic. And I'm not used to the way real pros do this. When we did student shows at Newcomb, it mattered, but not in the same way."

"How are you sleeping now?"

"Not too well," she said, and smiled at him. "Though I think that little problem may get taken care of tonight."

"Caro—have you thought any more about seeing a psychiatrist?"

"No," she said emphatically. "Look, here's Mr. Dupuy, just aching to sell you something. Mr. Dupuy, I'd like you to meet Dr. David Selbin, an old . . . friend of mine from San Francisco."

"And have you come all this way to purchase a Hamilton?" Dupuy asked.

"Yes," David said. "This one." His hand gestured toward Caro's painting, but his eyes remained fixed on her.

"An excellent choice," Dupuy said. "You have good taste, Dr. Selbin."

"I have a good instructor," David said. "Caro's been helping me buy art since the day we first met."

"And now you are buying hers," Dupuy said. "Everything comes full circle in its own good time." He checked the catalog and said, "That one is eighty-five dollars, Dr. Selbin."

"Fine," David said. "May I leave the painting here until tomorrow?"

"But of course. In fact, if you wish I will pack it and ship it for you, Dr. Selbin. If that is more convenient."

"I'll let you know," David said. He maneuvered Caro through the crowd and down the broad hall that led to the street. There was a small alcove midway; he pulled Caro into it and kissed her, feeling her instantaneous response. "If it weren't for the fact that we're going to celebrate your opening, I'd say let's skip dinner and go straight to your place," he said. He kissed her again. "You aren't going to make me go to a hotel, are you?"

"No," she said. "You're right. I am all grown up now. It's just—in New Orleans, where people know me—" She stopped. There was no need to go on. They had had this conversation too many times before. As long as she was at Newcomb, and had other girls in the house on Calliope Street, there had been enough valid reasons to make her refusal to allow David to stay there or to stay with him at his hotel stick. Now the housemates were gone. Caro was very much on her own, and only social convention stood between them.

She took his arm and moved toward the gallery entrance. "I really do want a drink, darling," she said.

They got into Caro's car and headed out of the Quarter for Commander's Palace, Caro chattering about anything that came to her mind, David seemingly intent on his driving. When they were settled over their drinks, he took her hand and began to caress her palm.

"Tell me about not sleeping."

"There's nothing to tell. I've been keyed up about the show—"

"Any nightmares?"

She stared down into her drink, focused on the orange slice and maraschino cherry decorating it. "Some."

"Same old thing?"

"Same old thing."

Her flat tone hid the terror behind her admission. David's hand tightened on hers. "Darling—it's been well over three years. If they haven't gone away by themselves—I really think you should talk to someone."

"I don't have anything against psychiatrists, David." She smiled sadly. "I just can't imagine that anything one could say would change anything."

"It wouldn't change it. It might make it lose its . . . power."

"I'm going to try my way a little longer," she said. "I don't have them as much anymore—sometimes not for months."

"All right," he said. "Whatever you think—"

She looked at him, her eyes suddenly filled with old pain. "I don't want to dredge all that up, David. I don't want to remember every detail. I'm busy forgetting it. And most of the time, it works."

"All right," he said again. He brought her hand to his lips and kissed it. "Promise you one thing—tonight, there will be no nightmares."

"There never are when I'm with you," she said.

"That should tell you something." He let it rest then, sensing that Caro had had all she could take of anxiety and tension. Watching her across the table, seeing her cool poise, he wondered again at the maelstrom of feeling beneath her calm surface. No one seeing her at the gallery, or here at the restaurant, would see anything but a beautiful young woman in a beautifully cut silk dress the exact color of her blue eyes, whose string of pearls and kid gloves announced as clearly as her manner that she lived in a rather special world. Nor, David knew, did anyone but himself and her stepfather know that when Caro put away her overalls and work shoes, her heavy gloves and her assortment of bandannas at the end of the war, she had not been able also to put away the memory of those years at the shipyard, and return to Newcomb unchanged. She had seemed to slip back into the familar collegiate routine as easily as she slipped back into her wardrobe of plaid skirts and cashmere sweaters. Only Beau and David knew that Caro still had nightmares, still woke trembling and shaking on the near edge of hysteria. Only they knew of the stack of sketchpads filled with her efforts to exorcise her demons. Those drawings were very different from the calm strength of the landscapes in this show; it was the very discipline that held those night monsters at bay and allowed Caro to get on with her real work in the beneficent light of day that David believed would ultimately release her from them.

David had a whole folder of her sketches; they might almost be a graphic journal of their courtship. At first, when he was settling into practice in Phil Jacobs' clinic, and Caro was groping her way back into painting, the visits had been fairly far apart: Thanksgiving, part of the Christmas break, a few days at Easter. But then they both mastered the challange of their postwar lives, and flew to one another at least once a month, taking turns making the cross-country flight. It was possible, they learned, to live between visits. He wrote every day, sometimes twice a day, so that often Caro got a letter from David in the morning and another in the afternoon. She wrote almost as frequently; her letters were longer, often illustrated, and so the correspondence balanced out. They talked on the telephone once a week, on Sunday afternoons. Sundays became identified in their minds as the day you said good-bye. Sunday was the last day of their weekends together, Sunday was the day they heard each other's voices—but still across a distance, still miles and miles apart.

For both of them, this was a solution for the duration only. They had picked up the term used in the war, adapting it to mean when Caro finished school, when David was a full partner. Now she had finished school, following her June graduation with a tour of European galleries and museums, returning to New Orleans to open a studio and join Dupuy's gallery. There was nothing to stand in their way now, David told himself. And before he left New Orleans, he would tell Caro so.

Skye let his eyes rove idly over the gallery crowd, watching their reactions to the various works. He was proud of Caro, delighted with the way almost everyone who passed in front of her paintings stopped and looked at them, and then turned to the catalog to learn more. She deserves it, he thought. God knows she's worked hard enough.

Then, seeing David and Caro leave, he broke away from the people he had been talking to and walked over to Caro's favorite work for a last look. A woman stood in front of it, taking notes. Skye stared at her. There was something distinctly familiar about her . . . It couldn't be, he told himself firmly. Just a girl with Natalie Watkins' hair . . . her build . . . The girl turned her head and he saw the familiar profile.

"Natalie!" His voice boomed through the room. Heads turned, and Natalie swirled around.

"Skye! Skye Langlinais, for heaven's sake!"

"What in the world are you doing here?" he said, crossing the space between them in three long strides. Then he had her in his arms, kissing her without thinking. For the briefest instant her lips met his and she kissed him back. Then, as though on a signal, they broke away.

"You first," he said. "What are you doing in New Orleans? And here, of all places?"

"I live in Baton Rouge now," she said. "I'm a reporter at the *Morning Advocate*. There's a Baton Rouge native in this show—and the editor said people in Baton Rouge would know Caro Hamilton, too."

"She's my stepsister," Skye said.

"I remembered," Natalie said. Color flooded her face. "I thought—I thought you might be here, Skye."

"But you live in Baton Rouge! And you haven't tried to get in touch with me?"

"I haven't been there that long," Natalie said. "I finished my degree in journalism at the University of Virginia in June. Then I spent the summer looking at options. Uncle Paul invited me to spend a couple of weeks in St. Francisville—and then talked me into applying for a job on the *Advocate*. I guess what really persuaded me was the political situation here—I've been fascinated by Huey Long since I was old enough to follow politics. I wondered what the state would be like with his brother Earl as governor."

"An art show seems a far piece from politics," Skye said. One quick glance told him that the diamond that had shone on her left hand in England was gone. Questions crowded his mind; he caught her hand and said, "We have years to catch up on. Have dinner with me, can you?"

She seemed to hesitate. "What about you, Skye? I know why you're here—at the opening. But what have you been doing?"

"I'm in law school now. I got through prelaw as fast as they'd let me, but I still have two years left."

"You're at LSU?"

"Right." He thrust his hands in his pockets and stared at her. "I still can't get over the fact that you didn't let me know you were in town. If you weren't such an old friend, I'd be mad as hell."

"I thought you'd have done what you said you were going to do," she said.

"What was that?"

"You said you were going to come home and marry your girl."

"Oh. Yes, I did say that, didn't I? Well, I didn't." He looked at her hand. "For that matter, what about you? You were engaged."

"Nothing came of it," Natalie said. "He married someone else—a nurse he met after he was wounded."

"I'm sorry to hear that," Skye said, feeling the leap of his heart that denied his words.

"Those things happen," Natalie said.

"About dinner," Skye said, covering the pause that suddenly developed. "Most of my family is here—we're all going to Commander's Palace to celebrate Caro's show. Please come."

"I don't want to barge in on a family party—"

"You're not barging in. There's always room for one more. Come meet everybody." He took her hand and guided her to where Beau and Caroline stood talking to Émilie and her her husband, Fielding.

"I would like to introduce you all to Natalie Watkins," he said. His voice made the name special, and his eyes glowed in a way Beau and Caroline had not seen for a long time. "This is my stepmother, and my father," Skye said to Natalie. "And my sister Émilie and her husband, Fielding Horton. I've invited Natalie to have dinner with us. She thinks she's barging in, but I told her we always have room for one more."

"Of course we do," Caroline said firmly. She took Natalie's hand. "I'm so happy to meet you. Skye wrote so much about you when you were both stationed in England during the war."

"We had some good times together," Natalie said. "But, really, Mrs. Langlinais, I don't want to intrude—"

"Nonsense. Everyone knows the Langlinais meals are movable feasts—we can change the place, the number of guests, anything—to accommodate our wishes. And what we wish now, very much, is for you to join us."

"Thanks, Mère," Skye said. Turning to Natalie, he said, "Please say you will. I'll be terribly disappointed if you don't."

"Now I've placed you," Émilie said suddenly. "You're Paul Watkins' niece, aren't you? He was telling Fielding and me just last week all about his niece who had come down from Virginia to work on the *Advocate*—but I didn't make the connection."

"Oh, you know my Uncle Paul?"

"We live not five miles from him," Fielding said. "Just north of St. Francisville at Magnolia Hill."

"That's a lovely old place," Natalie said. "I've driven by there dozens of times."

"Make Skye bring you to see us, then?" Émilie said. "He's got an eighteen-month-old godson up there he needs to come see more often."

"Thank you, I'd love to," Natalie said.

There was a pause, and Skye, testing its quality, felt the warmth of their circle extend outward, bringing Natalie in. A rush of happiness filled him. "I don't know about anyone else, but I'm starving," he said. "Didn't I hear the promise of dinner?"

"Absolutely," Beau said. "Émilie, why don't you and Fielding come with us? Skye, will you and Natalie round Gennie up and bring her?"

"Sure thing," Skye said. He held out his arm to Natalie. "It's so wonderful to see you again," he said warmly. "And don't think I'm going to let you off with just dinner. You're not rushing back to Baton Rouge, are you?"

"The story doesn't have to be in until Monday, so I made reservations at the Monteleon. I love New Orleans—"

"Let's hear some jazz after dinner."

"Fine. I'd love it."

"And then we can get coffee and beignets at Café du Monde."

"Wonderful."

"And tomorrow I'll take you to Brennan's for breakfast."

"All right."

"We can plan the rest of the day over breakfast."

"Yes, boss," Natalie said, and laughed. "Skye, it's so good to see you!"

"It's good to see you."

As the three of them drove toward Commander's, Gennie and Natalie began talking theater; Natalie had gone up to New York frequently during her years in college to see plays, and they discovered that she may have seen Gennie perform without knowing who she was.

"Of course I don't use 'Langlinais,' " Gennie said, laughing. "No one could pronounce it, and I gave up trying to teach them. I act under the name Gennie Langley, but don't pretend you remember it. I've only had very small parts—but they're getting better."

Skye listened to their conversation with a feeling of ease he had not known for some time. He had dated a number of girls in the last three years; sometimes, when he looked back, an astonishing number of girls. When accused of playing the field, he answered reasonably that he wasn't doing so intentionally. He was studying hard, cramming as many hours in per semester as he could—dating was a casual thing, something he did when the occasion demanded, or when a girl conveniently fell in his way. So that even though some of his dates met his family, the meetings had been unimportant. He had not felt attracted to any of them in any real way. It had been a long time since he'd met a girl who mattered to him. But Natalie was not like other girls. Natalie was different. From the first, he had felt his family responding to her. Which, he told himself as he parked the car, is pefectly natural. After all, I did write a lot about her. And I did talk about her a lot when I first got home.

"We had promised to keep in touch," he said, turning to Natalie. "And except for one Christmas card, I never heard from you."

"I thought you had married," Natalie said. "And were too busy for wartime friendships." She smiled. "Except for one Christmas card, I never heard from you, either."

Not until dinner was over and they were on their way back to the Quarter did he allow himself to ask the questions that had nagged to be answered all evening. "When did you find out about your fiancé? After you got back to the States?"

"No," she said. "That last week in England. I got a letter—oh, I guess a day or two before our picnic."

"You knew *then?* But you never said—"

"Skye, what was there to say?" She looked away from him, staring at the streetcar rolling past them.

"But you were with friends—we could have comforted you . . . done *something*."

She swung back to him and reached out her hand to touch his. "Oh, Skye. You were the last person I wanted to know I'd been . . . jilted. Especially after you announced your plans to get married." He could see color rushing into her face; she bent over her purse, and, opening it, pulled out her cigarettes. "I mean, it was a happy occasion, the war was over, everyone was looking ahead—I just didn't want to talk about my little problem."

He opened his mouth and then closed it again without speaking. What could he have said? Especially, as she said, in view of his own announcement. "Well, as it happened, I didn't know what I was talking about at all," he said. "Got back to find Rosalind engaged to a cousin she wasn't even in love with."

"Skye!" Natalie's shock reaffirmed his own long-ago feelings.

"Yeah, I felt the same way. I couldn't understand it."

"It doesn't make sense—"

"You'd have to understand Rosalind's people. I didn't, not then. I do now, I guess. They're Syrian. And they've kept to the old ways. They marry to strengthen family and business ties."

"Did she still love you?"

"I don't know." They had reached the Quarter, and he pulled into a parking place, then cut the motor. "To tell you the truth, Natalie, I'm not sure Rosalind ever loved me—or if I ever really loved her. If either of us knew what the word meant."

"You were both young—"

"No younger than you. Anyway," he said. "it's over."

"And?" On the sidewalk in front of Pat O'Brien's, the glow from the neon lights on the street gilded the edges of her hair; he remembered how she felt in his arms when they danced together and wished they had gone to the Blue Room to dance instead.

"And what?"

"And have you found someone to take her place?"

He thought of the girls, all the pretty, sweet, agreeable girls he had danced with and taken to movies and had dinner with. Played tennis with. Gone swimming with. Sailed with. They melded together into one girl, but she had no name, held no meaning in his life. "No," he said. He took her hand. "Have you found anyone to take the lieutenant's place?"

"No," she said. As they entered the nightclub, she continued, almost too low for Skye to hear her, "But I've learned something. I've learned never to rush into anything like that again."

He did hear her, but what his mind settled on was not the words. Words, as he learned in law school every day, mean only what we agree that they mean. What he settled on was her tone. It held the determination that is fired by hurt and shaped by sorrow. Well, he thought, I don't want to rush into anything, either.

"Where are you going?" David asked, catching Caro's arm the next morning as she sat up and swung her legs over the side of the bed.

"To make coffee," she said. She leaned over and kissed him. "Don't you want coffee?"

"Only if you promise to come right back," he said, pulling her down to him.

"Maybe I won't leave," she said.

"That's a much, much better idea." His arms closed around her, and she sank back into the world that existed only when they were together. It was a small world, no larger than their bed, but it contained, during the times they were in it, all that either of them had ever wanted.

Later, when they both got up and went to the kitchen to make coffee and scrambled eggs, Caro thought regretfully that somehow, that special world was much too fragile; it seemed hardly able to endure past the bedroom door.

"Shall we eat on the patio?" David asked as he beat the eggs.

"No, let's eat inside," Caro said, keeping her eyes fastened on the water she was dripping into the coffeepot.

"It's a gorgeous day—why not?"

"I'd rather not, David," she said.

"Wait a minute—let me guess. You don't want the neighbors to see a man coming out of your house this early in the morning."

"I know you think that's silly. I'm sorry. I see no reason to upset them—"

"I didn't say I thought it was silly. Come on, Caro, I don't enjoy scandalizing old ladies."

"I didn't say you did," she said.

"We're not going to have a fight, are we?" he said, coming over to the stove and getting out a pan for the eggs.

"We certainly are not." She kissed his ear, letting her tongue run around the edge. "If you want to eat outside, we will. A little scandal in her life is probably just what my dear old neighbor needs."

"I have a much better idea," David said. "We'll take it back to bed."

"Should I be suspicious of that?" she said archly. "Oh, David, why do you have to leave? I want to have breakfast in bed, and lunch in bed, and dinner in bed—"

"You could come with me," he said.

For a moment she concentrated on putting plates and utensils on a big tray, pouring coffee and taking the biscuits out of the oven. "All right," she said. "Let's talk about it." She took the coffee and he followed, carrying their breakfast. They sat cross-legged on the bed, the tray between them. "When you say I could come with you—what do you mean?"

"Caro, ever since I got out of the Navy—I've been ready to marry you. You know that. It's you who's held things up—"

"To finish my work with Miss Clements. To give you time to get established."

"All right. Both those things have happened. You're finished. I'm established. So come out there and marry me."

"Or marry you and come out there."

"It's the same thing."

"Not really." She set down her cup and looked at him. "It's not the same thing. And that's the whole problem."

"I'm afraid I don't see how a change in wording—"

"But it's what that change means, don't you see? It's one thing to go out there—and then marry you. It's another thing to marry you—and then go out there. I want to be married here, David. In front of my family."

"Of course. I know your family will want a big splash—sorry, I don't mean that the way it sounds. I mean they'll want all the trimmings. And why shouldn't they? You do too, I imagine. That's fine, I can go along with that."

"It isn't fine, though. We couldn't marry in church. And unless you promise to bring the children up Catholic, David—we couldn't even be married by a priest."

He leaned over and took two cigarettes from the pack on the night table, lit them both, and handed one to Caro. "I had hoped that didn't matter so much anymore, Caro." A film of smoke blew up between them. "Then come out and marry me. We can do it another way. Leave the Church out of it."

"If we leave the Church out of it, I may as well not be married at all."

"The State of California seems to think it can legitimatize unions."

"That's not what I meant. David—what about the children?"

He looked about the room. "I don't see any children. We may not even have children."

"But don't you want children?"

"Yes, I want children. But, Caro! I want you a hell of a lot more. I'm not ready to bargain today's happiness against the chance that we'll have children."

"Why wouldn't we have children? I'm perfectly healthy, you're perfectly healthy—"

"Lots of perfectly healthy people don't have children." He laughed, and she heard an undertone of bitterness she had not heard for a long time. "I have an idea. We'll adopt children, children who have already been baptized—or who are already Jewish." He looked at her, mimicking the expression of someone who has just been struck by a thought. "I know—we'll adopt some of the children who survived the camps. Kill two birds with one stone, so to speak."

"David!" Her shock changed to concern; David's face was contorted with pain, and she pushed the tray aside and took him in her arms, cradling him against her. "Oh, darling, I'm sorry. David, I love you. We'll work it out, David. Really. It will be all right, you'll see. There has to be an answer—"

"I hope so," he said. He lifted his head and looked at her. "Because if I lose you, Caro, I'll lose the only thing that matters to me in the whole world."

"You're not going to lose me, David."

"Then marry me."

"You don't want me to marry you like this," Caro said.

"Yes, I do."

"No, David, you don't. Can't you see? If I abandon something that's such an important part of me—ignore it as though it has no meaning—I'll be leaving a part of me outside of our marriage. There'll be a hole, David, a hole I can't expect you to fill."

"It sounds so hopeless, Caro. I understand what you mean—it would be as if I were to abandon a part of my heritage."

"It can't be hopeless. I've just got to think . . ."

He took her hand and held it against his chest; she felt his familiar warmth, the way his hair curled softly over his flesh.

"There's something else, David," she said slowly.

"Something else?"

"I'm afraid of being absorbed. I'm afraid of leaving everything I've done for three years—all my friends, my family, my home—for a life that is so much *your* life."

"San Francisco's one of the most artistically sophisticated cities in the country. You could paint to your heart's content. God, Caro, what would absorb you?"

"You. Your work. Your friends."

"My friends love you, Caro."

"I've met Phil and Sarah Jacobs," Caro said. "And that other couple, I forget their name."

"They loved you," David repeated stubbornly.

"And I liked them. But, David—that's not enough to build a life on."

"Dammit, Caro! You would be marrying *me,* not my friends!"

"I'm a doctor's daughter, David, remember? I know how much a doctor's wife is left on her own—and I need to be sure, David. I need to be sure that I'll make that time mine—that I'll use it to keep Caro going. That I won't lose her."

He leaned back against a pillow and stared at her. "You've been doing a lot of thinking."

"Of course I have. Haven't you?"

"Not as much, apparently. I guess I hoped—" He frowned. "It was an unrealistic kind of hope. I see that now."

"You hoped when I graduated, I'd put some of my other notions away."

"Something like that."

"David, did you ever think—maybe part of the reason you love me is some of these very notions you wish I'd get rid of?"

She saw a light come into his eyes, a smile break across his face. He held out his arms and she went into them. "Dammit," he said as he kissed her. "You're right, you know. But listen—do you think you can use some of that famous New Orleans voodoo to get this monkey off our back? Because I'm telling you, Caro Hamilton—one way or another, you've got to come to San Francisco. I want you so much. I can't live without you anymore."

"I can't live without you, either," Caro whispered. And kissed him as if sealing their souls.

17

JANUARY 1949

"But what a wonderful house!" Natalie exclaimed as Skye turned into the drive that led up to the farm. The house sprawled at the far end, it's long porch clear of the vines that sheltered it in summer. The shutters framed shining windowpanes, and smoke drifted up from a massive chimney set in the center of the high-pitched roof. "You said you lived on a farm!"

"Well, it is," Skye said. He cocked an eyebrow at her. "You didn't think I lived in a log cabin, did you?"

"Of course not! I guess I really didn't think about it at all," she said.

"But somewhere deep down underneath, you wouldn't have been surprised if I'd brought you to a house built up on piers with the swamp licking at its toes," he teased. He pulled up on the concrete parking apron and came around to help her out. "Never mind. No matter how sophisticated and citified we Langlinaises appear—when outlanders come down here for the first time, they always expect to find that all the stories about Louisiana are true. I'll never forget Émilie mad as a hornet because a girl I brought home from LSU expected to find everyone speaking an incomprehensible patois and wearing dresses made out of flour sacks."

"Why is that, do you suppose?" Natalie asked. She paused and looked at the Langlinais house, cloaked with the stillness of the January afternoon. "Why do we cling to our notions of what other people are like, despite all evidence to the contrary?"

"Do you mean why do we ignore what our head tells us and listen to instinct? Primitive memory?" He shook his head. "I don't know. Even in prison camp, I had a hard time adjusting what I learned about my German guards to what I'd always thought about Germans. You know, the images from *The Student Prince.*"

"Yes," Natalie said, and reached out and squeezed Skye's hand. Her quick sympathy moved him; not a little of Natalie's attraction was this shared past. She was the only person he knew now who had directly participated in his life during the war. She was the only person to whom a reference to that time did not have to be fully explained. And though he did not dwell on those years, he had found, in these few months they had been dating, that it was very comfortable to be with someone connected to that time.

Then Caroline came onto the front porch, André behind her.

"I shot the teal we're having in the gumbo, Skye!" André cried. "Papa got some too, but I got just as many as he did."

"André had his first hunt this morning," Caroline told Natalie. She put her arm around her youngest son's shoulders affectionately. "His father says he's like all Langlinaises—an absolute natural."

"Listen, fellow, I want to hear all about that," Skye said. "Sounds like I'd better look to my laurels."

"I'll show you your room, Natalie," Caroline said. "André, bring Miss Watkins' bag, will you?"

When Natalie came downstairs, Beau and Skye were out in the kitchen shucking oysters. She watched in fascination as they pried open the shells, skillfully twisting off one half and then plumping the oyster in the remaining half onto a bed of ice.

"We eat off the land at home, too," Natalie said, perching on a stool near Skye. "I think I was in college before I realized that not everybody just went outdoors and came home with supper."

"Then you live in the country too?" Caroline asked.

"On a plantation outside of Charlottesville. I grew up with a houseful of brothers—I'm not sure anyone realized I was a girl until I hit my teens."

"They could hardly mistake it then," Beau said, and smiled.

Natalie felt suddenly at home, as though this were just one in a chain of Friday nights she had spent in this place, with these people. So at supper, when Skye passed her a steaming bowl of gumbo, she looked at it and blurted without thinking: "But aren't you Catholic?"

"Sure we are. Why?"

"There's meat in there—and it's Friday," she said, blushing. The table had grown suddenly still, and she could feel Beau and Caroline and André looking at her.

"That's not meat, that's teal," Skye said.

"I don't understand—"

"Well," Beau said, "it's like this. Most wild ducks, yes, we'd have to say they're meat, and we couldn't eat them on Friday. But teal?" He shrugged, the Langlinais shrug Natalie was beginning to learn signaled a rule these Cajuns made when the ones the rest of the world observed didn't suit them. "Teal eats like a fish. Water plants. Minnows. Like that. So how can something that eats like a fish be meat?"

Natalie joined in the shout of laughter that greeted Beau, but she was still puzzled. And even when Caroline assured her that Father Richard, the pastor of St. Martin of Tours Church, was enjoying some of this very gumbo for his supper, delivered by Caroline that afternoon, Natalie felt confused. Somehow, these people bent rules that others followed—and bent them for no reason other than that life was better for it.

"You really know how to live down here, don't you?" she said to Skye on Saturday morning, when they drove into town to visit his grandparents. Claude and Alice Langlinais welcomed her with open arms; in the course of the morning, one story followed the other as tiny cups of dark black coffee flowed from Alice's seemingly endless pot. When she passed freshly baked blackberry tarts, made from berries she had put up last summer, she said apologetically, "My pastry's not the best in the world. I always stir it too much after I add the liquid."

"My Mama used to tell Alice that every time she ate one of her biscuits or pies," Claude said, patting Alice's hand. "Now Mama's gone, Alice says it herself—just to keep in touch, you know?"

Natalie felt the rich presence of all those past lives permeating the room where she sat with Skye and his grandparents, as they did every room at the farm. The fullness of family love, and loyalty, that seemed to inhabit every aspect of the Langlinais domain. "I love it here," she said as they drove to New Iberia for lunch. "It's totally different from Virginia—and then again, it's very much the same."

"I'm glad," he said. When they drove back to St. Martinville, she sat a little closer to him, and when his hand reached over and took hers, she let it stay there. She went to her room for a nap, and spent the quarter of an hour before she fell asleep thinking about Skye.

They had begun dating right after Caro's show in October; at first they had gone out mostly on Saturdays, because Skye's study load and her irregular schedule at the newspaper allowed little else. Gradually, they had begun to see more of each other. Although Skye still called ahead of time to ask her out for Saturdays, he had fallen into the habit of calling her on the spur of a moment when his studying was going particularly well and he could take an hour or two off.

"You're a mighty agreeable girl," he told Natalie on more than one such occasion. "Most girls won't go out at the last minute—they'd rather sit home than let a guy think they aren't all booked up."

"I've never believed in cutting off my nose to spite my face," Natalie said. "Besides, that's all pretty silly, isn't it?"

She had not been able to tell from his quick agreement whether he understood that she meant playing games about being all dated up was silly—or whether he had left with the impression that this relationship didn't mean enough to her to dissemble about. There was a space between them, a distance, that they seemed to have agreed on without having to discuss it. The space was to stand in, to observe from. To move forward from, if either or both of them decided that they were ready to risk disappointment.

Natalie was beginning to think the space might become a barrier. She liked Skye. She would rather be with him than with any man she knew. And yet, she remembered the way she had felt about Steve, her ex-fiancé. The way she had not been able to look at him without actually getting weak. The way the sound of his voice on the telephone had been able to completely undo her. Skye did not have that effect on her. Nor, she had to admit, did she apparently have that effect on him. As she slipped into sleep, her mind caught on one small question: if all that were so—did she want it to change?

Like a shell ejected from a mortar, the black cock leapt straight into the air, spurs glinting. The red cock sprang an instant later, talons extended, yellow eye fixed on its enemy. They met in midair in a flash of gleaming strikes and flying feathers, each falling back to the dusty floor of the cockpit without having drawn blood. Their trainers came forward and soothed them, whispering familiar words and sounds close to the plumed heads. The crowd around Skye and Natalie momentarily relaxed, lighting cigarettes and opening bottles of beer.

"For heaven's sake, Skye!" Natalie said, leaning back against the rough edge of the bench behind her. "It's . . . it's terrible and beautiful at the same time. I've never seen anything like it."

"Not sorry you came?"

"Not yet. It'll make a wonderful color story—"

"Better not be too specific about the location if you're really going to write about this," Skye said. "It's as illegal as it can be. Illegal to transport these birds across state lines, illegal to train them to fight, illegal to have them fight—and illegal to bet on the fight."

"But that's the point, isn't it? To bet on which one will be left when it's all over?"

"That's right," Skye said. He gestured toward the birds, poised now at either side of the ring. "By the end of this, one of those two cocks will be dead. And his owner will be out a lot of money."

Natalie turned back to the pit and watched the two cocks circling each other, each waiting for the other to make the first aggressive move. The two cocks jumped at the same time. At the apex of their leap, their talons found targets. The black cock squawked loudly and jerked downward in an awkward fall while the red cock spread his wings and half-flew, half-leapt, after his victim. The trainer grabbed him just in time and held him while the wounded cock's trainer examined him, probing gently beneath the black feathers that glistened with blood.

"What will happen now?" Natalie said. The crowd had begun to roar, a ragged, disjointed cacophony of hoots and jeers, mixed with encouraging yells and cheers.

"The red cock was hurt too," Skye said. "See? Up high on his throat?"

Like a crimson necklace, a band of blood shone in the bright lights that flooded the pit.

"Can't they stop it?" Natalie cried. "If they're both hurt—"

"No," Skye said. "But it'll be over fast enough now."

Both cocks fairly exploded from their trainers' grasp, attacking each other in a flurry of strikes, their wings extended, canopies of black and red. Their yellow talons and beaks drew angry marks in the dust-filled air. Then the red cock jerked backward, stood motionless for a moment, and fell, wings folding like a fan. Blood pulsed from his chest and red-gold feathers drifted silently down, making a pattern in the stained dirt. The black cock flapped his wings, crowing loudly above the yells and cheers of the crowd. Cries of victory resounded through the small building. Natalie saw men digging into their pockets, slapping money into palms. She looked back at the pit. The dead cock had been picked up by his trainer, who carried him carefully out of the pit, as though he were still alive and could be healed. Friends came out to meet him, offering condolences. The victorious cock strutted proudly, the wound in his chest forgotten, and the blood of his opponent still staining his spurs.

"Do you want to leave now?" Skye asked quietly.

"Do you mind?"

"Not at all." They pushed their way to the end of the row and went down the wooden steps that took them to the passage that led outside. Natalie found that she was holding her breath; the very air seemed tainted with blood, and she stood in the cold, fresh air, breathing deeply once they were outside.

"More terrible than beautiful, finally, isn't it?" Skye said.

"Yes," she said. She took his arm and let him guide her over the rough ground to his car. "I guess I'm not as tough as I thought I was."

"Still going to write the story?"

"I don't think so. I . . . I don't think I could have the necessary detachment."

"Cockfights bring out different things in different people," Skye said. "I don't seek them out—but it's expected that we show up once in a while." He helped her into the car. "You'll like the *fais-do-do* we're going to. We're expected to go to those, too—but that's a pleasure."

She did not need to ask who "we" were, or why they were expected to show up. Over the months since she had met Skye's father, she had spent a great deal of time in the newspaper morgue, where all the back issues of the papers were kept, reading up on his career. She had come away with a feeling somewhere between awe and real affection: Beau Langlinais emerged as an almost heroic figure, standing up for what he believed in, opposing what he felt was wrong and would hurt his constituents. Time and again, he had put his honor on the line. And time and again, it had made a difference. Skye told her the story of his father's romance with his stepmother, and her fascination with the Langlinais family grew even deeper. But something bothered her, too. She could no longer look at Skye without seeing the heir to the family name, the family position, a position of status, money, and power. Yet when she looked in the mirror, the face that looked back at her did not seem to belong to a fairytale princess, someone brought up to stay home in the castle while the prince had all the adventures. Instead she saw a very ordinary girl with average looks who was trying to make her way in a world that kept women and politics as separate as it possibly could. And the more she learned about the Langlinaises' place in Louisiana politics, the more firmly convinced she became that her place in Skye's life would be as a pleasant companion.

She thought of Virginia, the placid houses lining the James River, the order, the serenity of those lives. The gentlemanly air that permeated the university. The pride of a state that had given so much to the governance of the nation. She thought of her own upbringing, in the middle of a family of brothers. She had ridden with them, hunted with them, shared their adventures in the wooded hills that surrounded their land. She had grown up with a tough-minded honesty, in a household where both Natalie and her mother spoke with directness, and where no subject was considered unfit for ladies' ears.

Natalie's father taught economics at the University of Virginia while her mother ran the plantation; Natalie's earliest memories were of her father driving off to college while her mother went out to supervise the plowing. A house full of hounds and heady conversation, a life of easy freedom and an abundance of male companionship. Looking back, Natalie realized with a start that except for her stint as a WAAF, she had never really lived among women at all. She had commuted to the university, driving in with her father each day, using the time to and fro to talk about everything under the sun. Every male topic under the sun, she thought wryly. Not for Natalie long talks about the latest Paris designs, already again dominating the fashion scene. Not for her an afternoon of girlish confidences over Cokes and cigarettes.

But I wouldn't have wanted to grow up any other way, she thought now. I may be a tomboy—but I like it. Her innate honesty forced her to examine that statement. Because that was the other thing that bothered her. The women in Skye's family, from Caroline to his sisters to Caro, were so darn feminine. It wasn't just that they were all pretty—more than pretty, beautiful. It wasn't just that they dressed well. It was the way they carried themselves, the way they moved, the small gestures that gave them that ineffable something that could only be called charm. And charm, Natalie thought, is, as James Barrie so well expressed it, what, if a woman has, she doesn't need anything else. And if she doesn't have it, it doesn't matter what else she does have. If asked, Natalie would have said that she did not possess that kind of charm.

"Penny?" Skye said, smiling and handing her a cigarette.

"Sorry." She smiled back and drew deep puffs of smoke, tasting the faint traces of perfume her fingers gave to the tobacco. Skye switched on the radio, and she focused her attention on the sounds coming from it. At first, they made no sense. Then she realized that the announcer spoke in French, a patois unfamiliar to her that she had difficulty understanding. The talking stopped, and music began, a strange, jangly kind of music with a strong, regular beat.

"That music is called zydeco," Skye said. "It's a blend of old French and African and some Spanish and even German music traditions."

He turned the car into a gravel parking lot surrounding a long, low wooden building with one small blue neon sign hung high over the doorway. "This is probably the best *fais-do-do* around," Skye said. "I think you'll find this bit of Cajun culture more to your liking than that cockfight."

"What does *fais-do-do* mean?" Natalie said. She saw an occasional buggy drawn up between the parked cars, the horses standing patiently in the shafts.

"Literally, it means 'make sleep,' " Skye said. "People bring their babies and put them to sleep all around the room." He reached out and touched her hand. "Now, stay close to me."

The noise when they entered the room was astonishing: a wild swirl of music from players grouped at the far end of the room; people clapping;

people dancing, heels coming down hard on every beat. A baby crying. The hum of people talking.

"Goodness!" Natalie said, her mind fleeing to the sedate dances of her college days.

They were suddenly surrounded by people, men and women who seemed to appear out of the music itself, smiling shyly until Skye moved around the circle, grasping hands and calling them by name.

"*Mais,* when you finish down to LSU, Skye?" one woman said.

"I've got one more year after this one, Mrs. Hebert."

"Cher, I don't know how you stand it that long, me!" the woman said, putting her hand in front of her mouth and laughing.

Skye laughed too, and slapped a man standing near him on the back. "I wouldn't be able to stand it if I couldn't come home every now and then to have some real food and dancing," he said.

"Look at Althea," Mrs. Hebert said, pointing to a dark-haired, dark-eyed girl standing at the edge of the circle. "See how she's grown up, Skye? When you came in, she said to me, she said, 'Mama, I'm going to ask Skye to dance. What you think? You think he will?' " Mrs. Hebert put her hands on her hips and gazed at her daughter. "Okay, Althea, Skye, he's here. So ask, all right?"

"She doesn't have to," Skye said. He moved through the path the crowd made until he stood before the girl. "Althea, may I have the next dance?"

Natalie stood with the others, watching the two of them take the center of the floor. When the music started, a change seemed to come over Skye. She could almost see the easy manner he wore in Baton Rouge and New Orleans drop away; his body seemed to gather into itself, operate as though on springs, as he took Althea into his arms and began to dance. The music called for a fast two-step, which seemed simple enough. But there were variations; hops, skips, dips, arm and head movements that made the dance more complex. And something else. An intensity in the way partners looked at each other, eyes never leaving the other's face. A communication between their two bodies, even when they were a foot apart. People around her were singing along with the musicians, and she strained to hear the words. *"Jolie blonde, jolie fille, chère petite chérie, mon cher coeur, tu m'as délaissé, tu es partie avec quelqu'un, en Louisiane; tu m'as laissé dans ma douleur."* Something about a pretty blond going away—she looked around the room. The walls were unfinished wood, and the beams that supported the roof were bare. The tables had no cloths, the chair seats were woven rush. A primitive, rustic place. And yet—and yet despite its rawness, despite the jeans and khakis the men wore, the simple skirts and dresses of the women, there was a spirit here that drew her to it at the same time it made her realize how very different this world was. The women, whatever their ages, moved with a kind of grace that made their bodies soft, open. She knew that she looked well; the wool jersey dress she wore was a deep, rich green that contrasted well with her hair and eyes. More than one man cast admiring glances her way—certainly she had no reason to feel less attractive than the other women here.

She watched as Skye swung his partner out and back again. Althea's body moved easily, and though her feet flew through the changing steps of the dance, her eyes never left Skye's face. Something about the way she looked at Skye, something about the way her body seemed to curve to his—then Natalie knew what was different about these women. They wanted to please the men. They sought the men's admiration with every gesture and glance. Not in a fawning way. Not in a way that lessened them. But simply as though they found in men something they could find nowhere else, and did all they could to attract them.

Skye looked different, too, dancing opposite Althea. His shoulder muscles rippled under his shirt, and his long, lean legs looked hard and strong as he leaned his body back and bore his weight on his thighs. This was a Skye she had never seen before; more intense, more attractive, more compelling than the Skye she had met in England, and had found again in Baton Rouge. And, dammit, she thought, as the accordion drew out a last long chord and Skye bent over Althea's hand, thanking her for the dance—it's his own people, his own turf, that brings that out in him. And that being the case—just where does that leave me?

Caro went to the open window and stood looking into the courtyard. She refused to watch the man behind her pull one after another of her paintings out of the stack beside him and place it on the easel in front of him. From time to time, she heard small sounds, but whether they denoted approval or not, she couldn't tell. And although she kept telling herself, over and over, that his opinion didn't matter that much, of course it did.

"Louis Koenberg has the best gallery in San Francisco," David had told Caro, calling as usual on Sunday. "He'll be in New Orleans next week, and he's going to Charles Dupuy's gallery to look for new artists. I showed him your painting—the one I bought last fall. He didn't say much, Caro. But he did say it showed promise."

"David—I've heard of Koenberg. He's one of the best in the business. He's not going to want to fool with me."

"Will you let him make that decision?"

"All right."

"Listen—if Muhammad won't come to the mountain, the mountain will just have to go to Muhammad, right? And then maybe Muhammad will move on out here."

She hung up the phone with her emotions in turmoil. Just thinking about showing her work to a stranger with that kind of expertise made her uncomfortable. That was the first thing, easily resolved. Koenberg would come, look at her work, either like it or not. It was the second thing that made her pace up and down the hall, restless, unable to concentrate on the book she had been reading before David called.

Even if Koenberg didn't like her work, David would continue to press her to come out to San Francisco. Their visits, letters, and phone conversations since October had begun to revolve around one theme: since neither of them could get past the religious differences, she should move, set up her studio—and let things develop as they would.

On the surface, this seemed reasonable enough. Her work was portable, David's was not. Furthermore, San Francisco's own California School of Fine Arts, under the leadership of Douglas MacAgy, was becoming the forerunner in the new abstract and nonrepresentational painting. And although Caro's work was very different in style, still, to be in a city where new trends were developing made every kind of sense.

Two reasons had made her indecision seem plausible. First, if she left New Orleans, she left a very good connection in Charles Dupuy; without a gallery, she would have a difficult time entering the San Francisco art world. And second—she had a strong feeling that was almost a conviction that once she was out there, far away from everything that affirmed her own roots and beliefs, she would give in gradually, accede to David's point of view, marry him in a civil ceremony—and be left to face whatever consequences that brought.

But if Louis Koenberg liked her paintings, he might very well offer to represent her. Which would be an open door to moving to San Francisco. That would solve the first of the two obstacles. Part of her wanted more than anything else to do just that. To see David every day, to have him part of her life. It was at one and the same time the most wonderful and the most frightening thing she could imagine. Frightening because she was afraid she would give in to David because of the sheer distance from familiar things, familiar friends. Not that David would deliberately try to persuade her to marry him outside the Church. It was herself she could not trust.

She suspected that her self-doubt went back to that terrible Sunday at Walter's when she had shot a man—not to wound, but to kill. It didn't matter that both Père and Walter had told her she had not really aimed for a fatal spot. It didn't matter that they both claimed repeatedly that her action had been instinctive, that she had been protecting Walter and

Henri. In her own heart she believed there had been one split second in which she could have aimed for the man's arm, or leg—could have wounded him, and stopped him all the same.

And so she was not sure she could trust her instincts. If she moved to San Francisco, she would have to be very careful.

"Well, my dear," Koenberg said, coming up behind her. "I can see why Dr. Selbin suggested I look at your work. You're very good, Miss Hamilton. Very good indeed."

She spun around and looked at him. He had been only a small, distinguished man in a gray suit until now. Now she saw the sharpness of his eyes, the keenness in his face, the vitality in his long, supple fingers. "I . . . Thank you," she said.

"Thank me when I've made you rich and famous," Koenberg said. "I want very much to handle your work. Now, shall we discuss our arrangements over lunch?"

"Arrangements?" Caro looked wildly at her paintings, ranged now against the wall behind the easel. One work was still in place on the stand, an oil painting of the cemetery at Beau Chêne. Koenberg took her arm and steered her toward the painting.

"This is an intriguing work for many reasons," he said. "The strength of the composition, the reduction of colors to black and white, with only the barest suggestion of green—the light, which is almost an absence of light—already, it has given me much to think about. But it is also intriguing because of these." He pointed to stiff wreaths of roses which decorated the two tombs in the foreground. "I cannot remember ever seeing anything like them except perhaps in Mexico, where there are many folk artifacts associated with the Days of the Dead. Are these something similar? Or are they your own touch?"

"Oh, no, they're very real. Women around St. Martinville—where our family's plantation, Beau Chêne, is located—make them and sell them on All Saints' Day."

"But what are they made of? In the paintings, it is difficult to tell."

"They have a wire base. The flowers are made of crepe paper. And then the whole thing is dipped in wax. I've never seen them in the family cemetery at Beau Chêne, but I wanted them to carry out an idea—" She stopped. Either Koenberg saw what she meant, or he did not.

"Exactly," he said, nodding. "And it is this juxtaposition of cultures which makes your work exciting, Miss Hamilton. You are a fine artist, with unquestionable talent and craft. But where you will leave others behind is with the mass of material you have gathered. Imagine!" He gestured at the paintings along the wall. "Here we see, one might say, a spectrum of a culture's soul—as seen through the sure eye and understanding heart of an artist." He winked at Caro and laughed. "You see, I am already composing the material for the catalog of your first show. Now, come along, I am more than ready for my lunch."

"First show! Mr. Koenberg, are you really going to take me on?"

"You're not committed to Dupuy?"

"No, I don't have a contract with him. I just show things here, and he gets a commission on what he sells. How . . . how soon are you talking about?"

"Let me see. This is January. Oh, I think we could open your show the second weekend in May."

She let out breath she had not known she was holding. "Then I have several months."

"Yes, you have several months. And it will not be nearly enough time to meet the people you must meet, to get enough work done to fill my largest room. I hope you are a person who can settle herself quickly—we have much work, you and I."

"But that means moving right away—"

"If we wish to have your show before I close the gallery for the summer, yes."

"I'm not sure I can leave that fast—" I'm not sure I can make that decision, she thought. She followed Koenberg out of the gallery and stood on the sidewalk beside him. He was looking at her with an expression she could not read; he offered her his arm and began piloting her toward the oyster bar at the end of the block.

"Miss Hamilton. Am I mistaken in what I see in your work?" He did not wait for her to answer, but fastened his eyes on her face. "Because what I see is the work of a dedicated artist."

"Yes. Yes, I am."

"Then, Miss Hamilton, please explain to me why you are behaving like some coy girl being asked to the senior prom. I am not a suitor, Miss Hamilton. I am not flirting with you. I am a businessman, attempting to make a business arrangement. If you are not ready to discuss such an arrangement, we will have a pleasant lunch and bid one another good-bye."

She couldn't imagine why she had ever thought Louis Koenberg a soft, plump man with little personal force. He seemed to fill the sidewalk, to dominate the space around her. She lifted her chin and looked him in the eye. "I am a dedicated artist," she said. "I apologize. I'm—well, just so surprised. I'm very glad that you like my work, Mr. Koenberg. And if you really want to represent me, I'm ready to start packing this afternoon."

He took her hands in both of his and laughed. "Good. Now you sound like the Caro Hamilton Dr. Selbin led me to expect."

Suddenly realization hit her. The famous Louis Koenberg, owner of one of the most prestigious galleries in the country, liked her work. Was going to represent her. And was as glad to have her as she was to be with him. She began to walk faster, feeling that she could hardly wait to reach the restaurant and find a phone. It was only eleven o'clock in San Francisco; David would still be at his office. She rehearsed what she would tell him. Finally, only one thing seemed necessary. "I'm coming out there, David. Meet my plane."

The next three weeks seemed to comprise one long day broken by occasional sleep. Caro did not have to close the house on Calliope Street; Raoul, practicing pediatrics now, was more than glad to move in, and Henri, who was working on a Ph.D. at the University of Chicago, reserved one room to be used when he came down to New Orleans. She packed personal items she wouldn't be taking with her in neatly labeled boxes, unable to escape feeling that she was sealing an entire segment of her life and storing it away in the big closet at the end of the hall. Caroline insisted on a farewell party, a reception at Beau Chêne so everyone could see Caro off. And then there were lunches with friends in New Orleans, a hurried day in Baton Rouge with Skye, a weekend snatched with Émilie and Fielding in St. Francisville. By the time Caro got on the plane, and watched New Orleans recede into the distance as the plane soared into the winter sky, she was exhausted.

She dozed on the long trip west, coming out of a half-sleep to take a lunch tray from the steward. She had been dozing again when she heard the pilot announce the approach to San Francisco. She took out her compact and redid her makeup, powdering the dark circles of fatigue that ringed her eyes, and freshening her lipstick. As she stood in the aisle waiting to leave the plane, it dawned on her that she would not be flying back to New Orleans in a day or two. She was committed here—at least for the next several months. Perhaps for a lifetime.

She hurried down the aisle, putting doubt behind her. As she went down the steps, breathing in the brisk air and searching the waiting crowd for David, she let one emotion rule her: how much she loved him. Then she saw him, pushing his way forward, taking a position by the opening in the chain that held the crowd off the field. She broke into a run, darting past the slower passengers ahead of her—then she was in his arms, clinging to him, feeling his lips against hers. And hearing him whisper, as he kissed her again and again, "Welcome home, darling. Welcome home."

18

JUNE 1949

"One thing about all this smoke," Beau said to Natalie. "It drives the mosquitoes away."

He dipped his brush into the rich sauce simmering on one side of the grill and drew it slowly over the roasting beef. The wood had burned down to glowing coals, but as the fat dripped from the beef onto them, it made thick smoke that hung around the grill as though suspended from the branches of the nearby oak.

"It smells gorgeous," Natalie said. "In fact, it made me forget what I was sent out here for. Mrs. Langlinais wants to know if you need another beer."

"Barbecuing is thirsty work," Beau said. "Tell her yes. And ask her to find something for me to snack on before I begin tearing at this beef."

"I've never seen so much food in my life," Natalie said. "I'll fix you a sample and bring it right out."

"Thanks, *chérie,*" Beau said. He watched Natalie walk back up to the house, long legs well-tanned, her shirt knotted loosely around her slender waist. Hell of a good-looking girl, he thought. Skye's got the Langlinais taste, all right.

"Mr. Langlinais does want a beer," Natalie said to Caroline, who stood tasting a big bowl of potato salad she had just finished putting together. "And he says if he isn't fed soon, he's going to go on strike, and none of us will have any supper."

"I'll go rescue him," Caroline said. "Here, Natalie, taste this. More salt, do you think?"

Natalie took the spoon Caroline handed her and judiciously tasted the salad. "I think it's just right," she said, dropping the spoon into the sink where pots and utensils sat soaking.

"Put it in the refrigerator for me, will you, please?" Caroline said. She picked up two cans of beer from a big ice-filled cooler, stuck them on a tray already laden with cheese and crackers, and headed out the back door.

Skye stuck his head in the door leading from the central hall. "I've just beat the stuffing out of Fielding at gin," he said. "You want to take on the champ?"

"Watch out," Natalie said, laughing. "I used to make movie money playing with my brothers."

They went out to the front porch where Fielding and Émilie and Raoul and his date had gathered. Fans set in the high ceiling of the front porch battled the June heat, and bright canvas awnings provided protection against the blazing afternoon sun.

"I'm beginning to think Henri doesn't exist," Natalie said as she sat across from Skye and watched him shuffle the deck. "I've still never met him. Did he stay in Chicago all summer?"

"No, he's off on a trip with some of his friends from the university. Been gone almost a month now."

Natalie cut the deck and held up her card. "Beat that," she said, showing Skye the ace of hearts.

He cut a ten of spades and handed her the deck. "Your deal." He picked up a pencil and wrote their names across the top of the score pad. "What shall we play for?"

"What do you usually play for?"

"Fielding and I played for a hunting trip," Skye said. "He now owes me a weekend at his place."

"Virginia's a little far to go to pay off a gin debt," Natalie said.

"Tell you what. Let's play first—then the winner can decide what the stakes are."

"All right." She shuffled the cards and dealt them, then arranged her hand.

"Does Henri like Chicago?"

"I guess so. Wouldn't stay there if he didn't."

"It crops up in the news now and then," Natalie said. She discarded a card and watched Skye pick it up. "Some of the students—and faculty—at the university have some associations that keep getting them into trouble."

"Henri's never said a word about anything like that," Skye said. He pulled a card from his hand and carefully laid it on the table. "What kind of associations?"

"Some people call it a hotbed of Communism. There was a conference in Chicago, oh, about eighteen months ago. Caused a big stir. People who fall under the progressive and liberal labels met to bury the hatchet—and ended up split into worse factions than before."

"I seem to remember something about that," Skye said. "It's getting so you can't pick up the paper without reading about somebody being called a Communist."

Natalie pulled a card from the deck and placed it in her hand. "One faction calls itself the Progressive Citizens of America—they're pretty definitely pro-Communist. The others are the Americans for Democratic Action—they're anti-Communist, and loudly vocal about it, too."

Skye put down his hand and looked at Natalie. "Why do I have the feeling you are telling me all this for a reason?"

She looked at him unhappily. "It's just—well, there probably isn't anything in it—I don't know what made me think of it—but one of our reporters was at that conference. He'd been assigned to do a series on the effects of the Loyalty Order—so he went up to Chicago to talk to some of the people there, see if they'd been accused under it."

"How does Henri come into it?"

"It's really nothing. A week or so ago, a few of us were sitting around the newsroom. It was one of those lulls, nothing much coming in over the wire—and someone began talking about that man up in Baker or Jackson or wherever it was that was accused under the Loyalty Oath and had to go before a hearing, and of course we began kicking the whole thing around, how it looks like the House Committee on Un-American Activities is really getting out of hand. Then the reporter who'd been to Chicago said that we'd be surprised at the people who had questionable affiliations that were overlooked because of who they were. When one of us accused him of making allusions he couldn't prove, Tom—the reporter—replied that one of our very own legislators had a stepson who'd been at that conference in Chicago; that since the conference was full of Communists, perhaps Communists were Henri Hamilton's cup of tea."

"The devil you say!" Skye's voice exploded in anger; he gripped the edge of the table and leaned toward her, his cards forgotten. "What's that guy's name? I'll cram that little piece of libel down his throat for him."

"You don't think Henri was at the conference?"

"Dammit, your reporter was at the conference, Natalie! Since when does attending a conference imply that you're guilty of disloyalty?"

"It's getting pretty bad, Skye."

"Maybe in other parts of the country. But not down here. Even when the Ku Klux Klan was at its height in the rest of Louisiana, it couldn't get a toehold in south Louisiana. The region is so Catholic that if the pope sneezes we all take out our handkerchiefs. This is the last place we'll see Communism."

"But Henri goes to school in Chicago, Skye."

He saw the worry in her eyes and made himself calm down. "Look, Natalie, I know when you hear the stories day after day, the House Un-American Activities Committee seems to be going crazy. But I assure you, Henri would never get mixed up in the Communist movement. He's kind of scatterbrained sometimes—but he's a Democrat—when he's political at all." He picked up his scattered hand and straightened the cards. "I appreciate your telling me. But there's nothing to worry about."

"Good," Natalie said. "It's just that we see a lot of stories about what the House Committee on Un-American Activities is up to that never reach the public. It's scary, Skye. It really is."

"A blatant grab for power, a lot of it." Then he smiled, and touched her hand lightly. "You've done a great job of distracting me from the business at hand. I can't remember a thing you discarded."

"Good," she said. "It doesn't matter, because I'm going out." She spread her hand on the table, laughing at Skye's rueful face. "Did I catch you with lots of points? I hope so—I intend to win this game."

"Deal, madam, while I total the damage."

But even as he added up his cards, and noted Natalie's score, he made a note of another kind—to warn Henri that even in Chicago, eyes were watching if you were prominent enough.

Later, when supper was over and the sun had dropped from the sky, leaving only a pink glow to light the world by, Skye and Natalie walked over to Beau Chêne. "The moon will be up soon," he said, taking her arm to guide her over the root-marked path. "Beau Chêne's always beautiful—but by moonlight, it's magical."

They walked around the house, feeling almost spellbound by the richness of the June night. Sun-warmed roses had released their scent during the long summer day, and it still hung in the air, mixing its sweet perfume with the smell of freshly cut grass and jasmine. The pink brick walls glowed white in the moonlight, the columns rising like ghosts from the dark shrubbery at their base. The couple climbed the stairs to the upper gallery and stood looking at the alley of oaks, still, silent, under the moon.

"I can see why your stepmother hung on to this place," Natalie said. "It has that same feeling some of the great houses in Virginia do—a sort of direct tie with the past." She shivered and looked behind her. "I almost expect to see an early DeClouet step out of the woodwork."

"You never did tell me what I owe you," Skye said. "For the game of gin."

She turned and leaned against the railing, her eyes on the floor, not meeting his. "I guess I haven't really thought about it. Why don't we let it go?"

"Can't do that," Skye said. "You beat me fair and square; I always pay my debts."

"Dinner, then," she said.

"We go out to dinner all the time," he said.

"A special dinner. Someplace we've never been."

"I have an idea," he said, watching her face. "Why don't we have dinner at the Grand Hotel? Have you heard of it?"

"No."

"It's a famous resort near Mobile—built on a point between Mobile Bay and the gulf. A nice drive along the coast. What do you say?"

Skye saw the question in her eyes. "Sounds like a long way to drive for dinner."

He paused, hanging at the edge of the words that would change everything between them. "I thought we might make it a whole weekend," he said.

Her face was suddenly vulnerable; she turned away from him, staring out at the moonlit lawn. The calm of the scene contrasted so violently with the tumult of her emotions that it no longer seemed real. Beau Chêne wasn't real. This night wasn't real. What Skye had said wasn't real—she turned and looked into his eyes.

"Well?" he said.

"Yes," she whispered.

And then he pulled her to him. Her skin was soft, supple, the sun's heat still held in its smooth silk. Lights set on the corners of the house and in lanterns on posts made the gallery a stage; he felt this moment slip out of time. He kissed her gently, covering her mouth with his, tasting the faint tang of pepper traced on the edges of her lips. Then her lips moved under his, and he felt her arms slip around his neck.

How easy it is to love her, he thought, pulling her closer still. How wonderfully easy it is to be loved. The last jagged edges that had held his two worlds apart slipped quietly into place, and made a solid whole; there was no longer a "before" he went to war and an "after." There was only a continuity, a slim ribbon that guided him forward, held now in Natalie's golden hands.

He heard Natalie murmur something, and lifted his head. Her eyes reflected the shadowed light. "Remind me to play gin with you more often, Skye Langlinais," she said. But her eyes, solemn, filled with wonder, did not match her light tone, and he bent to kiss her again. He knew that for both of them, a whole new world had begun.

Caro took the glass David handed her and sipped the wine slowly. Then she held the glass at eye level and looked through its clear, rose-tinged contents at the view from the redwood deck that seemed to hang from its hillside straight into the cool California air. The bay stretched before her, but the perspective was different from that of her apartment near Russian Hill. Seen through the wine, distorted by the curvature of the glass, its perimeters narrowed, its color changed, and instead of being the gateway to the Pacific, San Francisco looked like a small, closed world huddled into itself. The idea made her smile. David, standing next to her, his back to the bay, smiled back. "Having a good time?"

"Wonderful," she said.

Phil and Sarah Jacobs had invited them over for an informal evening with only one other couple, Jake Rubin and Mollie Haskell. Caro already knew Phil and Sarah well; given the sheer number of people she had met over the past few months, the Jacobses had achieved the status of old friends. Like Caro, Mollie Haskell was an artist. When Sarah issued the invitation, she had added, "You and Mollie should have a lot in common. Mollie just had her first big show last March."

When they were introduced, Mollie mentioned Caro's show at once. "I saw your show at Louis Koenberg's. I liked it. Some interesting ideas."

"It's not exactly what everyone else out here is doing," Caro said. "When I look at other people's work, I almost wonder what Koenberg sees in me."

"I don't," Mollie said. She was a large woman whose abundant red hair was tied back with a multicolored scarf; she wore a lavender lounge suit sashed with the same vivid print as her scarf, and her arms were laden with slim gold bangles. "You're good. Damn good."

"Not many critics said so," Caro blurted. She tried to think of something to say, something to cover that moment of self-revelation, but Mollie was smiling at her in a way that said she understood.

"Look, honey—you're brand-new. Even if Koenberg did discover you, the critics are going to make you pay your dues."

"That's what Louis said," Caro said.

"He's right. Anyway, that review in the *Examiner*? I'd cheerfully wring your neck if I thought it would help me get a review like that." Mollie leaned closer to Caro. " 'Miss Hamilton does not simply paint the landscapes, the people, native to her own Louisiana. She does not simply paint things that she "knows." She also paints things that she does not know.' Listen, Caro—whether you know it or not, that was strong stuff."

"Thank you. I—to tell you the truth, I'm still having a little trouble seeing myself the way people out here do. Being taken seriously."

Again Mollie nodded. "Sure. For years, you've been sweet Caro Hamilton who can also paint. When she's not doing the deb bit. I'm not from the South, but I'm from a family that has its own ideas about Mollie and what she's like." Her laugh was warm, and Caro felt the last vestige of reserve melt. "What they actually want me to do is become a dental assistant and work in my Uncle Harold's office. I tried to pacify them by using his denture samples in a series of oils—somehow, they didn't seem appeased."

Caro joined in the laughter that greeted Mollie's story. She reached over and took David's hand, squeezing it. "I like your friends," she whispered to him. She saw Mollie's eyes on them, quizzical, almost amused.

"Hey, David! Jake!" Phil called from the stone barbecue pit at the edge of the deck. "If you want to eat, you'd better come give me a hand."

Mollie watched the men walk away, the quizzical look still in her eyes. She sipped her drink and looked at Caro over the rim of her glass. "Do you live together?"

"I beg your pardon?"

"You and David. Are you living together?"

"No!"

Mollie held up her hand. "I don't mean to pry. I rush fences, go where angels fear to tread, that kind of thing. Jake and I do."

"Do you mind telling me why you ask? Because it really doesn't seem to me that it's any of your business," Caro said, trying not to sound stiff, trying to find the proper tone that would let Mollie know she liked her just fine—but found her questions unanswerable.

"Of course it's none of my business," Mollie said. She seemed as cheerful as ever, as though Caro's reaction bothered her not at all. "I'm just curious. The way David has talked about you—as if you were the most incredible woman he's ever met—I mean, the man has no perspective where you are concerned at all. I thought that if he was that much in love with you, it would be natural for the two of you to be living together."

"Where I'm from, people don't live together until they're married," Caro said. Her eyes went to Jake, standing with Phil near the pit.

"No, Jake doesn't love me the way David loves you," Mollie said. "We get along all right—needs are met, as the saying goes. But David—" She shook her head. "We think a lot of him. He's the kind of guy that once he's your friend—well, you don't want him to be hurt."

"I have no intention of hurting David," Caro said, suddenly angry.

"I didn't mean that." Mollie stopped talking and stood rattling the ice in her glass, staring out at the bay. Then she turned and looked at Caro, eyes intent, voice low and determined. "I'm just trying to say—we're ready to like you, too, Caro. Love you, even. You've already earned our respect, because David loves you—and he respects the hell out of your work. So many of us—of David's friends—have been anxious to meet you." She smiled. "Sometimes my tongue gets in the way. Sorry if I came on too strong."

"It's all right," Caro said. Impulsively she reached out and took Mollie's hand. "Thank you for what you said. I'm flattered. And very grateful."

Mollie looked at her glass. "I'm on empty. Are you ready? Let's get another drink—and then let's find a spot and talk about art."

As she followed Mollie across the deck to the bar, her mind drifted back over the past few months. There had been the first hectic weeks; finding an apartment, unpacking the boxes that straggled after her, setting up a studio. And getting accustomed to the new patterns of her life. Her world had both expanded and narrowed. The exterior world was bound by the path between her apartment, David's, and Koenberg's gallery. She knew little of the city beyond the restaurants they had eaten in, the theaters they had attended, the parks they had picnicked in on her earlier visits. Now she did not have time even to go back to those familiar places; every hour that she was not with David was spent at the easel or with Koenberg. For the first time since she and David had met, she did not resent the demands of his profession, because hers was equally demanding.

But if her exterior world shrank, her interior world broadened. There was a new freedom in her relationship with David, a freedom born of her distance from New Orleans and all its reminders of the conventions that bound her. There was a luxury in knowing so few people, and having so few to answer to. Her leisure time was her own, and if she worked hard, if she spent hours staring at a canvas, concentrating on the painting that would take shape there, she found that when she did leave work to be with David, she had never been so happy, so fulfilled, in her life.

She knew that somewhere ahead of her lay a less intense time, a time that would be less demanding in terms of adjustment—but perhaps more demanding in terms of routine. But for now—for now she was still flushed with her first success, still confident that moving here was the wisest course she could possibly have taken.

David saw her crossing the deck, and came to her side.

"Here," he said, "let me pour you some wine."

"I like your girl, David," Mollie said.

"I'll drink to that," he said. He held out his glass to Caro; she lifted her glass to touch his, then sipped her wine. She glanced up and caught an image of the two of them reflected in a prismed mirror hung in a west-facing window to catch the sun. The mirror revolved slowly on its long, thin wire, its three shining sides forming an elongated pyramid. Their faces were small, crowded into the narrow space, and she peered at the image intently, seeing the vision in the mirror as reality and the solidness of the world she stood in as the dream.

Then she felt something spring into being inside her; a canvas, blank, then filled with form and color. She leaned forward, staring into the mirror, etching into her mind what its rigid planes did to the contours of their flesh. Her hands felt for tools that were not there, and she longed to be in her studio, framing in the outlines of the painting waiting to be born.

"Caro?" David said.

She closed her eyes, and still saw the broken planes, the splinters of reality, all the fragments she would use to make a new whole. It was fixed, there was no way she would lose it. She opened her eyes and took David's hands. "I'm famished," she said. Another hour with these nice people, she thought. And then home. They would make love, and David would go back to his apartment near the hospital. She would lie on her big soft bed, draperies pulled wide so she could watch the bay. She would fall into a sweet, gentle sleep, and when she woke, the clear golden light would fill her studio, and she would stretch a new canvas and place it on her easel and begin to bring out of its emptiness the vision that existed now only in her mind. She squeezed David's hand and kissed his cheek. "Oh, David—I'm so glad I came."

19

JULY 1949

Skye slowed the car for the turn into the gates of the Grand Hotel, carefully negotiating the curves in the drive that ran between well-kept lawns up to the sprawling resort. Cockspur and zinnias held up their brilliant heads, thriving in the July heat; in the distance there was the glint of sunlight on water.

"We're staying in one of the cottages," Skye said to Natalie, pointing at a small building standing in the midst of its own square of hedged-in lawn. "The Grand Hotel is a golf resort, and a lot of the guests get up early. I thought we'd get off by ourselves where we wouldn't be disturbed."

"Yes," Natalie said. She wore sunglasses that covered her eyes, but her voice sounded tense, and her jawline looked tight. Her hands were clasped together in her lap, twisting her handkerchief.

"Natalie," he said gently. "If you don't want to go through with this—the cottages have living rooms. And couches that pull out. If you change your mind—it's all right. I'll understand."

Her hands loosened, and one of them touched his arm. Although Skye did not show his anxiety outwardly, beneath his poised exterior he felt surges of doubt himself. The idea had seemed so right that night at Beau Chêne. But now he wished that he had not made such a production of their first night together. Far, far better to have simply let one of their evenings in Baton Rouge end, sweetly and naturally, in bed. To purposely drive all this way, for three days . . .

"I'm not going to change my mind, Skye," Natalie said, looking at him intently. "I know what I want. And I want you. I'm just a little nervous. And tired from the drive. A swim and a shower will make a new woman of me."

"I like the one I've got," he said seriously, and was rewarded with a smile that almost relaxed Natalie's tense face. He pulled the car up under the hotel's porte cochere and got out. "Wait here," he said. "I'll get the keys." She watched him vanish inside, and thought again how careful, how thoughtful, Skye had been. The cottage gave them privacy, the way Skye had registered protected her.

She refused to look past this weekend; she had not questioned whether this was a prelude to a new phase in their relationship or just a way for them to get each other out of their systems. She only knew she was intensely attracted to him and that she could no longer put those feelings off. She suspected that part of the attraction they had for each other came from their past; when Skye felt frustrated about his student status, when she felt her position as neophyte female reporter too humbling, they could get together and find in each other's memories more mature selves. She knew how many missions he had flown, she knew what it was to listen to reports measuring the destruction you had caused—and then go back and do it all over again. She knew what it was to lose a friend by violent death; she knew the Skye that no one else did. And he knew her. And while she did not believe that those few years would retain the significance they had now, for the moment they still loomed large. For the moment she still had to bite her tongue when the crack political reporter who had sat out the war because of his eyesight needled her because she wrote about ladies' teas and club meetings. She would not soon forget the day he had found a story she had written, a practice piece based on a political scandal in Ascension Parish, and read it aloud to the newsroom. She had stood her ground, refusing to let his gibes make her cry, but her cheeks had flamed in anger. She could have told him of driving through bombed-out London streets, of, in the last days, ducking rubble tossed in the air by the silent V-2's that sailed out of an empty sky, death and damage in their wake. She said none of those things. She clenched her fists and thought of Skye, and took the ribbing, took the joking, took the hazing she knew she must if the men on the paper were ever going to accept her. It had begun to pay off; the city editor "borrowed" her from Society once in a while, throwing her scraps of stories to rewrite, and once even sending her out to do one live. I can wait, she thought. I can outwait all of them.

"All set," Skye said, getting back in the car. A bellman came out of the hotel and got in the back seat.

"Down the drive, around the building, and take the first left," he said.

"It's one of our nicest cottages, Mr. Langlinais. Got the best view of the water."

They followed him inside, and waited while he opened windows on the water side and turned on the attic fan that pulled a warm breeze through the room. "It gets nice and cool in the evening," he said. "There are a couple of small fans in that closet if the attic fan isn't enough."

And then he was gone, tucking the bills Skye had given him in the pocket of his starched jacket. Natalie and Skye stood looking at each other, equally uncertain of the next move.

"You said you wanted to swim?" Skye said.

Natalie stood in the doorway between the living room and bedroom. The cottage was furnished with a mixture of white-painted wrought-iron and wicker pieces, with cushions, draperies, and bedspread of a gaily flowered print. Bright cotton shag rugs covered the tile floor, and a large fern filled the empty hearth of the fireplace.

"It's beautiful, Skye," she said. She could taste a hint of salt in the breeze coming in from the gulf. "To tell you the truth—if I can have that shower—I think I'll skip the swim. I'm suddenly so tired all I want is a nap."

"Why don't you shower, and I'll call room service to send over some iced tea and a plate of fruit and cheese."

"Fine," she said. She closed the bedroom door and stood for a moment, trying to determine what she felt. Anxiety? Concern? Mostly she was happy—to be here, with Skye, the night, the weekend to themselves. A weekend like no other weekend before. She began to shuck off her clothes, kicking them into a neat little pile and stuffing them in the bathroom hamper. She let the water run long and warm, felt the cleansing suds on her back. When she stepped out, her skin was glowing.

She reached for the batiste gown and kimono she'd bought for the trip, a white gown with sprigs of violets and deep ruchings of lace. She tied the satin ribbon of the kimono around her waist and went into the living room.

Skye stood at a window staring out at the water that lapped against the seawall. He heard the sound of her bare feet on the tile and turned; a look of tenderness and desire came into his face, and he covered the space between them, arms outstretched. She went into his arms, lifting her face to his kiss.

"The tea's on its way," he said after the first long kiss. "Give me five minutes in the shower . . . and then . . ." His voice caught, and she felt his lips again on hers. Then he broke away from her and vanished into the bedroom. She heard the bathroom door close, imagined the rush of water, imagined Skye naked under the shower, the water beating against him.

When the waiter arrived with the tea, she poured it into an ice-filled glass and drank, the chilled liquid seeming to enter her blood and slow it. Back in Baton Rouge, the newsroom was bustling with activity: typewriters clacking, phones ringing, people scurrying back and forth. Here, time did not exist. There was only sunshine and silence, solitude—and Skye. She heard the bathroom door open and set down her glass. Baton Rouge, the newspaper, were far, far away. She did not have to be on guard here, she did not have to forget that she was a woman. Beyond that door Skye waited: as she went to him, she felt all the other roles drop away. Her step quickened, and she almost ran into his arms.

He lifted her and carried her to the bed, lowering her carefully onto it. And then he was beside her, his mouth covering hers, his hands gently stroking her. She slipped her arms around him and traced the line of his spine with light fingers. How gentle he is, she thought. How tender. She could feel the full strength of his passion beneath the tenderness, waiting for her response. She could feel her own response building. Then all at once she felt as though they had been in bed together many, many times before; they already knew each other, were already attuned to their own private rhythms, their own private needs. She was no longer anxious, no longer concerned. "I want you," she said. She sat up and pulled her gown up over her head; he took it and lifted it from her body. Again the look of tenderness and desire in his face, again his arms reaching for her. . . . As she went to him, one last thought came to her mind. The question of whether or not they were only trying to get each other out of their systems was quite meaningless, at least as far as she was concerned. Skye Langlinais had settled even more deeply into her being, had become an essential part of her life.

The city editor rapped for attention. "All right, you guys," he said. He looked at Natalie, sitting in a chair against the wall. "And Natalie." She could see heads turn; this was the first news-staff meeting she had been asked to attend, and although she had told herself not to look for either acceptance or rejection, just to get the job done, she could not help reading her colleagues' faces. Most of them looked neutral; as Skye had told her, except for a few people whose prejudice outran their judgment, their own lives kept everyone too busy to worry about someone else.

"What we're doing here is a section on the anti-Long forces. Earl's not the same kind of man Huey was—but in his own way, he's able to hold the center, keep people in hand. And, of course, a lot of the same old faces lurking in Huey's background are in thick with Earl—they don't give much of a damn who's spreading the butter, just as long as their slice of bread gets its share." He began to give out assignments; one writer would summarize Huey's rise to power, another would write about the passing of the scepter to Earl. The meat of the section would be individual features about the men who resisted Earl Long; central to this group, the editor said, was Beau Langlinais. "His is probably the most interesting story, his position aside, because in the early days of Huey's career, Langlinais was one of his staunchest supporters. So a feature on him can represent the gradual disenchantment of a whole segment of people." He looked at the reporters in front of him, then let his eyes rest on Natalie. "Watkins, you take Representative Langlinais. It's going to take some time, so I told the ladies over in Society they were just going to have to do without you for a while."

"Yes, sir," Natalie said, trying to keep the jubilance out of her voice. Thank heaven, she thought, her mind already on the story, she had done so much background research on Beau Langlinais already. She would review her material, she decided, and then make a rough outline of what she wanted to do. Talk it over with the editor, talk with Beau—she went back to her desk with her mental list of steps already made. There were a few items to clear up and turn in to Society before she could devote full time to the new assignment; she settled down and began to write, picking up speed as her fingers typed the familiar phrases—"flowers placed at vantage points"—"Alençon lace trimming a full skirt of tulle over satin"—"those in the house party were"—Lord, she thought, pulling a sheet of copy from the machine and adding it to the stack at her elbow, if I do well on the Langlinais story, I may never have to write this sort of pap again.

She was finished with everything by lunchtime, and went to the coffee shop to get a Coke and eat her sandwich with a feeling of celebration. She thought she sensed a difference in the way the reporters gathered there greeted her; whether she imagined it or not, she felt an acceptance that she had not felt before, and she joined two men who waved her over instead of sitting with the woman who wrote real-estate copy as she normally did. Tom Burns, the top political reporter, came in as the other men were rising to leave. He had drawn the background story, the recap of Huey Long's career, and was embarked on his usual grousing.

"I shouldn't complain," he said, popping the top off his soft drink and sprawling in a chair opposite Natalie. "I can just pull a bunch of stuff from the morgue, piece it together, write a new lead—and presto, all done." He took a long swallow, peering at Natalie down the length of the bottle. "Nice little assignment you've got," he said. He set the bottle down and wiped his mouth. He put his arms on the table and leaned across it. "You know what that assignment is, don't you?" When Natalie said nothing, continuing to regard him with polite interest, he laughed. "It's a setup."

Natalie looked at her watch and shoved her chair back. "I've got to go. Been nice talking to you, Tom."

As she rose, Burns's hand shot across the table and grasped her wrist. "Hold up, Watkins. You might as well listen to what I've got to say."

The coffee room was empty, and something about Burns's tone made Natalie slowly sink back into her chair. "All right. But look, Tom—you don't have the greatest track record with me."

"Okay. I don't. I've given you a fairly hard time, Watkins. But you took it. I respect that. So I'm going to give you a break and tell you what our boss is up to. He's testing you, okay?"

"I don't get it."

"He knows damn well you and Skye Langlinais are seeing each other." He saw her quick flush and laughed. "Come on, girl. You work on a newspaper. You think we don't know everything that goes on in this town? Anyway—he wants to see if you can be objective. Write about the great Beau Langlinais without making him sound like the Second Coming."

"My seeing Representative Langlinais's son has absolutely nothing to do with my job," Natalie said. Even as she spoke, she was conscious of the relief she felt. She had read just about every story she could find about Beau Langlinais, and nowhere was there one item that he would want to hide or forget.

"Well, good," Burns said, tipping his drink to his mouth. He winked at her. "You owe me one, Watkins."

"I'll remember that," she said.

She returned to her desk and began making notes, deliberately forcing every consideration but the story at hand from her mind. She soon became thoroughly engrossed, and the list of questions she needed to answer grew longer. By the time she quit for the day, she felt reassured. The subject of her story might well be the father of the man she loved in private life—but it was his public life she was writing about. And that, she thought, her mind leaping to the evening ahead, could not possibly affect her relationship with Skye, or with his family. Still, she thought as she dressed for dinner, maybe she wouldn't tell him about the assignment just yet. Maybe she'd let him read it when it came out, and be pleasantly surprised. A nagging corner of her mind suggested that this course might not be wise—and then another thought overrode it. After all, wasn't Skye enjoined, in every course he took, to remember that there were two rules paramount if a lawyer were to survive? The first was that he never become emotionally involved in a case, and the second was that he never reveal what he learned as an attorney to anyone without a right to that knowledge.

Journalism is a profession too, Natalie thought. And if I'm going to be a professional, I've got to play by the rules. If anyone understands that, Skye will.

Caro slipped the small ring over the nail David had driven into the wall and straightened the gold frame. "Am I being totally ridiculous?" she asked.

"Certainly not! How many artists your age—hell, *any* age—can frame a check for three thousand dollars from their very first show? And from Louis Koenberg. That's first-class, Caro."

"Louis gave me a funny look when I asked him if I could have the canceled check. He laughed and said I was a sentimental Southerner."

"You keep painting the way you are and you'll paper your walls with his checks," David said.

"He's going to put on a two-woman show for Mollie and me in the fall, did I tell you?"

"No! That's great. I'm glad you two get along. Mollie and Jake are two of my oldest friends. But I was a little worried how you and Mollie would jell."

"In so many ways we couldn't be more different. But I like her honesty—and I like her work."

"When in the fall is your show?"

"Mid-October, I think. Louis was going to check with a couple of other people and then firm up the schedule."

"I guess she'll join Jake after it opens—I can't imagine Mollie missing an opening."

"Wait a minute," Caro said. "I've missed something. Where is Jake going?"

"Didn't you hear him at dinner the other night? He's going to Israel."

"Israel!"

"He was telling us all about it—"

Caro shook her head. "I must have been helping Sarah. I don't remember a thing about it. How long will he be gone?"

"He's moving there. Mollie, too, from what I understood."

"David!" She sat on the couch and drew him down next to her. "Why are they moving to Israel?"

"To help out. They feel they have to," David said. As a newly created country, Israel needs all the help it can get."

"Mollie's a painter, David. They need painters?"

"They need anyone they can get. Anyway, Jake's an engineer. God knows they can use him. As for Mollie—everyone over there is doing manual labor. Part of it is sheer necessity. They've got to get the land in shape. But part of it is pride. For a long time, my people have been thought of as living off their brains and the labor of others." His eyes suddenly clouded, as though seeing a vision that came between him and Caro. "We've also been thought of as people who couldn't and wouldn't fight. I guess Israel itself disproves that theory. Now we're going to make the desert bloom. And if we have to prove we can fight, we'll do that too."

She caught his hand, feeling that she was drawing him back into the room. "Are they moving there for good?"

"They don't know. Jake's going to try it, see how it goes."

"And Mollie? What about her work? Will she still paint?"

"Mollie will do what she needs to do," David said. "She comes across as pretty carefree, but underneath, Mollie's quite a gal. I'm not worried about Mollie."

Again Caro felt a distance, but this time it was she who seemed to withdraw. She and Mollie spent a lot of time together; because they met as artists, it was art that consumed the greater part of their talk. She thought she knew Mollie's commitment to her work; it was greater than her own, and Caro felt humbled by it. Unlike her own relatively easy path—a fine art education paid for by her family, ample money to live on whether she sold anything or not—Mollie had paid her way at every step.

"It's simple," Mollie had said. "If I would do what my family wants, they'd pay for it in a minute." She shrugged. "Art's a frill, a luxury. Luxuries you buy for yourself."

And so Mollie gave lessons and worked in an art-supply store, and painted at odd hours. And already she was having her second show in a year.

"If she leaves now, David, she'll lose all the momentum she's built up. New artists are coming out of the walls. She might never have such a chance to make it again."

His eyes told her how foolish she sounded. "You don't understand, Caro. Mollie can do something a lot of American Jews can't. She can go to Israel and be part of the most important, valuable thing that has happened to us in centuries. Caro, don't you know what Israel means? A chance to live in our own land, free of persecution and hatred. For God's sake, I didn't think I'd have to explain it to you!"

"David—I'm sorry," She stopped. Although he was only scant feet away, she felt that the space between them was infinite. There was a wall there, a wall built of her lack of comprehension, of his passion for a land he had never seen. "No, I guess I don't know what it means, David. I don't suppose anyone who isn't Jewish can."

He saw the hurt in her face, and took her in his arms. "You understand better than you know, darling. I wouldn't be here if you didn't."

She curled against him, letting his familiar body reassure her. And again she realized there was no barrier stronger than their love for each other, no wall their passion could not crumble.

"Do you really have to go to the hospital now?" she said, slipping her hand inside his shirt.

"Well, maybe I can fudge a little," he said, pulling her lower on the couch.

This time it was she who led their lovemaking, her mouth searching his, her hands stroking and caressing him to bring him to her strong desire. She felt a wildness she had never felt before; she could not get enough of him, she wanted to possess him entirely, to take all of him into her, to feel possessed by him in return. At one point she sat up, breathless, staring down at him as though she had never seen him before.

"You're incredible," he said.

As she leaned back over him, she caught sight of their image in the mirror hanging opposite the bed. Her artist's eye saw the forms, the composition, the flesh tones: her blond hair framing her flushed face, the contours of her body curving softly, David's dark head against the white pillow.

She held the picture as she began to kiss him, working her way from his throat to his chest. She felt the sudden rise of passion, and moved so that he could enter her. As long as we have this, she thought, nothing can ever separate us.

When David finally left, she sat for a long time looking out at the bay. Over the months, it had become more than just a body of water whose surface changed with the wind and the tide. It had become a presence, something that kept her company during the long hours when she was alone. She had come to know it almost as well as she knew the landscapes of her youth: time and again, she looked at it, feeling her response to it as part of her growing attachment to this place.

She had believed that David was attached to this place too. And yet, when he spoke of Israel, there was something in his voice . . . She remembered the way he used the word "we." He clearly identified himself with Israel and her people. As of course he should. Still . . . She sighed and looked at the bay, as if its calm could ease her spirits. But tonight the bay had no answers. It lay shimmering under its veil of moonlight, a dark sheet of impenetrable silver glass. Finally, she had no answers, either. She did not understand why it mattered to David that she thought Mollie's art more important than planting fields in Israel. For that matter, she did not understand how Mollie could chuck her career and move there. None of this should matter, none of this should impinge on her life. On her life with David. It shouldn't. But somehow—it did.

"Natalie?" Beau Langlinais's voice was warm and friendly. "My secretary said a reporter from the *Advocate* was on the line—I didn't realize it was you."

"I'd like to make an appointment to see you," Natalie said. "I've been assigned to do a story on you as one of the leaders of the anti-Long people—I've done the background. Now I'd like to talk to you."

There was a small pause, and then Beau spoke, his voice still warm, still friendly, but with a different note. "So this is a business call," he said. "All right, let me look at my book." There was a longer pause, and then he was back on the wire. "Do you want to talk over lunch? We could meet at Mike and Tony's tomorrow—"

"I'd rather come to your office, if that's all right," Natalie said. "I need to make notes—and Mike and Tony's is always so crowded."

"That's true," Beau said. "You probably wouldn't even have to print the story—it would be all over town before the day was over. All right—how about ten o'clock day after tomorrow? Does that fit your deadline?"

"That's fine," Natalie said. "Thank you very much, Mr. Langlinais."

"I'll be happy to see you," Beau said. "You can tell your editor he has my gratitude. Being interviewed by you should be pure pleasure."

She hung up feeling a little off-center. It's because you have always known him on a purely social basis that making the changeover to business seems strange, she told herself. And of course, Beau Langlinais did not mean being interviewed by her would be a pleasure because he expected her to go easy on him. He was being gallant, the usual gallantry that demanded ladies be complimented, even in a purely business transaction. She had grown up with that kind of gallantry in Virginia, and she had found it here. It was not insincere, it was just part of the territory. But, she thought, catching sight of Tom Burns on the phone at his desk across the room, that gallantry also asks for something back. It asks that I be different from Tom Burns, that I don't pry and poke and demand and pester. It asks that even if I am a reporter, I never forget I'm a lady.

With Burns's warning in mind, she had gone back over the files on Beau line by line, searching for the slightest hint of wrongdoing or alliances made for his own profit. There had been none. His enemies said Langlinais wasn't necessarily that good a man, it was just that he had all the money he could ever want and had no reason to steal. His allies said his acts were the measure of the man; Beau's integrity was real, and not a product of his wealth. The question of who was right, his allies or his enemies, could not be answered, and Natalie had abandoned that line early on. Her angle for the feature was not particularly new: the main question would be why Beau Langlinais spent so much time and energy in Louisiana politics when his experience should tell him his cause was almost useless, and when the life he left behind was such an enviable one. In other words, Natalie thought, recognizing the cliché—what makes Beau Langlinais run?

She hoped the interview would tell her.

"I've told Nancy to hold my calls and give us an hour," Beau said, ushering Natalie into his office and closing the door. "Will that give you enough time?"

"It certainly should," Natalie said. She took the chair he held for her and flipped open her notebook. "As I told you on the phone—I've read just about everything the paper has in the files on your career—so I shouldn't have to bother you for those details."

Beau folded his arms and leaned forward on them. "So what can I tell you?"

She laid her pad in her lap and looked into his eyes. They were so much like Skye's that for a moment she lost the objectivity she was determined to maintain. Then she turned her mind to the business at hand, told herself to forget everything but the fact that she was a reporter with a story to get.

"Why did you support Huey Long at first?" she asked.

"I suppose I believed in what he wanted to do," Beau said.

"Your father didn't."

One eyebrow raised, and he smiled at her. "You *have* done your homework. Most people don't even remember that."

"So why did you?"

"I believed in what Long wanted to do," Beau said again. "His cause seemed to be a good one . . ." He lifted his hands and shrugged. "That's it."

Natalie put down her pencil and looked at him, trying to phrase the next question so it would come out the way she intended. "Mr. Langlinais—do you mind if I say I find that just a little hard to accept? From what I gathered—you and your father were really poles apart when it came to Huey Long. And frankly, from what I've seen of the kind of family feeling you Langlinaises have, I somehow can't see a man as young as you were throwing his support behind a candidate his father didn't like and didn't accept—unless there was some powerful emotional reason."

Beau looked at the pencil in her hand. "Are you one of those reporters I can't go off the record with, Natalie?"

"No, sir."

"So if I give you the real answer—you'll let me give you another one that isn't a lie—but maybe just isn't the deepest kind of truth?"

"Mr. Langlinais, you don't even have to give me the real answer. I'm surprised no one's ever wondered before why you didn't follow your father, why you risked a split with him."

"For one thing, Papa kept his mouth shut, didn't make it worse than it was. For another—well, I wised up soon enough, I guess." He smiled a little ruefully. "With, I have to admit, my father's help. The reason I first got on Long's wagon was the simplest motive of all," Beau said. "Revenge."

"Revenge! Against whom?"

"I'm sorry. I really can't tell you that, Natalie. It involves someone else—it's not a story I ever go into. Let's just say I had been hurt, badly hurt—and I saw in Long a way to get back at the person I blamed the most."

"That would be Mrs. Langlinais's father," Natalie said softly. "Charles Livaudais."

His head jerked back, and he stared at her. "You put two and two together very well. Yes, that's exactly who it was. He was the attorney for a couple of the big companies Long went after as public service commissioner. I thought the more I helped Long, the worse it would be for Livaudais."

"Did it work?"

She saw an old, old pain fill his eyes and wanted to take the question back. His hand went up to shield his face, and she saw his mouth tighten. "I'm sorry. I shouldn't have pressed—"

From behind the screen his hand made, he spoke, his voice so low she had to lean forward to hear him. "Yes, it worked. Livaudais's kingdom came tumbling down all right—by the time it did, I had other reasons to hate him. And by then, nothing that happened to him seemed enough." He seemed to force himself to look at her. "I can't talk about that part of it, Natalie. Not off the cuff, or as a friend—not at all."

"I've really gotten off track," she said. "Look, I've got plenty of other questions. Let's go on—"

He held up his hand. "Wait a minute. I learned a great deal from that experience. I learned that while personal motives often compel us to take up causes—if we don't learn to set them aside, they'll eventually distort, even poison, everything we do." He took a breath, and his face relaxed, became calm again. "I've tried never to forget that, Natalie. No matter what my personal stake may be—I back off, try to take the long view."

Her pencil was flying across the page; when he stopped, she said, "Could I use what you just said?

"Natalie, I trust you. So long as you don't mention Mrs. Langlinais or her father—even hint that our personal situation was involved—write what you want to."

"Tell me your impressions of Long," Natalie said, turning to a fresh sheet. "What do you remember thinking when you first saw him?"

She scribbled notes for the rest of the hour, filling several pages. Beau was a good storyteller; he had a flair for the small details that made Long come alive, and his insights into why Long had such impact on otherwise rational and seasoned men would pull her whole story together. She rose and thanked him with real gratitude. "You may very well be responsible for getting me off the society page and into the work I want," she said, holding out her hand.

"That won't write itself," Beau said, gesturing at her notebook. "I've watched for your byline, read a couple of pieces you've done. I'm in good hands, Natalie." He came around the desk and took both her hands in his, bending to kiss her cheek. "And so is Skye."

She felt suddenly comfortable, as though the task of being friend and observer at one and the same time were not impossible after all. As she got into the elevator to ride down to the Capitol's first floor, she thought, with a sense of relief, that what Beau had told her was off the cuff was really a private matter that was of no legitimate interest to anyone. As far as what he had hinted at . . . but she shut off the curiosity. She had the makings of a good story now, and if it did not fulfill its promise, she had no one to blame but herself.

20

AUGUST–SEPTEMBER 1949

Natalie's story on Beau Langlinais ran on the second Sunday in August; it began in a box on the front page, and carried over for almost another full page inside. There were several pictures of Beau at various stages in his career, beginning with one of him taken with Huey Long under the Evangeline Oak in St. Martinville after the speech that gave the final impetus to Long's successful gubernatorial campaign.

"You're his spitting image," Natalie told Skye, holding the edges of the paper down against the breeze from the fan set near the bed. "It's astonishing."

"Strong genes," Skye said. He leaned closer and kissed her. "Any girl who marries me will have to like my looks, because all our sons are guaranteed to look just like me."

"Poor things," Natalie teased, slipping her arms around his neck and kissing him back. She broke away and picked up the paper again. "I don't mind admitting that seeing my byline on the front page of the Sunday *Advocate* makes me so proud I could pop."

"It should," Skye said. His mouth moved to her breast.

"Seriously, Skye," she said.

"Seriously, Natalie." He sat up straight and smiled at her. "I'm almost as proud as you are, although I didn't have a thing to do with it."

"But that's why I feel so proud, Skye. That I did it alone." Her amber eyes darkened with her intensity. "One thing about growing up with a bunch of brothers—you think you can succeed in a man's world. At least, when you have the kind of brothers I do. Actually, I guess I didn't realize there *is* a man's world—my parents didn't have that kind of marriage. They were partners in every sense of the word. Daddy had his teaching,

Mother had the plantation—they had lots of time together, lots of sharing." She shook her head. "I was in college before I realized that not all marriages are like theirs."

"Natalie, ever since I've known you, you've more than held your own at whatever you do. I've always found that very attractive."

"I know that, Skye. You've never given me anything but encouragement. But you're a rarity, do you know that? Most of the men on the paper—well, their attitude ranges from Tom Burns's open hostility to mild ragging to total neglect. And, dammit, I'm going to show them they're wrong."

"About what?" Skye said, lying back on his pillow.

"About their biases! About their prejudices that tell them any writer who wears a skirt automatically can't understand anything more complicated than recipes and raising babies."

"Aren't you being a little unfair? There're some fairly well-known women journalists in this state—they seem to do all right."

" 'Some fairly well-known women journalists'—oh, Skye!"

"All right, I guess that did sound a little condescending. But, Natalie, you can't take on the entire male bastion." He pointed to her article. "Read again what you quote Papa as saying—about not letting personal emotions distort dedication to a cause."

"Touché," she said. "But it's hard, Skye. Sure, Tom Burns gave me one tip—but he still takes every opportunity he can find to try to trip me up. If I were a man, he'd never think of doing that."

"Or if you weren't such an attractive woman," Skye said. He reached for her and pulled her down next to him.

"What's that supposed to mean?"

"Surely you see the sexual element in their behavior. You're a good-looking woman, a very sexy woman—what they want to do is flirt with you—but you're also a colleague, and a damn bright one. So they take their frustrations out on you any way they can—from teasing you to ignoring you."

"That's terrible!" she said. "And so unfair!"

"I didn't mean to upset you," Skye said. "I just meant to give you my own observations."

"I'll get over it," she said. "Forewarned is forearmed, Skye. Their attitudes, after all, are their problem. All I've got to worry about is mine. And I can promise you, it's going to be purely professional."

"Good," Skye said. He wanted to make love again, wanted to pull the sheet away and stroke her tense muscles until they relaxed and responded, but even as he touched the sheet, he hesitated. The air seemed heavy, thick with something more than just the punishing humidity, and he changed his mind. There was a whole day ahead of them, a day to bury what had just occurred. Maybe they could drive up to St. Francisville and swim in the dammed-in creek on Émilie and Fielding's place. By the time they drove back to Baton Rouge, the heat would not be quite so terrible, and the fan that hummed steadily in Natalie's bedroom window might even pull in a real breeze from the cooling river.

"I'm starved," he said, getting out of bed and pulling on his shorts. "Why don't you shower and dress while I make my famous pancakes?"

"Okay," Natalie said. But she stayed in bed, sheet still covering her, ostensibly rereading her article, until Skye was safely out of the room.

Jake Rubin looked appreciatively around the restaurant, taking in each detail of its lush appointments. "This is a real send-off you're giving us," he said. "Eat well, Mollie, my girl. It'll be a long time before you see the likes of Ernie's again."

"That's good news for my waistline," Mollie said. "I intend to make Mollie shrink while I help the desert bloom. Been carrying this baggage too long."

"I wish you could put off leaving until our opening," Caro said. "It's only three weeks away."

"Time and Israel wait for no man," Mollie said. "Or woman. Either my pictures sell themselves to the reviewers and buyers or they don't, Caro. People don't buy art because they like the artist. Not our kind of buyers."

Caro opened her mouth to say something, and then sipped her drink instead. There were times when she simply did not understand Mollie Haskell. Since she had met her, she had believed Mollie to be more dedicated to her work than she, more willing to make sacrifices. And yet, just on the brink of taking a giant step forward, she was pulling up stakes and leaving. With no new work of hers to show, Koenberg would have to replace her with another artist. And whether he would have room for her when she got back—if she came back—was a risk Mollie would have to take.

She saw Mollie rise and pick up her purse, and got up to follow her. Weaving through the tables of the dining room, she felt the richness of aromas, textures, colors, and glittering surfaces that made dining here so memorable. The lavish use of red velvet and gilt, the mirrors, the fashionable clothes and sparkling jewels of the women, the quiet assurance and command of the men—all these combined to make a world so much like the world she had left behind in New Orleans that she realized all over again why certain places in San Francisco could make her so happy.

She went to the ladies' room to find Mollie standing at the dressing table sponging her skirt. "Everything I own is a record of my social life," Mollie said. "I don't think I've gone through a single evening without spilling something or burning a hole in something." She let the skirt drop, and lit a cigarette. "So," she said. "What's on your mind?"

"Nothing," Caro said.

"Sure there is. You still can't figure out why I won't stay a few weeks longer—why I'm leaving before our show opens."

"Mollie—I know Jake's project is ready to get off the ground. He needs to be there, so of course—"

"So of course I'm tagging along? Is that what you think? That I'm changing my life to follow Jake?"

"No, not the way you put it. I don't mean you don't want to go for your own reasons. I just meant—if you weren't going because of Jake, couldn't you go at a time that suits your own work a little better? Because whatever you say, Mollie—you know a lot of people *do* like to know the artist, do like talk about a work before they buy it. And you're right—I really can't figure out why a few weeks makes any difference."

Mollie crushed out her cigarette and looked at her skirt. "Almost dry." She picked up her purse. "Okay, let me see if I can help you understand. In the first place, Caro, my work, my life—they belong totally to me. As for following Jake—we're going to be living in a kibbutz, but whether or not it will be the same kibbutz, I have no idea. As for the opening—Caro, I bought and paid for the right to be an artist. I am an artist. And if I choose to put the active part of being an artist aside for a while to do something else—well, I've bought and paid for that decision, too. Now we'd better get back before they send a search party. Come on."

The evening's spirit was fueled by Jake's exhilaration as he talked of the work ahead of him, the conditions in Israel. Caro tried to imagine the life waiting for him and Mollie, a life that would have its share of danger. "All kibbutzim are armed," Jake said. "If any of the surrounding countries starts anything, we can defend ourselves."

"To think that Israel can't be left alone," Caro said. "After all the Jews have been through."

"We've been the favorite scapegoats for a hell of a long time, in a hell of a lot of places," David said. "Perhaps this is the end of that."

There was a strong current of anger in David's voice; Caro saw the instant response in Jake and Mollie. "No more," agreed Jake. "We're back in Israel, and by God, we're going to stay there."

"I'll drink to that," David said. "In fact, I'd like to propose the first toast of the evening, if I may." They picked up their glasses. He touched his glass to Jake's, then to Mollie's, then to Caro's. " 'The Lord God of your fathers make you a thousand times so many more as you are, and bless you, as he has promised you.' "

Caro touched her glass to Mollie's, to Jake's, then drank with them all. And though she tried to tell herself that the moment of unity David's toast created held each one of them in its warmth, she could not help but feel that while three of them had been born into that unity, she was part of it only so long as she was part of David Selbin's life.

They parted from Jake and Mollie long after midnight, stretching the evening with a nightcap in a small bar near the wharf. By the time they reached Caro's apartment, they were both tired; knowing that David had been up since dawn, Caro suggested that he stay over. She held his face in her hands and looked at him with concern. "You look exhausted, darling."

"I'm pretty beat," David said, unfastening his cufflinks. "Had a long day, of course—but I guess a lot of it is emotion, too. God, Jake's been like a brother. I'm going to miss the hell out of him."

"I know," she said. She undressed slowly, still feeling keyed-up; by the time she slipped into bed beside him, David was sound asleep. She curled against him with her arms around him, soon falling into deep slumber herself.

She was awakened sometime later, coming suddenly into consciousness. The room was still dark and silent. Then she heard a moan, long and drawn out. She shifted onto her elbow and looked at David. He moaned again, and in the dim light that filtered in from the hall, she could see that his face was twisted, contorted in a grimace of pain. He cried out then, and woke, eyes staring at her uncomprehendingly. "Darling," she said, putting her arms around him. "David, it's Caro. Darling, are you all right?" She saw reason slowly return. She reached over and turned on the bedside light. "What was it?" she asked.

David sat up and got a cigarette from the pack on the table by the bed and began smoking, his eyes fixed on the wall opposite, his breathing still hard. She put her hand on his chest and felt his heart pounding; gradually he quieted, his pulse slowed. She kissed his cheek and asked again, "What was it, David?"

"Shouldn't have had that last drink," he said. "Set the monsters loose."

"The same dream?" she said.

"Another version." He sounded more exhausted than he had when they went to bed several hours before. She heard the terrible fatigue in his voice and cradled him against her.

"Want to tell me about it?"

"I think I'd rather try to forget it," he said, putting out his cigarette and reaching for her.

"Yes," she said, putting her arms around him.

They began to make love, slowly, carefully, letting each kiss, each caress, carry them further from the horror that had waked David, closer to the world that kept them both safe. Caro could feel him begin to let go, and knew that he was beginning to bury the dream back where it had come from. But it would come again, as it had come for the last year, always the same theme, with only the details different. David dreamed of hideous death; its victims were David's relatives, still lost in the maelstrom of war's aftermath. Caro knew that his family was searching for traces of them through every avenue available, but with six million dead, those avenues were choked with similar appeals, similar desperate inquiries, and thus far they had learned nothing. The birth of Israel in May of 1948 had renewed their hope; among the masses of exiles heading there, surely there would be some survivors, surely there would be news.

Caro thought that if any of his family had survived, they would have gotten in touch with their American relatives, but when she ventured this view, David had protested that their first concern would be to find each other, to collect what fragments of their lives and property might remain—and to begin to rebuild. "Maybe only the younger ones are alive," he said. "They could easily not even know how to get in touch with the family over here." She privately thought that David was clutching at straws, but since, if she were in a similar place, she would undoubtedly do the same, she said nothing more.

He began to avoid the topic himself; it was then that the dreams began, as though his denial by day must come out sometime. There was no pattern to them, nothing that seemed to trigger them, and sometimes the interval between them was as long as a month—or as short as a week. Sometimes, too, he wanted to talk them out, pouring out the terror like a dark stain. But most of the time he wanted to leave them behind, to refuse to give them space in his waking life.

And Caro, who had occasional dreams herself, in which a man fell bleeding at her feet, understood. It made her feel closer to him to know that they both carried wounds whose scars had not quite healed. But because her work truly *was* helping her, because that afternoon at Walter's when she had killed a man figured less and less in her dreams, and almost never in her consciousness, she believed that David's work of healing others would, ultimately, heal him.

Now she pressed against him, willing her warm flesh, her eager passion, to pull him back into a world where pain was not deliberate, and hope was still real. "I love you," she whispered.

He gave a long, shuddering sigh, and she knew the last of the demons was gone. "I love you too," he said. "Oh, God, Caro, I love you more than anything in the world.

The last vestige of her unease vanished too, and the small doubt Mollie's words had raised died. Mollie was a free agent; as she said, she had bought and paid for her art, her life. But I am not, Caro thought. Nor do I want to be. I am bound to David; I can't separate my love for him from my art, from the rest of my life. I can't live in compartments, shifting from one to the other without a backward glance. David and I can make a life that holds everything, a life so filled with love and good work there is no room for monsters. And at that moment, as close to him as she could be, she believed with all her being that this was true.

The phone rang, and Skye reached out to answer it. "I'll get rid of whoever it is," he said to Natalie. "Hell of a time to be calling."

Natalie looked at her watch and yawned. Almost midnight, and she had to be at the paper at seven-thirty. She yawned again, and pushed a pillow behind her, mentally reviewing the week ahead. There was that trial in Pointe Coupee, and a meeting in Livingston Parish of a group formed to ban books. "Watch out for loonies," Tom Burns had told her. "Some of those people think *Huckleberry Finn* should be censored."

She heard Skye exclaim something, saw his hand gripping the phone. "What? All right, hold on. Start from the beginning, Henri. And take it slow. I'm taking notes." He gestured wildly at Natalie, and she handed him a pad and pencil, eyes intent on his face.

"What is it?" she mouthed.

He shook his head, pressing the receiver closer to his ear, jotting words and phrases on the paper in front of him. "I'm going to call Papa right away. Are you going to be at that number? I know he'll want to talk to you. Okay. And look—try not to worry, will you? Those people have made mistakes before. Papa will know what to do. Yes. Sure, Henri, anytime."

He hung up slowly, staring at the paper in his hand. Then he turned and looked at her, his face dazed. "Henri's been subpoenaed by the House Un-American Activities Committee," he said.

"No!"

"Happened a couple of hours ago—he went right to a friend's place—was calling me from there." Skye shook his head. "Poor Henri. The best advice seemed to be to get hold of Papa."

"So he called you."

"Said he hated to wake everybody up by calling home. And to tell you the truth, he—well, he hopes Papa can take care of it without his mother ever having to know."

"Oh, Skye! I don't think there's much chance of that! Those things always get out."

"It's not as though he'd been subpoenaed here," Skye said. "He's in Chicago. No one here's ever heard of the silly little group that got him in trouble."

"What are the charges?" Natalie asked.

"He joined some damn study group," Skye said. He was pacing up and down the living room, covering its small length with quick, energetic strides. "Said they study philosophy, forms of government, that kind of thing."

"That sounds harmless enough."

"Oh, hell, Natalie, I'm sure it is. That's not the point. It seems that the organizers of the group are on a couple of lists that make them prime targets for Senator McCarthy and his friends. It's the same old thing—hang out with the wrong gang and when they hang, you're going to be swinging from the same rope." He stopped and stared at the telephone. "Well, I guess there's nothing for it but to call Papa. I'd wait until morning, but Henri's a wreck. This happened to a friend of his a couple of months ago—the man lost his job before the hearing was even held. It's a hell of a situation when every standard of justice we've ever known in this country is tossed to the winds."

"I wonder if the friend . . . gave Henri's name," Natalie said.

"Don't think he hasn't already thought of that. He's sitting up in Chicago feeling that he doesn't have a soul left he can trust."

"Thank God he's got you," Natalie said.

Skye finished giving the operator his father's number and waited impatiently for Beau to answer the phone. There was no chance Mère would take the call; too many people phoned Beau at all hours, and years ago, he had taken over what he called the dog watch.

"Papa? This is Skye," he said. "Listen, are you where you can talk? No, no one's hurt or anything. Could you go to another phone? I don't want Mère to hear this."

There was a silence, and then Skye began to speak again, giving his father the details of Henri's situation, reading from the notes in his hand. "He was going back to his apartment. I told him you'd call him there." Skye listened, then nodded. "Good, Papa. I told Henri to try not to worry, that you'd know what to do." Another pause, during which Skye's face became grave. "I know. It's a mess. I agree—Henri must have had some indication the group at least sympathized with Communist causes—but, hell, that's a long way from trying to overthrow the government. You know as well as I do that the vast majority of the people hauled before those hearings no more have treason and sedition on their minds than you and I. All right. Keep me posted. And, Papa—thanks."

He hung up and came to the couch, where Natalie still lay. "Papa's going to call Henri. He says he doesn't know what he can do until he finds out how bad it is. Of course, he's got some powerful friends in Washington—" Skye shook his head and lit a cigarette. "Needless to say, mum's the word on this."

"Yes," Natalie said. "It's late, Skye, and we both have a long week. Can you take me on home?"

"Sure." He watched her for a minute, then went over and took her face in his hands. "Natalie. Is something wrong?"

"No—I'm just tired, that's all. You know I always drag the last weeks of September until the cool weather gets here." But she did not meet his eyes, and he studied her, still puzzled, as she started toward the door.

"Wait a minute. Is this thing about Henri going to be a problem?"

"How do you mean?" she said. Her tone and her face told him he had found his answer.

"With the paper. With your job. I mean—this is a story."

"Skye, I overheard a private conversation—two private conversations—while a guest in a friend's home. As far as I'm concerned, they were completely off the record."

"Maybe Papa will get the whole thing over and done with before it ever reaches the public. I sure as hell hope so."

"Me too," she said. They were both quiet as Skye drove her home through the silent streets. His thoughts were with his father, who was already deciding which of the many wheels at his disposal were the right ones to turn, and with Henri, sitting in lonely misery so far away. Natalie's thoughts wrestled with a truth that seemed to loom larger and larger the longer she tried to evade it. It was all very well to promise herself she would be objective and not let her professional commitments come between her and Skye. But now, for the second time, something she had learned in confidence put a strain on that commitment. She had rationalized her promise not to write what she had learned from Beau with the reasoning that it was none of anyone's business if Beau Langlinais had supported Long in order to ruin a man who had hurt him. But Henri Hamilton's subpoena was *news.* And although Skye might be optimistic that it would be handled quietly, Natalie had no such hope. The instant Henri's name got to the press in Chicago, the papers would pick it up here. And she was giving up a chance for her paper to scoop everyone else.

Natalie dressed for work the next morning with a heaviness she could not attribute to the humidity that weighted the still September air. Until news of Henri's subpoena reached the *Advocate* newsroom and was out in the open, she knew she would feel a sense of dread, of anxiety; she left her apartment and drove to the newspaper feeling more and more disturbed.

The normal office bustle greeted her, and she soon slipped into the day's routine. She made a few calls to people in Pointe Coupee to confirm information included in her trial feature, wrote the final version, and then began to read the background on the censorship group in Livingston Parish. It was just before noon that the city editor walked by her desk and asked her to come into his office. Although she felt a premonition of what she was going to hear, she followed him, hoping futilely that this was just another assignment and had nothing to do with Henri Hamilton.

His first words confirmed her fears. Closing the door, he went to his desk and perched on a corner near her chair, tapping his cigarette against his palm. "Got a story here I think you're the right person for," he said. "It concerns Henri Hamilton, one of Beau Langlinais's stepsons."

She tried to keep her face immobile, to show professional interest only, but something must have tipped him to her feelings. "Watkins, why do I think you already know what I'm about to tell you?" When she remained silent, he said, "Henri Hamilton was subpoenaed in Chicago yesterday by the House Un-American Activities Committee. The charges are association with known Communists, and the list of organizations he's supposed to be involved with is as long as a damn laundry list. Now, did you know about this?"

"Not in my professional capacity," she said. She could hardly open her mouth to speak; her mouth was dry, her tongue was stiff.

"Now, what the hell does that mean?"

"I happened to learn something about that by the accident of being with a . . . friend. I was in a personal, confidential situation at the time—"

"Dammit, there's no such thing!" the city editor said. "You knew damn well we'd have that news today. You've lost us a chance to beat the other papers in the state with this story."

She moistened her dry lips and coughed to clear her throat. "I knew the story would reach Baton Rouge. But I didn't feel I could violate my friend's trust."

"Watkins, I know you see Skye Langlinais. You don't have to play coy games with me. The question is—if you can't be objective about the

Langlinaises, why in the hell didn't you tell me when I assigned the Beau Langlinais story to you? What did you cover up there?"

"Nothing!" She stood up and faced him, her temper barely controlled. "I didn't cover up a thing."

"Maybe. But it'll be a long time before you get an assignment like that again, Watkins."

"That's not fair. You said yourself it was a good story—solid, well-written—"

"What was there was solid. I don't know about what wasn't there."

"What are you talking about?"

He reached behind him and pulled a copy of Natalie's story on Beau Langlinais off the desk, and began to read. " 'Beau Langlinais's early commitment to Huey P. Long was sparked by a personal experience that left him convinced Long was the man to follow.' He put the story down and looked at her. "You don't say what that personal experience was, Natalie. Didn't Beau Langlinais tell you? Or did you just not ask?"

"I—he told me. It . . . it just didn't seem really . . . relevant."

"In whose judgment? Yours?"

"It was too distant—"

"You should have let me be the judge of that."

"Then why the hell didn't you ask me at the time? You read the story before it went in—"

The city editor shrugged. "The story was okay without it. And at that time I thought I knew where your loyalties lay, Watkins. You'd been begging to be in my bailiwick—I thought you had better sense than to hide something."

She stared at him, speechless.

"Never mind. I've given the Hamilton thing to someone else. Get back to work."

"But—"

"You've got deadlines, Watkins, and so do I. Now, get back to work."

When she entered the newsroom, she felt a hush descend over it. It's my imagination, she told herself, walking back to her desk with her head held high and her hands deliberately relaxed at her sides. They couldn't possibly know I've just been reprimanded, she thought. Then, just as she was about to sink into her chair, Tom Burns's voice cut through the small hubbub that had begun again. "Hey, Natalie! Would you explain the exact relationship between Henri Hamilton and Beau Langlinais?"

She stood frozen, for the second time that morning unable to speak. Then she sat down and rolled a piece of paper into her typewriter. She began to type: "Now is the time for all good men to come to the aid of the party. The quick brown fox jumped over the log." Over and over she typed the meaningless phrases. And by the time she had filled a page, she was calm again. She took out a fresh sheet of paper, put it in her machine, and began work on a real story. She would not let herself think about what Tom Burns would do with the story on Henri. Whatever it was, it would be merciless, filled with innuendos, almost gleeful in its tone. She didn't know whether Tom Burns particularly disliked Beau, or if he simply disliked anyone he envied. At any rate, she thought, I'd better warn Skye that the lid is open and a pretty ugly can of worms is about to crawl out.

21

OCTOBER 1949

"There," Skye said, holding a long taper against the tinder and kindling. "That ought to catch."

"The first fire of the season," Caroline said. She stretched her hands toward the hearth. "Why do I never feel really warm unless there's a fire burning?"

"Primitive instincts," Beau said. "I don't know about anyone else, but I'm starving. Caroline, if you'll serve up the gumbo, I'll open the wine."

"Can I help?" Natalie said, springing up from her place near Skye.

"You can toss the salad," Caroline said. "And, Henri, if you'd just set up some of those tray tables—"

"Sure," Henri said. He raised his head, but immediately sank back into lethargy, staring into the flames that were licking the pecan logs, catching the rough edges and settling down to a steady blaze.

"Here, I'll help you," Skye said gently. "Mère keeps the trays in the hall closet. Come on, fellow."

Beau watched them leave the room. His hands were busy with the wine opener, but his mind played over the events of the last few weeks. He had flown to Chicago the day after he'd received Skye's call. He had remained until the crisis was over. Even now, he was not sure what it had cost him in terms of political favors exchanged to get Henri off. Calls to friends in Washington, a desperate bid to all the people who owed him for past favors—obligations to him that he could have used to benefit a score of other causes. Henri had had to go through the hearing, but the teeth of the administrators conducting it, people far down in the hierarchy, had been effectively pulled before the hearing ever began, and Henri had left it exonerated.

Exonerated, but hardly free. The University of Chicago had not asked Henri to resign his position as a lecturer in the philosophy department—that had been Henri's choice. No matter what arguments Beau had used in Chicago and his mother had brought up when Henri was home again, Henri was adamant. He could not stay in Chicago. He no longer trusted anyone he knew there. He could not stop thinking about the picture of him that had been presented at the hearing, the picture of a man so naive he had not known that a great number of his friends belonged to the Communist party.

"If I'm that stupid, I shouldn't be turned loose in a classroom," he told Beau.

"Henri, there was no alternative but to disclose your naiveté. If anyone in that hearing had felt you knew the political affiliations of the leaders of that study group, there'd have been hell to pay."

"There already has been," Henri said, tossing down a sheaf of clippings and going to stand at the window, body rigid, head turned from Beau.

Beau had not needed to read the clippings. Tom Burns had a field day with Henri; he had pieced together a profile of Henri that made him look like a weak, self-indulgent rich man's son, and although Burns had not come right out and said so, the implications were clear: people who lived in ivory towers thought they could afford friends no common man would give the time of day to. Burns had also gone over Beau's life, particularly when the results of the hearing were announced. Next to the article that reported the hearing was a boxed feature that speculated as to why Beau Langlinais's stepson had gotten off when so many other people with far fewer associations had been found guilty. The feature made Beau sound like a power-mad politician who would stop at nothing for his own ends; although Burns was correct in his assumption that Beau had pulled every string he could to affect Henri's hearing, the portrait of Beau he had painted was completely inaccurate. When Natalie read it, she had been overcome with guilt and sorrow.

"No one blames you, Natalie," Skye said. "Burns has a burr in his saddle. He explodes every once in a while. It was just Papa's bad luck to be caught in the flak, that's all."

"But if I had said something to Jack Lawton about Henri's subpoena when I got to work that morning, he'd probably have given me the story, Skye."

"Natalie, you did what you believed was right. And I'm very thankful you did. Look, I don't know if I could have handled reading all this stuff with your byline."

"I wouldn't have written it," Natalie said. And she realized that she was right. She wouldn't have. There had followed a period of consternation, a time in which she had to think about her own journalistic ambitions and her love for Skye Langlinais. The atmosphere in the newsroom grew more hostile than ever, and although she knew that Burns and his sharp tongue made most people want to stay neutral, neutrality was not what she wanted. When she had heard of an opening on the *Times-Picayune,* she applied for it—and got it. She would begin on November 1, in another week.

Despite their efforts to make the meal by the fire a cheerful one, the pauses between one topic and the next one became longer, the conversation more forced; Henri did not enter into it at all, answering direct questions with monosyllables, spooning up his gumbo in an abstracted way that made it clear to all of them that he did not know where he was or what he was doing.

"I'd like a walk," Skye said when the kitchen was clean and Caroline announced that she was dead for sleep and was going up to bed. "Natalie, Henri, how about it?"

"I want to talk with Père," Henri said. "You two go on."

"Wait up for us," Skye said. "We'll make hot buttered rum when we get back."

They got jackets and whistled for Marq, who bounded ahead of them down the steps and out into the frosty night. The farm was suffused by the orange glow of a harvest moon; the tips of the field grass seemed burnished with light, making waving shadows of rippling silver. Trees stood in black masses against the sky, swaying and bending before the autumn wind. The stillness of coming winter gripped the land. Birds nestled deep in their nests, and on a fencepost, an owl waited for its prey.

"God, it's beautiful," Skye said. They linked arms and struck off across the lawn, heading for broad pasture beyond.

"I'm worried about Henri," Natalie said. "He . . . he seems so lost."

"I know," Skye said. "His whole world's been destroyed." He helped her over a stile, then scrambled down beside her. "Speaking of which—so is mine. I still can't accept that you're moving to New Orleans next week."

"Skye, I couldn't stay at the *Advocate.* This job with the *Picayune* is a lifesaver. It was just a matter of time before Lawton sent me back to the society page. And I'd have had to quit then, anyway."

"Why didn't you tell me?"

"I'm sorry. It was right in the middle of all the hurrah. He called me in and said he hoped things would settle down but that I had to realize that if my presence in the newsroom continued to be a disrupting factor, there was nothing he could do but have me transferred out."

"Damn him!"

"He didn't blame me, Skye. He knew Tom Burns was out to get me, but he has a newspaper to get out, and a cub reporter isn't important enough to enter into a war against his best man."

"You should have told me, Natalie! Hell, I'd have gone down there and given Burns something to remember."

"Skye. It doesn't matter anymore. I've taken care of it by quitting and moving on."

"I don't care. He shouldn't be allowed to get away with intimidating you—going after you—"

"Oh, Skye. It happens to a lot of people."

He stopped walking and took her in his arms. "All I care about is you. And now you're moving seventy miles away!"

"Seventy miles isn't so far, Skye. Besides, you're in your last year of law school. You'll study better without me to distract you."

"I have an idea," he said, drawing her to him. Her cheek felt cool against his, her body warm and solid in the thick jacket. "Marry me, Natalie. Stay with me."

She did not answer him, only lifting her head to kiss him, tightening her arms around him. Finally she pulled away and took his hand. "No, Skye."

"Natalie, I love you. I want you to marry me."

"Because I'm moving?"

"Because I want you. I want to be with you every day, every night, for the rest of our lives."

She put her hand across his lips. "Shh. Skye, it's not time for this."

"What are you talking about?"

A sudden gust of wind blew against them, scattering dry leaves over their heavy shoes. "Let's go back," Natalie said. "I'm getting cold."

"All right. We'll go inside. But I'm not dropping this, Natalie. It's too important to me."

She went ahead of him into the warm house, filled with the aroma of woodsmoke and spices. The hall light was on, and one shone on the landing, but the house was quiet, and when they went into the living room, they found a note from Henri propped against the mantel: "Went up to bed. See you in the morning. Henri."

"That's that," Skye said. "Throw another log on the fire and stick the poker into the coals," Skye said, "while I get the fixings."

He waited until they were settled on a rug in front of the fire, hot mugs in their hands. "All right," he said. "Now tell me. Why won't you marry me?"

"I haven't accomplished what I set out to do yet, Skye."

"Natalie—"

"Darling, let me finish. Please." She shifted away from him, leaning against the sofa. "I've worked hard to be a journalist. Even in college, I had to keep proving myself. I did get named managing editor of the newspaper—but of course a boy was editor. And when an exam-stealing scandal broke, I had to give the story to a male reporter—even though I was the one who uncovered it—because it happened in a fraternity."

She saw him begin to speak, and held up her hand. "Skye, believe me, I'm not holding any grudges. But, dammit, look what's just happened to me. Next to Henri's problem, I guess it's pretty small. But I was getting a toehold. I was a reporter writing real stories, handling real news. Now—" She sipped her drink and looked away from him, but not before he saw tears glistening in her eyes. "Now it's all to do over again."

"Not if you marry me," he said stubbornly.

She swung around to face him. "I can hardly believe you said that," she said. He heard the sadness in her voice and moved across the rug to sit beside her.

"Darling—what's keeping you from marrying me? Is being a reporter that important? Do you mean to give up everything in the world for it?"

"Is being a lawyer important to you?"

"That's not the same . . . I'm sorry. I can't say that, can I? Because I really don't know how important your career is to you. Except that right now it's more important than our love."

"I don't know if it is or not," Natalie said. "Darling, try to understand. I don't even have a career. Not right now. I had the beginnings of one. And I have the chance to start a new one. To find out if I can even make it, for heaven's sake."

"Make it? Of course you can make it. You're damn good, Natalie. You know that."

"I can write. But maybe I lack some essential quality—the thing that makes Tom Burns, as arrogant and awful as he is, such a top-notch reporter. A kind of toughness—"

"You're tough enough. You don't lack anything."

"I don't know that, Skye. But I'm going to find out."

"In New Orleans."

"The *Picayune*'s a bigger paper than the *Advocate*. It's a great opportunity. If I fail to take it—I'm afraid I'll always regret it."

"But you won't regret not marrying me."

She caught her breath and stared at him. "What's gotten into you, Skye? You're acting—dammit, Skye, you're acting almost as arrogant as Tom Burns! Are you offering to give up law school? Are you offering to abandon something you've dreamed of for years? How dare you make this an either-or proposition!"

"I don't mean it that way, Natalie. I'm sorry if I sound arrogant. I'm sorry if I seem to put my ambitions ahead of yours. I . . . I don't think of you as a reporter, Natalie. I think of you as the woman I love more than anything in the world."

"And I love you."

"I guess I thought that when two people love each other as much as we do—they would just naturally marry," he said.

"Skye, you have a year of law school left. Can't we just . . . put marriage on hold? Until you've finished?"

"It seems I'm going to have to," he said. "I can hardly march down the aisle alone."

Her anger died, and she leaned toward him. "I'm sorry, Skye. I don't want to hurt you—"

"You're right, Natalie. I can't ask you to give up your ambitions because they get in the way of what I want. I guess at this point, I can't ask you anything."

"You have my love," she said, and kissed him.

He held her close, kissing her eyelids, her cheeks, finally covering her mouth with his and pulled her down to lie on the rug beside him.

We're close, so close—as close as we've ever been, she reassured herself. But as the fire died low behind them, and an edge of chill entered the room, she couldn't help but wonder if seventy miles were not a very long distance after all.

Caro idled down the street, stopping at almost every shop to peer inside, reveling in the special atmosphere of San Francisco's Chinatown. She loved to come here; it was the quickest trip to an exotic land she had ever made, all the way to Cathay and back in one afternoon. Her favorite tea shop was just ahead, and she walked a little faster, looking forward to a peaceful hour.

The wind chimes hanging in the doorway tinkled as she brushed past them, a soft Oriental welcome that reflected the serenity of the shop. Caro sat at her usual table and ordered tea, watching with lazy pleasure as the woman who brought it tilted the small teapot over her cup and filled it. "Thank you," Caro said. The woman bowed, then moved away silently, her heavy socks gliding noiselessly over the tile floor.

The tea's taste blended well with the smell of incense from the brass censer swinging gently in the light breeze. From the next room Caro could hear voices. A guide was explaining the meanings of various curios ranged around the walls to a busload of tourists; she heard the guide telling someone to rub the Buddha's stomach, it would bring her fat babies.

Her own stomach seemed to be suddenly hollow. She felt aware of all the soft places inside, as though her body were something separate from her, something that had a life of its own. What would it be like to be pregnant, to have a baby taking shape there, beginning with a tiny seed and then dividing and growing, occupying its own space? She would encase herself in the glowing silk kimono she had just brought, making a bright cocoon for herself and the baby, sitting in solid peace like the ivory Buddha on the shelf across the way. While the baby grew, she would spin pictures, using the threads of her life and David's, until the baby would not know where one began and the other ended. David would like that, she thought. David would like that very much. And so would she.

She sighed. The idea of a baby was fine. The reality still posed the old questions, raised the old conflict. The baby would have to be baptized Catholic, if Caro were to remain true to her religion. And brought up Catholic as well. David would not only have to agree to this; he would have to promise it. Promise to let his children attend Catholic schools. Watch them mourn on Good Friday for the death of a Christ David's religion denied. And while it was all very well to think about these promises in the abstract, before a child was actually born, when the child was real, it would be a different matter. Could David not want his children to follow his beliefs? How could he not mind being the odd man out in a family of Roman Catholics? Which brought her squarely back to the central dilemma. Any compromise she offered or accepted would undermine her entire belief. She had heard of at least one Jewish-Catholic family in which the boys were Jewish and the girls Catholic, but she knew of no priest who would agree to such a solution. She knew of no priest who would marry them if David did not make those promises. And if she were not married by a priest, she would not be married at all. The baby would not be blessed. It would be born to a mother who did not have the strength to stick by what she knew she must, a mother who wavered when she should stand fast.

The warmth of the teacup reminded her to sip her tea. You're too hard on yourself, David had told her. Do you really think your God would deny you because you didn't dot every I and cross every T of the law's letter? And then he said something she kept coming back to, because it seemed more true than anything else she knew. "Anyway," he had said, bending over her and holding her in the intense gaze of his blue eyes, "you and I are more married than if we'd been blessed by the pope himself. What we have between us is permanent, Caro, whether anyone ever pronounces the words over us or not." Yes, she had said. Yes. So they could go on the way they were. They did not have to be married—the words would not change anything, for better or for worse. Unless she had his baby. Unless she decided that the hollow place inside her was not doubt about whether she should make this final commitment, but simply a womb waiting for life.

From the back of the shop she heard the hesitant notes of a piano, a few chords, and then a solid pattern of scales. She peered through the screen of beads hanging in the doorway, and saw a small girl perched on a stool, tiny hands plucking at the keys. The shopowner stood behind his counter, his long black braid swinging gently as he nodded his head in time to the music.

"Is that your little girl?" Caro asked the Chinese woman who had brought her tea.

"Yes," the woman said, and smiled and bowed.

"I used to play," Caro said. "When I was a little girl."

The woman smiled again. The tourists' voices diminished, faded, and stopped. A pocket of peace, this afternoon in Chinatown. A stroll down narrow streets, browsing in shop windows, making idle purchases. A sandalwood fan, a silk kimono. A packet of incense, a tin of jasmine tea. She smiled, thinking of how she would welcome David. Incense burning, tea ready to brew. Herself naked under the smooth silk, its rich folds falling away from her body. She looked at her watch. Time to sketch the shopkeeper, time to make a few strokes that would hold the little girl at the piano, time to draw a woman rubbing a Buddha's tummy. And then home. David.

She finished her sketches and her tea together, then stuffed her pad and pencil into her big canvas bag and stepped out into the street, filled now with people. It was late afternoon, the last week in October; a chill wind blew up from the bay, and many of the passersby wore thick quilted coats and tunics, hands buried in deep sleeves. I'll make a fire, she thought. Throw the incense on the wood. She could almost smell the rich smoke, she could almost feel the room, a temple now, ready for celebration.

The phone was ringing when she let herself into her apartment, and she picked it up, hearing her mother's excited voice at the other end of the wire. "I have the most surprising news," Caroline said. "You know Henri's been so down—he's been talking to Father Richard, trying to deal with all this—and yesterday he came home from a long session and said he'd made up his mind. Caro, he's joining a group the Diocese of Lafayette is sending to a mission in Guatemala!"

"Guatemala! Mother, for heaven's sake!"

"I know. I was absolutely bowled over. But the more Henri talked, the more sense it made. He's always been fascinated by archaeology—there're some old ruins near the village, and he can poke about in them. Then he and Beau had a long talk about it. Beau says Henri feels he has to make amends for all the trouble he's caused."

"Poor Henri," Caro said. "This is probably the best thing in the world, though. A different environment, good work—"

"He's feeling a little better, now that he's made his decision. I wish you could come see him off, Caro. I know he'd love to see you."

"Of course I'll come," Caro said.

She heard the weariness beneath her mother's excitement, and thought again of the long weeks of worry and strain before Beau had finally brought Henri home. "Mama, Henri's all right now. He's going to be fine."

"I know." Caroline laughed a little, forcing herself to sound cheerful. "Someone said something the other day that I find is all too true. A mother is only as happy as her unhappiest child."

"Well, we'll all be happy this weekend."

"I will. Can David come, do you think? I know what a doctor's schedule is like, but of course we'd love to see him."

"I'll see," Caro said. "I'll call you tomorrow and let you know my travel plans."

They finished their conversation, and Caro laid the fire and put the tea things out. When the fire was burning well, she sat on a cushion near the hearth breathing in the incense's sweet smell, thinking about Henri. She pictured him in the Guatemalan jungle, a tiny figure on a dense mat of green. He'll be all right, she thought. He's a perennial student. He'll find things to occupy his mind. So it's over; all the weeks of anxiety, the phone calls, the waiting for the worst while hoping for the best—another chapter closed, she thought.

She heard David's key in the lock and rose from her cushion. "Oh, good, you're home," David said. He held a letter in his hand which he gave her as he took off his coat. "From Jake," he said. "He sounds like he's on top of the world."

Caro skimmed the letter quickly, taking in the enthusiastic description of life on a kibbutz. "He does sound happy," she said. "I'm glad."

"Yes," David said. He took the cup she handed him and sniffed the air. "You've been to Chinatown."

"I had the loveliest afternoon sketching," she said. "And when I came home, Mama called. David, Henri's going to Guatemala! To work in a mission there. Isn't that astonishing?"

"Sounds like it might be just what he needs," David said.

"He seems to think so. Mother wants me to come home for the weekend. Henri's leaving in the middle of the week, and she's gathering everyone together for a send-off. Of course she wants you, too, if you can get away."

"I'd planned to go to a lecture on Friday night," David said. "A rabbi who's been in Israel is speaking at the synagogue."

"We'd need to leave here Friday, David. Would you mind very much missing it?"

David turned his cup slowly in his hands, looking into its shallow bowl as though the tea leaves held the answer. "Caro, it's more than a lecture. It's—well, it's kind of a recruiting talk."

"Recruiting? For what?"

He raised his eyes and looked at her. "Israel."

"Israel! What? David—are you thinking about going to Israel?"

"It's crossed my mind. To be fair—yes, I've given the idea some thought."

She sank back onto the cushion, staring at him. "But, David—for how long? And why didn't you say something before?"

"There wasn't anything to say. There isn't now. As I said, the thought of going to Israel has crossed my mind. I have given the idea some thought. So far—that's all I've done."

"I can't believe you've been thinking about leaving me without saying a word about it."

"Caro. I think about a lot of things. So do you."

"But this is important, David. Just this afternoon, I was remembering what you told me about you and me being more married than if the pope himself had blessed us. And now you spring something like this on me!"

"I haven't made up my mind to go. I feel I should. I feel almost compelled to go. But I'm not sure I can. Or will. The only thing I've been sure of is that this is a decision I have to make—alone. Because if I bring you into it, Caro, I know I won't go."

"If you really felt you had to go, David, I wouldn't stand in your way," she said. "And considering the fact that you've kept all this to yourself, I don't think I *could* stand in your way."

"That's not fair, Caro."

"*You're* not being fair!" She leapt up and confronted him. "You talk about bringing me into your decision. Don't you know I already *am* part of your decision? Just as you're part of every decision I make. Isn't that what love is?"

"Caro—that's not what I meant. God, don't you think you're at the center of all of my thoughts? Do you think I *want* to leave you?"

"Then don't."

"It's not that simple," David said. He sat on the sofa and leaned his head wearily on its back. "Every time I read a letter from Jake—every time I hear another lecture about Israel, see another story—I feel that I'm . . . not doing what I'm supposed to be doing. Not . . . carrying my weight."

"What about the money you give to Israeli projects? They need money, too, David."

"That's true. And I've told myself that over and over again. But, Caro. It's not enough. Money is just . . . money. Look at Henri. He could send money to that mission. But he's not. He's going there."

"It's not the same thing at all, David."

"But the idea is. If I send money . . . How can I explain it?"

"You don't have to. You want to give something more important than money. You want to give your time, your energy. A piece of your life. And a piece of mine as well."

"Caro—I'm not choosing between you and Israel. Don't put this on those terms."

"I'm not putting it on any terms at all. I'm trying to . . . adjust, David. First to the idea that you kept this from me—and second to the idea that you probably will go." She felt as weary as he looked, but she did not sit beside him, taking a chair near the fire instead.

"The only reason I didn't tell you is that I need to make this my own decision, Caro. I can't go in spite of you. I can't go because of you. Can't you see that?"

She read the unhappiness in his eyes and could bear it no longer. She rose and went to him, sitting near him and putting her arms around him. "Yes, I do see that. I . . . I'm being selfish, David. What you feel you have to do is directly opposed to what I want—but I won't ask you not to go."

"You couldn't be selfish, darling. Not in a million years. You'd every right to expect me to discuss this with you, every right to expect me to consider you. I'm afraid I've made a mess of it, blurting it out this way."

"There's never a good way to tell bad news," she said. "Would it—would it be for a very long time?"

"It's hard to say. At least six months."

"Six months! David—then I'll go with you," she said impulsively.

"Darling, that's not possible." He kissed her, his eyes pleading for her understanding.

"Why not? Mollie Haskell went with Jake. Do you think I'm too weak to help?"

"It has nothing to do with that, Caro. Mollie and Jake aren't even living together. They see each other maybe once a month."

"So?"

"So that's all right for *them*. They both went to Israel for reasons having to do with commitment to what Israel is, rather than because of their commitment to each other. But you, Caro—you'd be going only because of me. And that wouldn't work. If you weren't where I could keep an eye on you—and the chances of that are minimal—I'd worry. You'd be lonely."

"In a kibbutz full of people?"

"In a kibbutz full of Jews," he said. He stroked her face with a touch so loving, so gentle, that it brought tears to her eyes. His eyes were solemn, almost sad. "Darling, I know how you feel about Jews. I know where your sympathies lie. But you've no idea how fired-up the people in Israel are now. I'm afraid it would be—well, I'm afraid you'd feel very alone, that's all."

"You mean I wouldn't fit in."

"It's more complicated than that. We're bound by a kind of pain, a pain that marks the soul. We're used to everything from snubs to outright persecution; it makes us seek each other out, even when things are going well. When they're not going well—when there's a crisis—that same bond makes us stick together tighter than glue."

"And not just anyone can get in, is that it?" She tried to keep anger from her voice, but he heard it and grasped her arms.

"Caro, you wouldn't be kept 'out.' It's more than that. You just couldn't get in."

"Then I guess there's nothing else to say," she said. "My family will be sorry not to see you this weekend. But under the circumstances, I think you'd better not miss that lecture."

"May we compromise? Get either a late flight out Friday night or an early one Saturday morning?"

"David, do you really want to go to New Orleans with me?"

"Of course I do!"

"So you will come back to me."

"Come back?"

"From Israel. This isn't the beginning of . . . the end for us."

"How can you ask me that?"

"I need to know, David."

"Of course I'll come back. With this . . . compulsion—whatever it is—out of my system. And you still very much in it."

"I hope so," she said. She nestled against him, and felt Jake's letter, tucked into her kimono pocket, brush her like the stiff wings of a bird. Something seemed to brush across her mind, a sensation of a dark figure, large and formless. There was no tingle in her fingers, no urgency to reach for pen or brush, and she knew that whatever the dark figure meant, the time for it to be born had not yet come.

Nor, she thought sadly, lifting her face to David's, was it time for their baby to come.

22

JANUARY 1950

Well, Caro told herself, getting up and going toward the small Christmas tree glowing in her big window, there's no point in prolonging the agony. This is the twelfth day of Christmas, and time to take the tree down. It was raining outside, a soft rain that slid down the windowpane, obliterating the world outside. Which suits me fine, she thought.

David had been gone less than a month, but already her loneliness, her need for him, was almost more than she could bear. The six weeks before he had left for Israel had been incredibly hectic, with the normal tasks of a major upheaval complicated by their emotional parting. By the time she had seen him off, just days before Christmas, she had been exhausted, so strung out that she had almost not gone back to Louisiana for the holiday, afraid that even the family rituals and love would not assuage her sorrow. She had gone home, finally, because the alternative seemed so pointless. And her week at the farm had been an oasis after all. Not only because of the soothing familiarity of her family and the holiday routines, but because she realized that hers was not the only life facing change.

Henri was settled into a Guatemalan village, teaching the Indians to read and happily exploring Mistec and Zatotec Indian ruins. Gennie was getting married to a man who taught economics at Columbia University; Beau and Caroline planned to fly up to New York in early January for the wedding, and the rest of them would see the couple when the play Gennie was in finished its run. "And then I'm coming back to kick off my campaign for Congress," Beau had announced. He had put an arm around Caroline and hugged her close. "Our campaign," he amended.

That announcement had occupied most of their conversation. As far as Beau was concerned, now was the ideal time for him to run. "I'm getting restless," he admitted. "I see the Dixiecrat movement splitting the Democratic party. There's a lot to do in Washington, and I want to be part of it." The election was in November, and already Beau had his campaign organization in gear. Caro left for San Francisco knowing that her mother would be almost totally absorbed for the next eleven months in Beau and the election, and a small part of her felt deserted, as though the momentum that moved Père and her mother forward were pushing them far away.

And David was gone, vanished in a crack of time, caught by forces too strong for either of them. Her loneliness seemed almost unbearable: she could not wake without thinking of David waking too, halfway across the world. She fought the mood, embarking on a routine that included fresh air and exercise, as much sleep as she could manage, visits with friends. So that by now, the sixth day of January, she was beginning to learn to live with the reality of David's absence.

She put the last ornament in its box and tucked it into the waiting carton, then sealed the carton with heavy tape. There was room in the big storage closet at the end of the hall for it, despite the cartons of David's personal belongings. David's substitute at the clinic was subletting his apartment, and to make room for his tenant, David had left several boxes in Caro's safekeeping.

Lifting one of the square boxes, she glanced at the neatly typed card taped to the top that identified its contents. "Family Records," the card read. She put the box aside, thinking that if it contained papers and photographs, it might be better stored somewhere else. She carried it back to the living room and set it on the cleanly swept hearth.

Her curiosity getting the better of her, she decided to open it. He's probably lugged this stuff around with him for years, she thought, expecting to find the high-school yearbooks, the scrapbooks, the memorabilia people maintain despite the fact that they never look at them again.

The first item was a large black ledger, with nothing to indicate what it contained. Idly she flipped open the cover and turned to the first page. A list of names—of numbers—filled the page. She realized that this must be an index of some kind, that the numbers were pages in the ledger, and she curiously turned the page. A woman's name was written at the top, her birthdate and birthplace entered neatly beneath it. There were several photographs; they were of the young woman at various stages in her life. Below them was a caption written in David's familiar well-formed hand: "First cousin on mother's side. (See family tree, Appendix A.)"

Then she saw the last line on the page, and the chill rain that still slid down the windowpanes seemed to enter the room. "Died at Buchenwald, sometime in March 1941." She clutched the ledger against her, knowing now what its pages held. She could not look at them, she did not want to know—but of course, she did. Sixty-five pages, sixty-five names. Faces that belonged to members of David's family. Young girls in tea gowns; young men in tennis garb. Old women carrying their years with grace, their jewels with quiet pride. Men solid with prosperity. The line "in the midst of life we are in death" sprang into her consciousness as she went through the pages, at first rapidly, as though to know the worst and get it behind her, and then more slowly, reading each sparse entry, feeling the agony it hid. Buchenwald. Dachau. Auschwitz. The names seemed to make an awful tolling in her head, each one beating against her as though with a huge metal clapper. She let the ledger fall into her lap and wrapped her arms around her shaking body. A low moan escaped her lips. Something tugged at her, a memory—clippings she had made, articles she had kept. She got up and went into her studio, pawing through a box that held years of miscellany. And found her own file of horror.

Stories ripped from newspapers about the victims of Hitler's mad dictums. Articles torn from *Life* magazine, with photographs of stacked corpses. Interviews with soldiers who had liberated the death camps. The same photos, the same words—Horror. Horror. Horror.

She held the file against her, as though her own warm flesh could negate the terrible aura of death it held. Then she carried it into the living room, and sat again by the fire, spreading its contents on the floor. She went from ledger to folder, matching David's family with the terrible camps in which they died. This stack of bodies might contain David's Aunt Anna; that oven might have cremated his Cousin Josef. An emotion she had never felt before rose in her, compounded of anger and fear and an agony of grief. She pounded her fist against the floor, and her lips formed her own denial. No. This could not be forgotten, this could not be allowed to slide into the past. Her mind seemed enveloped in a cloud of red mist, and through the mist she saw dark figures forming. This time, she knew what those dark figures were. This time, she knew the paintings they meant to be.

For a long time she sat staring into the fire, letting the figures inhabit her mind. She no longer needed to look at the ledger pages or read the folder's contents. Both were now a part of her. She did not know when David had learned of his relatives' fates; that was not important. What was important was that now she understood what impelled him to go to Israel. What was important was that she make him know that she did, and that her understanding came out of her love for him—but that it just as strongly came out of her love for mankind.

Her fingers felt the way they did when she was ready to paint—alive, almost separate from her, as though their skill lived apart. She could feel her anger and fear and grief breaking through some hard barrier, making an opening that led to a space she had not yet explored. She felt that the exploration would take a long time, and that it would consume all her energy. There would be none left for the small series of paintings she had been working on, a series developed from sketches she'd made on various trips to Beau Chêne. Elegant paintings, subtle paintings, paintings hinting at richness—paintings that might describe the lives David's people, too, had lived—before Hitler.

An idea exploded inside her, filling her with light. She saw those elegant paintings in that harsh light, and knew, suddenly and clearly, what it was she would do. And then, mindless, ruled by that light, that emotion, she went to her studio and began to work.

"Another election year, another dollar," Ben Roberts, the *Picayune*'s city editor said, glancing at Natalie. He looked at the press release in his hand. "Beau Langlinais is throwing his hat into the Third District race—there's going to be a big barbecue in St. Martinville to kick off his campaign. Our stringer will write that up, Natalie, but I'd like you to do a sketch on him. Write it so we can use about twelve column inches in the country edition and cut it to about six for the city edition."

"I . . . I know Mr. Langlinais fairly well," Natalie said. "I—well, I date his son Skye."

"This is just a biographical sketch, Natalie. Even a positive bias won't affect that."

"I just wanted to be candid about it from the beginning," Natalie said.

"Your professional conscience is a better monitor than I am," Roberts said. "Let me know if you need anything. I'll want this by Friday."

"Fine."

She had her *Advocate* story about Beau Langlinais in her personal files, but to get a slant on how the *Picayune* had treated him over the years, she went to the morgue after lunch and began her research. Beau's candidacy had a significance greater than his position in his own district and the state. As a moderate, he stood against extremes at either end of the Democratic party, supporting neither the Dixiecrats at one pole or the ultraliberals at the other. Which made his race one that party officials around the nation, but particularly in Washington, would be watching. And that meant that anything written about him might well be picked up by the news services; even a simple biographical sketch took on more importance in that light.

Natalie found what she wanted and made extensive notes. As she went through the files, she found additional information about the Langlinais family: social events reported, wedding announcements, birth announcements, obituaries—her eye stopped at one of these: Françoise Alicia Langlinais, July 16, 1922. Rapidly she read the death notice; Beau Langlinais's sister, she realized. She had died at a very young age. With a feeling almost of reverence, as though she could feel the family's grief coming through the yellowed page, she slipped the obituary back in the file. She was almost out the door before she thought of someone else she had meant to look up. Charles Livaudais, Caroline Langlinais's father.

Swiftly she found his file and began to skim it. The Livaudais file, like the Langlinais one, was a mixture of both business and social items. The Livaudaises cut a wide swath in New Orleans society, Natalie concluded, looking at yet another picture of Mr. and Mrs. Charles Livaudais at yet another dinner or ball. There were pictures of Caroline, too, ending with the one of her as a bride. After that, the file was slimmer, with longer periods between items. And then she came to the last one, Charles Livaudais's obituary. She saw with shock that he had killed himself—"dead by his own hand," the article read. And what a sign of his fallen status, she thought, that no one had kept that fateful line from public view. The *Picayune* was, however, still circumspect, and no details of the suicide were given in the news article that supplemented the formal notice. But the *States-Item* is a horse of a different color, Natalie thought. I'll bet they have a lot more—and I'm just curious enough to go find out.

Several days passed before she found time to visit the other newspaper, where a friend took her into the *Item*'s morgue. There she found her expectations fully realized. The *Item* described the site of Livaudais's suicide as a "love nest," with speculation as to how long he had been established there, supported by interviews with neighbors, who had seen him on the street frequently, and although they had never seen him with anyone, had seen a dark-haired girl going into the house from time to time. Given that small bit of cloth, the writer had made a full sail, letting his imagination carry him into realms of supposition that disgusted Natalie with their hint of voyeurism and total disregard for decency.

How awful for poor Mrs. Langlinais, she thought, stuffing the file back into place. Of course, she wasn't Mrs. Langlinais then, she was still Mrs. Hamilton, and Beau Langlinais was still married to his first wife, Louise.

She stopped short, remembering Beau Langlinais's words last summer: "Livaudais's kingdom came tumbling down, all right, but by the time it did, I had even more reason to hate him." The wet cold of January must have penetrated even the thick walls of the building, she thought. She felt chilled, and she hurried out of the newspaper office to find the nearest coffee shop where she could get warm.

She sat over her cup, feeling warmth steal back into her bones. What a morass of sorrow and scandal even the most fabled lives seem to conceal, she thought. To cheer herself up, she thought of Skye, and of the invitation she had received from him to go to St. Martinville for the weekend. A weekend in the country was just what she needed, even if it did include a campaign barbecue. But as she went back to the *Picayune,* she could not help but wonder about Charles Livaudais's death, and the fact that something besides his opposition to Beau had made Beau Langlinais hate him so much.

"I want to show you something," Skye said, holding his hand out to Natalie. "Get your jacket, we're going to take a drive."

"It better be good," she said, "if you're taking me away from this fire."

It was Sunday afternoon. They were all tired after the big campaign barbecue, experiencing the letdown after hours of excitement. After eleven-o'clock Mass and a noon dinner, they had scattered: Beau in his study, Caroline napping, André off with a friend, leaving Skye and Natalie to drowse by the fire until it was time to start back to Baton Rouge and New Orleans.

She remained silent beside Skye as they drove through the crisp day. The fields on either side of the road were barren, and only the live oaks were still in full leaf; the other trees held bare arms up against the wintry sky, their myriad fingers splayed. "Even in winter, there's a kind of beauty out here, isn't there?" she said as they entered St. Martinville.

"The country never loses its charm as far as I'm concerned," Skye said. He turned into a side street near the church and parked the car in front of a building that Natalie recognized as being Beau Langlinais's law office. "Here we are," Skye said, coming around to her side to help her out.

She followed him inside, watching while he opened a door and held it wide. *"Entrez, mademoiselle!"* he said with a flourish, bowing her into the room.

It was an office like any other: a desk, comfortable chairs, a long table, bookshelves. Then she saw the pictures on the desk, and on the credenza behind it. Beau and Caroline Langlinais. The Langlinais children. And her own face, looking back at her from the desk. "Skye—Skye, is this your office?"

"Sure is," he said, beaming. "What do you think?"

She sank into one of the chairs placed near the desk and stared at him. "But—you haven't finished law school yet!"

"I only have one course left," he said. He perched on the desk in front of her. "I got to thinking—seems kind of silly to be stuck in Baton

Rouge all week when I only have that one seminar on Monday afternoons. When Papa said he was going to run for Congress, we decided that, while I can't practice yet, I can begin to take care of some of the family business—and look after the private clients he has, at least in terms of getting things ready for Papa to handle."

"I didn't realize your father had that many private clients."

"There are a number of families he looks after. It's not the most exciting kind of law, but at least I'll be getting the feel of it. What do you think?"

She stood up and put her arms around him. "I think it's wonderful. It's a great office—the only thing I question is that enormous picture of me."

"You're my inspiration," Skye said. He pulled her close and kissed her.

"Wait. You're going to be down here most of the time now."

"Well, yes. That's the whole point."

"Then we'll almost never see each other. Going back and forth from Baton Rouge to New Orleans is manageable—but this will be impossible, with my schedule."

"That's the main drawback," Skye said. "I'll keep my apartment in Baton Rouge, and I'll be there one day a week for class. I'm sure other reasons for going there will come up."

"But when you do finish—you'll practice here."

"Of course."

"I . . . I had a silly kind of hope you might . . . move to New Orleans."

"Natalie, Papa's had a sign reading 'Langlinais and Langlinais' since I entered law school."

"I know. I said it was silly." She picked up a bronze letter opener and ran her finger along its edge. "Maybe I should ask Ben Roberts to let me be a stringer down here."

She saw the quick hope in his eyes and was instantly sorry. "I shouldn't have said that, Skye. I'm beginning to make a little headway at the *Picayune*—I'm going to be there a while longer."

"I never thought you wouldn't," he said. "You might enjoy being a stringer here more than you think. Small towns can produce some good stories."

"I'm sure of that." She replaced the letter opener and pretended to study the bas relief on a pair of bookends. "I want—I want to make a name for myself, Skye. I want people to see my byline and recognize it. I guess that sounds pretty—I don't know—glory-hunting. But it's not glory I want. It's—"

"Success," he offered. "Accomplishment. Look, Natalie, you have as much right to want those things as I do. I'm not happy that your job is in

New Orleans and mine is here—but if that's the way it is, that's the way it is."

She felt suddenly uncertain. "I'm going to miss you," she said, wanting to hear him say the same words.

"I always miss you," he said. He pulled her to him, kissing her with the familiar passion that closed out everything but Skye. She pressed against him, letting all thought melt in her answering desire.

"Let's leave now, so we can get to New Orleans sooner," he whispered.

"Oh, yes," she said.

"I don't have class until three o'clock tomorrow," he said.

"I don't have to be at the paper until noon."

"I think we can manage to put the time to good use," he said.

They did, spending a luxurious morning in bed that seemed better because the rest of the world was at work. But when Skye left for Baton Rouge and she caught the streetcar to work, she added on the distance from Baton Rouge to St. Martinville to the miles that had marked the space between them. He's getting further and further away, she thought. And then another thought came to her, one that almost frightened her. You're about to find something out, she told herself. You're about to find out whether your love for Skye or your career is more important. Because while he says he'll come see you often—and maybe he even will, at first—by the time he's been practicing six months, how much time will he have free? And how much will he even want to come?

23

APRIL–MAY 1950

Beau Langlinais paused on the steps leading from the gallery to the front lawn, watching the party surge around him. What had begun as a small gathering to welcome Henri home had blossomed into a reception for all their old friends and relatives; the party had been moved from the farm to Beau Chêne, where a number of houseguests were already staying.

He made his way slowly down the steps, pausing to speak to people on the way up to the gallery where a band played for dancing, intending to find Caroline and get her to come dance with him. He stopped to speak to young Dr. Jaubert, the son of the old doctor who had treated the Langlinaises for years. "Paul, good to see you," Beau said. "Glad you could make it."

"I almost didn't," Jaubert said. "An ugly case this afternoon—young woman died after an abortion." He had lowered his voice, but Natalie, standing in the shadows of one of the tall columns, overheard him, and turned in time to see Beau's shocked face.

"An abortion! Who performed it, Paul? Do you know?"

Dr. Jaubert moved closer to Beau, and Natalie leaned against the column, wondering if she should let them know she was there.

"Has to be that same woman whose work crops up from time to time."

"Dammit, can't you get her?"

"I'm going to try this time," Jaubert said. "I've already talked to Conrad. He's willing to prosecute if I can get a solid witness. He's tired of bringing her to trial and having it explode in his face."

"I'll talk to him," Beau said. "He's a good district attorney, but he doesn't have a lot of help. Maybe I can do something."

"Beau, you're campaigning for Congress. You don't have time to get involved with a mess like this."

"I'll be the judge of that, Paul," Beau said. Natalie could not see his face, but she heard the deep anger in his voice, and was puzzled. Why would Beau Langlinais get mixed up with what could only be a highly emotional, tension-filled trial? If, she thought, remembering the doctor's words, it even got that far. She saw Skye coming toward her with two glasses, and went to meet him, leaving Beau and Dr. Jaubert with their heads together in low-voiced conversation.

"What's the matter?" Skye asked. "You look upset."

"Nothing," she said. And then, because the tenor of Beau's conversation with Dr. Jaubert really bothered her, she said, "I overheard your father and Dr. Jaubert talking just now. A girl died of an illegal abortion today—and it sounds very much as though your father's going to help prosecute it."

"You're joking! In the middle of a campaign?"

"That's what Dr. Jaubert asked him. Skye, he sounded dead serious."

"It beats me," Skye said. "Must be that woman who operates between here and Breaux Bridge. She masks her operation by calling herself a midwife, but I guess everyone knows what she really does."

"For heaven's sake!" Natalie stopped in the middle of the lawn, her eyes wide with shock. "You mean it's known that the woman performs abortions, and no one does a thing about it?"

"You've got to catch her, Natalie. The girls that live—well, they're not about to say anything. The girls that don't—most of the time, their families aren't going to say anything either. They don't want to add shame to their grief. I guess the difference with this one is that she died at the hospital, and Jaubert was there."

"It sounds like a mess," Natalie said. "I admire your father wanting to do something—but it seems very ill-advised."

"The district attorney may be able to handle it," Skye said. "The whole thing will hinge on whether they can get a witness. If they can't—" He shrugged. "They've got no case."

"Even though the girl died."

"They've got to be able to place the girl in the woman's house, with the instruments in the woman's hands. Once before she was brought to trial, and the state's witness decided at the last minute to change her mind. And there went the case."

"Somehow, I don't think of things like that happening out here," Natalie said. She waved her hand around her, taking in the glowing Japanese lanterns that lit the grounds, the laden tables, the entire gracious scene. "This should be proof against that kind of ugliness."

"Well, it's not," Skye said. "I don't suppose there's a corner of the world that is." He smiled at her and added in a challenging tone, "I told you small-town stringers come upon newsworthy stories."

"I realize that," Natalie said.

"But the call of the big city is still too strong?"

"Skye—"

"Sorry. I won't pester you. Now." He took her face in his hands and kissed her lightly. "But I won't promise that once I'm all graduated and settled here I won't mount a campaign you'll find hard to resist. Even if I have to cook up some enormous story to tempt you with."

"Is Skye giving you trouble?" Henri said. "Sorry. Am I interrupting something?"

"Yes," Skye said, "but since you're the prodigal son this evening, I'll forgive you."

"Henri, you look so good," Natalie said. "Life in Guatemala must have agreed with you."

"I was surprised at how well it did," Henri said. They had all remarked the change in his appearance. He seemed taller; he was certainly heavier and darker, his muscles developed and his skin tanned. He walked vigorously and spoke with a new energy that seemed to have utterly dispelled his tendency to be moody. "In fact, the whole life at the mission became so attractive that I made a decision. I'm going to talk to Mama and Père about it later—but if you don't mind, I'd like to try it out on you first."

"What is it?" Skye asked.

"I've decided to become a Jesuit," Henri said.

"A priest!"

"Does it shock you? It kind of shocked me at first. I mean, I never really thought of myself as the type of person who becomes a priest."

"I wouldn't think there was any one type of person," Skye said. "I think you'll be a fine priest." He slapped Henri's shoulder and grinned. "At least in the confessional you won't be one of those priests who act like they were born wearing cassocks."

"There's Caro," Henri said. "I'd like to tell her, too." He caught her eye and beckoned her over to them. "I've been sharing some news with Skye and Natalie," he said. "I'm going to enter the Jesuit seminary."

"Henri! But that's wonderful!" She hugged him and kissed his cheek, her spontaneous enthusiasm lighting her face.

"It's a little scary," he said. "But since it takes twelve years to become a Jesuit, I'll have plenty of time to think it over."

"You'll be fine," Caro said. "I can't say I ever thought about you being a priest—but somehow, it has the right feeling about it. One of those ideas that the minute you hear it, you know it's sound."

"You're a love, do you know that, Caro?" Henri said. He sounded choked, and Skye could see that he was about to be overcome with emotion.

"You haven't told us a thing about Guatemala," he said. "What was it like, Henri?"

"Primitive, of course. But beautiful, very beautiful. You'd be amazed, Caro, at some of the native crafts. I brought some of the weaving done by the Indians near Oxaca. And then the ruins—" Henri was off on what both Caro and Skye knew would be an anthropological and archaeological survey of Guatemalan culture. They smiled at each other.

"Good old Prof Henri," Skye whispered to Caro.

She laughed, and nodded her head. Henri was going to become a Jesuit, she thought, mulling the idea over in her mind. The Jesuits were famous for the extensiveness of their religious and intellectual training. They might also be called the Talmudists of the Catholic Church, she thought. Another idea came to her and she turned to look at Henri speculatively. Not right now, of course. It was too soon to ask him. But after he'd been in the seminary awhile—mightn't she give him a problem to pose to his teachers? If you had a couple who loved each other very much, and the man was Jewish and the woman was Catholic—how could they marry so as to satisfy the religious principles of both?

Caro lifted the last painting and set it on the easel, then stood back to look at the double line of works filling the East Gallery of Koenberg's facility. She had returned from Louisiana the last week of April and had worked with the same intensity that had kept her at her easel for long hours daily during January, February, and March. Now, at the end of May, the series was finished. She had deliberately not viewed it in its entirety until now, when she felt finally detached from the creative process and able to be at least a little objective.

At first she could not separate the thirty paintings into entities; she saw only color, shape, form. Then, slowly, her vision focused, and she picked out individual points: this bit of shading, that bit of composition. Her breath seemed to fill her body; she was caught by the force emanating from her work—for one long moment she was at one with it, her soul embracing its spirit, her essence part of her work's light. She hung on the edge of conviction—could it really be as good as she thought it was?

So intense was her concentration that she did not hear Koenberg come in behind her. She had asked him to set up thirty easels, to let her place the new series in the order in which she wanted them viewed before he saw them. Now he came into the East Gallery and stood quietly, seeing first the impact of the whole series. His eyes ran rapidly down one row, up another. Caro had angled the easels slightly, so that a viewer entering the East Gallery could follow the double line, ending at the large central painting that dominated the crux of the two lines. As the theme emerged, as Koenberg realized what it was he was looking at, an almost unbearable tension gripped him. "My child," he said, moving forward and taking Caro's arm. "My dear child—what is this you have done?"

"Is it . . . not good?" she asked, turning anxiously.

"That word has no meaning when applied to this," he said. He took her hand, and she could feel her own intenseness coming back to her from him. "Let us look at them. Let me see what this is that you have been working on so long. If individually the works hold up to the impression of the whole." He patted her hand. "Let us begin."

The first five paintings had come out of those elegant sketches she had done at Beau Chêne. They showed people drinking tea in airy gazebos, playing croquet on lush green lawns, dancing in golden ballrooms, sailing on bright blue seas, dining by candlelight. The colors used were soft pastels, the light clear and shadowless. Lifting the works from the ordinary was a certain tautness in the body lines, a certain intelligence in the faces. The vitality that flowed through them charged them with an energy that made the viewer ask: And then? And then?

The same figures appeared in the next five paintings, again presented in familiar settings. Picnics in forest glades, women tying on hats, two mothers walking with their children—but in this set, the figures were slightly apart, their faces averted, their bodies carving out separate spaces on the canvas. The light had lost some of its clarity; shadows obscured the outer reaches of each scene, and the vitality that had charged the first five paintings had subtly changed, until there seemed to be two forces in each canvas, opposing each other and creating conflict.

The conflict intensified in the next five works. The mothers walked past each other, their children huddled against them. People dining in restaurants had their backs squarely to each other, a young lady rejected a suitor's bouquet, an employer stood frowning over a worker. There were no pastels in the palette of colors. Each had been darkened with ombré, and the shadows at the edges of each scene were now dominant, seeming to emerge from the very beings they obscured.

Koenberg sucked in his cheeks, making little kissing noises in the air. "I had no idea," he said. "You said you were working on something new—something very big. But, my dear Caro, this is marvelous. Do you have any idea just how marvelous it is?"

"No," she said. "I . . . Oh, Louis, is it really good?"

He bent and kissed her cheek, then looked at her solemnly. "It is much better than good, Caro. Much, much better." He patted her hand again and then tucked it beneath his arm. "Now—let us see the rest."

The large painting at the angle was dark in the center, and lit at the edges by a fiery light that glowed with red-gold brilliance. The figures were only shades lighter than the dark foreground, emerging as two tight groups in angular formations that opposed each other, splitting the paintings in two. In the next four paintings, the figures from the earlier scenes returned, in the same settings. But the gazebos now had machine guns mounted in them, the croquet wickets were crushed under marching boots, refugees flooded the golden ballroom, and the sailboat was loaded with people and their possessions, the people desperately bailing to keep the boat afloat. Light and shadow chased each other across the canvases; the composition was tortured, and the clear conflict had become chaos.

The five central paintings in the line showed railroad stations with lavish private cars on a siding and cattle cars of human beings on the main track; women from the earlier paintings lived in brothels serving uniformed men; children who had romped in forest glades cowered in alleys with yellow Stars of David stitched to their clothes. In the last of the group, a small cluster of worshipers gathered around a Catholic altar, furtively looking over their shoulders for the stormtroopers who patrolled outside.

And then came the last five, and Caro felt Koenberg's fingers tighten on her arm, digging into her flesh until she could feel his nails through the cloth of her sleeve. She tried to see them with his eyes, tried to see them for the first time—the naked women, trying to cover themselves with bony hands. The children walking two by two toward a small square building. The men digging a common grave under the guns that would be used to execute them. And then the last painting. The fiery red-gold light that had darted through each of the last fifteen paintings filled this one. It burned everything before it—shards of teapots, the mast of a sailboat, fleeing human figures—the flames seemed to leap from the canvas and lick at the viewer, threatening to devour anyone who came too near.

Koenberg turned and took Caro into his arms. His face was against hers, and she could feel his tears mingling with her own. "My child," he said. "My dear child. I did not know that you knew."

Caro felt the tension that had kept her stretched into sleeplessness all last night let go, and she allowed herself to relax against the old man's shoulder. He was openly sobbing now, and she knew he was thinking of his own friends and relatives who had not escaped the red-gold flames called the Holocaust. "I . . . I wasn't sure I did," she said. "I felt . . . almost presumptuous."

"Presumptuous!" He stood straight and gazed at the paintings. "My dear child, you have taken what was a terrible experience for our people—and you have made it a part of all mankind." He bent and kissed her cheek. "David will be very proud," he said. "We must wait to have the opening when he returns."

"Oh, Louis, could we? He's due home in a little over a month—"

"But of course we will wait." He smiled down at her. "For such an artist, is there anything I will not do?"

24

JUNE 1950

Ben Roberts stopped at Natalie's desk and handed her a sheaf of copy. "What do you make of that?" he asked.

She read the pages quickly, trying to keep the emotion she was feeling from showing in her face. The story had been written by the *Picayune* stringer in St. Martin Parish; it concerned the trial of a local midwife accused of performing a fatal abortion, but its focus was on Beau Langlinais, who had joined the prosecuting team by being sworn in as an assistant to the district attorney. "I don't know," she said, giving Roberts the copy.

"Doesn't it seem strange to you that he'd get himself involved in something like this?" the editor said. "Middle of a campaign, emotional issue, local family's name dragged in—"

"I agree," Natalie said. "It does seem strange. But after all, Beau Langlinais is well-known in that district. It's not as though he has to start from scratch in his campaign. I suppose this trial is important to him."

"Must be," Roberts said. "I'm not going to blow this thing out of proportion. Not even going to send anyone down there. Let the stringer handle it. Tell you what I think, though."

"What's that?" Her hands were poised on the keys of her typewriter, ready to get on with the story she was writing.

"I think Beau probably has a friend who lost a daughter through an abortion. Something like that. He's emotionally involved—why else would he take this on? You can hardly come out and say a thing like that—but it would be the best reason I know for his involvement during a campaign."

"You're probably right," Natalie said, and went back to her story. She and Skye had never discussed the abortion trial again after the night of Henri's party; what she knew of it, she had learned from the papers. The dead girl's parents had agreed to testify, and the case seemed fairly solid. The story she'd just read had been a summation of the trial as it went to the jury. Beau's final speech had been impassioned, and Natalie found that the sound of his voice as he talked with Dr. Jaubert, so filled with anger, stayed in her mind all afternoon. She left work late, walking toward the streetcar stop through the warm June evening. The pavement was hot, and the small breeze stirred up dust from the gutters and bits of paper from the street. A long, cool shower and a long, cool drink, she thought. Skye had taken the bar exam today; she looked at her watch and counted the time left before she could expect him here in New Orleans.

"I'll be there with my shield or on it," he had told her. Of course he wouldn't get the results today, but she had champagne chilling anyway. Skye had graduated in the top five percent of his class; celebrating his passing the bar might be premature, but it was safe.

While she was brushing her hair and putting on fresh makeup something Ben Roberts said struck her. "Beau probably has a friend who lost a daughter through an abortion." The hand holding the tube of lipstick paused, and she stared at her face in the mirror. Was it a friend? Or had Beau Langlinais himself lost someone that way? Not a child. Who?

Stop it, she told herself. This is exactly the aspect of journalism you hate, all the legitimate questions that lead to dark alleys like a crow to carrion. The image disgusted her, and she switched on the radio and made herself think of something else. But her mind had hold of the question of Beau Langlinais's trial, and it wouldn't let it go, no matter how hard she tried to put it elsewhere.

Skye arrived just as the evening began to cool: she took that as an omen. By earlier agreement, they gave the night over to celebration, beginning with champagne and steaks grilled on Natalie's tiny patio, and progressing to a night of lovemaking. Skye was tired from the exams but exhilarated that the final segment of his long preparation for the law was over. "Do I look different?" he asked, raising himself up so he could see himself in the dressing table mirror. "I feel very old and very wise."

"You look very sexy," Natalie said. "In a wise kind of way," she added teasingly.

"Say, I forgot to tell you because I was so involved thinking about the exams. I got a letter from George Harris, the black pilot I met in Biloxi."

"He was in the Ninety-ninth Pursuit Squadron, wasn't he?"

"Yes," Skye said. "What a memory. Well, he's coming to Louisiana in a week or so to interview at Southern Law School. He's been working with his father in insurance—but George thinks he'd like to get a law degree. Be good to see him again."

"I can just see you trying to take him to the Heidelberg Hotel and getting turned away at the door."

"I'm going to tell him to come to my apartment. It's a hell of a note when two old war buddies can't even go drink a beer together. I'll just lay in a supply, and we'll have our reunion at home."

"I'd like to meet him," Natalie said, and when Skye looked at her, eyebrow raised, she said, "No, really. He's another little part of what makes you tick, Skye. And I find myself fascinated by each one."

"Let's see if I can fascinate you here and now," he said, turning to her.

Several days later, while checking a date of birth at the Bureau of Vital Statistics for a biography on an early civic leader, Natalie found herself going to the files for the year 1922. Stop this right now, she told herself, even as she flipped through the cards to find the deaths recorded on July 16. Her hand pulled a death certificate with the name "Langlinais, Françoise Alicia" from the file, and then stopped. She could put the notice back where it came from, take her information, and flee back to the *Picayune*. Were it not that the Bureau of Vital Statistics had remained in New Orleans when many other state offices had moved to Baton Rouge, the St. Martin records would not even be here. I have to know, she thought, and took the notice over to the light so she could read the faded ink. She scanned the lines until she came to the cause of death. "Internal hemorrhage from causes unknown," she read. She slumped against the sill, feeling sick. She heard Beau's voice: "Oh, yes. Livaudais's kingdom came tumbling down. By the time it did, I had other reasons to hate him. And by then, nothing that happened to him seemed enough."

She thought of Charles Livaudais, of the house on Dumaine Street, and of the dark-haired young girl neighbors reported having seen going there. Oh, no, she thought, stumbling back to replace the file. My God.

All the way back to the *Picayune* an image she had once formed of her career in journalism kept returning—her mind like an iceberg, the depths hiding the ugly bits and pieces of other people's lives, with only the tip clear and pure.

"George is late," Skye said, looking at his watch again.

"He probably misjudged how long it would take to get here," Natalie said. "You know how it is when you're driving in a strange place."

"Still, he said he'd be here by midafternoon. It's almost six."

"He could have had car trouble, Skye."

They had both driven into Baton Rouge at noon, meeting at Skye's apartment. By the time they had shopped for groceries and had lunch, it was nearly three o'clock. They had been waiting for George minute by minute ever since.

They played a game of gin, and had started on a second when the telephone rang. "George," Skye said with relief, and reached to answer it.

"Hello," he said. He heard a faint voice, its clarity blurred by the cacophony of noise in the background. Then the voice became louder, and he heard George, sounding at once strange and familiar.

"Skye, is that you?"

"George! I've been worried to death. Where the hell are you?"

Natalie saw Skye's hand tighten on the phone.

"You're *where*?"

"In the West Feliciana Parish jail, Skye. I was arrested a couple of hours ago. They say I killed a woman. Some white lady."

George's voice stopped, but the fear it held pulsed in Skye's ear.

"All right, George," Skye said, making his voice steady. "I'm on my way. Don't say another word to anyone, you hear me? Let me talk to whoever is in charge."

His free hand tapped restlessly on the table while he waited; when he heard a new voice on the line, he spoke rapidly, biting the words. "This is Skye Langlinais. I'm George Harris's attorney. Langlinais. What's that? Yes. He's my father." Then Skye's face reddened, and his gray eyes were suddenly furious. "Watch yourself," he barked into the phone. "And take good care of my client, you hear me? I'll be there within the hour—and he'd better be all right."

Skye slammed the phone back into the cradle. "George is under arrest," he said. "They're holding him in the St. Francisville jail. I've got to get there right away."

"Skye, my God! What for?"

"He's charged with rape and murder."

"Oh, my God! But he was on his way here—"

"That's all I know. I'll just toss my gear together and let you close the apartment if you don't mind. And could you call Émilie for me? Tell her what's happened—and that I'm going to need a place to sleep tonight?"

"Of course. Skye, there has to be a mistake."

Skye returned to the living room moments later, his overnight bag swinging from his hand. The bleakness in his eyes made her weak. A line of stories, of headlines breaking horror into manageable syllables, rose before her. Lynchings. Beatings. Kangaroo courts. Her mouth was dry, her throat constricted. "You go on, Skye. I'll see to things here. And I'll call Émilie." She rose and went to him. "But, Skye, for God's sake, call me in New Orleans as soon as you know anything!"

"I will," he said. He put his arms around her; she buried her head in his chest and clung to him for a moment before letting him go. And then he was gone, running down the steps, tossing his bag in the back of his car and heading down the driveway in a spray of pea gravel.

She let the screen door bang behind her and sat disconsolately on the couch, a freshly lit cigarette in her hand. Smoke still drifted up from the cigarette Skye had crushed out hastily, and she reached over and finished putting it out, feeling the paper tube break and crumble against the glass tray. She felt numb, as though only by paying attention to the smallest details could she absorb the larger one: George Harris, on his way to a reunion with his Air Force buddy, had been arrested for rape and murder. Of a white woman.

And Skye, just over a week away from his bar exams, was hurtling up U.S. 51 to St. Francisville, a shining knight whose armor was his innocence and whose only sword was his belief in his friend.

The forty-minute drive to St. Francisville gave Skye time to get hold of himself and to review what it was he had to do. The first thing, of course, was to see George. And then he must have George brought before the judge, so that bond could be set and a trial date determined. If, he thought grimly, this can't be cleared up and the charges dismissed immediately. If George were freed, it still would not be over—Skye would make the arresting officers defend their behavior, would make them prove to him, in a court of law if necessary, that George was not just picked up and brought in because he was a strange black man driving through a place where everyone, black and white, is known, and where strangers, especially dark ones, had better have answers for any curious questioners.

If George were not freed—and he felt that he must prepare both of them for this—then his work was clearly cut out for him, a whole summer of it, in all probability. His thoughts flew to his father, back on the campaign trail now that the abortion trial was over. The jury had voted for conviction, but the vote had been hard-bargained for, and now that the first tide of moral righteousness has passed, people blamed Beau Langlinais for airing in public something long tolerated secretly as not really good, but often necessary. The dead girl's parents, finding that testifying against the woman had been rewarded with an open discussion of their daughter's shame, blamed Beau for talking them into going to the prosecutor to begin with. All in all, Beau had gotten little for his pains except the honest praise of his friends and a few others and the almost universal opinion that he had stuck his nose into something that did not concern him. No, he couldn't ask Papa to get involved in this one.

The last thing his father needed now was to defend a black man accused of raping, then killing a white woman. The storm that would create could damage his campaign. If Skye even hinted he needed help, his father would be there like a shot. I'll just have to go it alone, Skye thought, pulling up in front of the courthouse and heading around to the jail.

He gave his name to the man at the desk, and stood waiting until the sheriff came out of an inner office and stood in front of him, taking his measure.

"So you're his lawyer."

"I am," Skye said. "And I'd like to see my client now, please."

"You're going to see him. Just hold your horses. I want to make sure you and I understand each other." He waited a moment, but when Skye said nothing, he went on. "The way I see it, I've got a job and you've got a job. My job is to make sure your client is around to stand trial, and your job is to see to it he cooperates with the system we've got here. I'm not making any judgments about your client, I don't give a damn about him one way or the other. He's here, he's my prisoner. But I get the idea that he thinks he's a little better than the common run of niggers we get in here. And what you need to make sure he understands is that, while it don't matter to me what he thinks, he's going to make his life pretty miserable if the white deputies and the black trusties get the idea he's too high-and-mighty to fit in. I don't have to say any more, do I?"

"I think that covers it," Skye said. He was grateful for the drive; his temper was in check now. He followed the sheriff into the row of cells with outward calm.

George lay on the bare mattress that covered an iron cot bolted into the brick wall. "Skye! Thanks for coming."

"You couldn't have kept me away," he said. He waited until the sheriff had vanished back into his office before sitting next to George on the cot.

"All right, George. We don't have any time to waste. I want you to tell me the whole story, in as much detail as you can remember. Take your time. Don't leave anything out."

"I didn't do it, Skye."

"I believe that."

Harris stared at Skye; his eyes brightened, and Skye felt that whatever mechanism had helped George cocoon himself from the reality of his situation was reversing itself. George's vitality seemed to be returning. Thank God, Skye thought, because that and George's courage were the only allies they had.

"I drove into Louisiana on Fifty-one, coming down from Natchez," George said. "I'd packed a lunch, and I ate in the car about halfway between Natchez and St. Francisville. I didn't plan on stopping again until I got to your place." There was only the slightest pause, but Skye knew what the pause meant. George had packed a lunch because there was nowhere he could buy a meal; he did not plan to stop because, except for the open country, there was nowhere he would be welcome. Skye forced his mind away from the thought of traveling in the summertime without being able to go into a roadside café for a cool drink and a wash.

"All right. Then what?" he said quietly.

"The car began to heat up. I have trouble with it from time to time, there's probably a slow leak somewhere. Since I didn't know how far I was from a service station, and damn sure didn't want the radiator to boil over out in the boondocks, I decided I'd stop at the next place I came to and see if I could get some water."

George swallowed, and licked his lips, as though remembering how he had felt that morning, on a hot, empty road, with car trouble, and no help in sight. "I thought I was lucky—around the next curve was a farmhouse, fairly neat-looking place. I pulled up into the drive—not too far, just in from the road—and went up and knocked on the door."

The air in the cell was close, stale, but Skye was transported to the still morning, to George standing on a strange porch knocking on a strange door, the silence of the unfamiliar and unknown sealing him away from the road. "This man answered the door, and I asked him if I could get some water from the faucet. I could see it from where I stood. He said go ahead, but to be sure I turned it off good when I finished. He watched me while I got the can I always carry out of my car, and filled it, and then funneled the water into the radiator. Then I left."

"What did you do then?"

"I kept driving on toward Baton Rouge. I passed through St. Francisville, must have been maybe ten miles on the other side when I hear sirens behind me, and I look, and there's a couple of cars bearing down. There's no one else on the road, and although I don't see how they can be after me—I stop."

Again the thick, hot silence of the deserted country road seemed to close about them; Skye could feel sweat trickling down his back, and he imagined sweat pouring down Harris's face and arms as he waited for the men to leave their cars and approach him.

"They told me to get out of my car with my hands up. They searched for weapons, and then they handcuffed me and brought me on in. One of the deputies drove my car—I guess it's out there somewhere."

"I'll see that it's released to me," Skye said. "I'll get it put somewhere safe."

"Does that mean you think I'm stuck here for a while?"

"I won't know a thing until we get before the judge," Skye said. "I haven't even talked to the sheriff yet. I wanted to hear your story first, get my perspective from that rather than what they'll tell me."

"They're going to tell you a lot," Harris said. "It's a hell of a story, Skye."

"I better talk to them now," Skye said. He rose and looked down at Harris. "You need anything?"

"Other than getting out? No, I'm all right."

"I'll leave these cigarettes," Skye said. "And I'll be back to see you before I leave."

The quick panic in George's eyes frightened Skye too. "Look, I know some people up here who have some influence. I'm going to call them, have them make it clear that you're to be guarded like the crown jewels, all right?"

George's eyes went to the barred windows. "Thanks. Those bars look like the kind that can keep me in, all right. But I'm not sure who'd they'd keep out—if anyone was bound and determined to get in."

"No one's going to get in," Skye said. "And if we can get before a judge tomorrow, you might be out on bond by afternoon." But as he rapped on the cell bars for the deputy, his early hope that this could easily be cleared up was almost gone.

"You see your client all right?" Sheriff Lockwood asked, putting the slightest derisive emphasis on "client."

"Yes, thank you," Skye said. "I've heard what he has to say. Now I'd like to hear why he's here."

"You know why he's here. He raped and murdered Whitney Hale's wife, Merlene."

"Is that what he's charged with?"

"Don't play games with me, Langlinais. You know damn well that's what he's charged with."

"I haven't read the charges. I haven't read any statements—"

Sheriff Lockwood opened a file folder, removed a sheet of paper, and shoved it at Skye. "There's the charges. You see what Hale says. His daughter saw Harris leaving the lean-to, he ran in, found his wife beaten, raped—and dead."

"Where was Hale when this alleged attack took place?"

"You want to read the whole thing?"

"I'd like to."

"You'll have to wait until tomorrow. It's not typed up yet, won't be until the morning."

"All right. In your own words. Where was Hale?"

"In a field. His daughter was between the house and the field. She sees the nigger coming out of the lean-to, she yells at her pa, he runs after him, the nigger gets in his car and hightails it out of there."

"And then?"

"Then Hale finds his wife, like I said. She's a mess—the coroner says he hasn't seen many worse." The sheriff looked at Skye. "You sure you want to handle this case, Langlinais?"

"And then what?" Skye said, ignoring him.

"So then Hale calls us. Tells us to look for a nigger driving a forty-nine Chevy sedan—yellow with white sidewalls. Fancy damn car. I guess he can afford a fancy white lawyer."

"And that's it?"

"You want pictures? Busy as he was beating up on Merlene, he didn't have time for pictures."

"Could I make a few calls?"

"You going to run up my bill?"

"They're local," Skye said.

The sheriff shrugged, and Skye picked up the phone. When he was connected with Émilie, he spoke in a loud voice, making sure that the sheriff, who was reading the paper, heard him. "Émilie. It's Skye. Did Natalie call you? Right. Listen, I'll be there in about an hour. My client is a little concerned that this incident might have people . . . stirred up. I wonder if Fielding would mind coming down here? I'd like him to meet George, give him a little reassurance. Would he do that, do you think? All right. I'll wait."

"You having a party down here?" the sheriff asked when Skye hung up.

"I asked my brother-in-law to come meet George Harris. You probably know him. Fielding Horton?"

"You kin to Fielding?"

"His wife is my sister."

"Fielding's all right," the sheriff said. He took the papers from Skye and stuffed them back in the folder. "I hunt some with Fielding." He looked at Skye. "You're not dumb, are you, Langlinais?"

"I hope not," Skye said.

"Listen, you could have just said you were kin to Fielding. You didn't have to get him down here."

"I want him to meet George," Skye said. "If that's all right with you."

"Oh, it's all right with me," the sheriff said.

They smoked in silence until Fielding arrived, large, blond, skin and hair showing the effects of hours in the sun. "Sorry there's trouble," he said, holding out his hand. He held up a paper bag. "Émilie sent some sandwiches and things. Tide your client over."

"Thanks," Skye said. "Sheriff Lockwood, would you take us back?"

Sheriff Lockwood came around his desk, hand outstretched. "Fielding. Your brother-in-law and I have been talking about this case. I guess you heard all about it on the news—it's not a good one."

"Murder never is," Fielding said. "I haven't had a chance to talk to Skye, so I'll tell him now. We're civilized people up here, and our prisoners don't have to fear for their lives."

"That's right," Lockwood said. "Of course, sometimes people get excited, try to stir up trouble—"

"And the rest of us dampen them down," Fielding said. "Let's go see Harris now, Lockwood."

The pile of half-smoked cigarettes at George's feet testified to his nervous state; he stood up and greeted them when they entered the cell, but he seemed agitated, not at all the man forcing himself to be calm that Skye had left a half-hour earlier.

"It's hitting me," he said, grasping Skye's hand. "Oh, Lord, Skye, I'm scared."

So am I, Skye thought. So am I.

"What's gotten into the Langlinaises?" Ben Roberts said, sitting down at the table in the coffee shop where Natalie sat. "First Beau gets himself mixed up with an abortionist's trial and now dammit if Skye Langlinais isn't defending a Negro accused of rape and murder up in West Feliciana. I want you to go on up there and cover this trial."

"Ben, you know I . . . date Skye."

"That's not going to affect the outcome of the trial."

"Why me? It's not that big a story."

"It could be. It's not as if George Harris were some local man who's been in trouble before. He's got a good background, he served in the Air Force, saw action in the war—hell, Natalie, I think this can be a good story." He drained his mug and looked at her over the rim. "The war changed things in this country for good. Men who were in the service won't go back to second-class citizenship. There's no way to predict what will happen up there—but whatever it is, it might just be a straw in the wind of things to come."

"Skye talked about that same thing during the war," Natalie said. "How you couldn't ask a man to defend rights and privileges he didn't have."

"I agree." He stood up. "Now—you can book in at the hotel up there—"

"I have an uncle in St. Francisville. I can stay with him."

"Better and better. Things get hot, you call me. We'll send an artist up, some photographers."

"It's all so ridiculous, Ben. Here George Harris is on his way to meet Skye in Baton Rouge—and he's supposed to have stopped and killed a woman?"

"Doesn't matter what I think. Only matters what the jury thinks. Get some money, Natalie. You'll need to eat." He set his empty cup down and left the room, leaving Natalie to finish her lunch. But the chicken salad was tasteless, the Coke suddenly flat. She dumped the remains of her sandwich in the trash barrel and went back to her typewriter, part of her mind already in St. Francisville with Skye.

He called her that evening. She could hear the frustration in his voice; enough had come out at the hearing that afternoon to make it impossible for George Harris to walk away, and the judge had refused to set bail.

"The district attorney, a guy named McPherson, quoted the daughter of the dead woman as saying that not only did she see George coming out of the shed where they found her mother's body, but he was holding his pants up and running like the dickens." Skye sighed, a long, exhausted sound that made her want to hold him. "So then McPherson looks at me, and looks at George, and looks at the judge, and says that he doesn't know how anyone else feels, but he doesn't want to see a nigger—pardon me, *Negro,* running loose on bond who can't keep his pants buttoned when white ladies are around."

"Oh, Skye!"

"The judge didn't like it any better, I'll say that for him. Name's Charles Rowland. Papa says he has a good reputation. But he still didn't allow bond."

"So George is still in jail."

"I asked for a speedy trial, and thank God, we've got a fairly early date."

"When?"

"End of July. Trial starts the twenty-fourth."

"That's almost five weeks. Does that give you enough time?"

"It's got to. The longer this thing sits, the worse it's going to be. Little place like this, a rape-murder's not just a nine-day wonder. I won't go into the grisly details, but the body was a mess, and when the jury sees the pictures—it could be all up with George. What's driving me nuts, Natalie, is that he didn't do it. You'd think the fact that he's educated and talks well and has a good war record would be in his favor—but it's not, to most of the people up here. If he's not Step-and-Fetch-It, then he's an uppity black, and they can't handle that. Fielding's helped some; I'm not afraid of George being lynched anymore. But I don't have any illusions about what's going to happen when the trial begins."

Natalie shifted the receiver to the other ear and then lit a cigarette off the end of the one in her hand. She was smoking too much and eating too little; she could attribute it to the heat, and to job pressures, but she knew the real trouble was that she wanted Skye. "Skye, you may be new, but you're good. You're smart, you're tough—and when you get your teeth into something, you don't let go."

"That may be. But a lot of people think I'm on the wrong side of this particular war. What's worst of all is that I know how scared, I mean really scared, George is. I can feel it in the cell with us. His fear. Mine. But I get to walk out: he has to stay, and I guess that's the worst of all. Every time I step out into the air, a free man, I realize all over again what it must mean to be black. Which is presumptuous, because there's no way I can. I keep thinking of your feeling that we Langlinaises live in a kingdom—and though you're too polite to say so, that we wear golden blinders, that we don't know how the rest of the world lives."

"Skye—"

"Wait, Natalie. I'm tired and I'm scared and I want you so badly I can hardly stand it, but there's something I want to tell you."

"All right." The smoke curled up around the telephone, a gentle veil closing her in with the sound of Skye's voice.

"Maybe we do seem to live in a kingdom, but if we do, we're dedicated to spreading what we have into other lives. And now I have the chance to test that, Natalie. I have the chance to see if I can make justice work. Only, when I see how great a distance there is between what I think of when I think of justice, and what these people think of, I do get discouraged. And I've broken the first rule for lawyers—don't get emotionally involved in a case. I'm in this up to my neck. I feel like so much is riding on it—George's life! And a lot of my beliefs." He stopped suddenly, paused, then said her name. "Natalie? Natalie, are you still there?"

She swallowed the sobs that choked her. "Yes, darling. I'm here."

"Are you all right? You sound funny—gosh, I didn't mean to make a speech—"

"I'm crying, Skye. But I'm all right. I'm fine. Ben Roberts has assigned me to that trial, Skye. I'm going to be right there, every single minute of it."

She heard a strangled sound, then muffled noises. She held the phone lightly, gently, cradling it against her as she would cradle him. "Are you all right, darling?" she said softly.

"I am now," he said. For the first time since he had gotten George Harris's first frantic call, he believed that he really was.

25

JUNE 1950

The first few weeks of June were among the happiest Caro had ever spent, in a way new to her. The period between the completion of the series and the opening existed out of ordinary time; busy with invitation lists, copy for the catalog, she spent a great deal of time at the gallery, and slipped away from her tasks again and again to study her work. Her first sense of accomplishment at finishing the momentous project had deepened; now she took each painting separately, standing in front of it, taking in each detail, plumbing the depths of her being to find its source.

A particularly pleasant day was spent in the company of the photographer taking pictures for the catalog and slides for her files. He was open in his admiration of her work, talking fluently about its finer technical points. At the end of the afternoon, as he was leaving, he put out his hand and shook hers vigorously. "You're one hell of an artist," he said. His eyes swept the paintings again; then he smiled at her. "And a hell of a human being."

In an odd way, she felt pregnant, or as she imagined pregnant women must feel at the very beginning. Fragile, and yet resilient and strong. Breathless, hovering at the edge of a vast new territory whose peaks could be but dimly seen and whose valleys could only be imagined. She knew that new work was stirring inside her, beginning to take life. She knew that very soon she would no longer be content with these small routines, these quietly similar days. But except for the fact that she still did not have David, this final period of waiting for him, with her work behind her, had a sweetness she could almost taste, a warmth she could bask in.

Not since high school and the countdown to graduation had she so literally counted the days; David's return date was June 30; her show would open on July 5. She posted a calendar next to her bathroom mirror, marking off another day before she went to bed each night. The solid red lines marching toward the month's end were a barometer of her mood; the longer the line of red, the higher she soared.

One evening she came home late, having gone out for an impromptu meal with Koenberg. He had smiled secretively at her the entire day, and she knew he had good news for her, news he would impart in his own time and in his own way. Whereas a year before she would have been almost mad with impatience, her new serenity made it easy to let Louis take things at his own speed. Whatever it was had already happened; her knowing or not knowing could not affect or change it. And if the news were good, why then her anticipation of it made it even better.

"I have taken a few small liberties with your work," Louis announced at supper. Louis had picked a neighborhood restaurant that cooked seafood brought in fresh each day; the same people ate there regularly, and it was yet another of the places that made San Francisco feel like home. "I have been bringing people in to look." He broke into a broad smile and reached across the table to pat her hand. "Caro, a very good gallery in Los Angeles wants the show. And another one in Santa Monica after that. I have not yet heard from my friend at Carmel, but I—"

"Louis!" The implications of what he was saying struck her, and she could only stare at him wide-eyed and speechless.

"But why would they not want this show? It is unique, wonderful in concept as well as execution."

"I never dreamed—Louis, I don't know what to say."

"Eat your abalone," Louis said, pointing to her plate. "You're letting it get cold."

She automatically picked up her fork and began to eat, her eyes still fixed on his face. "But, goodness, Louis, we must be talking about showing this series the entire fall!"

He looked at her, a cautious, considering look. "There is something else."

"More?"

"My friends and I—we believe that a series of prints should be made of this series. A very fine series, original plates, hand-pulled, all very well done."

"I don't understand—Louis, for heaven's sake! What in the world are you talking about?"

"Caro. This series is not something that can be broken up, painting by painting. It would lose all meaning. Surely you agree?"

"Of course. I never even thought of anyone buying it, Louis. That's not why I did it—"

"My dear Caro, the reason you did it is clear. The thing speaks for itself. But prints—prints would be salable, as an entire series. They would be affordable."

"But who would buy thirty prints, Louis? And of such a subject?"

"My friends and I can think of many places. To begin with, Jewish organizations have already asked to auction off a set of prints, with the money raised to go to Israel. The prints themselves would be donated to a synagogue, or hung in the organization's offices."

"Louis, you mean you have already spoken to such people? And they . . . they want my work?"

"Caro. Don't you know yet what it is you have done? You have taken an unspeakable horror, and if you have not made it comprehensible, you have at least made a beginning. A very large beginning."

"I don't know what to say, Louis. I . . . I'm overcome."

"There is only one word I want from you, my dear. Yes."

"Oh, Louis. Yes. Of course, yes."

She had driven home on a stream of exhilaration that seemed part of the night around her; the stars of the summer solstice hung brilliant in the sky, and she thought with pleasure that it was Midsummer Night's eve; June 20, and only ten days until David came home. A magic night, she told herself, taking her mail from the letter box. A night to throw wide the windows, sip wine, and gaze at the stars. She tossed her purse on a chair and riffled through her mail, discarding everything but the letters. One from Henri, one from her mother—and, oh, good, one from David.

She put them on the coffee table and went to her bedroom to change. The silk kimono, she decided, pulling its rich folds around her. She got a glass of wine and took her letters with her into her studio, settling in her favorite rocker placed so she could watch the bay. She read Henri's letter first, tales of life at the seminary. Her eyes misted from time to time at his seriousness and commitment. He mentioned a Father Connolly several times, and she made a mental note. Perhaps that was the priest to cut through the Gordian knot that kept David and her tied to their dilemma; well, they would see.

Her mother's letter gave a sketchy account of the abortion trial, saying little other than that Père had won, but that it had cost him, and that she had persuaded him to take a week off from campaigning to come to San Francisco for the opening of Caro's show. Skye had passed the bar exam, and was already involved in his first case, a murder trial. I have faith in

Skye, and so does his father, her mother went on. And though it's about to kill Beau to keep his hands off, he's promised he'll let Skye handle this one by himself. The letter ended with more cheerful news, and Caro put it away to read again later. She now turned eagerly to David's, which would, she was sure, tell her exactly what flight he was taking to come home.

The letter began abruptly. David's usually clear handwriting was hurried and almost illegible. But the meaning of the first stark sentences was immediately plain. "Jake's been wounded. A Syrian shell caught his crew; one man died, another probably won't make it, and Jake lost a leg. He's in a hospital here in Jerusalem—" She picked up the envelope and read the postmark before turning back to David's letter, her eyes not able to move fast enough. "—and in the old medical phrase, 'doing as well as can be expected.' His spirits are all right—Jake's tough. But what he doesn't know is that the other leg may have to go too—they operated, but it's still iffy. I can't leave him, Caro. I called Phil Jacobs and he says they can hang on a while longer. It's sort of day-to-day right now—" The letter fell in her lap, and she stared out at the bay.

For the last few months she had suspected that David was not really ready to come home. He had still written as though he was—but the spirit beneath the words was reluctant, and with every letter, she had felt his commitment to Israel grow. And yet, every letter was filled with his love for her, his need for her.

She got up and leaned out the window, breathing in the scent of roses blooming in the bed beneath the sill. She gazed at the water, sparkling under the moon, glittering with starlight. The night was silent, hushed. Caro took one deep breath after the other, as she tried to ease the terrible pain gripping her heart. When she was calm again, she picked up David's letter and finished reading. Again the protestations of love, again the avowals of his need for her. Which she knew he meant. She knew, too, that unless he could find a way to reconcile what he saw as his duty to his people with his love for her, they would be stalemated forever.

That can't be, she thought. She rose and went to her desk, removing a flight schedule and reading it quickly. Months ago, shortly after David had left, she had had her travel agent list the flights she could take to reach Jerusalem. "It makes me feel better to know I can be there quickly," she had said. If she packed quickly, if she called the agency first thing in the morning . . . Thank God I have a current passport, she thought. She stuck the schedule in her pocket and went to get her luggage. As she packed, she composed the telegram to send to David. "Whither thou goest, I will go," it ran. "Will arrive Jerusalem 8:30 P.M.

your time, TWA Flight 642. Please make reservations your hotel. Love, Caro."

Just before she closed her suitcase, she went back to her studio and stood holding the set of slides of her new series. She stood for a long time, feeling the small weight of the thick stack. Then she slipped them into a case, and carrying them to her room, tucked them in.

26

JULY 1950

Skye surveyed George Harris, taking in the conservative cut of his gray suit, the quiet pattern of his wine-and-blue tie.

"Will I do?" George asked. He turned slowly, head tilted and hands placed mockingly on his hips. "Is this what the nigger who knows his place wears to court?"

"George," Skye said. "I know how you feel, but—"

"No, you don't know how I feel," George said angrily. "There is no way in the world you could know how I feel."

"All right," Skye said, holding his body rigid as though to make a hard container for his own rising anger. "I don't know how you feel. I can't know how you feel. But I know one thing. You've got to keep your temper in check. Because if you don't, George—you'll do yourself in."

"I'm already done in," George said. His anger died, replaced by a note of fear that clutched at Skye's heart. "You think I don't know this trial is just going through the motions? If that bitch keeps telling that story she made up—it'll be all over."

"I'm going to try to get her to tell the truth," Skye said.

George's harsh laugh filled the cell, echoing against the brick walls. "The truth! What truth is that, Skye? White man's truth? Or black man's truth? They're not the same, Skye. No way are they the same."

"Maybe, just this once, they will be," Skye said. He fought the words that tumbled against his lips. He remembered what Natalie had said when he had complained that he didn't know how much longer he could take the D.A.'s apathy on the one hand and George's wrath on the other. "But you're all George has, Skye. God, Skye, when I think of what he's up against—"

Yes. There was always that. A small bright room with a green door. The chair, heavily wired. The quick slitting of trousers so clamps could be attached to bare skin. The hood slipped down over the face.

Still, Skye thought, I have enough to deal with without George letting me know how much he hates being in my debt. How much he hates the fact that he had to call on a white lawyer to defend him, even if that lawyer is a friend. Dammit, he's as biased as anybody. But with reason, he thought. With reason. And George was right. Skye did not know how it felt to be black; he could not really even imagine it. He had no idea what it felt like to go hungry because no restaurant would serve him. He did not know what it felt like to drive miles and miles without sleep because no hotel would house him. He did not know what it felt like to see two water fountains in department stores, with the better one marked "White Only." He did not know what it was like to hold the muscles sealing his bladder tight because there was no place to go to relieve himself. It was when that terrible awareness of all the things he did not know came over him that he asked himself the toughest question of all: was he defending George Harris because he truly believed him innocent—or was he defending him to prove he himself was not prejudiced, was not one of the oppressors?

As they followed the trusty down the hall and up the stairs to the courtroom, Skye made himself push those thoughts away. His feelings would be useless, even harmful, in court. He forced himself to focus on reason, on the evidence, instead. He tried to turn himself into a weapon that could cut through the thin mail of lies that shielded the truth, and set George—and himself—free.

He settled at the table across from the one occupied by the D.A. and one of his assistants, and took papers from his briefcase. His hands were trembling, his heart pounding in his chest. He felt George's stillness; it was as though George were part of the chair he sat in, a dark statue placed in the courtroom. The hum of voices and laughter rose around them. People passed to and fro to the big coffeepot simmering on an electric plate at the clerk of court's elbow and stopped to exchange pleasantries with the D.A.

Skye had clipped a letter from his father at the top of his brief; he reread it now, though he had long since committed it to memory. Beau had written it when Skye had first taken on George's case and had let his father know he intended to do this one alone. "Dear Son," the letter ran. "There are times a man knows how much he loves his son. There are times he knows how proud he is of him. There are times he knows how much he respects him. This is one of the times when I know and feel all three. Papa." He felt a surge of energy that seemed to steady his hands and his heartbeat.

Turning, he looked around the room. The benches were filled, crowded from end to end with people from miles around come to see the show. He felt eyes on him, saw the curiosity, the interest. Could almost hear what they were whispering to one another: so that's the nigger's lawyer. So that's the white man he got to defend him. Hmmm. Seems like he'd have better sense. Understand he *wanted* the case. Wasn't appointed at all.

He turned back to his papers, giving George a reassuring smile. "They're a little informal up here. Allow things city courts wouldn't sit still for."

"So I've heard," George said. His voice was dark with memory, and Skye remembered the fear that had sat with them that first evening, until Fielding had come, and the specter of the Klan was put to rest. Both Skye and Fielding had been shocked at the depth of George's fear. Against every argument they could muster, George could muster fact. A lynching here. A burning there. An execution somewhere else. As nothing else had ever done, that night with George Harris had brought vengeance and blind hatred alive, set them dancing like hooded figures down the mazes of Skye's brain. Truths he had denied, truths he had turned his eyes from, became pellucidly clear. Two codes of justice. Two systems of law. Separated by a fine line of color.

"There are higher courts, George," Skye said. "If the verdict goes against you—I'll take it as high as I have to."

"On what grounds?" George said. He cast a glance over his shoulders, and froze. Skye, watching the impassive black mask slide over George's face, felt his own face contort. What must it be to look at a room full of people and see them as deadly enemies? George swung back, again immobile. "Even a Langlinais has to have grounds, Skye."

George's angry tone separated them, set Skye on one side of that fine line of color and George on the other. Damn, Skye thought. Then Natalie entered the courtroom, a camera slung around her neck, a briefcase weighting her arm. He half-rose, then sank back down. He couldn't greet her here, couldn't establish their relationship for the court to see. He saw her look for him, read the message in her eyes. Good luck.

"If it comes to that, I'll find grounds," Skye said under his breath as the clerk called them to their feet. "If I have to hire a detective to do it."

George raised an eyebrow and pulled his lips into a tight line. Hire a hundred detectives, his eyebrow seemed to say. What good will it do, when there's nothing to find out? When it's her word against mine?

Skye sat through the preliminaries with a growing sense of displacement. The wall behind the judge was a long row of many-paned windows, crowned by half-arches of glass set into heavily carved molding. Each open window framed another segment of bright summer sky—one pure blue, with only one branch of a live oak breaking it, another a mass of pine. The air in the courtroom was heavy, barely stirred by the fans set on platforms around the walls. Skye's hand left wet marks on the table, and he took out his handkerchief and wiped his hands, face, and neck, wondering how the judge could stand to wear robes in this heat. The sultry air made him sleepy; the courtroom did not seem real. He heard the drone of the D.A.'s questions to prospective jurors through a haze of heat. Then Skye found himself questioning the jury pool, going through the motions of finding those who were in any way at all George Harris's peers. The noon break came swiftly, as though the clock had run faster than the sun, and left it hanging at midmorning in the bright hot sky.

"I'm going to try to find a cool spot," he told George. "This heat is terrible—I can hardly think straight."

"I'll see you later," George said. He disappeared through the small door near the witness stand, flanked by two guards. Skye kept his back to the people thronging out of the courtroom, not wanting to hear their questions, nor to meet their eyes.

Then he heard Natalie's voice. "I wonder if I could ask you a couple of things, Mr. Langlinais?" she said, and he turned and faced her, feeling suddenly pulled back into this time and this place.

He made a show of looking at his watch. "The recess isn't very long. Maybe we can talk over lunch?"

"Fine," she said, stuffing her pad and pencil into her bag and holding the gate for him.

They pushed their way past the people opening brown paper bags, extracting wax-paper-wrapped sandwiches, pulling out apples and candy bars.

"If I'd known there was a picnic, I'd have come prepared," Natalie said.

"Actually, Émilie did put up a lunch for me," Skye said. "I thought I might want some space. Not have to eat in a crowd."

"Let's walk over to the graveyard," Natalie said. "It's one of my favorite places around here."

Skye shucked off his coat and loosened his tie, then rolled up his shirt sleeves as he followed Natalie down the sidewalk and across the street, around the old church drowsing in the sun, and into the cemetery beyond it.

"I get such a perspective here," Natalie said, perching on the low brick wall that surrounded a family plot. "Read all these old names and dates and realize my problems aren't so important after all. Or won't be, given a couple of hundred years or so."

"I wish I felt that way now," Skye said. He took the lunch packages from his briefcase and opened them, spreading them out on the narrow ledge. "I feel absolutely useless, a pawn in a travesty that no one will stop—but that I'm stuck with performing in anyway. And no one *will* stop it. You know that as well as I do."

She watched him for a moment, and then said quietly, "What do you think of the jury selections so far?"

He took a bite of his sandwich and chewed slowly, thinking about the four jurors chosen that morning. "The former schoolteacher might not be too bad," he said. "At least she has some intelligence."

"Will her sympathies automatically be with the dead woman?"

"Natalie, what I'm up against is that *everyone's* sympathies will be with the dead woman. She's white. George is black."

"I thought you might object to that farmer," Natalie said, taking the pear Skye offered her.

"The guy that looks like Hale?" Skye remembered the farmer's eyes, the shock that had gone through him when he realized that there were two men in the courtroom this farmer hated—one was George Harris, but the other was Skye.

"I wanted to. But we have eight jurors to go. I might find worse than him."

"He seemed so hostile, almost as though he didn't like you, either, Skye."

"That's what I found out this morning," he said. "Something I didn't know before. I'm not an asset for George, any more than his education and good English are."

"Why do you say that?"

"I'm seen as an oppressor—an enemy who lives off the fat of the land while they make do with the bones."

"Oh, Skye, surely not? Just because you're—well, who you are—"

"That's the way these people look at it. My defending George is just one more 'privilege' rich people have. They know I'm taking this case on without pay. And they hate me for it."

"Ask for a change of venue. For God's sake, Skye, get the trial put somewhere else!"

"It wouldn't matter. It would be the same no matter where it was held. This is just one more engagement in a long battle between the haves and the have-nots. I should have seen that, gotten someone else to defend George."

"I hate to hear you talk that way—"

"I hate it too. Worse than you do, because I'm stuck with trying to make a system work in the face of hatred and blindness and ignorance—"

"Oh, Skye!"

Her hands closed on his, her eyes burned into his. He saw his own doubt reflected in her face, and reached out to touch her.

"Sorry. I haven't been in practice long enough to be able to detach myself from it. If I saw any chance—but my one hope is breaking that girl's story, and you know good and well what will happen if I get rough with her."

He felt Natalie's fingers stir in his, and was reminded of how long it had been since they had made love together. He had hardly left St. Francisville since George was arrested, putting everything else aside to stay close and prepare his case. Natalie had been stuck in New Orleans, coming up for one weekend early in July. He suddenly wanted to forget this pointless game of a trial, to pick her up and carry her off to St. Martinville, to live in the golden kingdom that could be his. Then he thought of his father's letter. Love. Respect. Pride. He had been given the first, but he had earned the others. And, by God, he'd not renege now.

"Skye, I've been thinking," Natalie said. "About the daughter." She looked at him, caution slowing her words. "How would you feel if I tried to talk to her?"

"What do you mean?"

"I'm familiar with people like her. Girls from those dried-out families who barely scratch a living. I ran into a lot of them when I worked one summer on a service project in the Blue Ridge Mountains. Sometimes, if you can approach them right—"

"Natalie, there's also something called tampering with a witness."

She looked at him with a look he couldn't quite comprehend. "Does that mean you don't want me to talk to her?"

"It means I don't want to know about it if you do," he said. He stood up, watching crumbs fall into the thick ivy that covered the ground. "I don't know what she'd tell you that she hasn't blabbed to everyone who will listen," he said. He sounded so dispirited that Natalie's own resolve intensified.

"Skye—if she goes on the witness stand with that story—"

"Don't I know it," he said. The bleakness of his eyes made a mirror in which she saw the motherless girl giving the jury the last nail to hammer into George's coffin. With her as their excuse, they would find it not only easy but also necessary to find George Harris guilty, and to recommend that he be put to death.

The words blurred before Skye's eyes, words that seemed more and more meaningless the longer he looked at them. He tossed the brief aside and sank back against the big leather chair. Closing his eyes, he let the breeze from the fan Émilie had placed near him cool him. The trial was now in its second day; the jury had been sworn in that morning, and already the D.A. had begun to put his case, carefully presenting the thin strands of circumstantial evidence that would, given the situation, likely prove strong enough to make a rope around George Harris' neck. Skye felt racked by his emotions; nothing he could recognize as the truth had yet emerged in court. The D.A.'s opening remarks had set the stage: the ingredients necessary to convict an accused of a capital crime had been blended to fit the jury. Motive and opportunity—stumbling blocks that should have required solid evidence, evidence beyond the shadow of a doubt—had proved not to be stumbling blocks here at all. George admitted he had gone up to the house, knocked on the door. There was opportunity. As for motive? What black man needed a motive to violate and kill a white woman? Was that not the threat that lay beneath all the racial rules, all the prejudices and prohibitions? George was not a person; he was one of a class of predators. Skye, taking the measure of the jury's reaction, saw conviction in their faces, and knew that his cause held little hope.

He could not remember when he had been so tired, and though he knew it was the fatigue of depression, still, its weight dragged at him, made his head ache and his shoulders tense. Tomorrow he would have to take the floor, attempt to answer the unanswerable, try to get past the flat pale eyes of the witnesses and somehow uncover the truth. He remembered George's bitter words: White man's truth? Or black man's truth? It was no good to tell himself that legal truths were above everyday reality. It was no good to tell himself that legal truths were stronger, because they were bound by principles, rules, and procedures. They were bound also by people. What he needed now was only one truth—from a witness who had no intention of supplying it.

He thought of the way Crystal Hale sat close to her father, white-blond hair skinned tightly back from her face, tongue nervously, incessantly running over her lips. He knew she was lying. But he wondered. If she were the daughter of a plantation owner, a girl who had gone to private schools and whose closet bulged with clothes out of *Glamour* and *Mademoiselle,* would he still think she was lying? Perhaps not. Girls like that would have little reason to lie. But the girl he would face tomorrow did have a reason. If you lived in a jungle, you learned to use its methods. If you yourself fell victim, you learned to victimize others. Any intruder into the familial circle would be seen first as an enemy. As she saw George. And Skye.

He heard voices from the hall. Émilie's. And then another—Natalie! Even as he got up, he heard the study door open. Émilie poked her head in. "Natalie's here, Skye." She pushed the door wider and stood back, letting Natalie in. "Y'all want some iced tea?"

"That would be wonderful," Natalie said. Her face looked pinched, and there was a weariness in her eyes that seemed to mirror Skye's own.

"I'll be right back," Émilie said, closing the door behind her.

"Sit down, won't you?" Skye said. "That chair will get the breeze from the fan." They both seemed gripped by a tension not of their own making; they looked at one another silently; then Natalie spoke, her voice low and hesitant.

"I . . . I have something to tell you," she said. Her eyes were still filled with a chilling compound of fatigue and horror. "About the girl." He watched a slow flush rise up from her throat. He could think of nothing that would account for Natalie's state. For one panicked moment he was afraid she was going to tell him that George was a liar after all, and that Natalie had proof Crystal Hale was telling the truth.

"She's been . . . Skye, she's been sleeping with her father."

"Natalie, what are you saying?" The sound of his own voice, steady, normal, surprised him. He was still trying to come to terms with what Natalie had said; all the questions that must now be asked were forming, and he could feel his mind begin to race. If this were true . . .

"Let me start at the beginning," Natalie said. "I kept coming back to one thing—what could possibly make that girl lie?" She looked at him, and he saw reason returning, chasing out the ugliness her eyes had mirrored. "Of course, that's what was driving you crazy too. What you hoped to get out of her when she was on the witness stand. But I agree with you—there's little possibility of getting her to admit she's lying in open court. Not with the father there. I kept going over all the reasons she might lie. She just plain hates Negroes? Or she didn't know what the truth was—who had killed her mother. But nothing seemed to ring true. So I decided to do a little investigating. I dropped by the school yesterday afternoon and found a teacher who was willing to talk to me about her. Crystal didn't stay in school long—the minute she was sixteen and could drop out, they never saw her again. And when she was there, she was almost invisible. One of those washed-out girls who sat in the back of the room and did as little as possible. Not even enough to get by, really—she was only in the ninth grade when she quit. The only reason this teacher remembered her at all was that she taught home ec, and Crystal showed some small interest in that." Natalie shuddered, a quick movement that seemed to jerk her body back to life. "You see. I . . . I already had an idea about what might be going on out there. As I told you, I've seen girls like that. Situations like that. You'd be surprised—I guess you would, God knows I was, if 'surprised' is the right word—how much . . . incest there really is. So when I heard how passive Crystal has always been, how withdrawn—no friends, isolated from contact with people her own age—I thought the chances were pretty good that my hunch was right. This teacher said the Hales didn't go to any local church—they belong to some off-brand sect that's long on hellfire and damnation and short on love and mercy—they travel about thirty miles each way on Sundays to go to services."

Skye saw Crystal's flat, pale gaze as clearly as though it were she, rather than Natalie, who sat across from him. A gaze enclosed by bigotry and ignorance, sealed by violence and perversion. "But you said you *knew* she was sleeping with him? How?"

The door opened and Émilie bustled in with a tray. "Here's your tea," she said. "And some cheese and crackers. Skye hasn't been eating well." Then she caught the terrible tension in the room and stopped. "I'm sorry. I'm rattling on—I'll leave you alone now, all right?"

"Émilie, thanks," Skye said, his eyes never leaving Natalie's face.

Natalie waited until the door closed. Then she said, "She told me." She ducked her head as though shaking off a memory she wanted to be rid of. "I'm not proud of the way I got it out of her, but, God, Skye, there's a life at stake."

"What did you do?" He felt shaken, his whole perception of the case, of the course he must take, jolted into a new path. If Natalie was right . . . But he would not allow himself to hope. Not yet. Whether Natalie realized it or not, there was a very long distance still to be traveled before George Harris was free.

"I dashed to the ladies' room at noon recess, praying she'd come in too. Which she did. While she was washing her hands I went up to her and told her I represented a New York magazine that wanted an exclusive interview with her and that I would pay her five hundred dollars for an hour of her time. She didn't turn a hair. She just looked at me with those terrible eyes and asked when did I want to talk to her. I said why not now. Court was recessed for two hours, there was more than enough time. She agreed. I didn't ask her about her father, but she volunteered that he was doing some business in town during the recess. I told her I had a fancy picnic in my car and that we'd drive somewhere where we could be private. Then, to make sure she didn't change her mind, I took out two hundred-dollar bills and gave them to her as an advance."

"Natalie—"

"Wait, Skye. We drove to the park on the bluff, and I spiked her Coke with enough Jack Daniel's to kill a horse. She got tighter than a tick, and when I started asking her about her boyfriends . . ." Natalie stopped talking, pressing her hands against each other as though she were compressing some awful memory into a manageable flat packet. "Then I asked her point-blank if she had ever slept with one of her boyfriends, and she got this awful look on her face, and said she didn't have any boyfriends. I said all girls had boyfriends. She still didn't say anything, and I'm afraid I got rough—I said she probably couldn't attract a man, and that did it." Natalie's face crumpled, the ugliness she had held at bay finally breaking her. "Oh, Skye, it was horrible! Once she got started, she went on and on. I couldn't have stopped her if I'd wanted to."

Skye went to her and held her, feeling the rigidity of her body fighting him, realizing she was thinking about the violent images Crystal had drawn.

"Will she remember what she told you? And more important—will she tell it again?"

"Oh, Skye, I don't know. I haven't got past what happened. I drove her back to the courthouse, full of coffee and food and peppermint to hide the smell of bourbon, and then I headed my car out of town and kept driving until almost dark—and then I came straight here to tell you."

"I've got to think what to do," Skye said. "How to use this."

"I know I tampered with a witness," Natalie said. "But I had to, Skye. I just had to."

"Natalie, if you knew how grateful I am that you did!" He pulled her closer and felt some of the stiffness leave her. "I finally have a wedge, something I can use to get some leverage."

"But how, Skye? If she talks at all—she'll deny everything."

"There's always the father," Skye said.

"He's bound to lie, Skye. My God, incest is a crime, aside from everything else."

"If I catch him off-guard—dammit, Natalie, what else can I do?"

"I don't know," she said. She sank back into her chair, chin resting in her hands. "But if you try and it doesn't work—things will be worse than before, won't they?"

"I think things are as bad as they can be right now," he said. "I don't like using a dirty weapon, but it's what the situation calls for. And I'm glad you got it for me." He sat beside her and took one of her hands in his. "Now I have a suggestion. There's not a thing I can do tonight—and I'm as weary of this whole business as I've ever been of anything in my life. What say you and I put it out of our minds and spend a nice quiet evening right here? I'm sure Fielding won't mind if his study is put to frivolous use."

"There's nothing I'd like better," she said.

They put more logs on the fire, stacked Sinatra and Whiting on the record player, turned off all but one lamp, and found each other all over again. "It's always like the first time all over again," Skye whispered, feeling Natalie's body move under his hand.

"I think it always will be," she said.

He let all thoughts of the trial go; Natalie's smooth flesh was his defense against tomorrow, his passion for her now stronger than his fear.

Later, when she had left to go back to her Uncle Paul's, he walked through the silent house to his room, passing doors behind which Fielding and Émilie and their children slept. This is what I want, he thought. A home. A wife. Children. This was what he wanted, all right. And all too soon, he would learn if it was what she wanted too.

27

JULY 1950

Skye backed away from the witness stand, carefully measuring the effect his last question had had on Whitney Hale, who stared back balefully at him. He had slipped the question among a score of routine ones, hoping to surprise Hale into an unthinking answer.

Now he repeated the question, enunciating each syllable slowly, commanding the courtroom's attention. "Why would your wife invite a Negro man into her home?"

Hale's hands gripped the edge of the stand, and his eyes burned into Skye as though wishing he would melt. "Who says she did?" he said finally, the rough edges of his voice cutting the words into almost unrecognizable shapes.

Skye felt the first small surge of hope; balancing on the balls of his feet, feeling suddenly light, agile, he leaned forward. "Your daughter," he said.

Hale licked his lips, a movement so reminiscent of his daughter's that Skye was reminded of the images he had been trying to deny, images in which this man and his daughter mimicked in terrible perversion the acts that most people used in love.

"He must have pushed his way in," Hale said finally. His voice sounded the same, but it was as if a hood had come down over his eyes, the hood men wore when they were deliberately lying, and the surge of hate became a wave.

Skye picked up a sheet of paper and read the words written there. " 'Question from the district attorney to Miss Crystal Hale: "What happened after you saw the man knocking on the front door?" Answer: "I saw my mother open the door. He said something to her, and then she opened the door and he went inside." ' " Skye rolled the paper into a thin shaft and pointed it at the witness. " 'She opened the door and he went inside.' I repeat, Mr. Hale. Why would your wife invite a Negro man into her home?"

"She must have had a reason," Hale said. He seemed reduced to something primitive, something beyond the precepts of normal men.

"But what reason?" Skye said. He controlled his voice with an effort. The pent-up tension of the last weeks edged his question. "All he wanted was water for his radiator—and as you well know, Mr. Hale, any Negro male with any sense at all knows better than to go into a white woman's house. Particularly if she's alone." He rolled a shaft of paper between his hands, then again pointed it at Hale. "You and your daughter are asking this court to believe that a woman like your wife, all alone in her house by your admission and your daughter's admission, opened the door, found a strange Negro man on the doorstep, and asked him inside. Neither of you seem to think that the least bit unusual—and I won't accept that." He spun around and faced the jury. They were staring at him as though he had thrown wide a window and let the summer storm raging outside into the room. "And I don't think you'll accept it, either. You know as well as I do that every white woman in this state—in this region—is brought up to fear Negro men. Brought up to fear the very thing we are told happened to Mrs. Hale." He saw agreement steal across their faces. The former schoolteacher nodded, a sudden involuntary jerk of her head that, like a string, seemed to pull the jury into a cohesive unit. He felt as though the end of the string was in his hand; he could pull it, twist it, lead the jury exactly where he wanted them to go. He smiled at the jurors, and then turned back to Hale. "Perhaps," he said, his voice more gentle, "perhaps your wife was an especially charitable person. Perhaps she intended to . . . give the defendant something." He let his voice drop, let it become insinuating. "A glass of water? A sandwich? What do you think, Mr. Hale—was your wife in the habit of inviting strangers in to feed?"

"She wouldn't wait on no nigger," Hale said. The intensity of his hatred shocked even Skye.

"But she asked him in. For some reason none of us can understand."

"I don't have to understand it," Hale said. He suddenly rose, a long, thin figure silhouetted against the bright lights that fought the storm-black skies outside. "That nigger killed her, he done it, and that's all there is to it. Asking me a lot of durn-fool questions won't change that."

"It might," Skye said. Fatigue settled over him like a leaden case, one of those moments during an exhausting campaign when will alone is not enough to conquer lack of sleep, constant stress. He felt dizzy, as though the terrible forces that ruled Hale's life were focused on him, attempting?

to destroy him, too. He looked up, made himself meet Hale's eyes. "Your daughter's testimony is the only thing that puts George Harris in that lean-to. By God, Mr. Hale, you're going to give me a reason why your wife would ask a strange Negro man into her home or you'll be in this court until you do."

"How should I know what my wife was thinking?" Hale demanded.

Skye heard a rustle of papers behind him, and then the D.A. spoke. "I've been thinking the same thing. Your Honor, I've listened while my colleague drew this line of questioning out—after all, this is a capital crime, and I want to be reasonable and fair. But I have to confess that I fail to see why it's so important to know what reason Mrs. Hale might have had for opening the door to the defendant. Isn't it sufficient that she did?"

Skye's heart slowed; he could almost feel it pausing, waiting for the judge's answer. He remembered what both Fielding and his father had said about Judge Charles Rowland: a fair man, a conservative man, a gentleman of the old school. He watched light bounce off Rowland's silver head, watched his blue eyes focus first on Hale and then on George Harris.

"I don't agree with you, sir," Rowland said. His fingers came together, a small temple where he might worship truth. "There are many nuances in this trial that have little to do with evidence, and everything to do with community attitudes and prejudices. You know it, I know it, Mr. Langlinais knows it—and certainly the defendant knows it. Now, I can't allow you to have it both ways, Mr. McPherson. I can't allow community attitudes and prejudices to work for you when you want them to, and yet ignore them when they support another view. If we are going to automatically assume that Mr. Harris, while driving to an important interview, suddenly took it into his head to rape and murder Mrs. Hale, on a simple impulse resulting from the fact that she was a white female and he is a Negro male—then I think we are going to also have to automatically assume that Mrs. Hale would have seen him as a natural enemy—and would never in this world have opened that door to him."

"Are you presenting the defense's case, your Honor?" McPherson snapped.

"I can allow myself a little leeway in my own court, Mr. McPherson," Rowland said. "If you object to the way I conduct things here, there are remedies open to you."

"I beg your pardon, your Honor," the D.A. said. "We all want to be fair, of course." He sank back into his chair and murmured something to his assistant.

"Let me repeat the question, Mr. Hale," Skye said. "Why would your wife have invited a Negro man into her home, particularly when she was alone? Or if she didn't open the door for him, why would your daughter say she had?"

Hale coiled his lean body into a tense line, his thick tongue running over his lips as though lubricating them for a particularly arduous task. Then he sprang, his arms flailing, stark black against the pale wall behind him, a figure out of a dark dream, a relic of an unspeakable past. "Because they are whores," he said. "Both whores."

The D.A. jumped up. "Hale, get hold of yourself. Your Honor—"

But there was no stopping the words welling up from Hale's poisonous mouth. A mixture of biblical judgments and common filth assailed them. And punctuating the tirade, that one syllable, shouted over and over again: Whores. Whores. Whores. The court reporter dropped her pen and held her hands over her ears; Rowland raised his gavel and struck his desk, again, and again, and again.

A shrill cry sliced the room in two. Crystal Hale fought past the people filling the bench where she sat. Although she had listened impassively throughout the trial, her face was now a red circle of rage. "He done it!" she screamed. "He done it to me and he done it to her. Then he killed her."

Hale's terrible gaze centered on his daughter. "Whore!" he screamed back. "Corrupt daughter of Satan—"

Natalie reached Crystal and took her in her arms, turning the girl's face to her chest. Guards reached Hale and yanked him from the witness stand. One clapped a huge hand over Hale's mouth and then jerked it back, staring at the bright drops of blood marking the place where Hale had bitten him.

Judge Rowland's gavel was a tom-tom, calling his court to order. McPherson, who almost crouched in his chair, was blank with shock.

"McPherson! Get your witness under control, sir! *Now!*"

McPherson rose and approached Hale, who struggled between the guards, his head thrown back. He was almost inarticulate now. Words were splintered, their syllables uttered out of sequence. His voice was hoarse, raging, so that each sound had the same raw shape.

"Get hold of yourself! *Hale!*" McPherson said something to the guards and stood back as they force-marched Hale out of the courtroom to the parish jail. Suddenly there was again silence.

Judge Rowland broke it. "Mr. McPherson. Mr. Langlinais. I am going to recess this court for two hours. I want to see both of you in my chambers—immediately." He looked past them to Crystal, who sat beside Natalie, still cradled in her arms. "And I want Miss Hale available for clarification of some of the things we've just heard."

"Your Honor—" McPherson began. He flinched before the anger he saw in Rowland's face. "Yes, your Honor."

Skye gathered his papers together and shoved them into his briefcase. Beside him, George Harris sat immobile, his hands clenched in his lap. Throughout Hale's outburst, George had become more and more rigid; when Crystal stood and began screaming, he had almost stopped breathing. Skye had reached over and gripped his wrist, had whispered intensely, "Stay still. Try to be calm. Trust me."

Now George let out his breath, a rush of air that almost palpably released him. "Man," he said in a low voice. "Did you know what was going on?"

"Yes," Skye said.

"Does this mean . . . am I going to be . . . free?"

"It should," he said. He turned and faced George. "But stay still, George. Don't say a word. Lie low and be patient just a little longer. All right?"

"All right," George said. He stood up and walked between his guards to the small oak door, his back straight, his head tall.

Skye heard someone behind him and turned to see Natalie. "Skye, you were wonderful. I kept holding my breath, I kept praying he would break. It's all right now, isn't it?"

"I hope so. Of course, I still have to convince Judge Rowland. And it depends on how willing Crystal is to talk—though my guess is that Hale is still talking, that he won't shut up for a long, long time." He saw the disgust he felt mirrored in her face as they both remembered Hale's flood of filth. "I'd better go. It's never a good idea to keep a judge waiting. Right now, it's a particularly bad idea."

"Good luck, darling," she said. "I love you."

"I love you," he said.

McPherson was already in Rowland's chambers when Skye entered, slumped in a chair smoking a cigar, his eyes narrow with anger. "That was a hell of a stunt you pulled in there, Langlinais," he said when Skye walked in.

"It was no stunt," Skye said. His earlier weariness had lifted, but something else weighed on him now, and he sank into a chair opposite McPherson.

Rowland leaned forward and peered at Skye. "Did you know Hale would react that way?"

"I didn't know what he would do, sir. But I've been worrying at that question since this began—" He shook his head. "If my client was innocent—then someone else was lying. There had to be a pretty powerful reason for that lie."

"But incest!" McPherson said. "My God, Langlinais, what a can of worms you've opened up."

"Worse than executing an innocent man?"

"I didn't mean that. I just meant—hell, do you think for a minute Hale is going to give us a statement, all cut-and-dried?"

"Hale isn't my problem," Skye said. "Harris is." He looked at Judge Rowland. "May I tell you what I think happened, sir?"

"That's what I'm waiting to hear," Rowland said.

Rapidly Skye sketched the theory he and Natalie had conceived. "It appears that Hale has been . . . molesting his daughter for some time. Probably since she was a very small girl. I don't know whether the mother realized what was going on or not. Maybe she just never did anything because she was afraid, or because of her own terrible passivity . . ." Skye shrugged. "However, it seems that she did not protect Crystal against her father. Until that day. Crystal says that on the day her mother was murdered, her father was working around the house. He approached Crystal, and took her into her bedroom. Later the door opened, and her mother found them—and began screaming at both of them. 'Out of her head' is the way Crystal described her. She said that her father left her and went for her mother, dragging her out of the bedroom through the kitchen. Crystal could hear her mother screaming, but she didn't get up off the bed. Then the noise grew fainter, and she dropped off, fainted—anyway, the next she knew, she heard voices. She peeked out of the bedroom door and saw her father standing in the doorway talking to a Negro man who was on the steps outside. Then the Negro went away. Her father came back inside, and took her back into the room . . ." Skye blinked and looked away, trying to blot out the pictures that crowded the room. He took a breath and continued. "After a while, her father told her something terrible had happened, that a Negro had killed her mother. That she must tell the sheriff, when he came, that she had seen her mother letting the Negro into the house."

"Mr. Langlinais, how did you get Miss Hale to tell you all that?" Judge Rowland asked.

"She didn't tell me. She told a . . . a friend of mine. Natalie Watkins."

"That *Picayune* reporter?" Rowland looked at Skye sharply. "All right. Miss Watkins can tell me herself how she happened to get a witness in a capital crime to talk to her."

"Your Honor," McPherson said, "that sounds like tampering—"

"Mr. McPherson. I'll deal with that later. Right now I'm going to talk to Miss Hale. And then I'm going to get Dr. Monroe from Baton Rouge to talk to her. He's a psychiatrist there, he's done a lot of court work. My secretary's already called him. He'll be here after lunch. Then we'll both talk to Hale. If all this proves out—your client will be freed by morning, Mr. Langlinais."

"Your Honor. Do you really believe this tale?" McPherson said.

"I'm suspending belief," Rowland said. "And disbelief. Until I've talked to the Hales. You'd better stick around, you need to be in on those interviews." He smiled at Skye. "You go on. I'll let you know what happens. You look beat, son."

"I'm beginning to feel better," Skye said. He got to his feet, wondering why he did not feel elated. He had no doubt that George would be freed, that in the morning he could walk out of that cell and into the world a man once more in control of his own life. It was not until he had reached the entrance of the courthouse, and was opening his umbrella against the rain pelting down from a sea of clouds, that he recognized the leaden feeling inside himself for what it was. Powerlessness. Helplessness. The knowledge that except for a lucky break—Natalie snooping into Crystal's past—he would never have broken this case. And George Harris, instead of being set free, would have been strapped into the electric chair at Angola Prison and jolted into eternity.

The umbrella seemed a frail shield against the storm's ferocity. Skye hurried down the steps and across the street to a small coffee shop where Natalie waited. He sank into a seat opposite her and signaled the waitress to bring him coffee. "Well, I think it's going to be all right," he said. "Rowland's going to talk to Crystal and Hale. And he has a psychiatrist coming up from Baton Rouge to talk to them, too. McPherson's madder than a wet hen, but Rowland's got a tight grip on the case now. I think maybe it's all over but the shouting."

"Thank God!"

The waitress put his coffee in front of him, and he drank it gratefully, needing the caffeine's stimulus.

"You all want something to eat?" the waitress asked.

"A couple of hamburgers," Natalie said.

The girl went away and Natalie took Skye's hand in hers. "You look exhausted, darling. All these weeks of tension—"

"I'm pretty tired," he said. He set his cup down and closed his hand over hers. "If it hadn't been for you . . . God, Natalie, if you hadn't figured out what happened . . ." He could taste the coffee rising in his throat, and swallowed hard. He did not want to believe that George Harris would really have been executed for a murder he did not commit. The implications of that were too awful; he wasn't yet ready even to think about them. He smiled at Natalie, weariness tugging at the corners of his mouth. "I guess this is what they call a 'benchmark' case in a young lawyer's career. One he can cut his wisdom teeth on."

"You need a vacation, Skye."

"You're right on my wavelength. Do you think you could get a couple of days off? Go back to the Grand Hotel?"

She started to say something, changed her mind, and nodded. "I imagine so. Not until after next week, though."

"That's fine. If this all works out—I'll go back to St. Martinville, get things squared away there—" He stretched his shoulders, trying to ease their fatigue. "God, it'll be good to get away. The summer's almost gone—"

"Yes," she said.

Their food arrived and they talked of other things, letting the high excitement of the morning subside. Then Skye went back to the courthouse and Natalie went to file her story.

"Roberts wants to talk to you," the rewrite man told her when she finished giving him her notes.

The close air of the booth was stifling; she pushed open the door and stared sightlessly at the dusty leaves, the weeds growing in the roadside ditch. Then Ben's voice boomed in her ear. "Looks like the trial turned into a big story after all," he said. "I picked up an extension and heard what you told Sam. Look, I'm going to want more. A sidebar on Harris himself—"

Natalie took her pencil and pad from her bag and began making rapid notes; Ben wanted at least three features on principals in the case. A photographer would arrive tomorrow, and she was to stay on the scene. "I don't guess I need to tell you that you'll get a front-page byline," he said. "And I wouldn't be at all surprised if the wire services picked this up."

She waited for the exultation to come. Maybe I'm just too tired to feel it, she thought. I've worked so long for just this kind of break—why doesn't it seem more important? Even as she hung up the phone, the answer came. These days with Skye, working by his side, had tipped the balance. She could write anywhere, but his law practice was set in St. Martinville. If he asks me to marry him now, she thought—and then stopped, feeling suddenly chilled despite the heat. If he asks me.

He loves me, she told herself. He says so, he shows it. But perhaps he's discovered that a long-distance love affair is perfectly all right, and that he doesn't need to marry me at all.

28

JULY 1950

Nothing was the way it was supposed to be, Caro thought as she dove into the hotel pool and began a steady crawl toward the far end. Except for her reunion with David the day of her arrival—that had been all she had dreamed of. David met her plane, and his first welcome was all she could want. She felt the same passion in his embrace, the same eagerness in his response to her; they had gone straight to the hotel and to bed, hardly speaking the first intense hours, but so close that they did not have to.

Where had that gone? Because within twenty-four hours of her arrival, David seemed abstracted, distant, behaving as though she were a not terribly convenient houseguest he must amuse. Remembering how lonely his distance made her feel, how unhappy, she stroked harder, kicking her feet rhythmically, feeling her muscles unwind. The cool blue waters washed over her, removing the dust and fatigue of the day, a day spent with Mollie Haskell, who had traveled into Jerusalem from her kibbutz to see Jake.

They had lunched at the hospital, returning to the hotel to spend the afternoon "gabbing," as Mollie called it. Now Caro was alone again, as, she reflected ruefully, she had been most of the month she had been in Jerusalem. Unless, of course, she was off on an activity David had arranged for her. At first she had been enthusiastic about the tours, even though they were almost always under the guidance of other people, since David himself worked long hours at the hospital where Jake was a patient. She had been out to visit a kibbutz, traveling the road out from Jerusalem that paralleled the Jordanian border for some of its length, falling into respectful silence when they passed the rusting remains of armored trucks still gallantly arrayed in fading wreaths and ribbons. These were, she had been told, relics of the convoys that tried to bring food and ammunition through the Arab blockade to relieve Jerusalem's starving, besieged defenders in 1948.

The kibbutz had generated honest enthusiasm; its people combined a sense of serious purpose with a joyous spirit that made the day one of the pleasantest she had spent. Even Jake was in a better mood than David, she thought, turning to swim one last lap. He joked about being peg-legged, drawing improbable contraptions he vowed he would have built instead of wearing the usual artificial limb. But David, except for his real happiness when Jake's remaining leg began to heal, except for the times when he lost himself in making love, was withdrawn, quiet, almost morose.

And that, she told herself, is the last straw. She had held in her disappointment over missing the opening of her show; she had not even told David it was happening. When she made the decision to come to Jerusalem, she had told herself she would give it her best efforts: she would stay long enough to make sure of what was going on with David, long enough to make sure what the future held. But this morning's mail had brought a sheaf of clippings from Koenberg, the critical response to her show. She had read them with growing humility and wonder: was this *her* work they were talking about? "Powerful" . . . "Compelling honesty" . . . "Masterful execution" . . . "A subtle talent." At that moment, she had wanted more than anything else in the world to have David there beside her, to be able to hand each clipping to him, to watch him read them, to see him smile, to see his eyes fill with love and pride—and feel his arms around her as he spoke to her of both.

She stood up at the shallow end, angry tears streaming down her already wet face. Koenberg had sent something else, a report of the first auction of the prints he had had made. It had been held at the gallery a week after the opening; it had made thirty thousand dollars, a sum which even now was on its way to Israel. She had sat staring at the figures, trying to realize that it was her work that had brought that money in. And would continue to do so. The last item in the packet was the list of other galleries that would show the series, each with an auction already arranged.

Koenberg's note had been brief. "My dear Caro—we need you here. Read all these and you will see why. Everyone wants to talk to you, everyone wants to interview you. Please come home."

She had put the clippings, the report, Louis's note, back in the envelope, and tucked it next to the envelope that held her slides. Then she had gone to the telephone and made reservations two days hence to fly home.

I'll tell David tonight, she told herself, climbing up the ladder and wrapping herself in a thick towel. He may well have work here—but I have work too. And I've got to get on with it.

She went upstairs, showered and dressed, then sat on the balcony that opened off her room waiting for David to come. She could see the walls of the Old City from where she sat, the part of Jerusalem still in Arab hands. David had taken her up to the roof of the Franciscan Monastery of Notre Dame soon after she arrived; it gave, he said, the best view of the Old City. He had pointed out the landmarks: the old University of Jerusalem, the empty and abandoned Hadassah Hospital, the Damascus Gate, the Mount of Olives, the Garden of Gethsemane, the Church of the Holy Sepulcher . . . She had peered through field glasses at each place, feeling an increasing sense of unity, of continuity—standing there with the hot wind blowing over her, she had felt at one with the city and its people, and had turned eagerly to David, certain that he felt this same thing.

He had not seemed to understand her meaning, and she had let it drop, feeling a growing insecurity, a growing bewilderment. She felt neither insecure nor bewildered now. She was angry, angry at David and angry at herself, determined to bring the issues between them out into the open, once and for all, and to finally know just where it was they stood.

When David finally arrived, he looked so hot, so tired, that she almost relented. He's worked like someone possessed for over six months, she told herself, going to him and taking him into her arms. Don't hit him with all this now. And then she saw, in a sudden flash of revelation, what it was that was wrong. David was working like one possessed. He did not have the joyous spirit of the people at the kibbutz, or of Jake and Mollie. David did not really want to be here. And he was driving himself to work harder to make amends for that fact.

Of course, she thought. Of course. That explains everything—why he has treated me so strangely, why he's so withdrawn. He did not want to be reminded of her, of their life in San Francisco. He was punishing himself. "David," she said. "Let me fix you a drink while you shower. You look so hot—I want to talk to you about something important, and I want you to be refreshed."

"A shower is exactly what I need," he said. "The drink sounds good too." He disappeared into the bathroom, and she fixed their drinks, then waited on the balcony, feeling a kind of numbness at her center, as though her new understanding of David was too much for her yet to absorb.

He came out to her barefoot, dressed in a short terry-cloth robe, and sank into the chair opposite her with a grateful sigh. "So," he said. "What do you want to talk about?"

"The topic that has absorbed the great majority of my attention for a very long time now, David. You and me."

"Caro—"

"David, I will not be put off. You told me, last December, that you were coming out here for six months. All spring, you held to that. You even had a departure date, for heaven's sake!"

"I couldn't leave Jake—"

"No one asked you to leave Jake. I understood that, David. But I understand something else, something I think you know and just won't face."

"What's that?" he said. His face was in shadow, but his voice told her that he was not ready for this, he did not know exactly what it was she was going to say, but whatever it was, he did not want to hear it.

She thrust her chin out stubbornly and pushed on. "I don't think you really want to be here, David. And I think you're finding reasons to stay on because you feel guilty. You think you're some kind of monster because you'd really rather not be here, because you'd really rather go home."

"That's not true!"

"I think it is true," she said. "Look, David, even Jake with one leg is happier than you are."

"Happy! What the hell does happiness have to do with anything? Caro, I didn't come here to be *happy*."

"My point exactly."

He stood up and glared down at her. "Caro, Israel is only two years away from all-out war. *Two years!* I've been overworked since I got here—first in Ein Gev, and now in Jerusalem. Too much to do, too few supplies—and you say I'm not *happy*? Caro, that's not worthy of you."

She rose and confronted him. "And your attitude's not worthy of you. Dammit, David, when I say you're not happy I don't mean that you don't go around singing and telling jokes. Though come to think of it, one of the most memorable things about the kibbutz I visited *was* the amount of singing and laughter. What I mean is something much deeper than that. David, almost everyone I have met here is content with his or her place in life. People are content with what they are doing. With the country they've created and are building. I don't sense that in you. You *don't* feel good about yourself. Satisfied with what you're doing."

He turned from her and went to the balcony edge, staring toward the far horizon. She ached to go to him, hold him, take him inside to bed, where for a small space of time they could create the world that was always there for them. But she stood her ground. It had taken a long time to get to this point, and now that they were here, she would not retreat.

"You're right, Caro. I'm not . . . content. And I don't feel good about what I'm doing. Oh, at one level, I know I'm doing needed work. But it . . . it doesn't get beyond that level. I . . . I don't get anything out of it, Caro. And you're right about that, too. It's killing me."

She let her breath out in a long, slow sigh and went to stand beside him. "David. You've been here six, almost seven months. You've made a contribution. Darling, come home with me. Please."

"Is that what you want? For me to give up?"

"Give up? This isn't the only way to help Israel, to help your people, David! Obviously, it's not the right way for *you*—"

"So that gives me an out, is that it? I'm not 'happy,' so I can pick up my marbles and go home?"

The sheer force of his anger pushed her away from him. She stood in the corner of the balcony, staring at him. "David, that's not what I meant. You're not going to be any good to anyone if you keep making yourself do something you don't really want to do."

"Goddammit, Caro! Did my family 'want' to go to Dachau? To Buchenwald? Did they want to suffer? To die with no dignity? My God, Caro, is that your measure of life? That I should do what I 'want' to do?"

"No, it's not, and you damn well know it, David Selbin! But it's not my fault you're carrying a load of guilt because you didn't die too!"

She could not see his expression, but she saw the slump of his body, saw the way he turned again to the rail and clung to it, and was instantly sorry. "David . . . David, I'm sorry. That was—I shouldn't have said that."

"No, you shouldn't have," he said quietly.

She gathered her courage and moved closer to him. "I shouldn't have said it because that's something you have to realize for yourself. That's an issue between you and your own conscience—I'm sorry I interfered."

"Now, that's an interesting apology," he said. "So you think I'm interrupting my life, separating myself from you—all because I feel I have to pay for still being alive."

"You haven't been yourself for months, David. Your letters have been different, and God knows you've been different since I've been here. As you very well know, the only place we still communicate well is in bed. And I have a feeling that even that isn't going to work much longer." She picked up her glass and headed toward the bedroom, then paused in the doorway. "I've made reservations to fly home day after tomorrow. I had hoped I might convince you to come with me—or to follow me very soon—but I see there's really no point in pursuing that now. You're too wrapped up in your own arrogance, your own private hell, for me to get through to you. I'm sorry, but that's the way it is."

"My arrogance! You're a fine one to talk, Caro."

"You are arrogant. You are intolerant. Do you think you're the only person in the world who has ever suffered? You've set yourself apart in your own special world of prejudice and pain and you won't let anyone in, even when they bring love and compassion."

"You keep refusing to understand, Caro."

"It's you who keep refusing to understand, David." She was suddenly very tired. The weeks of being in a strange country, left to strangers the greater part of each day, had caught up with her. She was weary to her very soul, weary and sad, and she let both feelings show in her face and her voice. "You think I don't understand that someone like you, a doctor, a man who reveres life and who works to preserve it, to save it, has a special horror for those who so ruthlessly and barbarically defiled it. You think I don't understand that you feel you have to show there is still reverence for life, that the Nazis did not wipe that out when they slaughtered six million Jews—among them so many of your own family."

He started, and she nodded. "I saw your . . . ledger, David. I . . . I can't tell you the effect it had." She thought of the slides, slides he still had not seen. "I had thought I could show you—but never mind. That's not important now. What is important is you, David. Somehow, some way, you've got to see that you're trying to prove to yourself that life is still important, still worth living, no matter what the risk. I can't do that for you. No one can. I can only hope—and pray."

He was silent for a long time, and then he said, more quietly, "You've been doing a lot of thinking."

"I've had a lot of time to think," she said.

"Yes. Yes, I guess you have. Well. So you're leaving day after tomorrow?"

"Yes."

"I . . . I guess I won't see you again, then. I was going to tell you—I'm going out to a kibbutz a hundred miles from here. They need someone to train staff to run the infirmary—"

"Of course," she said. "I understand."

"Caro—"

"David. I do understand. Truly, I do." She smiled, a small, sad smile. "You know, in a way, what you've chosen is easier on you than the other course."

"What do you mean?"

"Well, David—I always thought, when I was a little girl listening to the nuns talk about the martyrs, people who died for their faith, that if you could just stand the pain, dying that way would make up for everything. All the little and big sins—much, much easier than having to try to be good every day."

"I'm not being a martyr," he said, and she could hear the anger still burning strong.

"I don't use the word in the sense some people do," she said. "I think the martyrs the nuns were talking about were people whose own view of themselves demanded they make that kind of sacrifice—I think the view you have of yourself now demands that you be here. All I meant was, there's a lot of suffering at home, David. A lot of work to be done. Only, it's constant and it's lonely. As you know far better than I."

"You've made it clear you think I'm running away from something," David said. He was only a few feet from her, but he might as well have been miles. "You have a right to your opinion, Caro, but if you don't mind, I really don't want to hear it anymore."

"No, I'm sure you don't." She held out her hand, feeling as though she were holding some object quite separate from herself. "I . . . I'm very tired. And I know you are. Good night, David."

He looked at her hand, then took it, held it briefly, and let it go. "Good night," he said. He strode past her to the door, then turned. "I guess I should have said . . . good-bye."

"Yes," she said. "Good-bye, David. Good luck."

"You, too," he said. He vanished into the dim room; she heard the clink of coins, the rustle of fabric, as he dressed. Then he was gone.

The numbness had spread, holding her in a protective wrap that would not let pain and sorrow through. She packed quietly, tucking shoes into their flannel bags, folding lingerie into its case. Her hand fell on the envelope of slides, and she picked it up, staring at it. Then she took it and the envelope from Koenberg and wrapped them together, addressing the package to Dr. David Selbin in care of the hospital.

Skye maneuvered Natalie through the couples scattered over the tile dance floor to a position near the bandstand and a better view of the moonlit waters of Mobile Bay. "Now," he said, "if this night isn't made to order, I don't know what is. Sweet music, moonlight, a beautiful woman in my arms—this is what comes of living right."

She smiled at him and nestled closer. The evening was magic; the whole weekend had seemed under some kind of spell. She had never felt so close to Skye, so happy, so content. Something is different, she thought, feeling the easy meshing of their bodies in the rhythms of the dance. An ease, as though barriers have fallen without my even noticing they were breaking down.

The band began again, and they continued to dance, bodies and heads close, anticipating the hours ahead. Natalie herself did not know just when the change in her had taken place; there was a time when she had thought of the Langlinaises as an entity, something Skye belonged to and carried around with him; but now Skye was just Skye—and her feelings for him had nothing to do with his family, but only with Skye himself.

The trial had of course played a large part in this change. She had seen a Skye she had never seen before; the man in that courtroom was very much his own person, capable of carving his own path, and in a strange way that she did not yet understand, she had fallen in love with him all over again.

She had returned to New Orleans bemused, abstracted, acting, she told herself, exactly like an adolescent in love for the first time. She had wanted to talk her feelings over with someone, but there was no one here she felt that close to; on an impulse, she had called Caro in San Francisco, but there had been no answer. She must still be in Israel, Natalie thought, when calls on successive days proved fruitless.

And so she had wrestled with herself, making her examine her work and the way she felt about it. She had to admit that her first enthusiasm was well-tempered; journalism still challenged her, but she saw it more clearly now. If she stayed on, she would have to keep growing. She would have to become the kind of reporter Tom Burns on the *Advocate* was, or like the top political reporters here. Not abrasive, as Tom was. But keen. Aggressive. Able to be objective. Or to write from a defensible bias. She would not be able to openly espouse a cause. She would not be able to come out for a political candidate, work in campaigns. For all the doors that would be open to her, a number would be closed. And sitting in that courtroom in St. Francisville watching Skye battle, not only the case on the docket, but generations of ignorance and prejudice as well, she had realized that there were causes that were important to her. And that the pen in her hand might not be the mightiest weapon if it were guided by the newspaper's viewpoint.

She had come to a decision before she left New Orleans with Skye, but the decision depended, in great part, on what would happen here. She brushed her lips against his cheek and heard him whisper in her ear, "Would you mind if we let this be the last dance?"

She kissed him in answer, and they left the dance floor, leaving the brightly lit terrace behind them as they walked back to their cottage. It was the same one they had had last summer, and already it seemed theirs alone, the place she would always remember, no matter what the future held.

Skye caught her hand as she headed toward the bedroom. "Wait," he said. "Let's sit out here. I—would you like some champagne?"

"All right," she said. "Shall I just change?"

"Stay as you are," he said. "I've got the champagne chilling. Sit down and I'll bring it right out." He went into the small alcove off the living room that held a tiny refrigerator and she heard the clink of glasses and ice. And then he returned, bearing a large silver tray. It held a silver cooler and a vase of roses; he set it on the table in front of her and began to work the cork out of the champagne.

"Skye—what is this all about?" she said.

"Shh," he said. He caught the first flow of champagne in a glass, then set it down. "Forgot something," he said. He went to the radio in the corner and switched it on; she recognized Dick Martin's voice, and smiled.

"How many dates do you think *Moonglow with Martin* has scored?" she said.

"I don't know," Skye said, smiling. He came back, poured their champagne, and handed her a glass. "I'd like to propose a toast," he said. "But I need to ask you a question first."

"What is it?" she said.

"Well, I'd like to propose a toast to the future Mrs. Skye Langlinais—but she hasn't said yes yet."

Natalie felt her heart begin to beat faster, and saw her glass tremble in her fingers. She looked at him, amber eyes glowing. "Is this the beginning of that campaign you warned me about?"

"Does it need to be?"

"No," she said. She set down her glass and took his hand in hers. "I've been doing a lot of thinking, Skye, but I—well, I didn't know how to tell you without . . . without seeming to push you. I got a lot of glory out of my stories about George's trial. And a chance for a promotion. But I've decided that's not what I want to do with my writing, Skye. I don't want to write about what other people are doing. I want to write to make things happen. I'm not sure just what that means yet, but I think it does mean that I don't have to be tied down to New Orleans."

"Does it mean you will marry me?" He smiled again, and took her into his arms. "Natalie. Will you marry me?" he said, lowering his mouth to hers.

She just had time to say yes.

Skye felt a new sensation, a feeling of oneness with Natalie that he had long wanted, but had not had before. He was almost awed by it, almost overcome by this sense of being totally united with the girl he held in his arms. It seemed to him then that when Natalie had said she would marry him, she had drawn back a curtain that had hidden the truly golden kingdom, the one that between them they would build.

29

OCTOBER 1950

Leaves of every color—scarlet, lemon, purple, orange—carpeted the lawns stretching around the canopy Paul Watkins had had placed to shelter the altar where Skye and Natalie would be wed. The decision to hold the wedding at her uncle's plantation rather than at home in Virginia had been readily agreed to by her family; she had not been in Virginia for a long time. Most of her girlhood friends were scattered; it was much more sensible to have the wedding in Louisiana and let her family travel there.

August and September had vanished in a flurry of wedding preparations that coincided with the waning months of Beau Langlinais's campaign. Had Caro not flown in from San Francisco for the last two weeks of September to help with the final details of the wedding, it might never had gotten put together. But now the day itself had arrived; October 1, a day seemingly created for the occasion.

The cool, clear air and brilliant blue sky against a backdrop of dark pines made Paul Watkins' grounds a perfect setting. Natalie, standing on the gallery that overlooked the back lawn on the afternoon of the wedding, turned to Caro and said, "I keep pinching myself. I can still hardly believe this is happening."

"I'm so happy for the two of you, Natalie," Caro said. "I've got things to do downstairs. I'll be up to help you dress in a little while."

Natalie watched Caro hurry away, and turned slowly to go to her room. Caro had not mentioned David since she had arrived two weeks ago, except once, when she had said, in a tone that brooked no questions, that she had left him in Jerusalem at the end of July, very committed, very involved. Caro, of course, had been busy herself. Her show had been featured in several cities in California, and other cities across the country were showing interest; these two weeks were the only hiatus Caro would have for another few months.

Except for Beau and Caroline, who had flown out for the opening, the family had not yet seen the show, but they had seen the slides, and if the wound left because she had not been able to share her work with David was still raw, her family's response had done much to assuage it. Watching the slides projected, they had all been openly moved. Père had come to her and taken her hands in his and said, speaking as though every word were coming from someplace he had never revealed to her before: "The most selfless courage is to take on someone else's pain. You're very brave, darling."

I will never understand the breakup of David and Caro's relationship, Natalie thought. Of course it's easier for me and Skye to reconcile my being an Episcopalian with his Roman Catholicism—there's really not that much difference, and I'll probably end up going to church with him anyway. But if they really love each other, how can they do this to themselves? She realized that Caro, in fact, was not standing up to it very well. She was impressed all over again by Caro's courage in attending the festivities before the wedding, when every day must be another arrow in her heart.

The wedding was set for six in the evening, with the priest from St. Martinville coming to perform the ceremony. Hurricane lanterns on tall beribboned posts made an aisle for the wedding party to walk down; additional lanterns hung from trees and standards, blending their glow with the light of the young moon.

Caro, Émilie, and Gennie served as Natalie's attendants; they wore waltz-length gowns in a scarlet taffeta, a brilliant background for Natalie's ivory satin dress.

Caro went through the ceremony in a daze; two weeks of putting Natalie and Skye first, added to her grief, her fatigue, were almost more than she could bear, and she thought gratefully that in just a little while it would be over. There was the reception to be gotten through, the parting with her family tomorrow—and then a quick trip back to New Orleans, and a plane back to San Francisco. And then . . . then more appearances at more galleries, more interviews, more hands pressing hers, more people crying, exclaiming, praising . . . But none of them David.

She made herself stand straight and concentrate on what the priest was saying, taking Natalie's bouquet at the altar so Natalie and Skye could hold hands while they made their vows. When the ceremony was over, Caro followed them back up the aisle and took her place in the receiving line, keeping a practiced smile on her face.

Now the faces that pressed around her were familiar, friends who had driven over from St. Martinville for the wedding, friends from New Orleans and Baton Rouge. Henri appeared and handed her a glass of champagne, looking clerical and correct in his black clothes. His favorite teacher had come with him; Caro had met him earlier and had smiled wryly to think this was the man she had hoped would help her and David marry. As if that matters anymore, she thought, sipping the champagne. The guests had all been through the line, and she was free to mingle, but she had nothing left to say to anyone, no small talk at all, and she ducked out of the crowd and walked toward the front of the house, finding a chair pulled up in the shadows of the porch, and settling herself there.

She could hear the orchestra tuning up, could hear the hum of voices rising as the reception gained momentum. I wonder if I'd be missed, she thought, if I just went up to bed? She closed her eyes and began to rock, the slow movement calming her, inducing her to sleep.

The sound of a motor wakened her; she sat up and looked through the dark at the headlights coming slowly up the curving drive from the road. Someone who lost their way and missed the ceremony, she thought, rising. She went to stand in the light so that the latecomer would see her, and know that this was the right place.

The car stopped at the edge of the circle of light from the porch and the driver got out, a tall, lean figure that moved quickly toward her. Something about the figure seemed familiar, and she stepped forward, peering into the gloom. Then the figure began to run, and she heard her name. "Caro! Caro!"

David! It couldn't be David. But it was. Her heart beat faster; already she was running to meet him while still denying it could be he. As they met, breathless, unable to speak, they clasped each other and kissed the long months of separation away.

In that one moment, the world changed and fell into place. The music, the faint laughter in the background, no longer made Caro sad. There was singing in her world again, and laughter, and love. She clung to him, not willing to let him go. "Oh, David," she said. "I thought I'd lost you."

His arms tightened around her, and she felt at peace: this was what it meant to be happy, this is what it meant to be loved.

"You almost did," he said. "But your pictures! You were right, darling. So right."

"Shh," she said. There was time for that, time to talk about the things that had kept them apart. Now, this night, she did not want to think of any of that. There was only one thing, one person, she wanted, and by a miracle of love and grace, he was in her arms.